Wild Rose

A Wildflowers of Scotland Novel

By

Sherrie Hansen

Donna,
To Wildflowers,
Sherrie Hansen

Published by Blue Belle Books
Saint Ansgar, Iowa

Blue Belle Books
PO Box 205, Saint Ansgar, IA 50472

Copyright 2013 by Sherrie Hansen

For information regarding bulk purchases of this book, digital purchase and special discounts, please contact the publisher at BlueBelleBooks.com

Cover design by Tracy Beltran
Photo by Sherrie Hansen

Manufactured in the United States of America
ISBN 978-1675330203

To Susan Decker, for sharing your wonderful son with me and making my dream of visiting Scotland a reality. I never would have discovered St. Conan's Kirk and Loch Awe without your generosity.

To my niece, Victoria, for masterminding Rose and Ian's daring escape.

Chapter One

Rose fussed with her hair and hoped the wind that was skipping over Loch Awe and whistling up the spires of St. Conan's Kirk hadnae messed it up. It was nae that the breeze didnae feel nice – it did. She just wanted to look her best. Who could blame her for that? She was nervous enough already.

Where could he be?

She hated being stood up, and with good reason. It had been two years since she'd stood waiting, and waiting, and waiting at her and Robert's favorite restaurant. When he hadnae shown up, she'd been angry – thought he'd gotten too busy at work, forgotten she was waiting, or worse yet, remembered and blown her off.

How could she have known he was dead?

Here she was again. So it was a church and nae a restaurant. A man she didnae know all that well instead of her husband. The emotions felt the same. She was peeved. So peeved she could almost forget what it was like to feel abandoned, to hurt so badly she could barely keep her head aboot her.

She took a deep breath and tried to relax. The rhododendrons were just beginning to bloom, and in all her favorite colors. She'd never been able to wear pink – nae a good match with her auburn, almost red hair – but she still loved the hue, especially in the spring.

He was almost an hour later than he'd said he'd be. She peeked through the hedge and tried to see round the bend that led to the village.

What were the odds that two men she was supposed to meet would die en route to their rendezvous point? She paced up and down the path that led to the church, squelching her nervous energy only long enough to look at a bee dipping into a rhody that was a lovely shade of lavender. And then, she was back at it, scanning the roadside for Digby's car, checking the time on her mobile every few seconds, and imagining the worst.

She'd been waiting for an hour – plenty long enough for Digby to get there even if he'd been temporarily detained at work, gotten a speeding ticket, or stopped by the mini–mart to buy her flowers.

Besides, the man had a mobile.

She clicked hers open and pressed the green button twice. Still nae answer.

Where could he be? And why now? Was it because she'd been too intimate with him? Nae intimate enough?

"Excuse me, ma'am."

She blinked and looked in the direction of the voice, but the sun was in her eyes, and all she could see was a soft sheen of light backlighting the silhouette of a very tall man. Too tall to be Digby. She raised her hand to her eyes to shade the light but the sun was still blinding, clinging to his head like a halo.

"Forgive me," the man said, just as she saw his collar, the white square gleaming brightly between the black, and thought, shouldnae it be me saying that?

"Sorry to intrude," he continued. "I couldnae help noticing that ye seem to be looking for someone."

So much for her and Dig having the place to themselves. Of course, as of this moment, there wasnae a "them" anyway, so it mattered little if they had privacy. Besides, she had been going to tell him that they couldnae do it again, that it was too soon, that what had happened shouldnae have. Not yet. That didnae mean she didnae want to be alone with him, to do something. She probably did, eventually. Just nae so much, or quite so fast.

"I was meeting a friend," she said.

"Ye've still plenty of time," he said. "Worship doesnae begin for another half hour."

The sun wasnae in his eyes, but behind him, illuminating her face. She knew, even without being able to see his eyes, that he could read hers perfectly.

"I didnae realize..."

"We've a small but active congregation," the man said, extending his hand. "Ian MacCraig. St. Conan's vicar." He nodded at a stone cottage with windows rimmed in tiny stones. It was mostly overgrown with creepers. She had assumed it was unoccupied.

She gave her hand, took his, and was surprised by his warmth. "Rose Wilson." Her hands had been perpetually cold ever since Robert had died. The only reason she'd come to meet Digby in the first place was to get warm. But holding hands with Digby didnae even compare to the heat this man radiated. "I'm nae from Lochawe.

Just up for the day from Glasgow."

She turned just enough to get the sun out of her eyes and looked up into his face. And started to melt. Warm times ten. Honest, intelligent eyes, longish hair the color of butterscotch. Wide shoulders perfect for shielding a companion. A genuine, concerned smile tinged with the slightest whisper of what? Guilt? Her mind flipped back a page. Forgive him for what? For startling her? For intruding on her reverie? For being concerned enough to acknowledge her presence? To see if she was in need of someone to talk to?

He had such a beautiful aura aboot him. So serene. So utterly masculine. She felt like she was in a dream, or starring in a film. She resisted the urge to pinch herself. The vicars she knew were old and gray – most, gone completely bald. This vicar – Ian – didnae fit any of the pastoral images she held in her mind.

Pastor Ian's eyes blinked wide open a split second before she felt a movement to her left. A stream of men streaked towards them, guns drawn. She could see them out of the corner of her eye. What the devil was going on?

In the moment it took to comprehend that they were slowly being surrounded by armed constables, her mind, ever agile, jumped to the conclusion that Ian must be a convict, recently escaped. Oh – my – God. Nae doubt "Ian" had killed the real vicar while he slept. It would have been a simple matter from there to don the poor gent's clothes. He was probably planning to take her as a hostage so he could escape across the border to England, make his exit on a ferry, and disappear on the mainland. It was the only explanation she could fathom.

That was when she realized he was still holding her hand, smiling at her with all the sincerity in the world. The man certainly didnae look like a convict. Perhaps he'd come to St. Conan's for sanctuary.

"Step away from the vicar." A voice boomed through a megaphone.

She looked at Ian and dropped his hand, fully expecting the constables to rush him once she'd safely backed away.

Instead, two strong arms wrenched her from behind, pulled her hands behind her back and slapped on a set of cuffs.

"What on earth?" she said, nearly toppling over from the shock of her capture.

Ian looked even more apologetic that he had before, with a little relief mixed in. Forgive him for what? For this? Had he called the police on her?

"I've done nothing wrong," she cried. "I'm nae sure what's going on here, but there must be some mistake. I'm Rosalie Wilson from Glasgow," she tried to explain when she wasnae struggling to stay on her feet, bucking this way and that as they pulled her over the rough terrain.

"She had nothing to do with the actual theft," the vicar was saying, following close at her side. "She was already gone when her man stole the artifacts."

Her man? Digby? What were they talking aboot? Digby wouldnae...

"Ye said she was on the tape," the constable said.

"The earlier part, when they were..." the vicar stammered.

The man holding her cuffs snickered.

Oh, God. They couldnae have a tape of her and Digby. Could they?

"Do ye want us to call ye a solicitor?"

"No," she said, sure of that at least. If Robert's barristers ever found out, or his sons, or the press...

Oh, God. How mortifying! How could she have? She'd risked Robert's good name, his reputation, and his millions, and for what? To feel a man's touch for a mere five minutes?

A man who appeared to be the ring leader of the hooligans who were herding her towards the car leaned against the vehicle with an amused expression on his face, and looked at her ... her... her breasts.

If she'd been blessed with the opportunity to get her hands on Digby at that moment, they'd have had reason to arrest her.

The little weasel! She certainly hadnae meant to get intimate with him when she did, but nae because she hadnae trusted him. *My God.* She'd taken up with a common thief, a con man, a criminal.

And the tape. How humiliating! Never in a million years had she ever dreamed... to have had her lowest moment recorded... and seen by who knew how many people.

The vicar rushed alongside her as the constable's men whisked her to the car, with – oh, God – bars on the back windows. "Is there a family member, a friend ye'd like me to call?"

She felt her cheeks burning just imagining what the vicar must think of her. "There's nae one." Which was a shame. She could certainly have used a hug and a little moral support aboot then. But she could hardly tell her mum, or Kelly and Kevin, that she'd been arrested, or that her new boyfriend had turned out to be a criminal, or that she'd been caught on some sort of tape, probably half–naked, her legs spread wide like some common hussy.

"Will ye come?" She turned to the vicar and watched as his cheeks flushed even redder.

"I'll get my auto and follow ye to the station."

The constable shoved her shoulder into the car and nearly shut her foot in the door in his hurry to lock her in the cramped back seat.

"Good thinking, assuming ye're planning to make a confession," he sneered.

"I've done nothing wrong," she said, knowing she had. But nae what they thought. She hadnae stolen a thing. What she had done was to throw her whole life down the crapper.

* * *

"I've only known Digby for a fortnight or two," she said for the twentieth time. "We met on the internet. I was widowed almost three years ago, and I felt like I was... was..." She struggled to go on. "I felt like I was ready to start seeing someone again." Someone who hadnae known Robert. Someone who didnae know Robert Junior and Rodney. Someone who didnae know she sat on the board of directors of an endowment worth millions. Someone she could trust to love her for herself. She gulped another belly full of air, rank as it smelled in the constable's office, and tried nae to give in to the urge to sob.

The man who'd been interrogating her for the last two hours asked her again what Digby's last name was.

"The emails I received from him were from Digby Bentworth. I had nae reason to think it was an alias. I didnae ask to see his driver's license. I trusted him."

More of the same odd questions, asked over and over again. They were trying to break her down. Couldnae they see she was already broken?

"No. I never went to his home. No. I never shared a hotel room with him. No. I never entertained him at my home." She set her jaw

5

stubbornly. "As I've told ye dozens of times already, we had only just met. What happened in the grassy spot under the flying buttresses was a fluke – the first time we'd ever, I've ever—"

"Hasnae this gone on long enough?" Vicar Ian MacCraig came to her defense, as he had several times over the last two hours. "The woman is clearly telling the truth. If ye've got nae evidence to the contrary, I kindly suggest ye let her go."

The interrogator ignored the vicar. "So ye had nae idea that yer lover was stealing architectural relics from the church?"

"He was nae my lover! And no! We'd met at the church twice before. The first time we visited, I admired the copper rabbit drain spout and the stained glass windows, and the interesting architectural detailing. The second and third times, I evidently didnae look up, or I certainly would have noticed that they were gone."

This brought another round of snickers.

She rose to her feet and planted her hands on her hips. What she wanted to do was to curl up into a ball and cry herself to oblivion. "Yes, I was on my back. But I'm sure if ye review the tape, ye'll find that I had my eyes closed through most of the afore mentioned proceedings."

"Too busy seeing fireworks," one of the deputies commented.

"Seriously, gentlemen. Is this really necessary?" The vicar stood and squared off with the constable. "If I'd known what disrespect ye were going to show Ms. Wilson, I'd have deleted the first half of the tape before I ever showed it to ye."

The catcalls and responses that followed were so gross that she forced herself to block them out.

"I must insist that ye cease this vulgarity immediately," the vicar demanded loudly. "If nae for Ms. Wilson's sake, then for mine."

She thought their fact–finding mission was aboot to start all over again, but this time, when their hoots and laughter died down, she was told she was free to go, provided she didnae leave Scotland, and with the stipulation that she would make herself available for further questioning as the need arose.

"I'll drive her back to her car." The vicar volunteered, securing her purse and ushering her to his vehicle.

"Thank ye," she said as they drove the few short miles to the kirk. The rhododendrons lining the road beside the parking spot she'd so innocently chosen were still in full bloom, but the colors had dulled, and several of the blossoms had wilted in the hot sunshine.

"He was never going to see me again, was he?" She'd opened the car door and was toying with the idea of getting out of the vicar's car, but hadnae acted on it. The horror of the day's events was just sinking in, and she felt numb, deflated, humiliated and dazed.

"I think it's reasonable to assume that nae everything the man told ye was true."

"But some of it? I mean..." Her voice trailed off. "He didnae need or ask for my help in committing the crime. He didnae involve me in any way. Can I safely deduce that his feelings for me were true, that what he said aboot me was independent of the lies he obviously told aboot the rest of his life?"

The vicar said nothing, probably wisely, but sat quietly, allowing her to talk.

"He said he loved me. He said I was beautiful."

"And truly, ye are," the vicar said.

"Ye think so?" she asked, as dully as the once bright rhodies.

"I have nae a doubt."

"Thank ye," she said in a voice that sounded absolutely piteous, even to her.

"I know the constable and his men were a bit unkind," the vicar said, "but the truth is, much of what Digby told ye may have been the truth. In the days to come, as the shock wears off, if ye should remember anything pertinent – a comment spoken in an offhand moment when the chap's guard was down – please contact the constable, or if ye prefer, me."

"Nae offense meant." She looked at him, really looked at him, for the first time since the nightmare began. "But what I'd really like is to forget the whole thing ever happened."

"I'm sorry ye had to be subjected to an interrogation, Rose, sorrier yet that ye had to learn these sort of unpleasant truths aboot someone ye'd grown close to."

"It's me who should be sorry," she said, looking deep into his eyes and seeing forgiveness, nae censure. "I'm so ashamed – nae only of what I did with Digby, but that ye were put in such an awkward position because of my actions. And sorry that ye missed yer church service."

"Dinnae worry aboot me," the vicar said. "I'm told the organist organized a hymn sing. All is well. Although I've nae doubt everyone is upset by what happened."

"Again, I am truly sorry for everything that's transpired."

"There's nae need," he said once more, his blue green eyes sizzling with compassion.

"I suppose ye have probably heard – and seen – worse." She tried to move her legs, but they just didnae seem to want to go.

"Much worse, as a matter of fact. So nae to worry."

"Are ye – could ye – if ye could grant me forgiveness–"

"No." He said it firmly, as though there would be nae changing his mind. "That would nae be my place. I'm nae here as yer pastor."

His collar said otherwise, but she didnae press the issue. She hadnae been to confession since before she'd married Robert. If it came right down to it, it made little sense to worry aboot one innocent romp when there was a whole list of other infractions unaccounted for.

He had such an earnest face. "If ye do remember anything at all, please ring me up immediately... If it werenae important, I wouldnae ask ye to revisit the horror of what happened today, but the truth is, St. Conan's has been struggling financially for some time now. There's been talk of ceasing our worship services by summer's end if donations continue to dwindle. The congregation is dear, but they do nae have much money to pay me, or to do the maintenance and upkeep the church requires. Losing whatever cash was in the donation box – and the artifacts – has proven very disheartening to all of us."

"I understand." And she did. Rose swung one, unfeeling–as–wood leg out of the car.

The vicar pressed a card into her hand. Once again, she was startled by the warmth of his touch.

"Do ye think Digby knows what happened here today? That he was watching from afar?"

"Anything is possible. The important thing is that if ye should hear from Digby, ye must contact the authorities immediately so they can sort things out."

"I promise." Rose nodded and mustered her strength. She could do this. The vicar squeezed her hand and a few moments later, she was driving toward home.

Chapter Two

Ian flipped through the hymnbook twice without seeing a single page. He was supposed to be selecting the hymns for next Sunday's worship service. Mrs. Dumphries was going on holiday and needed to have the bulletin printed by fourteen hundred hours Wednesday. *We're Marching to Zion? I Need Thee Every Hour?* How was he supposed to decide when his head was mince and he couldnae concentrate on anything for longer than two seconds?

Calm yersel, man. He hummed *"The Lord's My Shepherd, I'll Not Want"* quietly, absently, doubting the words for the first time. The Lord was nae less his Shepherd than he had been last week, or the week before. What had changed was that he couldnae stop thinking aboot Rose Wilson.

And it wasnae just her breasts, he reassured himself, although seeing them had certainly created a hunger for more. It was her vulnerability, her courage under pressure, the way she'd handled herself like a lady in the midst of what had to have been most humiliating circumstances, the way she'd turned the other cheek.

"Courage, Brother, Do Not Stumble!" he sang. Much as it pained him to admit it, there was nae denying that it would be best for all concerned if he never saw the woman again. Although, should she call, it would mean that she had a clue as to Digby's whereaboots, or information that could lead to his arrest, and that would be a good thing, would it nae?

"Oh, Love of God, How Strong and True..." He tried to concentrate on his task, really tried. *O Love, That Wilt Not Let Me Go?* He really should have asked what hymns the congregation had sung while he'd been with Rose at the constable's office. *Immortal, Invisible, God Only Wise?* The hymns alternately taunted and strengthened his resolve.

Surely Rose had friends and family who would help her through her ordeal. It need nae be him who comforted her. She was nae one to him, a mere acquaintance, certainly nae a member of his flock. He

9

had nae obligation, nae duty, nae ties to the woman at all.

Then why was it that he could nae stop thinking aboot her? He pushed her clumsily from his mind. He had work to do. Ladies Aid was the second Monday of the month. Preparations had to be made. And the quilters would be convening later in the week. He had tables to set up.

He'd seen quite enough of Rose Wilson, and his reasons for wishing to see more of her were so tainted that he couldnae begin to separate his ill–gotten carnal knowledge from his sincere desire to offer spiritual assistance. From now on, Rose Wilson would have to fend for herself.

* * *

By the time Rose hit the main thoroughfare, her numbness had abated significantly and anger had set in. Rose flipped open her mobile and redialed Digby's number. She didnae expect him to answer, but as long as she could call him and give him a piece of her mind, she was going to assume he was still picking up his messages and let him have it.

And she didnae believe he was dead for one second either.

If Robert knew... However inadvertently she'd acted, she'd put her entire life in jeopardy. Robert would be mortified. She was mortified.

And the tape. How humiliating! She felt her cheeks burning once again just imagining what the vicar had thought when he'd discovered what his tape had captured.

The vicar had been nothing but kind to her, another bit that stuck in her craw. She deserved his ire, God's wrath, and more. She thought of his gentle manner and guilt flooded her soul anew.

Would she have preferred that he had scolded her, berated her for her stupidity, condemned her as the worst of sinners?

The thoughts that streamed through her consciousness were as muddled as a stream filled with rocks and debris from the Highlands after a spring rain.

How she rued the fact that he had seen her naked. Kind and accepting as he'd been aboot it, it bothered her more that he had seen her spread on the ground than it did the men at the constable's office who had treated her like a shameless hussy. It bothered her more that the vicar had seen her naked than it did that slime, Digby. Unwise as her decision had turned out to be, she'd consented to let Digby see her naked. She'd given the vicar nae such right.

For a second, she felt a flash of anger towards him. He'd seen her naked against her wishes and without her knowledge. Nae that it was his fault. But his eyes had feasted nonetheless.

Her anger changed to guilt. He'd been so concerned, so chivalrous. He'd stood up for her, defended her, offered his help.

Her thoughts swirled around her like a tornadic waterspout. Her anger only started to abate when she replaced that emotion with another. Determination. She had to get the tape. She couldnae bear to know that it was out there, waiting to fall into the wrong hands.

The constable would probably insist that the tape be kept as evidence until Digby was caught and convicted. She knew that much from watching crime shows on the telly. But if the press ever got wind of that tape... worse yet, if it ended up on the Internet... She had to get the tape.

The question was how – and who she could appeal to for help. The police surely wouldnae assist her. They thought she was scum, just like Digby. Guilty by association. Besides, the constable nae doubt had a whole list of procedures to adhere to, which would pretty well rule out any of the possibilities she had in mind.

The pastor was her best bet. He was as highly motivated as she was to catch Digby, albeit for different reasons. He wanted his relics back. But he was also sympathetic to her plight. The vicar would understand and appreciate why she wanted the tape.

She thought aboot the pastor for just a second – Ian, wasnae it? She remembered the way his cheeks had turned red when he looked at her. Was it because he'd seen her naked?

She shook her head. It wasnae that she was ashamed of her body, although goodness knew, it wasnae much to look at – she was forty years old, for heaven's sake. She had all the classic signs of maturity – breasts starting to sag, a little belly she'd never had when she was younger, skin sprinkled with what she preferred to think of as freckles.

She could only hope the good reverend's security camera hadnae been high resolution. Or that the angle had captured her best features, what few were left.

Lord, what a horrible mess. It would be much easier – nae doubt for both of them – if she never set foot in the man's parish again. But pretty much everyone involved in this mess had seen the tape – seen her naked – and given the choice of asking the police or the pastor for help, she preferred the pastor.

She pulled into the Balloch Roundabout, circled past her turn, and headed back in the direction she'd come from.

She'd seen a little B&B that advertised wireless Internet alongside the road near Loch Awe – with her laptop, she could do what she needed to do here just as well as she could from home.

Her foot hit the brake. She'd almost forgotten Ginger. She flipped open her cell phone and dialed her sister's number.

"Hi Kelly," she said, trying to set aside her anxiety so her sister wouldnae detect the tension in her voice. "Um, aboot Ginger. Would it be a problem if I picked her up in a few days?"

"Ye said ye'd be back by early this evening."

"I know. But things didnae go quite as smoothly as I had anticipated, and it looks like I'm going to need to stay put for another few days."

"Sorry," Kelly said. "Nae can do. We've had a little disaster of our own and Kevin said if Ginger is nae gone by the time he's home from work, she's going to the pound."

She would have slammed on the brakes again, but a Renault was tailgating her. "He wouldnae. She's my baby."

"He can if ye dinnae pick her up before he gets home. And he will."

"How would he feel if I'd taken Jace to the adoption agency that time he bit me?"

"He was teething," Kelly sputtered. "He was one. He's a child!"

God, she hoped Ginger hadnae bit anyone. "Well, Lyndsie certainly knew better when she broke my snow globe. I told her nae and she just looked at me and grinned while she conked it on the edge of the coffee table. I know she was only two, but she certainly knew the meaning of the word no. There's still glitter in the carpet."

"I cannae believe ye're bringing all this stuff up. These are my children ye're talking aboot. My real, non–fur covered babies."

"I love them as much as ye do. All five of them. I'm just trying to illustrate that nae one is perfect. We've all done things we shouldnae have, or didnae mean to. We're all human."

"Which is Kevin's point precisely. She's a dog, Rose. Dog. She may be smart, but she's still just a dog."

She glanced in her rearview mirror. Still there. "So what did she do?"

"Ye know the daybed in Lyndsie's room? The one with all the pretty pillows that I made myself with Grandma's old buttons and lace and the pretty fabrics I got in London? Well, all that's left of them is a pile of tattered little scraps, none of them bigger than one half inch square."

Ouch. Nae wonder Kevin was upset. And Kelly. And Lyndsie. Her heart thudded in her chest. Poor little thing, Lyndsie. And Ginger, too. How scared, how terrified, how abandoned she must have felt to have done such a thing.

"I'm so sorry, Kelly. I'll buy ye more pillows. I promise." She swung her car into the next roundabout, ditched the Renault and did another U–turn, this time heading southeast, back toward Glasgow.

"Ye'll make me more pillows, by hand, with yer own little–used needle, thread and thimble," Kelly said. "And it's nae just me, but yer little niece Lyndsie that ye should be apologizing to."

"I'll make it up to her, I promise," Rose said, waiting for the other shoe to fall. There were always at least two shoes when it came to her and Kelly.

"There's more," Kelly said, after a tension–filled pause.

She glanced up, slammed on her brakes and just missed colliding with a lorry that was stopped, waiting for someone to make a left turn. "Just tell me," she said too loudly.

"She clawed the wood between each window all the way round the bay," Kelly said, her voice dreadful and ominous.

Kevin. Her nephews and niece, she could butter up with a few kind words. Even Kelly wasnae all that hard to win over. But Kevin... Kevin would hate her forever. Kevin, the poor, long–suffering garbage collector, who lived for his forays into his woodworking shop. Kevin, who worshipped wood – its grain, its texture, the colors he brought forth when he stained and varnished it. Good, loving, husband and father–of–the–year, Kevin.

"Kevin does know aboot the old forgive and forget adage, right?"

"It's nae an adage. It's from the Bible, right along with an eye for an eye and a tooth for a tooth."

"Kevin wants to gouge my woodwork?"

13

"He wants to strangle yer dog."

"I'll be there in two hours twenty," Rose said, passing a van on the only straight stretch of highway between Crianlarich and Tyndrum. "Tell Kevvy I'm so sorry."

"Kevvy, is it now?"

"I'm sorry. What else can I say?"

"Nothing. Just come quickly."

What choice did she have? She could hardly tell Kelly and Kevin that she'd been arrested, or that she had to help catch her former boyfriend, who had turned out to be a criminal, or that she was trying to recover a tape on which she was naked. All valid reasons, but none that Kelly would understand.

Fine then. She'd pick up Ginger, fabricate some sort of excuse aboot why she hadnae gotten back to Kevin and Kelly's when she was supposed to and make amends as best she could. She'd spend the night in Glasgow and return to Loch Awe bright and early. Hopefully, the B&B she'd seen earlier accepted dogs.

Chapter Three

The clatter of teacups interrupted Ian's thoughts. Granted, they were thoughts he shouldnae have been having in the first place, but that didnae make it any less irritating. The fact that he was exhausted didnae help – he hadnae slept more than four hours the night before. How could a man relax enough to drift off with thoughts – and pictures – of Rose Wilson bombarding his brain?

The voices of the ladies aid society echoed in his head like the drip of the proverbial faucet. The ladies from church werenae specifically trying to torture him by meeting the day after his run–in with Rose Wilson and the constables. The ladies convened bright and early every second Monday of the month, setting up tables in the rear of the sanctuary to wrap bandages and pack care packages for the soldiers in the gulf.

On any other day, he might have enjoyed chatting with the ladies, but today, all he could think aboot was Rose Wilson's naked body.

What was wrong with him? He'd never had any trouble keeping his mind free of unholy thoughts until Rose came along. What had she done to him? Nae only had thoughts of her and her breasts invaded his every waking minute – minutes that should have been spent in prayer, contemplation, and sermon preparation – but she'd made him compromise the very essence of his calling. When a man of the cloth was called upon to forgive, it was his avowed duty to grant absolution. By withholding the blessing Rose had asked of him, he had failed nae only her, but his entire profession.

"Pastor MacCraig?" Jessica Bennington waved a hanky at him. "The ladies were just wondering – have the elders been informed of the vandalism and given an accounting of the losses and damages sustained to the building?"

"They are aware that certain items were stolen. It was with their blessing that I installed a video camera in the first place."

At the mere mention of the word video, eleven sets of eyes lowered and didnae look up. That didnae prevent their heads from turning, or whispers from flying.

How was he supposed to stop thinking aboot the video when it was all anyone could talk aboot?

"Has Scotland Yard been notified then?" Margaret Ainsworth asked from behind long eyelashes, demurely down swept.

"I really didnae think it necessary to involve Scotland Yard until the local law enforcement agencies had a go at it."

"But if the stolen items are being sold on the mainland, and shipped across the Atlantic, it certainly qualifies as an International incident, does it nae?"

Karla Jacobs stood and held out both hands as if beseeching him to heed their advice. "It's possible our artifacts are on the auction block at Lloyd's of London even as we speak. If we dinnae strike quickly and preemptively, we may never see the items again."

"The police tell me it's unlikely we'll recover the items even if this Digby is caught," Ian said. "And the artifacts are nae really ours to begin with."

"The gall of the man," Esther Samuelson said. "Stealing from the House of the Lord."

"Wickedness in its basest form, that's what it is," said Phyllis McElfatrick. "Anyone who would steal the collection box right away from a church deserves to rot in hell."

Ian cleared his throat and briefly regained order. "Of course, I'd love to recover the relics as much as any of ye. But St. Conan's will go on with or without its copper gutters, with or without it's hand-carved baptismal font, with or without its stained glass windows, with or without its etched, stone panels, with or without Robert Bruce's bones."

The faces looking up at him said they were nae so sure.

"Ladies, ladies, ladies. The things that were stolen from us are but mere objects. The things we lost had nae monetary value to us, because we nae would have sold them."

"We might 'ave eventually, Reverend. We can barely pay our utility bills. And we're two months behind on yer salary," Esther said.

"Those things were our insurance policy," Sarah chimed in.

Ian shook his head. "Much as we love this magnificent old building, the heart and soul of St. Conan's is much, much more than anything ye see here."

"What aboot the press then?" Margaret said. "If we release the story in each of the major cities across Europe and the United States, we would certainly evoke a great deal of compassion – maybe even some monetary contributions."

"If we were to hold a benefit while sympathies are running high, it could be the answer to all our financial problems!" Ethel Connery exclaimed.

"The Bible says when life gives ye lemons, make lemonade," Millicent Wilder said.

"The Bible does nae actually..." Ian tried to say, but his voice was drowned out by the ladies missionary society marching to Zion.

That's when he caught sight of a fluffy–pawed cocker spaniel streaming through the door of the chapel, followed by the devil incarnate. Rose Wilson herself.

* * *

"Heel!" She tried again, a little louder. "Heel!!" Then she attempted to appeal to Ginger's greater powers of reasoning. "That's got to hurt yer neck, baby. Ye're going to strain yer vocal chords. Ye willnae be able to bark if ye keep this up. The squirrels willnae even be afraid of ye."

Ginger strained against her leash, unfazed, until Rose felt her arm very nearly being yanked off. "Be nice to Mommy," she pleaded, trying to sweet–talk the dog out of her frenzy. When that didnae work, she said, "Bad dog. Bad, bad dog", in her most shame–producing voice.

That was when she heard the words "release the story across Europe and the United States," followed by the most gut–wrenching phrase ever – "notify the press."

Ginger burst through the door of St. Conan's in an unbridled display of passion.

"Ye told them ye saw me naked? And now, ye're going to tell the press?"

A dozen or so heads turned to look at them in total synchronization.

"Ye cannae do that," Rose said, her voice echoing off the old stone walls. Great acoustics.

"Do we know ye?" the one who'd been rallying for a media blitzkrieg asked.

Pastor Ian, who looked almost as frozen in time and space as the stone carving of Robert the Bruce on the far side of the church, recovered and started across the room, shaking his head as he walked as if trying to warn her aboot some great, impending peril.

"Rosalie," she said, succumbing to the staring eyes of the church ladies. "Rosalie Wilson."

"The Rose Wilson?" a little voice squeaked from the back.

Oh, Lord. Someone had finally made the connection. They'd probably seen her and Robert's photo on the cover of the National Celebrity News when he died and put two and two together.

"This is the Rose in the video?"

Her heart stopped pounding and it felt as though every drop of blood in her entire body was rushing to her cheeks.

"Could I please speak to ye for a moment?" she said to the vicar, trying to ignore the holes that were being bored through her.

He followed her through the door, into the courtyard.

"Ye told them aboot the video? Because I thought we had an understanding, and it did nae include press releases and me having my reputation ruined."

"I dinnae tell them anything," he said, his cheeks looking as enflamed as hers felt. "My mother may have been involved in some way."

"Yer mother knows I was cavorting in the churchyard in the nude?"

"I'm afraid everyone does. My cousin, Sally, is the dispatcher at the constable's office. Sally told her mother. My aunt told my mother and so on."

"I thought it was going to be kept private."

"They have nae seen the video. As far as I know," he said, probably nae wanting to be caught in an inadvertent lie – which was very disconcerting. Ye could see it in his face – like, one never quite knew what Sally might do. "They've just heard aboot it, as far as I know."

"How comforting," Rose said. "Exactly how much have they heard?"

"They've been peering out the windows at the flying buttresses all morning."

Ginger rubbed against her, as if she could tell she knew what was coming. "Good Lord," Rose said.

"That He is."

"I did mean it that way," she said. "I mean, I know he is. Good, I mean. I just didnae..."

"I know," he said.

"I know ye do!" She clenched her hands and watched his cheeks – and his neck, and his throat flush a splotchy pink red. If he werenae a vicar, she'd have thought it was sexual flush. "Ye know everything. And it's downright frightening, if ye dinnae mind me saying so."

"I dinnae."

"Know everything, or mind me saying so?"

"Both. But in particular, mind ye saying so."

"Of course ye dinnae! Ye know everything, and ye're perfect, too."

His eyebrows shot up at that. "Ms. Wilson..."

"Rose."

"Rose, then. We seem to have gotten off on the wrong foot here, and while I regret the circumstances under which the wrong footing occurred, I'd like to think it might be possible for us to put this behind us."

"They know who I am?" she said, her face now feeling alternately hot and half–frozen with fear.

"I'm afraid so. I heard them discussing the fact that someone with such an old–fashioned name had certainly..."

"I get the picture."

"I'm sorry." He looked it, too.

"Nae all roses are old–fashioned, ye know."

"Certainly," he said. "There's a wild rose growing along the side gate of the parsonage."

"Even the prettiest roses have thorns," she said.

"Yes. They can be quite prickly, cannae they?" he said.

Ginger growled from deep in her throat. Rose turned just in time to see a woman with a large, floppy hat peer around the corner, then disappear when she realized she'd been spotted. "Is there somewhere where we might have a bit more privacy?"

The vicar looked out the window. "I would normally suggest the garden, but being as..."

"Fine." She realized too late how snappish she sounded and lowered her voice to a whisper. "I must have that tape, and I'm hoping, pleading really, that ye'll help me get it. What's happened here today just proves my point."

"Which is?" Ian asked.

"That if I dinnae get it back immediately, the whole world will soon know what transpired."

"Know and see," Ian agreed.

Just the thought of Robert's sons and former associates knowing what she'd done – or, heaven forbid, seeing her naked – made her feel like she might faint. If they ever found out, they would see her stripped naked all right, nae just of clothing, but of money, social standing, and respect.

"I dinnae blame ye for giving them the tape," she said, hoping that playing on his guilt as well as his sympathy would gain her an ally. "I knew ye did what ye had to do when ye turned it in."

"I was ethically bound to report it to the authorities." He sounded stiff and defensive.

"Yes. But now that ye're assured that I'm innocent, is nae my right to privacy also an ethical obligation? Ye know, because, well, are ye men of the cloth nae sworn to secrecy in regard to the private things, ye know, that ye're privy to?"

The pastor raised one eyebrow. "What happens at St. Conan's stays at St. Conan's?"

"Exactly!"

"What I'm told in confession, or in a counseling session, is confidential." He shifted his weight. "Nothing I was taught in seminary prepared me as to how to handle the occasional naked woman cavorting with a criminal in the churchyard."

Ginger wined disapprovingly.

"Ye make it sound like a game of Clue," she said, indignantly. "Rose Wilson, in the courtyard, with a candlestick."

He looked at her unapologetically.

"I'm nae some prettily–colored piece moving aboot on a game board," she cried, forgetting to keep her voice down. "I'm a flesh and blood woman with feelings, and a family, and financial concerns, and... Please!"

Ian shushed her just in time by pointing in the direction of the ladies meeting.

She continued in a whisper. "Ye've got to help me get that tape back!"

"I'll certainly do everything I can," he said stiffly.

"I appreciate yer help." She reached down and scratched Ginger's ear. "Do ye think they'll give it back?"

"No," he said. "Nae as long as Digby is at large."

"Then we need to find him," she said, letting the vicar think that she was resigned to the futility of his assessment of the situation.

Ian nodded. "The sooner he's apprehended, put to trial, and convicted, the sooner the tape becomes dispensable."

"But they'll have to use it to convict him? There's nae other evidence they could use?"

"The constable led me to believe that the tape is critical to their case. Believe me, I would na have turned it over otherwise."

"Of course. I believe ye." She believed everybody. She had even believed Digby. Why for Christ's sake wouldnae she believe a vicar?

"If it were me, on the tape, I mean, I wouldnae want... I am so sorry," he said. "If I had known ye... if I had known ye were..."

"What do ye mean?" she said, finally bristling. "Did ye think I was a common whore, or did my hair and nails and clothes at least signify that I might be a high–priced lady of the evening?"

"I was nae..." his face grew even more red. "I thought ye were an accomplice. I thought ye were here to take more artifacts. To be honest, I could nae imagine why the two of ye would stop to... to..."

She could feel her face muscles sagging, her momentary bravado fading to reveal the pathetic, defeated, miserable wretch she was.

"I never should have shown it to them in the first place. I should have found a way to edit out the part where ye..."

"This is nae yer fault. I'm the one who let him pull down my skirt. I'm the one who wanted to be touched so badly that I threw my morals to the wind and..."

"Rose," the vicar said gently. "Ye must nae blame yerself. Ye dinna know what he was up to. There was nae way ye could 'ave known."

He took a step towards her and slipped his arm around her shoulder without saying another word. The gesture felt awkward at first, his arm tight and unnatural, his entire gait distressed. And then, she felt him relax. His grip on her shoulder melted into the heat of her skin. He sighed, and the warmth from his body radiated though her sweater until she felt like she was enveloped in her Granny's old, calico quilt.

"I do," she whispered, seeking his left hand with her right. "Believe ye. I know ye meant me nae harm."

"But harm ye, I did," he said. "And I fully intend to make it up to ye – to help however I can, to stand by yer side, to defend ye. Ye have my word."

"Thank ye." And she meant it. She had to get that tape back. Now. Nae when Digby was caught. Nae when the trial had ended. Now.

Chapter Four

Ian looked at the utterly forlorn expression on Rose's face and then, at the sad, puppy eyes staring up at him and knew he had to do something. "I'd be honored if ye'd join me for a cuppa," he said. "Or a pint. Whatever yer fancy. There's a pub just down the way."

"But the ladies..."

"They will understand." The truth was, he doubted they would. She looked even less convinced.

"But, people will..."

"The first requirement of being a vicar is that ye have to develop thick skin."

"I could use a bit of cheering up," she finally conceded. "If ye're sure."

The only thing he was sure aboot was that he was probably losing his mind. "I am," he said, wishing he could offer her his elbow, but thinking better of it.

"We'll head out the main door then," he said, nodding to the north. Even if they could somehow escape the confines of the church without anyone seeing them, which was unlikely, if anyone from church happened to be at the pub – and it was almost certain they would be – talk of his rendezvous with Rose would be all over town by sundown. Nae that he cared what people thought of him – but he did have his career to consider. If the McNeely's son wasnae married to a cousin of his overseer's daughter's husband's, his superior might never know, but as he was, he had to count on nothing he did going unnoticed.

Rose's dog started to wag her tail as soon as Ian started towards the door. He motioned for her – and Rose – to stay. "If ye'll please give me a moment."

He heard a skittering of footsteps disappearing into the distance as he headed towards the spot where the ladies were working.

"Duty calls, then, ladies. I've need to tend to an urgent matter, so I must bid ye farewell for now."

"Is it her?" One of the women hissed conspiratorially.

"I'm nae at liberty to say, but I thank ye for yer concern," he said. "Carry on."

It wouldnae quell the tide of suspicion for long, but he hoped he'd confounded them enough for he and Rose to make their get–a–way.

He ripped his collar from his neck as he strode down the hall, tossed it on his desk and motioned for Rose and her dog to follow. She kept pace with his long, nervous gait so effortlessly that she made it look easy. Probably from having to keep up with her dog. An energetic one, that one was.

"I do nae want anyone to think ill of ye because of me," she said, when they were on the other side of the heavy entrance doors that led in and out of the kirk.

"I've been a pastor for almost half a decade, during which time I've had to learn nae to worry aboot what people think of me." He toyed with the idea of driving to Kinloch and taking her to the Boar's Head, but it was entirely possible that a parishioner would spot them there as well. And then it would seem as if he were trying to hide something. Which, of course, he was. If they walked down to the Tight Line, he could brush their excursion off as an inconsequential afterthought. Driving to the next town, being in a car together, the two of them and her dog, made the whole thing seem more like a date – an impression he definitely didnae want to give to Rose or the townspeople.

"I'm exactly the same person I was when I left home yesterday morning," Rose said out of the blue, "yet I feel ten years older and a hundred times more foolish."

For a second, Ian considered telling her that he'd forgotten he had a meeting and making a hasty exit. What was he thinking? He could nae even look at the woman without seeing those firm breasts, those puffy, kissable nipples, made hard as pebbles by the nippy breeze coming off Loch Awe...

"It has been a long couple of days." He willed himself to banish thoughts of her round bottom, her... "Lord have mercy." His voice eked out the words in a timber totally unlike his own.

She looked at him queerly.

"Forgive me," he said, trying to blink away his lust.

"Were ye talking to me," she said timidly, "or the Lord?"

"Neither, both... perhaps the world in general," he said.

"Never ever apologize for who ye are," she said, suddenly mentor and equal and champion of the underdog, which did nae make it any easier for him to resist her charm. "Ye've nothing to apologize for. If it were nae for yer gallantry at the constable's office yesterday, I'd still be behind bars."

So much for that plan. He wanted to think she was limited in her mental capacities, for something, anything, to be wrong with her. He wanted to feel an objective sympathy for all she'd been through, a brotherly concern. He did nae want to find her words wise and insightful, her intuition spot on, to be drawn to her emotionally or intellectually.

"If I learn nothing else from this horrid mess with Digby, at least I can say that on the same day my trust in men was destroyed, my faith in the goodness of God was restored," she said. "Thanks to ye."

Her chin quivered ever so slightly. He tried nae to look at the pale lids of her downcast eyes, or her eyelashes, resting demurely on her cheeks, and finally turned away lest her magic should bewitch him any further. *Ye can do this*, he told himself. The woman has been through a terrible trauma. What kind of a man would ye be if ye deserted her now, in her hour of need? One cuppa, one wee bit of lunch. That's it, and ye need never see the woman again.

"I dinnae know what I would have done if ye hadnae been there," she said, tilting her head and smiling faintly at him.

He resisted the urge to slap himself.

He was nae hero. That much, he knew unequivocally. To have looked on her nakedness was to have seen the answers to the final exam before the test. He was a cheater, of the worst kind. And – sorry to say – he hadnae just looked at the answers – he'd memorized them.

"Rose, ye must stop glorifying my actions," he said sternly. "I am very uncomfortable being cast as the leading man in this little drama we find ourselves engaged in."

"I understand," she said, looking as if she did nae.

The front door of the pub was open when they walked up to the gate. A noisy clatter of robust conversation, clanking dishes, and whirling fans reached out to greet them.

"After ye," he said, motioning her to enter.

"Thank ye, kind sir." She ducked to clear the *Mind Yer Head* sign mounted on the thick, dark timbers framing the door, made sure her dog's leash was bound up shortly, and stepped tentatively into the pub.

God help him. He'd always had a heart for bashful women. It was part of the reason he'd never married. The independent, assertive, sometimes brash women of his generation were wonderful to serve with, but when it came to romance... It wasnae because he was intimidated or felt emasculated, he simply felt nae attraction. But there was something aboot Rose, a softness, a shyness...

"What's ye're fancy tonight, Pastor?" Charles said, smiling broadly. "An intimate table for two?"

Intimate, he did nae need. He usually bellied up to the bar, but that wouldnae do with a lady on his arm – so to speak. He straightened his arm and pressed it tightly to his side, lest he should accidentally brush against Rose.

"May we have the table by the window?" Rose said quietly, pointing to a booth with a stained glass window above it.

Charles winked at him and started across the room.

Ian looked around the room and saw nae one from the constable's office. Nae one else would recognize Rose to be the woman who was in cahoots with the robber... or, the woman they'd thought was in cahoots with the robber.

He helped her with her chair and her dog settled in at her feet.

"What can I get for ye?" Charles said, winking again.

"Tea for the lady. I'll have a bottle of lager by the neck, please."

Rose started to speak as soon as Charles left to fill their orders. "I just want ye to know I'm nae in the practice of... I mean, outside, in full view of... or even in the first place... with a relative stranger."

"I'm nae the one to hear yer confession, Rose."

A young man wrapped up in an apron appeared out of the din, set down the pint he'd ordered, and poured Rose's tea from a pot covered with a tea cozy.

He waited to speak until their waiter was five or six feet away. "As I said earlier..."

"I need to talk to someone," she said. "I'd rather die than tell anyone I know what happened yesterday."

"I cannae..."

"But ye already know."

"I know, but... "

"There's nae one else I can talk to. Nae one else I can trust enough to..."

"Certainly yer family would understand if ye..."

"I think my sister would understand. Even if she didnae, she'd nae be one to judge."

He could sense there was a "but" coming.

"My brother–in–law..." She stopped and fiddled with her tea bag, winding the string around it until the air around them was steeped with the scent of fresh strawberries and rose hips kissed by the summer sun.

"If Kevin ever finds out aboot what happened, and he would – Kelly tells him everything, which is as it should be between a man and a woman, I mean, I've always envied the way that they share every little thing, ye know?"

He really didnae – much to his regret. "And yer brother–in–law – would he nae show ye the same compassion?"

"Nae. He's nae my biggest fan. He's threatened more than once to keep my nephews and niece from me. Afraid I might taint them nae doubt, given the little mishaps I'm prone to stumbling into."

He raised an eyebrow.

"Nae that anything like this has ever happened before," she said, her eyes opened so wide with feigned innocence that he had to stifle a smile.

"Of course nae," he said.

The smell of her tea toyed with his senses until he doubted he would ever taste a strawberry without thinking of the way she looked at that moment, sitting across the table, her eyebrows knit together with sincerity, so genuinely distressed, so eager to convince him that she wasnae the woman that anyone who viewed the tape would assume she was.

"When I say mishaps, I just mean little things like speeding tickets and that sort of thing," she said, a tad defensively.

"Yes," he said.

"Nae that I'm a consummate speeder or anything of the sort."

"I didnae infer..."

"Little things, like the time my neighbor and I got into–"

"Really, Rose," he interrupted. "There is nae need for ye to–"

"It was a minor altercation. Nothing more." She brushed a stray lock of hair from her eyes. "Nothing more. I can promise ye that."

He didnae say another word, assuming the quickest way for her to run out of gas was to let her speed down the motorway unhindered.

"What happened, on the tape, was nae what it might have appeared to be," she said.

"Ye can talk aboot it if ye'd like," he said.

She said nothing, but her eyes... her eyes snapped, sizzled, burned.

"Ye said it wasnae like that. What was it like?" He asked, wondering why he needed to hear it from her. He'd seen the video. He knew what had happened. He'd seen the passion, the hunger, the need. And nae just that. He'd seen her breasts, her nakedness, the vulnerability.

"It was..." she choked, coughed.

"Ye dinnae owe me an explanation."

"Maybe nae ye." She looked up at the sky.

"Oh, I see what ye mean." He brushed his fingers through his hair. "Again, I'm a vicar, nae a priest." And a man, he thought. *A man who's seen ye naked.* "Unless ye really need to unburden yerself..."

"I do," she said, her voice almost snappish. "It's been almost three years since my husband died, and there's been nae one in all that time."

"Until now," he said, gently, reminding himself yet again that he was nae allowed to feel superior because he had somehow managed to live without sex for five years running. It wasnae by choice after all – a vicar couldnae exactly run around having gratuitous sex. He hadnae taken vows of celibacy, but as an unmarried pastor, unless he planned to go against everything he preached on Sunday mornings, he may as well have.

"I was so starved for a little affection," she said. "I would have done almost anything for a little... and then, I found out I had a lump in my breast."

"I'm so sorry."

"Ye need nae be," she said. "I'm fine now. But for three long weeks I endured mammograms and ultrasounds and steriotactic breast biopsies, waiting and waiting and waiting, without so much as a hug."

"Or a caress," he said, wistfully.

"The day I met Digby, I'd had my biopsy. I was waiting for the results," she said, like that explained it all, her spreading her legs for a man she barely knew in a churchyard far from home where anything could have happened.

"It's the size of a strand of spaghetti," she said, her voice distant. "The sample of breast tissue they take from ye."

"I didnae know."

"The computer guides them in, so they get the right spot."

"They can do so much with computers nowadays," he said, still feeling uncomfortable talking aboot her breasts even though they had moved into clinical waters, which should have helped him forget the oh so soft, rosy–looking skin, the puffy nipples, the way her breasts curved away from her body and joined it again, the siren's song of her breasts.

"Lord help me," he said, nae realizing he had spoken aloud until he heard his own voice.

She gave him a curious look and flushed pink in her cheeks, as if she knew what he was thinking. She probably did.

"I was waiting to hear the results of the biopsy," she said. "My breast was still sore and tender. Digby offered to give it a kiss and make it all better."

Sure he did. She'd taken it as a sweet, considerate, almost motherly act. Ian didnae know this Digby, but he was a man, and he knew all aboot the lines men used to earn themselves the opportunity to see a woman's breasts.

"That's why, when Digby..." she stopped.

"I can imagine," he said, an understatement for her benefit, since he could do much more than speculate on what had happened next. He'd seen her in all her naked glory, there on the grass, under the flying buttresses.

"It had been so long," she said. "I felt like a garden, soaking up rain at the end of a very long drought."

Digby had rained on her all right, poured it on as thick as a deluge – to continue the analogy.

"I'm nae the type to succumb after one or two dates," she said, her voice more prickly than she'd been even when she'd been arrested.

She wasnae. He believed that much. He'd seen the way she'd spread her legs – slowly, fearfully, hesitantly, modestly – wanting to be touched so badly that she'd set aside her own morals and beliefs to do the unthinkable. That much he knew.

"I wasnae going to do it again. Nae any time soon."

He stuffed his hands in his pockets. "Probably a wise choice, knowing what we now know."

"But I didnae know."

"I know," he said.

"I'm very fortunate Digby didnae... I mean, when he gave, and didnae take, I thought that was proof that he was a nice man. Trustworthy." She sighed. "I feel like such a fool."

"Rose, ye must nae blame yerself. Ye dinnae know what he was up to. There was nae way ye could 'ave known."

An awkward silence followed.

"Is that it?" She looked expectant. "Dinnae ye need to say something official? Absolve me? Forgive me? Condemn me to hell?"

"Do ye have a pastor of yer own, Rose? Because I really cannae..." *How could he?* Because of her breasts — if for nae other reason.

"Fine," she said, huffing, pushing back her chair.

The easy thing would have been to just let her go. "Wait. Rose?"

She stopped and inched forward on her seat. "Yes?"

"Ye will let me know if ye hear anything more from Digby, will ye nae?"

"Of course." She hung her head. "I'll let ye know if he calls."

He nodded.

"I am truly sorry," she said, waving her arm as if to encompass her entire existence.

"Ye need nae be."

"I dinnae mean aboot Digby. I just meant, well, thank ye for listening. I know I ramble when I'm excited."

He smiled. "A wee bit."

"Ramblin' Rose. That's what my da used to call me when I..." She stopped.

Funny – he had already begun to think of her as Wild Rose.

A comfortable silence settled over them. If he hadnae been a minister – if she hadnae been a suspected accomplice to a crime against his church – he would have reached his hand across the table and given hers a squeeze.

Chapter Five

Rose looked up at the lofty beams and soaring ceilings of St. Conan's. In the end, she'd been persuaded to finish her tea and scones and to let the vicar walk her back to St. Conan's when they were done eating. Unfortunately, just as they were leaving, they'd run into a group of the same church ladies who'd been talking aboot her earlier. The vicar hadnae apologized verbally, but his entire demeanor begged their forgiveness, which did ease her conscience since she was really only using the poor gent to get the tape back.

She walked towards the altar. That was the thing aboot churches. If Christians really acted like Christ, churches everywhere would be filled with inspiration, forgiveness and honesty, wouldnae they? One should think, when ye entered the House of God that there would be nae deceit, nae rancor, and nae backstabbing. Sadly, it appeared that in those respects, St. Conan's was nae different than the rest of the world. It was quite disappointing.

She had to admit that the place did have a comfortable feel, though. Maybe it was the worn pews, the slightly dusty look of the floors, or the fact that the women had called the vicar Pastor Ian instead of Reverend MacCraig.

Because the other thing aboot churches was that while they were supposedly designed to lift yer spirits and inspire awe, more often than nae, they were more intimidating than welcoming. How had anyone come to think that austere, gothic cathedrals would make someone want to get to know God better? She looked down at her feet and climbed the steps to the chancel. She supposed the old stone floors, worn smooth with the gaits of all the saints who had gone before, could be construed as welcoming. They could also be cold and unforgiving. Anything that dropped on them would most likely shatter instantly.

She turned and looked up at the cherubs carved into the stained glass window and tried to focus on the warmth of being surrounded by angels and nae on the sharp shards of glass that had been used to form the design.

31

Pastor Ian had excused himself and gone to his office, and really, there was nae reason for her nae to be getting back to her B&B, which was a lot cozier than this place. She'd let Ginger off her leash and she was slipping and sliding around the smooth stone floors of the church like one of the three stooges doing a comedy shtick.

She wandered through the nave to the cloister. The low beams of the passageway gave her a more secure feeling, as much as stone and rough–hewn timbers could.

Things could definitely be worse, she reminded herself. So what if the church ladies were whispering aboot her behind her back? Only sticks and stones could break bones and nobody was throwing anything at her except words. At least nae yet.

But bones and brains were two different things entirely, and while her body was just fine, her feelings were definitely hurt.

She heard a noise and looked up to see Pastor Ian. She tried to put on a brave face, because she really didnae want him to feel any worse than he already did. But there was something aboot the man, something that compelled honesty, something that said, he already had ye figured out anyway, so ye might as well spill the beans.

And so, she did. What was the use of trying to pretend that things were anything other than what they were? She trailed her fingers along the rough patch of wall and looked up to find his eyes on her. "I've always been a popular sort, ye know – class president, rugby cheerleader, show choir – and I just dinnae... I mean... I thought my skin had toughened up after the past two, almost three years, of being a widow, dealing with my late husband's sons and an antagonistic board of directors where I work, but still, I find I'm ill equipped for all this negativity."

Pastor Ian touched her back in a soothing gesture. "It will blow over in a month or two, maybe sooner than that. Digby will be caught – or nae – and life will go on. We'll go our separate ways and nae one will even remember." Ian's voice was gentle and calming.

It was tempting. Nae more humiliation – well, none except what she got on a regular basis from the members of the board, Robert Junior and Rodney – but none more than she was used to.

But if she didnae find a way to get the tape, it would be out there forever, threatening to pop up and ruin her life at any time, coming back to haunt her – who knew when? That, she could nae live with.

But that was a topic for another time.

"I'd like to make it up to them somehow. The ladies, and the people of St. Conan's, I mean. I know I dinnae have to, but I want to. I could bring snacks to serve after church next Sunday." Her brain revved up and went into high gear. "I could bring strawberries dipped in chocolate. Oh – and I make the best mini–battenbergs. Or, I could do some bite–sized Victoria sponge with buttercream. They always get rave reviews when I serve them at parties. Even Kelly's boys – my nephews – Kelly is my sister – like them."

"Rose," Pastor Ian said. "It's truly nae necessary to–"

"I know! I could donate my sewing machine to the quilting guild. They do have a quilting guild, dinnae they? I never use it, and it's completely state of the art. All the latest – every kind of fancy gadgetry imaginable. The ladies would love it."

"As I was saying, nae one expects ye to–"

"I do have a few pillows to sew first though. For my niece, Lyndsie. Long story. But I could make them first thing next week and have the machine here by next Wednesday."

She couldnae just keep showing up. She had to have an excuse to be in town, to talk to Pastor Ian, to get the tape back. Okay. So she was a louse – dabbling with church ladies, pretending to be nice so she could get her hands on the evidence – but wouldnae anyone do the same?

"Can ye think of anything else?" She smiled at Ian in what she deemed to be her most contrite and sincere expression.

"If we could only catch Digby," he said. "That would set things straight, all right."

Her glance met his and stuck. Such a sweet, thoughtful, kind–hearted man. If only she had met someone like him instead of the likes of Digby.

"Can ye think of a way? I thought he cared aboot me, but when he didnae show up yesterday – well, I guess I can assume that I was wrong aboot that, too."

"Ye dinnae have anything he wants, something precious to him that he may have left behind on a previous, um... rendezvous, do ye?" The vicar asked.

Rose shook her head. "He's never been to my home. We've only had three meetings – in person. Most of our chatting and getting to know each other was done online."

"I dinnae know how to say this delicately, Rose, but knowing what ye now know, is it possible that he was planning to steal from ye as well? Jewelry? Assets? Cash?"

"I dinnae think he knew that I had any!" A chill ran down her spine. Was it possible that Digby knew who she really was?

* * *

The next day, Ian had put his feet on and was out on his daily trek – the same time of day, and the same place he'd been when Rose and Digby had been going at it under the flying buttresses – when he saw Rose's car parked alongside the Corrie Bank B&B.

He was set to make a hasty retreat when he caught a glimpse of Ginger's eager face rounding the bend, her furry paws mopping the pavement only a few dozen meters from where he stood. He looked up and saw Rose's equally eager face, which was a second or two after he forced himself to look away from her bouncing breasts.

They were sculpted in what appeared to be a bright pink, form–fitting sports bra.

Once she'd spotted him, he could hardly turn away from the woman and walk in the opposite direction, so he stood and awaited her approach.

"Pastor Ian!" She raised her arm high over her head and waived enthusiastically, which further complicated matters by doing all kinds of riveting things to her... *Ye have to stop this. Now,* Ian told himself sternly.

She drew closer, and appeared to be talking on her mobile. A few more steps and he could hear every word she was saying.

"No. He's just someone I met at one of the historic sites I've been investigating." Pause. "Mum, I would tell ye if he were someone special." She gave him an apologetic look. "No, I did nae tell Kelly I would be home today." Pause. "Yes. I promised her I would make Lyndsie some new pillows, and I will." Pause. "No, I have nae started them yet. But I will as soon as I return." Pause. "No, I'm going to need to stay another few days."

"Rose. What a surprise," he said when she finally put her mobile away. He crouched low to scratch Ginger's ears and waited for her to explain why she was still in Loch Awe.

Instead, she raved aboot the weather, asked him how many miles per day he walked, and told an anecdote or two or three aboot Ginger.

34

Was bumping into him the sole reason she was back in Loch Awe, or what was the woman up to now?

And then she got down to brass tacks. "I do have something I need to speak to ye aboot – nae worries – it's nae another confession. I promise ye that." And then she smiled, and the little dimples in her cheeks winked at him, and her rich auburn curls, accentuated by the wind and humidity, reached out to him like tendrils ready to latch on to a trellis and climb higher and higher – which was apropos, because he would have flown to the moon and jumped off the highest mountain for her if she'd asked it of him.

"Certainly." He struggled to keep his wits aboot him, his equilibrium intact. If they needed to talk, it would have to be later, when he'd had a chance to compose himself, and when she was dressed in something far more staid and conservative. "How aboot dinner later tonight?"

Chapter Six

Ian looked across the table at Rose Wilson and tried to compartmentalize his feelings – the physical attraction, the surge of emotions he felt each time she entered a room, and the more professional aspects of their relationship – and failed.

The woman was very vulnerable, that was all. She needed a friend, didnae she? He was in a position to help. That was his job, wasnae it? Sure, she wasnae a regular member of his congregation, but he was a pastor. How could he turn his back and walk away when she was so obviously distressed and in need of good counsel?

He watched her closely as she rambled on aboot this and that – as she had been the whole time they'd been eating dinner. To be honest, he'd loved having an excuse to stare at her, to gaze deeply into her hazel green eyes, to memorize the beautiful lines of her face and nose and chin – all points of interest that had been overlooked at their previous meetings.

Her olive green dress and the scarf she wore around her neck – a beautiful concoction made of unique yarns in shades of royal blue, pink, and greens – made her eyes dazzle. The collar of her dress was high and caressed the sweep of her neck just enough to be alluring. Her dress was nae nearly as overtly sexual as the clothing she'd worn – or nae – on any of their previous meetings. His eyes traveled down a notch and met with her scarf again. The way it swept around and aboot her chest essentially hid the fact that she even had breasts, which was a very good thing, indeed.

Rose Wilson was a very lovely woman. He doubted he would ever tire of looking at her. And a very complex woman as well. The things she'd rambled on aboot were intriguing to say the least.

But still, he wished she'd left her family out of it. How was he to maintain a sense of impartiality with thoughts of a doting young niece and impressionable young nephews and a concerned, respectable sister floating around in his head?

"Ian, I mean Pastor MacCraig–"

"I said ye could call me Ian," he said, and realized afterwards that his voice sounded a bit terse.

"Ian. Would ye mind if we went for a little stroll instead of eating dessert?" She lowered her voice. "Now that people have figured out who I am, I'm afraid that anything I say in these close quarters might be overheard."

He looked around the restaurant and spotted several men from St. Conan's ogling Rose as though she were still under the flying buttresses, stripped nude.

"Yes," he said nervously, because truth be told, he was still having the occasional image pop into his head. "I'll get the bill and we'll be on our way then. The walls do seem to have ears tonight."

Rose thanked him, and a few minutes later, they were walking along Loch Awe in the still bright light of the midsummer night. The rhododendrons were in full bloom now – lavender, fuchsia, and pink.

"Beautiful, are they nae?" Rose said. "I was just noticing them, too."

"I'm glad ye suggested a stroll."

"Yes. It was quite crowded in there, and I've something to say that's a bit indelicate." Rose motioned to a bench several yards up the path.

He voiced a silent prayer for divine assistance. What else could he do? He already knew far too many indelicate things aboot the woman, but if she needed a friendly ear, and she certainly seemed to...

"It's the video tape. I keep thinking aboot it," she confessed.

"I know what ye mean." He also felt the need to confess, although he let it rest at that.

"I'm just nae comfortable with it floating around out there, where the wrong people could get their hands on it at any time." She paused and looked in all directions as if to make sure they were nae being overheard. "I've come up with a plan to retrieve it. But I need yer help."

"As long as ye dinnae ask me to do something illegal." He joked.

She leaned closer and her mannerisms grew even more clandestine. "There is a piece of technology that erases video tapes. A powerful magnet."

"There is?"

"Yes. My plan is to purchase one and take it to the constable's office. I'm just so... I have to destroy that tape. If I dinnae, it will end up on the Internet. I just know it. And my mother, and Kelly and little Lyndsie will–"

"I promised ye that I would do everything in my power to make sure the tape is never seen."

"Yes. But it's already been seen. It's only a matter of time before–"

"But what ye're planning to do – it's against the law." He understood the urgency she felt, nae for fear of the same repercussions, but because he had seen the tape and understood the sheer embarrassment of it. "I agree that the content of the tape must never be revealed to the public."

"Thank ye," she stammered, apparently misunderstanding him.

"But while I do sympathize with yer plight," he searched for the words to correct her misconception, "that does nae mean I can condone breaking and entering or willful destruction of evidence, or—"

"I'm nae asking for yer approval." Rose's voice took on a rebellious tone. "I'm asking for yer help. I'll be the one to have the magnet. If it comes down to it, ye can say that ye had nae idea what I was up to. All I'm asking is that ye come down to the station with me and create some sort of diversion until I've gained access to the vault and erased the tape."

"But what will ye say? How will ye get them to let ye see the tape?" He chose nae to bring up the fact that she was asking him to lie.

"Leave that part up to me. The less ye know, the better." She did nae look confident. She probably did have a clue what she was going to do.

Every instinct that was in him screamed nae to get involved with the woman. But there was a smidgen – a part of him that desperately wanted to protect her honor. He barely knew her. But for some reason, he was determined to fight for her with every ounce of his resolve.

Rose inhaled deeply of rhododendron blossoms and what she supposed was whatever soap Ian had used to shower – the scent of cucumbers fresh from the garden mixed with herbs and a subtle, but very manly perfume. It cloyed with her senses. Which to be frank, was quite irritating. Her nerves were already over–stimulated due to the continuous adrenalin urge she'd felt ever since she'd learned of Digby's betrayal and the existence of the tape. She didnae need a man pushing her over the precipice.

She stood, and Ian seemed startled. "Well, I'd best get back to my room at Corrie Bank and get some sleep." *Best get back to Ginger before she felt abandoned again and had another rabies attack.* Come to think of it, her bed at Corrie Bank had been covered with beautiful pillows. Her pulse quickened and she looked at the stone wall between the bench where she and Ian had been resting and the previously non–descript churchyard she'd made infamous. She did her best to steer her emotions towards the cold, gray wall instead of the virile man in front of her.

She and Ian had been discussing their options for over an hour, going back and forth between the options – going in under cover of night or in full view of daylight, sneaking in or walking in right off the street as if nothing was wrong, he carrying the magnet that would erase the tape, or her.

The wall did its job and left her cold, but soon enough, she'd given into her impulses and glanced back at the man, this time, with a new respect. And yes, she now thought of him nae as a pastor, but as a man. Now that she'd gotten past his pesky collar and the embarrassment of knowing he'd seen her naked, she could see the determination in the set of his jaw and in the way he held his shoulders, broad and impenetrable. She could see the fiery passion in his green blue eyes. And she knew without a doubt that this chivalrous man, who barely knew her, was ready to fight for her with every iota of power available to him.

Trouble was, he had none. If it ever came to it, her step–sons would use their money and power to squash him like a bug. A vicar, a gentle vicar, a caring vicar, a loving, humble pastor, would be nae match for their cunning barristers and vindictive agendas.

* * *

The next day, Rose stood beside Ian a few feet from the outside of the constable's office in Loch Awe. "Ye're certain this is the best way?"

"Dinnae say anything more until we're in and out." Ian sounded stern. "They've probably got the whole place wired."

Somehow, she didnae think so, but she was in nae position to argue. Ian nodded covertly, which made nae sense, since they'd opted for the middle–of–the–day, out–in–plain–sight plan he'd favored.

If they'd selected her plan, she would have dressed in all black to blend in with the night air. She'd had just the thing, too – black leggings that were close cropped so as nae to catch on random tree branches or window hardware, a black blouse that had designer lines and would look good in the photographs if they were apprehended. Nae that she wanted to be caught, but having endured the stigma of being photographed nude, she felt very strongly aboot being appropriately dressed should she be featured in any sort of future documentary.

Which was a moot point now, because here they were in street clothes walking up to the front door in broad daylight instead of creeping up unaware. Ian had said it was impossible to compromise the security system at a town hall that did double duty as a jail.

"So it's yer job to distract them. Nothing more, nothing less," Ian was saying. "I'll take care of the rest. Just keep them focused on ye."

Imagining her naked was what they'd be doing, which in theory, should make her job easy. But of course, Ian was too polite to say so. Even so, she'd dressed the part in a tight fitting knit sweater that showed off her best assets.

She had her basic shtick memorized, but she was prepared to ad lib as needed.

Ian opened the door, held it for her, and waited for her to enter.

"Well, looky who we have here." The constable didnae rise. Nor did he look or sound particularly thrilled to see them.

"Could I speak to ye for a moment?" She smiled in what she hoped was a professional manner and sashayed to the constable's desk. "I have some questions aboot what to do if Digby calls me again."

The constable didnae seem excited. "He's called ye then?"

"Nae since before I found out what he was up to. But I fully expect him to, and I'd like to be ready, if ye know what I mean." She winked at the constable and tried to forget aboot what Ian was or wasnae doing with the magic eraser.

"Also, I've been thinking aboot the description of Digby that I gave ye the night ye interrogat..., er, um interviewed me, and I'm wondering if I might have inadvertently given ye some faulty information. I know it will be painful for me to see the tape, but if I could see it – use it as a means to refresh my memory – I feel sure that I could give ye some more detailed physical attributes than I did before."

The constable winked back at her. "Dinnae ye worry yer pretty little head aboot that. We've viewed the tape several times on our special digital imaging machine."

Her heart sputtered as she imagined them gawking at her, naked. Over and over again. "Which is?"

"A digital imaging machine? Oh, nothing ye need to worry aboot."

"Why dinnae I be the judge of that?" She tried to keep her voice sounding sweet and harmless. It was hard.

"Oh, it's just this little piece of equipment that magnifies the images on a tape so we can see each and every minute detail that the camera has captured. Ye know, zoom in close so we can spot a little scar or blemish. On this monitor, we can see every little hair, the pores on people's noses, any little thing that might give us a clue. Hard on the old eyes, but if it leads us to the perpetrator, well worth it."

"Okay," Rose said. Call her mortified beyond belief. Her brain felt absolutely numb as it grasped frantically to come up with another reason plausible enough to justify her need to see the tape. "Um, Pastor Ian also wants, ah, needs to see the tape so he can check on something for his insurance money. Silly folks are claiming that the buttresses are crumbling from natural causes, and have been for years, while Ian, um Pastor Ian feels sure that all of the buttresses were intact a month ago. If he can see how they look on the tape, then he could verify his claim and prove to the insurance company that the damage was recent."

"Interesting." The constable twirled his pencil. "And how does Pastor Ian maintain that the buttresses got damaged?"

"I suppose it was Digby, thrashing his legs around while he was... or me, leaning against them without even thinking aboot the damage I might be doing. Even thinking aboot it at all for that matter."

"Thank ye. Just curious, that's all."

"It's a mystery, all right."

The constable leaned back in his swivel chair, looking much too amused for her comfort.

Where was Ian in all of this? Had he been able to accomplish their mission while she was going on and on to the constable?

"So it's imperative that the two of ye see the tape."

"Yes," she answered, trying nae to sound too overjoyed. She gave her best effort at appearing distraught. "Painful as I know it will be."

"That's what ye were saying."

"So is there a viewer we might use? And a private room, if possible? As I'm sure ye can understand–"

"Oh, I understand, all right. Pastor? Would ye please come here for a second?"

Ian turned, and she saw his cheeks flame red, as though he'd been outside for too long on the coldest day of the year. Except that it was a cool summer day, and there was nae reason for him to be overheated, which left... Guilt. Shame. Ian looked for all the world as though he'd been caught red–handed.

Stop it! Right now! She wanted to hiss the words at him before it was too late and the constable caught on, but there was nae opportunity. *Please Ian. Ye've nae reason to look guilty. We've been through all of this. The tape is personal. It never should have been made public. It doesnae show Digby stealing anything. It just puts him at the scene of the crime. And I can do that!*

"So ye want to see the tape, do ye?" The constable reached out his hand as if to shake Ian's but instead slipped it inside Ian's jacket and pulled out the magnet.

Ian lowered his head and grimaced, guilt now written all over his face as well as staining his cheeks.

He didnae even try to defend himself. No, *"Well, for heaven's sake – what's that doing there?"* No, *"Well look at that, will ye? What on earth did I have in my pocket?"* Or, *"Must be a relic from the last time I wore this jacket, which had to have been three or four years ago, which was the last time I was this weight, in the summer anyway. That must have been the year I attended the magnet convention down in London."*

Nae anything. Ian just stood there, looking utterly ashamed, and said nothing.

And then, it became clear that he had lost his chance, because the constable started talking and didnae stop for a long, long time.

"Get me a fingerprinting kit," the constable said. "And turn the camera on so it's warmed up by the time I'm ready to get their mug shots."

"Yes, sir." One of the constable's underlings scurried off to do his bidding.

Sally, the dispatcher, who was cousin to Ian's mother, and quite possibly the leak that had resulted in half the village seeing her naked, looked both mortified and elated. The pastor arrested! Quite the horror! But, oh, what a juicy tidbit to impart to friends and neighbors. And let's nae forget, relatives.

"Rosalie Wilson, I hereby..." She was being read her rights to an attorney. "Ian MacCraig, I hereby..." Ian, too.

"Wait!" Her voice came out like the screech of an owl. How she sounded was the least of her worries. "There must be something we can do."

The constable sat back and smiled like his work here was done. She knew on some level that this was probably the point where the constable let her hang herself by doing the good cop / bad cop thing, or engaging in some sort of ultra–sophisticated psychological manipulations until he'd eked a full confession out of her, but she couldnae seem to stop herself.

"Pastor Ian was only trying to help me! It was my idea. I'm the one who talked him in to coming over here. Arrest me if ye must. Just, please, please let Pastor Ian go."

"Ye'd like that, would ye?" the constable asked her, as calm and unflappable as if he were out for a Sunday afternoon walk instead of in his office, aboot to put two perfectly innocent victims in jail.

"Of course I would," Rose snapped, waiting for the other shoe to drop.

"Well, here's what I'd like," the constable circled round his desk until there was nothing separating them but a few inches. "What I'd like is for the people of Lochawe to get restitution for the things that were stolen from them."

"But Rose had nothing to do with the theft." Ian's cheeks were still bright red. Now his eyes were glowing, too. The man looked more like a demon than a saint.

"Rose? What say ye?"

She said nothing, her rambling tongue stuck, for once.

"It would be such a shame if that tape were released to the public. Wouldnae it?"

"Ye wouldnae." Rose stared.

"Or even the newspaper. Just think what would happen if one of those English tabloids that everyone reads got a hold of yer story. Such tawdry rags." The constable shook his head as though he felt genuine sympathy for her plight.

"I sure wouldnae want to be ye if the news should ever break."

"Those photos would go viral in a nanosecond if someone were to post them on the Internet," the constable's chief deputy said.

"But this wasnae Rose's fault," Ian said. "Catch Digby and make him pay! It was he who stole the relics."

"That's Rose's contention. The only evidence we have is the tape, which places both of them at the scene of the crime. And somehow I have the feeling that if I ever do catch Digby and have the opportunity to interview him, he would be sitting here saying that it was Rose who did it."

"But he'd be lying," Rose whispered.

"I'm sure he would say the same of ye."

"Rose has nae reason to steal anything," Ian thundered.

"I'm sure the judge will take Rose's virtues into consideration after he's had a look at the tape and any other evidence or testimonies we acquire between now and then."

Rose bit her lip and hoped she was doing the right thing, or in this case, what the constable wanted her to do. If he was trying to trap her again, she was in trouble. Attempted destruction of evidence and attempted bribery would nae look good on her record.

"What if... what if I were to make amends then? Before we let this whole thing spiral out of control."

The constable smiled. "That's very generous of ye, Rose. Pastor, is it nae kind of Rose to offer?"

Ian did nae look happy. "If that's what ye say."

"Perhaps a sizeable donation to St. Conan's – to make up for the losses they suffered because of my poor choice in friends."

"I like the way ye think, Rose. Sally, a pen for the lady, please."

"Oh, but..." Rose stammered. "Ye thought... I dinnae have my checkbook with me, and..." *Was it possible to feel any more embarrassed than she already was?*

"I'm nae liking ye as much as I did a few minutes ago, Rose."

She lowered her eyes. "I get a stipend each month in just the amount needed to cover my living expenses plus a little extra for whatnots. It's nae enough to fund a savings account, and my flat and its contents are nae mine to sell. It's all part of the trust Robert set up for me before he died. I've got nae way to..."

"Book them." The constable said.

"This is ridiculous," Ian thundered. "Ye're blackmailing her."

"I have nae cash reserves. But the Foundation does," Rose said frantically. "I'm the one responsible for ferreting out deserving charities and researching appropriate places to disperse the foundations charitable giving allotments each month. If ye'll just give me some time..."

The constable's jaw was set and locked. "Two weeks. I'm giving ye two weeks from today's date."

Chapter Seven

The constable's words were still ringing in Ian's ears as he walked into the special congregational meeting that the deacons at St. Conan's had convened when they'd heard the news of his and Rose's failed attempt to recover the tape. Word of their near arrest had saturated the town and nae doubt, the surrounding areas.

Even after Rose had agreed to make restitution, the constable had detained them and interrogated them each in separate rooms. While he had nae idea what they'd said to Rose, he imagined that he finally knew some of the humiliation she'd been enduring all week.

When he'd tried to defend her virtue, they'd laughed at him, called him naïve and gullible. They'd told him she was a liar and would do anything to get what she wanted.

"She's using ye, Pastor. She's a common whore."

He cringed again, just remembering.

"The woman needs yer good name, yer respectability to give her credence. That's why she keeps involving ye."

But that wasnae it at all. He wanted to be involved. He was responsible for at least part of the mess Rose was in. And he still believed in her innocence.

So when the meeting was finally called to order, he told his congregation exactly what he'd told the constable. "I know it was a bit unorthodox, but there were good reasons for what Rose did under the flying buttresses. She explained everything to me and... and... And I believe her." He wanted to tell them aboot the lump in her breast, that beautiful breast, her fear, the aloneness she'd felt, her strong need to be held. He knew it was the truth because he felt it as deeply as she did. His triggers were different, but he felt it just the same.

But he couldnae tell them. Nae any of it. She hadnae just shared the details of her ordeal with him; she'd confessed. Her request for absolution had proved that much.

He couldnae. He had betrayed her once already by looking at the tape for his own gratification. He couldnae divulge her confidences, even if doing so would benefit her. He would just have to make them understand with his own words.

"I may nae be as experienced, or jaded as some of ye gentlemen are – but I know human nature just as surely as ye do, and I know she's telling the truth."

William MacCragon cleared his throat. "Pastor, nae offense meant, but is it nae possible that yer judgment has been marred by her... her..."

A muffled snort sounded from across the room, followed by a loud guffaw. He gave a stern look in the direction of the noise and said nothing.

"Just because ye're a pastor doesnae mean ye're immune to the wiles of a well–endowed woman," his head deacon said kindly.

"Likely more so than most," a gent who only came to church on Easter, Christmas and when there was an argument brewing, said. "He cannae go out and find a release for his built–up tensions like the rest of us, now can he?"

A few of the men laughed nervously. The women responded with disapproving looks.

"There are things I cannae..." He sighed and tried to hide his mounting exasperation. "And I dinnae mean sex. There are things I cannae say. But I can say, well... I've spoken to the woman directly. Ye're operating on hearsay. I've spent time with her, been with her..."

He realized his mistake too late. "I should nae have to defend myself. I've been yer pastor for three years. If I havenae earned yer trust by this time..."

"Dinnae go getting yer knickers in a bunch," Mrs. Clooney said loudly. "Nae one's questioning yer judgment."

But they were.

"Fine. Press charges against the woman if ye feel ye must. But I'm telling ye, as someone who knows more than he can say, that Rose Wilson is innocent."

There ye had it. He'd made his best case, done all that he could. It was out of his hands.

"I say she's just as guilty as the man who pawned the goods," one of the woman said after a brief silence.

"If nothing else, she's guilty by association," another of the deacons said.

"Pastor preached aboot that just last month," Phyllis, the 73 year old church secretary said, glancing at him for the approval she was sure she was aboot to receive.

While it was impressive that the woman had remembered one of his sermons for over three weeks, this wasnae the kind of guilt by association he'd been talking aboot.

He raised his hand. "What I said was to choose yer companions with care. That if ye choose to spend yer company in the presence of men who think adultery is acceptable, ye may be surprised to find yer attitude mimicking theirs."

"Exactly," Phyllis said, her voice full of sanctimonious censure. "She chose her companions very poorly. Now she has to pay the price."

A murmur of approval rippled through the room. Like it or nae, when Phyllis spoke, people listened.

"She dinnae know he was a thief," Ian said, trying to keep the edge out of his voice. "He conned her into believing he was in love with her. He told her he was from a family of means. He told her he worked for a charity. She did nae knowingly associate with a criminal."

"But a criminal he was, nonetheless," William said, sounding uncustomarily sage.

"The only thing she's guilty of is believing what the man said," Sarah Dumfries said.

The room stilled. Sarah's first husband had run off with the teenager who'd baby–sat the couple's one year old.

"Since when is being gullible and believing what a man tells ye a crime?" Sarah said, her voice wavering between impassioned and dull, her entire demeanor weary from waging the same battle.

"Exactly," Ian said. "I dinnae think I'm breaking any confidences to say that Rose lost her husband of seventeen years quite recently. If I know anything aboot human nature, and I believe I do, I would presume that Rose's grief made her vulnerable to this man's promises. How can we, in good conscience, condemn her for that? It's compassion we should be showing the lass."

A number of chagrined glances crisscrossed the room.

"Ye're sure ye've nae been hoodwinked by the lady?" William said.

"Sure as sure can be. Ye know I'm nae a betting man, but if I were, I'd stake my reputation on it."

* * *

"So ye're dating the woman now, are ye?" Phyllis's incredulous tone echoed back and forth across the sanctuary, bounced off the stained glass windows, veered left where the baptismal font used to be and rounded the corner at the sacristy.

"It's nae a date." He'd just been on his mobile with Rose. Unfortunately, Phyllis had come back from taking tea before he'd disconnected. "We have business to discuss."

"But ye're meeting for dinner."

"What? I'm to drive all the way to Glasgow and back without so much as a bite to eat?"

"And meeting the woman for dinner is different than going out on a date, um, how?"

"In ways I've nae need to explain to ye," he said, his patience finally spent.

"It's nae me ye'll have to answer to. It's yer deacons."

He looked away from her, nae trusting his facial expressions, and left the room. He resisted the temptation to slam the door.

He bowed his head. Might God grant him the same control when it came to the other temptations that assaulted him.

* * *

Rose fluffed the hair on both sides of her face and freshened her strawberry pink lipstick. Here she was, waiting again. This time it was Ian who was late. Only five minutes, which wasnae much, given that he was driving all the way from Lochawe, but still. Would she never learn?

She glanced over her shoulder. Still nae sign of him.

Good grief. What had she been thinking when she'd said she'd meet him?

The waiter who'd been assigned to the table she was supposed to be sharing with Ian came round for the third time and asked if she wanted something to drink while she waited. This time, she gave in and ordered an amaretto sour – the same drink she'd been sipping on when she'd found out that Robert was dead.

Nae that she had any desire to tempt fate, especially when it hadnae been very kind to her as of late.

She was sure Ian would be here soon. And really, there was every reason to try to get off on a better foot with the man. She did owe him. She'd almost gotten him arrested. Things had been very unsettled between them the last time they'd been together and they'd never had a chance to properly debrief after their ordeal at the constables office. And, she did need his help if she was going to put together a convincing application for the grant she'd promised the constable she'd secure for St. Conan's.

Although Ian – Pastor Ian – hadnae made clear his motivation for wanting to meet her for dinner, she felt sure his agenda was the same as hers. And really, everything was probably just fine, even though he was running a few minutes late.

If she could trust anyone, it ought to be a minister. On the other hand, Ian wasnae just any minister. He was the minister who had tried to help her recover the tape. He was the minister who'd almost gone to jail on her behalf. Unfortunately, he was also the minister who'd seen her writhing on the ground in the throes of misguided ecstasy.

She felt her cheeks flush, and honestly couldnae tell whether her blush came from perpetual embarrassment, or the sexual reverberations she seemed to get just thinking aboot sex – good or bad.

It was probably a good thing Ian was a minister. Even if they were to get involved – and she felt quite sure they wouldnae – there would be nae jumping the gun with him.

That's when she saw Ian MacCraig in a tweed, wool sport coat and a turtleneck sweater, looking every bit a man and nae at all like a pastor, gazing at her from across the room. The mait're de nodded and Ian strode in her direction, his muscular shoulders swaying to the movement of his steps, his face lit up in a smile.

Her heart fluttered. What was wrong with her? Just because the gent's collar was gone didnae mean that he still wasnae a man of God.

"Rose." He took her hand.

Such a shame the man was a minister. Such a shame aboot everything. Her reputation did precede her, after all. What future could they have?

"Rev. MacCraig," she said, sounding stiff even to her own ears.

"Back to that again, are we? Please, call me Ian. I'm here as a friend."

"Of course." *See?* She'd had high hopes – buried deeply under her cynicism – and for what? He'd made it clear in their first 60 seconds together that he didnae think of her in a romantic light.

Fine. If friends was what he wanted to be...

Then why was he still holding her hand? She looked up and met his eyes. Why was he stroking her hand with his thumb – lazy, random circles, gentle, firm with promise...

She snapped herself out of her reverie.

Ian squeezed her hand, then started to draw his away from hers. Even the lingering, almost imperceptible touch left her fingers tingling.

"May I?" He pulled out the chair opposite hers, waited for her nod, and took a seat.

He would be a gentleman. She had always had a soft spot for gentleman.

"So. Down to business then, I suppose." She cleared her throat and tried nae to look besotted with the man.

Ian ordered a spot of tea and they cleared the air aboot their mishap at the constable's office. When they'd chatted briefly aboot her plans for securing the promised funds, Ian leaned back in his chair, looked her square in the eye and said, "Now then, now that that's behind us, may we pretend that we've just met? Start over? Forget all the unpleasantness that's occurred and go back to the very beginning?"

"Why, certainly." She could feel her cheeks coloring, although really, there was nae reason. It was an innocent enough request.

"So, tell me aboot yerself."

Nae very original, but she admired his directness. "Ye already know more than most people."

"I'm nae talking aboot what's on the outside."

This time her cheeks went into an all–out flame. She could feel the heat burning its way into her brain. "So now ye want to know my innermost thoughts, do ye?"

"Only what ye feel comfortable sharing."

His voice was so calm, so reassuring. Nae wonder – the man must have had plenty of practice extracting confessions.

She opened her mouth and closed it again. "I, um..." She cleared her throat. "Have ye always been, I mean, why did ye become a minister?"

He laughed, apparently nae at her, but as though he were recalling some long ago memory.

"I started training as a barrister. I wanted to help people," he said simply. "Then one summer, I was hired as a legal assistant at an insurance company, where I assisted in bilking people out of settlements they well deserved."

That would explain the keen mind.

"The rest of the summer, I worked as a golf pro at Carnoustie."

That would explain the finely toned muscles in his shoulders and thighs.

"A friend suggested that if I wanted to help people with something other than their golf swing, that a better way to do it might be to go to seminary and enter the ministry."

"Ah." It sounded so formal. The ministry. Formal and purposeful. Self–effacing. She admired and envied him for that.

"What is it that ye feel called to?" he asked her.

"Called?" *Lately, to stay out of trouble.*

He smiled, probably the most sincere smile she'd ever seen, and said "I heard say once that what we are is God's gift to us. What we become is our gift to God."

"A lovely thought." She pondered the question for a moment. She'd certainly helped hundreds, maybe thousands of people in her capacity as the head of charitable disbursements at the Wilson Foundation. But it wasnae a job she'd been called to do. Although she loved what she did, she couldnae take credit for a task that had been thrust upon her by default. And, she really didnae want him to know any more aboot the foundation than he already did. Nae yet.

She looked straight into his eyes. "I had a heart to be a mother. Sadly, it never happened."

He nodded and gave her another smile, this one so tender that her heart almost melted.

"I've questioned God's intent in my own life in regard to that very issue," he said. "Why God gave me a heart so full of love for a wife and children, then never brought them into my life, I've never quite understood."

"Yer life's far from done," she said, laying her hand on his, her desire to comfort him so great that she could barely contain it.

"Ye have the gift of compassion then," he said, as though she had gotten an A+ on some secret test she didnae know she'd been taking.

That was when the waiter arrived with the Cumberland Mash she'd ordered. His Smoked Haddock Pie was steamy and fragrant. They were both silent for a moment as they arranged their napkins and settled in to eat.

He reached for her hand. "May I say grace?"

The differences between him and Robert, and most certainly, Digby, flashed through her mind like a documentary as he asked God's blessing on their friendship, their conversation, and the food.

What a gem he was! Listening to him, learning aboot him, sharing herself, it was hard nae to have her faith restored... in men, in God, in the world.

They spent the next hour and a half delving into this topic and that – the schools they'd attended, the jobs they'd held – catching up on pasts so long gone they were irrelevant, so dear they were as close as yesterday... which brought them to the present.

She would have preferred to linger in the past a bit longer, maybe forever. Oh well. She smiled, feeling more at ease, more accepted than she thought possible.

"So, how did ye stumble upon St. Conan's? Had ye been there before?"

She choked on her last bite of mashed potatoes so utterly and completely that it felt like air would never make its way into her throat again. How could she have forgotten?

She regained her composure, folded her napkin and tried to think of an excuse that he might actually believe. "Um, I hate to eat and dash," she said, so mortified she could barely speak. "I just remembered that I've an appointment." She stood and grabbed her purse. How could she have forgotten aboot the kirk? Her mind wove frantically from one damning fact to the next. For a moment, she was so flustered she couldnae even remember his name. But he would have been... would still be, unless he'd transferred his membership to St. Andrews or wherever it was that he was living now... a member of Ian's church.

"May I ring ye up again?" Ian said, looking bewildered.

"My schedule is simply a riot. I'm nae sure when I might have a spare minute."

"I see," Ian said, although it was evident he did nae.

"I really must..." she said, skirting the chair where he sat and easing away from the table as discreetly as she could.

"Sorry!" she said, and turned away from him, her heart beating wildly.

She didnae stop until she was in her auto, doors locked, out the parking lot.

What had she been thinking? She'd been wrong to get her hopes up in the first place. All she'd ever wanted was a good man. Someone who would respect her.

Ian would never be able to look at her without seeing her naked. Granted, the man did know a thing or two aboot forgiveness. That was obvious, or he never would have asked her to dinner.

She'd found a good man all right. But once he found out what she'd done...

She'd found the good man she'd always wanted. Trouble was, she wasnae good enough for him. Nae then. Nae now. Nae ever.

Chapter Eight

Rose clutched her leather satchel under her left arm and her purse with her right hand and walked into the board room at Wilson Enterprises, Ltd. *Dinnae be intimidated.* She tried to reassure herself. Nae one here had any way of knowing what had happened in Lochawe. Nae yet, anyway. She'd googled her name, St. Conan's, and a dozen other possible tags just before she left her flat and found nothing noteworthy.

"Rose," the eldest of her stepsons said formidably as she paused to survey the room. The board room had been redecorated in its entirety after Robert had passed, and this time, her opinion had nae been asked.

"Robert," There was nae need to add Junior now that his father was dead. She stepped quietly to his right and selected a seat four chairs down, on the same side of the table. Nae need to wave a red flag in front of the man by sitting where he had to look directly at her.

"Rose." The voice of the younger of Robert's two sons was neutral. Nae rancor, but nae love lost. He passed her chosen spot and selected the last chair on the right on the same side of the large, boat–shaped table.

She nodded. "Rodney."

The vacant chairs between them filled with the remaining board members – Robert's trusted business partners, a handful of cousins on the boys' mother's side, where their vast fortune had originated.

Winston Glenn, the chairman of the board and president of Robert's bank, called the meeting to order and passed out several handouts.

Rose's eyes glossed over at the sight of the precisely aligned columns of numbers, but she took each page in her hands and held them upright and gazed down at them as though she was absolutely absorbed in the financial matters at hand.

When Robert was alive, he'd always taken the time to explain each report, she assumed for her benefit, although he had never singled her out.

"Questions?" Glenn was as boring as a board, and a plain pine one at that. "Rose?" His voice was nae as condescending as Robert Junior's, but it wasnae exactly warm either.

She cleared her throat, gave a final glance to the papers and tried nae to let her discomfort show. "Just peachy." As peachy as one could be when she'd been taped in her birthday suit, cavorting with a common criminal.

"Robert? Rodney?"

Robert asked a question that was completely over her head. She smiled and nodded, as though she too felt concerned aboot the matter, and murmured her assent when the treasurer of the board responded. One of the cousins expressed concern over what he perceived to be the imminent fall of the European Union. A brief, sometimes heated, discussion ensued during which she wisely kept her mouth closed.

"Rose, what recommendations do you have for this quarter's grants?"

She slipped the papers she'd prepared from her satchel and decided to open with the orphanage she'd been researching in Renfrewshire. "Quarrier's Village was originally the Orphans Homes of Scotland and Mount Zion Church, known informally as the Children's Cathedral. It was constructed in the late 19th century by philanthropist William Quarrier. Sadly, today, the orphans' homes and even the church have all been converted into private housing. A charity under the name of Quarriers continues the work of the former orphan's home and is based within the village. They are desperately short of funds and in dire need of assistance."

"Wasn't Mount Zion Church of Scotland?" Robert, who didn't attend church anywhere to the best of Rose's knowledge, was subtly reminding them of his father's strong ties to chapel rather than church.

Fine. If Robert wanted to play hard ball, she was more than happy to engage him. "Quarrier was a devout Christian," she countered. "He even named the streets in the village Faith Avenue, Hope Avenue, Love Avenue, Praise Avenue, Peace Avenue and so on. His commitment to raising orphans in a Christian environment was always foremost in his mind."

"So let the Church of Scotland bail them out, if that's where their loyalties lie."

She glanced back at her notes. "In 2006, the Church of Scotland made clear that it could nae longer afford the upkeep on Mount Zion. To the pity of local residents, services were nae longer given in the church and had to be moved to a nearby home. In 2010, despite widespread local opposition, Mount Zion was converted to private luxury dwellings."

"Maybe they should have converted to Chapel," one of the cousins said. A titter of laughter circled the room.

Her blood started to boil. "Church – chapel. Chapel – church. Does it make any difference when there are hungry, lonely children aboot who simply need someone to love them?"

"They closed down the whole kit and caboodle in favor of private housing? Seriously? How was such a thing allowed?" Rodney wondered aloud. "Is nothing sacred these days?"

"Whilst the local authority rejected the planning application, the developer appealed to the Scottish Executive and won the planning permission," Rose said.

The room fell silent.

Rose met the eyes of those who typically supported her recommendations. "It's too late to save Mount Zion. The best we can do to salvage this situation is to donate funds to the charity that is trying to carry on the tradition of raising these dear little ones in the Christian faith."

"Maybe we should fund a private adoption of two or three of the little tykes," Robert suggested. "T'would give Rose something to do and provide Rod and I with the sisters we never had."

"What aboot Ginger?" Rodney's eyes were twinkling. He was teasing, presumably in a kind way. "Her curls are even the same color as mine."

She tried nae to show how flustered she felt, and moved on before anyone could insert another wisecrack. She'd learned the hard way that once she lost whatever advantage she had with Robert and his merry men, it was very hard to regain control. "There's another kirk, then, on Loch Awe, called St. Conan's, for whom it's nae too late – yet. St. Conan's was designed by architect Walter Douglas Campbell, great–grandfather of the Duke of Argyll and built from 1881 to '86, then expanded in 1907 to 1930, when it was first used for worship. The heavy oak beams in the cloister are believed to have come from the (then) recently broken up wooden battleships, HMS Caledonia and HMS Duke of Ellington. Um, I mean Wellington."

Oh, how embarrassing.

She cringed and ploughed on before anyone could respond. "St. Conan's boasts an eccentric blend of church styles, from Roman to Norman, and is built of local boulders, which were rolled down the hills before being worked. It consists of a nave, canopied chancel–stalls, a cloister, and several small chapels. Large, unsmoothed boulders of granite from nearby Ben Cruachan form the piers which carry the chancel arch. There is also a tower and spire. St. Conan's has always been known for unique architectural details like its metal rabbit head drain spouts and carved stone owls. The parish is functioning, but has been unable to pay their pastor for several months. Recently, they sustained demoralizing losses when the church was vandalized and the collection box and several irreplaceable artifacts were stolen."

"I believe I heard about it on the news last week," Rodney said.

Rose held her breath. Her involvement had nae been reported. She had nothing to fear, for now.

"Isn't that the place that has a larger–than life effigy of Robert the Bruce?" a cousin asked.

"Wasnae Robert named in honor of Robert the Bruce?" Rose piped up.

"I believe so," said another cousin.

"Am I the only one sensing a common theme here?" Robert said, his voice thick with sarcasm. "Found religion, have you, Rose?"

Leave it to Robert. The man knew full well that the foundation wasnae allowed to make contributions to religious institutions. "It's nae the church ladies I'm trying to subsidize here, Robert. All I'm saying is that if the congregation cannae even muster enough funds to pay their pastor, they're certainly nae going to be able to take care of the crumbling buttresses on the historic building that happens to house the congregation." She could feel her cheeks blushing to their trademark rose color. *Stupid prophetic name.* "There are dozens of old kirks all across Scotland in dire need of assistance. That's all. For some of them, it's already too late. Others can still be saved. Yer father was a lifelong fan of ecclesiastical architecture. It would break his heart to see these churches falling into ruin or worse, made permanently unavailable to the people of Scotland because they've been snatched up by private individuals."

"She's right," Rodney said quietly. "Dad always did have a soft spot for auld kirks."

"My research showed that more than a third of Scotland's churches – and chapels – worship less than 50 people a Sunday. The very things that make our lovely churches so historically significant make their upkeep a nightmare for a declining congregation. Both the Church of Scotland and the other larger, denominational church bodies rely on the same dwindling contributions that the local churches do, and are increasingly unable to help. Unless a new generation of philanthropists steps in, the future of these masterpieces of architecture is definitely at risk."

"So if it's historic preservations we're talking aboot, why St. Conan's?" Robert said briskly. "The kirk is barely a hundred years old. Does that even meet our requirements for historic preservation?"

Rose gulped back her frustration. The man disagreed with everything she suggested just to irk her.

"We donated to the restoration of the Willow Tea Rooms a few years back. Charles Rennie Macintosh didn't draw up the plans until 1904."

"So St. Conan's ekes by historically," Robert conceded. "I still question why we should be rewarding their obviously inept efforts at security with a contribution."

Her heart sank again as quickly as it had soared.

"If they had the funds to support a high tech security system, we wouldn't be having this conversation, now would we?" one of Robert's old business partners said.

Rose cleared her throat. "Ye're presupposing that there was a grandiose amount of cash in the collection box, and that the artifacts that were stolen would have been sacrificed for ready money. Neither assumption is correct. The congregation may be small and poor, but they are completely committed to preserving the historical aspects of their kirk."

Please, Rose begged of God. Under normal circumstances, she was perfectly fine being the fodder for Robert Junior's fun and games, but this time... She needed the foundation to grant the money to St. Conan's. The alternative was too unspeakable.

"But Robert was named after Robert the Bruce," she said feebly. "And his grandfather was a shipbuilder. He may even have worked on the HMS Caledonia."

"How did St. Conan's get Bruce's bone, anyway?" Her least

favorite of Robert's former partners drove another nail in her coffin. "And more to the point, if their security is so lax, should they be trusted to keep it?"

"Bruce certainly wasn't from Loch Awe, that's for certain. His body – or the rest of it anyway – is buried at Dunfermline Abbey."

"And his heart at Melrose Abbey."

She looked around the room, desperately trying to think of something to say that would tilt the outcome of the conversation in her favor.

One of the cousin's spoke before she had a chance. "Personally speaking, I'd like to have legal investigate the Quarrier orphans, and assuming everything checks out, proceed with a half million pound grant. As to the matter of St. Conan's – and by the way, great idea, Rose – I recommend a task force to explore which of Scotland's many needy churches are in most need of our assistance."

"Perhaps we could establish a ranking system to determine which of the congregations is in the most precarious position, and which have conducted the greatest fund raising efforts themselves."

"I like the thought of endowing those parishes who have tried their best to help themselves."

"Maybe our offer of assistance should be contingent on the congregation being able to raise matching funds."

No, no, no! The conversation swirled around her, a blizzard of cold words and stinging remarks. St. Conan's chances grew slimmer with every word that was spoken. There was nothing she could do. The board was set to take its annual summer hiatus and would nae reconvene for another three months. If St. Conan's received any moneys from the foundation, it would nae be until then.

"What aboot faith?" Rose heard a loud, confident version of her voice, and couldnae imagine what had prompted her to speak. It certainly hadnae been the side of her brain that was usually in control.

"What about it?" Robert said.

"Well," Rose said, while she mentally pled for the rogue brain–snatcher to return and say whatever it wished. "Well, shouldnae we be relying on it when we're making decisions aboot things pertaining to the creator of the universe?" She lifted her eyes and tried to look divinely inspired. "Shouldnae we be listening to our hearts instead of our heads? I've spoken to the pastor of St. Conan's several times, personally, and I assure ye, this is nae aboot facts and figures, it's aboot the power of prayer." She was starting to gather steam.

"What do prayers have to do with anything?" Robert asked, sounding more irritated with her than ever, if that was possible.

"The people of St. Conan's need a contributor now. Nae three months from now. Now. There are dangerous structural weaknesses in the church. The vicar is so concerned that he's been holding nightly prayer meetings to address their needs."

Okay, so if she didnae go to hell for cavorting with the likes of Digby without benefit of a marriage blessing, she felt certain that lying aboot a pastor having prayer meetings would earn her a spot. "It's a matter of imminent need. Imminent," she said again, because she could think of nothing more to say.

"Gerald, could we convene again two weeks from today, or will you be in Australia by then?" Rodney asked, taking the ball.

Thank ye, Rodney. She held her breath. Even two weeks would put her well past the constable's deadline, but a fortnight was better than the end of the summer.

Gerald checked his iPad. "Fine by me."

See? Nae worries. This was progress. The timing would be nip and tuck, but surely the constable would be patient with her if he knew funding was on its way, would he nae?

"You'll have to get more information from them if there's any hope of them qualifying for a grant." Winston Glenn frowned. "You'll need to find out why the church can't raise the money on their own, what kind of fund raisers they've held and are willing to hold, what improvements are needed and how critical they are to the soundness of the structure. We'll need budget projections, estimates, and a statement from a licensed contractor." He slid a paper across the table to the treasurer. "Have legal prepare a list of questions."

"I'll be happy to spearhead the task," Rose said.

"While you're at it..." Winston paused and exchanged a look with Robert. "Why dinnae you ask the vicar of St. Conan's to speak to us directly at the board meeting? That way, if we have concerns, he can address them without further ado."

"Certainly," Rose said. "I'm on it."

Robert snorted. Moments later, the meeting was adjourned.

Chapter Nine

"Can ye just say that ye've been praying nightly for a miracle for a month or more, should the subject come up?" Rose stood in the apse of St. Conan's surrounded by stained glass and cherubs and designs carved in stone, fidgeting with Ginger's leash. "That wouldnae be a lie, would it? Ministers do pray every day, dinnae they?"

"Of course." Ian walked towards the rear of the sanctuary. "I do pray aboot something at least once a day. And from this point on, I can certainly announce that we'll be having nightly prayer meetings to petition God to send a benefactor to ease our financial concerns." He hesitated. "We've been having regular fund raisers all along. Documenting our efforts and the inadequate funds that have resulted will nae be a problem." He grimaced and ran his fingers between his collar and his neck. "I'm more concerned with the imminent structural damages ye mentioned, to be frank. What if there are nae any?"

"Then we'll just have to create some." Rose kicked at the stone at the base of the missing baptismal font. "Ouch!"

"Hard as a rock," Ian said, while she clutched at her toe.

"The buttresses are crumbling." She pointed toward the Loch.

"Normal wear and tear of the elements," Ian said. "They're decorative. Non–essential to the structure."

She thought for a moment and tried again. "Every step going to or from the church is worn slippery smooth. That has to be a danger to the elderly among ye, especially in the winter, with the possibility of ice coating them," she said, her voice rising dramatically.

"Dangerous, nae doubt, but nae a matter of imminent structural concern."

"The whole outside of the kirk is overgrown with weeds. The roses look like they have nae been pruned in a year or two. The rhododendrons along the motorway are so tall and dense that many a prospective tourist probably drives right by without realizing there's even a church hiding behind them."

"We had to let the gardener go at the end of last summer. I do what I can as time allows. Rose, there's nae question that the kirk needs a lot of tender loving care that we've nae been able to give it, and I'd love to be able to re–craft the artifacts that Digby made off with, but I truly cannae think of a thing that would qualify as a structural concern."

"A rock has never fallen from the ceiling during services, endangering the innocent church attendees who gathered below?"

"No. I'm sorry, Rose. To the best of my knowledge, St. Conan's is built like a fortress."

"Are there any contractors who attend St. Conan's who might be persuaded to fudge on the truth a little then?"

"Rose. I want ye to get yer tape back. I want yer mind to rest and be at ease. And I must admit, I'd love nothing more than to see St. Conan's be the recipient of a sizeable grant. But I have to draw the line at purposely trying to hoodwink the board of directors."

Ginger followed close at her heels as she paced back and forth in front of Robert the Bruce's effigy. The translucent quality of his marble face and hands was a bit creepy. "I understand. I really do. I'm just a bit desperate to make sure the tape is nae released." She gave Robert a backward glance and shuddered. "We can focus on the safety issues then – crumbling buttresses, slippery steps, rotting wood, rusty hinges – accidents waiting to happen, a hornet's nest of liabilities, insurance aboot to be cancelled if things are nae remedied immediately... that kind of thing. I'll say that I was mistaken aboot the structural aspects – that when I heard aboot the safety issues, I just assumed..."

"I'd be far more comfortable if we stick to the facts," Ian said. "And it is true that if the money we collect at Sunday services didnae have to go toward the upkeep of the building and the grounds, the congregation might be able to pay my salary." He reached down to tickle Ginger's ears. "Old Man McDougall was an insurance adjuster until he retired last year. I'm sure he could compile a list of potential hazards and assign the price of repairing each one."

"That would be wonderful!" She turned to look up at Ian and noticed once again how blue his eyes were. "I sincerely appreciate all the help ye've given me."

"Nae a problem." He blushed. "I want to help."

"There's one other little matter that I need to speak to ye aboot."

"Yes?"

"I know these men. They place a great deal of importance on the efforts ye've made or are making to raise funds on yer own. And, Ian, well, I dinnae mean to disparage anything ye do or dinnae do to encourage giving, but I can assure ye, they're nae talking aboot a bake sale after the Sunday School program or dedicating an Easter lily for the front of the church. They're going to want to see evidence of some major fund raising efforts on the part of the church – events that have netted or have the capacity to net thousands instead of hundreds."

"The last church supper the ladies hosted raised £139.11. They were thrilled."

"I can help if ye'll let me," Rose said eagerly. "I've learned a thing or two in the years I've been associated with a non–profit – how to secure donations for auctions that will raise thousands, and more importantly, how to attract the right people to the events. Nae auction or event will be successful in terms of large donations unless ye have bidders with means."

"I'm nae sure what to say, Rose. They're nae a bit wealthy, but the people of St. Conan's are hard–working, proud folks. I'm nae sure they'll take kindly to some high–powered fundraising effort, even if it's on their behalf."

Rose's mind grappled for a solution. She had to make this work or the constable would reveal the tape for all to see – and life as she'd known it would come to an end. And she needed to do this for St. Conan's – and for Ian. It was the only way she knew to make amends.

"What if we just elaborate on something they're already doing? Ye said they quilt once a week – do they ever have quilt auctions?"

"Well, nae really. Most of the quilts the ladies make go to the African World Relief Missionary Effort. They strew the rest over the backs of the pews on the first Sunday of each month so people can purchase them if they wish."

"So if we use that idea and just embellish it a bit – have an official auction, invite the right people, spread the word to quilting shops across Scotland, serve something alluring like Sticky Toffee Pudding... I have a wonderful recipe, and it's Kate Middleton's fave, ye know."

Ian still looked uncomfortable, but she ploughed ahead. "It would be a good place to start."

"I suppose it would," he finally conceded.

* * *

Rose pasted a smile on her face and resolved to be the friendliest person on earth for the next five hours. She opened the hatchback of her MINI Cooper and lifted her sewing machine from the back end of her car. She wasnae the best seamstress in the world, but she could cut squares and pin and design colorful patterns. She was good at colors – blending, coordinating and making them come alive. *She could do this.* She could make a contribution and win the ladies of the church over at the same time.

She threw back her shoulders, straightened her scarf and marched into the kirk by means of the abbey. She wound through the entry, with its open beamed ceiling, and through the back door, which was propped open – a good thing since she was carrying her machine with one hand and the fabric pieces she'd collected from Kelly with the other.

She could hear voices as she grew closer to the rear of the sanctuary, where Ian had said the ladies would be sewing. She was just ready to call out a greeting when she heard a loud, sharp voice slice through the clatter of the others.

"Who does she think she is, anyway, telling us how to organize a fund raiser?"

Rose's feet stopped moving and her whole body tensed.

"City folks." A woman harrumphed. "Same thing happens every time one of them moves up here from Glasgow or Edinburgh."

"We ignorant country folk have to be re–educated aboot the right way to do things."

"Well, I for one am sick of it," another said. "Why dinnae they just stay in the big city where they belong and leave us alone."

"Probably cannae sew a stitch," one said.

"Ye wait see. She'll want to prance around, picking out the colors and suggesting new patterns and telling us what to do while we do all the dirty work."

She heard laughter.

"Dirty work? Why, Clara Mae, ye love everything there is aboot quilting. But I know what ye mean."

"I've been quilting for 70 years," another voice said. "She'd better nae try to boss me around."

"If we're lucky, she'll at least know how to cook so she can fix us lunch."

"I can almost hear the conversation now. Mince and tatties?" Whomever was talking mimicked a high pitched voice with an obvious Glasgowian accent. "Ye dinnae have any lettuce? Fruit? If only I had some fresh scallops and a little clotted cream! I have the best recipe for tri–colored seafood terrine. One layer is colored with corn, one with garden–fresh basil, and one with roasted red peppers. Such a delight," she swooned to the giggles of the other women.

"Sounds like ye know a thing or two aboot gourmet cooking yerself, Caroline."

"Right–o. Made it for my in–laws when they came up from Edinburgh a fortnight ago. Wasnae nearly as good as the mutton stew I made the night before they came."

The ladies laughed. In the moment of silence that followed, Rose heard footsteps behind her. She awoke from her mesmerized state, and knew she had to act fast lest she be caught eavesdropping.

Right foot, left, right, left, she prodded her feet, which felt nearly paralyzed. Enter with a brisk clip so it seems ye just rushed in and didnae hear a word of what they said.

"Hello, ladies!" she said cheerily, swallowing her tears and shoving aside the humiliation she felt. She swept into the room with a confident flourish and set down her picnic basket and sewing machine.

Most of the ladies just glared at her disgustedly – at least they were honest. She had to give them that. They were nae hypocrites.

One, whose mother had evidently taught her to be nice even when she didnae feel like it, said, "How was the trip up from Glasgow then?"

"Fine. Traffic was a bit touchy until I got past Dumberton." She held out her hand. "Rose."

"Amy. Always is," she said. "The traffic, I mean."

"Yes." She looked around the room, trying to hone in on some heat, some warmth, a modicum of sympathy, anywhere. Perhaps there was a tinge over by the stained glass, but it was barely perceptible. And then, like Tinker Bell's light going out, it too faded.

Or, it might have been wishful thinking all along.

A tall, stately woman with neatly coiffed white hair spoke next, her voice syrupy sweet, "So what would ye like to help with today, dear?"

"I thought, I thought..." she stammered, trying to reconcile what she'd planned to say and do with their expectations. Spur of the moment adaptations and last minute re–adjustments had never been her forte. *Just go with the flow,* she told herself. Nae big city airs. Nae gloating. Nae trace of superiority. *Just be yerself.* They'll love ye. Except that she'd never tried to impress – or un–impress – anyone. She'd been herself all along – just plain Rose – and they hated her.

"Um, I can sew blocks or strips," she said, almost choking. "I'm afraid I'm nae skilled enough to do triangles – I never can seem to get the points quite right. Really, whatever ye need me to do."

A pair of women along the west wall smiled, actually smiled, in a friendly sort of way. Nae mocking her, but accepting her. At least, that was the vibe she got.

They were outnumbered 20 to 2.

A short, stocky woman with yellowish white hair scrutinized her from head to toe. "So ye dinnae have a timetable, or a master plan or an organized outline for us to follow?"

"Nae a word," she lied, snapping her purse shut before they could spot the corners of the agenda she'd typed up earlier sticking out from the top.

"Well, then," a crisp, militant–looking, older lady said, pointing at one of the ugliest quilts Rose had ever seen. "This is a crazy quilt. Nae like pieces touching. That's the only rule. Mix and match at will. The more random the better."

"Carry on!" A second woman waved at the other ladies and nodded curtly at Rose. Like magic, the room filled with the whir of bobbins spinning, needles clicking against maladjusted plates and footpedals revving.

Rose lifted the lid off her machine, smiled bravely, and tried to remember which cord fit into which hole. There it was. And only three tries. This wasnae so hard.

A matronly looking woman approached her carrying one stack of squares in red and green plaids, and another of orange and black Halloween prints of the sort she'd heard they made in America. The woman broke the piles down into sub–categories of pink and red heart–covered Saint Valentine prints, and fabrics covered with blue and white snowflakes, green shamrocks, pastel Easter eggs, and May Day baskets filled with purple, pink and yellow flowers.

Rose's stomach lurched at the hodge–podge of clashing colors and hoped they intended her to make one mini–quilt for each holiday. Perhaps a set of twelve, one for each month. Certainly they didnae intend to put all of the fabrics in the same quilt.

"It's my own idea." The woman spread out a few more piles of fabric – summer–colored golf bags against splotches of yellow sunshine, blue skies and green grass, autumn leaves in red, orange and yellow, and bright red and green holiday motifs. Her face beamed. "It's an All–Inclusive Holiday Quilt."

"Good for any time of the year," Rose said, trying to mask her horror.

"Exactly," the woman said. "Nae need to switch quilts every time the season changes. Each one is filled with a lovely all–seasons batting that's light enough for summer use and warm enough for winter."

She was serious. Rose nodded, mortified beyond words.

"Resist any urge ye might have to align them according to the calendar. Crazy is as crazy does. The more mismatched the better."

"Do the quilts sell well?" Rose asked, trying to swallow.

"Ten or twenty pounds each – doesnae seem like much until ye multiply it by 20 or 30."

"Ye make that many, do ye?"

"We buy the holiday fabrics in bulk on clearance after each holiday. Since we only use a little of each kind per quilt, it goes a long way."

"So all the quilts are done in the same design?" Because actually, the pink hearts on the far heap and the blue and white snowflakes poking out from the stack in the middle would coordinate half way decently. "With all of the fabrics together in one quilt?" Her voice sounded high–pitched and desperate even to her own ears.

"Aye. It's our specialty. The beauty is, nae two are exactly alike. Why, we're known all over Argyle for our All–Inclusive Holiday Quilts."

"I'll bet ye are," Rose said, frantically trying to come up with a way to steer – well, guide, really – the ladies into coming up with some new color–coordinated designs in fashionable hues – say one of those nifty flying geese patterns or the ever popular wedding ring – without seeming pushy or condescending.

"I was at a quilt auction by Loch Lomond a few weeks ago," Rose said conversationally, like what she was saying hardly mattered and certainly didnae qualify as a suggestion of any sort. "The ladies in Luss were getting 500 quid a quilt on average. Of course, those quilts were made in the cutest calicos – one was strips of solids made up like a rainbow, another looked like a tulip garden, and my favorite – white on white with the most lovely quilted design. With all the talent ye've got here, I'm sure..."

"Told ye." A stage whisper sliced the air just as Rose's voice died down.

Twenty sets of eyes glared at her. It had taken them all of ten seconds to see through her scheme.

Rose busied herself by looking down at the mishmash of bobbins stored in the case of her sewing machine. So much for a windfall quilt auction and Sticky Toffee Pudding then. She selected a medium tone of tan that she hoped might match anything, lowered her head, and tried to remember how to align the bobbin properly. And kept her mouth shut.

Chapter Ten

The elevator was quiet except for the soft shifting of its gears and the slipping noises of cables sliding up and down their channels.

Ian smiled at Rose and tried to relax. "I feel very out of my element already, and we have nae even reached the fourteenth floor yet."

"I feel a bit nervous, too. And I'm nae sure why. I've been coming to board meetings for years now. And here I am today with an ally."

"A bit of a reluctant one," he admitted.

"Now ye know how I feel every time I walk into St. Conan's then, now dinnae ye?"

Ian smiled at her attempt at humor, but the more he ruminated on her remark, the more it bothered him. "I hope ye're nae serious."

"Oh, but I am. Ye spend so much time there, and I suppose, in the presence of the Lord in general, that ye must feel right at home hobnobbing with the Almighty. Did ye nae ever think that to the rest of us, it might feel a bit intimidating?"

"Ye make it sound like the kirk is still an Old Testament Holy of Holies. God is very approachable, and has been ever since he sent His Son to die for us."

The elevator dinged, and a few seconds later, they were stopped at the tenth floor. The door opened, but nae one came in.

He shrugged. The door closed. Whoever it was had missed their chance.

"So as I was saying, that's what Jesus' death did – bridged the chasm between a Holy God and a sinful people. Luther called it the priesthood of believers. We come as we are, nae priest or sacrifice needed, and pray directly to him."

"And that's nae the least bit overwhelming?" Rose fiddled with her hair, which looked perfect to him. "The man's given ye the best gift in the whole world, and now ye're invited to his house, and ye're trying to think of a host or hostess gift, and nothing ye come up with is in any way going to repay him or equal the gift he's given ye. I mean, it's nae like a bottle of fine whiskey or some homemade caramel shortbread is going to do. It's very intimidating."

"He only wants one thing."

"And what might that be?"

"Ye. Yer life. Yer heart. Yer love."

"Oh – that's all." She smiled and squeezed his hand.

The bell dinged again. They'd arrived.

"Dinnae let them rattle ye." Rose quickly adjusted the waistband of her skirt and straightening the lapel of her jacket. "Do I look all right?"

"Very professional. And lovely as well."

"Why thank ye, kind sir."

A receptionist escorted them to the boardroom, although Rose most certainly must have known the way. Was she nae allowed to roam the hallways at will, or was it him they did nae trust?

Although they arrived precisely at the designated time, even a few minutes ahead of schedule, the other board members all appeared to be waiting for them, almost as though they'd met earlier than the time they'd told Rose. Could it be that they'd wanted to discuss her without her being present? He gave Rose a keen look to see if the same thing had occurred to her, but her face was a carefully masked, corporate version of her normally warm, friendly expression.

Introductions were made all around, and the meeting was called to order. Suffice it to say that nothing that occurred during the brief go round did anything to set him at ease. Rose had assured him that the board knew nothing about what had actually transpired at St. Conan's, so he had to assume that the latent hostility that pervaded the room was due to some other matter, or, God forbid, the norm.

He was called upon to speak immediately, which further cemented his suspicion that the meeting had actually been underway for some time before he and Rose's arrival.

He stood and went to the podium at the head of the table. Winston Glenn took a seat at the vacant chair to his right.

He smiled. "Greetings from the people of St. Conan's and Loch Awe."

A few nodded. *So far, so good.* Rose had advised him to keep her out of things as much as possible, so to increase the odds of the board approving the grant, so he did nae mention her name in his presentation.

"St. Conan's is a small but enthusiastic congregation committed to living out nae only our Christian faith but the historic legacy we've been entrusted with." He went on to give a brief summary of St. Conan's significant historical and architectural points, then paused to take a sip from the water provided for him.

"The picture you paint is so rosy that it's hard to imagine why such a model congregation would need our help," Robert said.

Okay. So the claws were starting to come out.

"Quite the contrary." Ian set his water down and tried to reclaim the upper hand. "Our parishioners are either elderly and of limited means, or young couples with bourgeoning families who require the bulk – if nae all – of their expendable income. I only stress that St. Conan's is an active congregation because to me, it makes much more sense to invest in a building that is home to a goodly group of believers than one that has already been abandoned to sit empty, or one that functions simply as a stop for tourists."

"Makes perfect sense to me," Winston said, smiling in a way that was at least somewhat encouraging.

"Ye asked me to talk aboot the building's structural deficiencies and liability concerns." He passed out a hand–out with bids and repair estimates and went on to detail the supposedly imminent structural, safety and liability concerns the kirk was facing.

"It doesn't sound to me like the church has done anything to try to solve the problems of their own accord." Robert again, looking smug.

He was keeping him on the defensive, that was certain. "Again, I beg to disagree. I have here a report of the fundraisers we've held over the past five years, with the money we've earned at each one." He passed around the new papers. "Nae outstanding amounts raised, as ye can see, but again, I think it is quite clear that the congregation tries its best to do what they can."

"So what percentage of the population of Loch Awe attends Sunday services each week?" Robert grinned lazily from his high–backed swivel chair.

"11%. The same on average as the rest of Scotland."

"And am I right in assuming that the percentage we're looking at today has declined steadily in the five years you've been at St. Conan's?"

"Yes. That is the trend. Nationwide, attendance has fallen over 20% in the last 8 years," he answered honestly. He could bore them for hours with statistics aboot why the people of Generation X and Y were leaving the church, and the prevalent theories on what needed to be done to staunch the flow and reverse the trends, but somehow, he felt he could ascertain that facts and figures didnae seem to be what Robert Junior was interested in.

"Perhaps we could deduce that some of that is your fault." Robert delivered his punch line in such a neutral voice that its sting didn't hit until a second or two after he landed the shot.

"I'm as accountable as anyone," Ian said. What good would it do to start pointing fingers at those who shared the blame? Parents, declining morals in general, a more secular, materialistic society, the liberal worldview taught in schools, ridicule by people like Robert himself...

Was it better to speak or to play dead and see if Robert ceased his attack? The man seemed determined to hang him, nae matter what he said.

"Perhaps if your sermons were more relevant, there would be more people in church on Sundays, and more money in the offering plates. And assuming you're capable of improving your leadership skills, you wouldn't have to grovel for money at our door."

Everyone in the room, including Ian, was shocked into silence.

Rose was the first to gather her wits. So much for staying out it, then.

When she stood, her eyes were blazing. "Fine, Robert. Ye want to fight? I've taken the abuse ye've heaped on me for going on three years now. I know ye dinnae like me. I know ye wish yer father had never married me. Ye wish I would sneak off and slink down whatever hole I came out of. I get it." She inhaled sharply, as if trying to find the resolve to go on, and then spoke quietly. "I get it. I've endured yer disrespect because I know that yer father loved me with his whole heart. Yer father wanted me to be here, so every time this board meets, I tuck my emotions away and continue to do my job, per his wishes, because I would and have always been willing to do anything he asked."

"Obviously." Robert Junior smirked. "Everyone knows there's one sure way to a man's heart." A handful of the men laughed. "And I guarantee you, it's nae food."

A round of titters waged war with an equal number of protests.

Rose rolled her eyes. "Thank ye, Robert, for so deftly proving my point."

Ian shook his head. It wasnae his place to chastise them. He was the outsider here. Finally, Winston Glenn, the chairman, rapped his gavel. "Let her say what she needs to."

Rose nodded. "What I need to say is that I can accept the fact that it appears that I will continue to be the butt of yer jokes and innuendos nae matter what I do to prove myself, but I will nae stand by and watch ye treat a guest to our proceedings with such irreverence. Pastor Ian is a man of the cloth. He is highly educated, very compassionate, and extremely good at what he does. And if those qualities are nae credentials enough for ye, please bear in mind that he is an emissary of the Lord God Almighty. He deserves yer respect. If nae that, for some unimaginable reason, yer common courtesy."

Robert started to make yet another snide remark, this one directed to the balding man at his side instead of the group as a whole.

Rodney nudged his brother, finally spurred to action. "Give the lady a break, bro."

"Lady?" Robert's supposed stage whisper rang out as silence fell over the room.

That was it. Ian had had enough. He stood slowly, letting his long legs unfold to his full height. "I am neither yer father or your pastor. But I have come to have a great deal of respect for Rose Wilson, and speak, I must. St. Conan's is in need of a benefactor if our struggling parish is to continue to maintain the historic property we've been entrusted with. But desperate as we are for funding, I cannot in good conscience accept any monies from an organization that shows such blatant disregard for a woman so giving and caring as Rose Wilson."

"Well, that settles that." Robert stood with a self–satisfied smirk. "Meeting adjourned."

Winston Glenn rose again. "Robert, sit down. I'm not your father either – thank the good Lord – but if I hear one more harsh word out of you for the remainder of this discussion, I will have you expelled from the meeting. You disrespect your father with every word you say. It would grieve him horribly to see how you treat the woman he loved. As his friend, I will nae continue to stand by and listen to your hurtful barbs."

Robert's face smoldered with ire but he said nothing.

From what Ian could see, it was aboot time.

"Thank ye, Winston." Rose's voice eked out, barely audible.

Winston nodded at Rose and motioned for Ian to have a seat. "Now let's see what we can do about getting this man some money."

Chapter Eleven

Ian checked his calendar and updated his schedule. Now that Rose's dilemma had been dealt with, and the constable's threat was nae longer hanging over their heads, it was time to catch up on his regular duties. He had yet to prepare his sermon for Sunday, but he needed to work on the speech he was going to be presenting at the Argyle Ministerial Association's Retreat for Pastors. The date was only a fortnight away, and although he'd been mulling over what he was going to say, he hadnae had a chance to put his thoughts on paper.

He'd chosen the scripture and the topic he was going to speak on: Matthew 28, and the Great Commission. Scotland had sent many a missionary out in decades past, but modern thought had made the spreading of the gospel nothing short of politically incorrect.

Thank goodness, his audience should be more receptive than the one he'd endured in Wilson Enterprise's board room.

He was re–reading the text when his mobile rang.

"Ian?"

"Yes." He thought he recognized the voice. "Is this Benjamin?"

"Yes." The man was a friend who pastored the church in nearby Inveraray.

"What can I help ye with?" Ian sensed immediately that Benjamin was uncomfortable, and couldnae imagine why. Perhaps someone from Ian's congregation wanted to transfer their membership to Benjamin's. Many of their parishes were close enough to one another that if they liked a different pastor better than their own, or got something stuck in their craw, there was nothing to keep them from transferring their membership. It put the pastors, who knew one another well, in an awkward position, but they all agreed that it was better to be notified than nae. If Benjamin were calling to impart such news, it would certainly explain his discomfort.

"I wanted to call ye as soon as I got the news," Benjamin said.

"What news?" He tried nae to be alarmed. What could Benjamin be talking aboot? If something serious had happened to a member of his congregation, wouldnae a member of the family have called? Benjamin cleared his throat. "I'm sorry I have to be the one to tell ye..."

"Tell me what?"

"I'm afraid another speaker has been chosen for the Pastor's Retreat."

"Another speaker?" Of course, he was relieved that nae one had died, but why on earth would another speaker be selected for the conference when he'd already been asked?

"Am I supposed to, I mean, do they want he or she to share the stage with me? Do one of the keynotes? Introduce me?"

"Ian." There was a long, ominous silence. "They've asked Reverend Rathborn to speak at the conference instead of ye."

Rathborn? Instead of him? "I dinnae understand." *Why would they do such a thing?*

"It's nothing personal," Benjamin said.

"What is it then?"

"It's, it's the best thing for everyone involved given the circumstances."

"What circumstances?" The words burst forth more loudly than he had anticipated.

"The circumstances that have changed since ye were originally asked to speak," Ben said.

"And what circumstances would that be?" Unfortunately, he was beginning to suspect that he knew exactly what – or who – Benjamin was talking aboot.

"Ian, we all know that ye've been incredibly lonely these past few years."

"And that pertains to my speaking at the gathering in what way?"

"Ye know the policy, Ian. The senior manager looks the other way – as long as we dinnae flaunt our indiscretions."

"And I've been indiscreet in what way?"

There was a long silence.

"I'm going to say this exactly once, Benjamin. I have done nothing indiscreet with Rosalie Wilson or with any other woman. I am dating the woman, which to date, has included taking her to dinner, going on a few long walks, and talking on the phone. Last time I checked with our overseer, and more importantly, the Word of the Lord, none of that was a sin."

"We just assumed." Benjamin sputtered. "Given her reputation for..."

"I will be delivering my message at the convocation next week. If Reverend Rathborn would like to say the invocation, I would be more than happy to share the podium."

"But, but, but yer invitation has been rescinded."

"For invalid reasons. It's up to ye as to how ye'd like to explain yer faux pas to the senior manager. I will graciously accept yer apologies and try to forget this conversation ever occurred, but I will nae relinquish my spot on the agenda."

"But the overseer..."

The overseer can go to hell. Thank God the words never made it to his lips. But still, he could nae deny that it was what he was thinking.

His next thought was a chilling one. He'd made disclaimer after disclaimer, testifying to the fact that Rose had nae been the bad influence on him that they thought her to be, and yet, just a few weeks after meeting her, he was harboring vile recriminations towards his senior manager that prior to that time, he never would have thought. Sweet Lord, what was happening to him?

* * *

Maybe it was because Ian had been unjustly censured for seeing Rose that he was so determined to see her that evening. He'd had nae need to drive to Glasgow, nae pressing reason to give for his visit when he'd called Rose to see if they could rendezvous. But as it was his heart's desire, and since half of Argyle was already under the assumption that they were seeing each other, why should they nae be?

"Is something wrong, Ian?" Rose asked for the third or fourth time since he'd arrived at her flat, patting Ginger the way she did when she was nervous or out of sorts.

"I'm just fine," he insisted, glancing around at her living space, which looked exactly like her – classic, beautiful, charming, in some ways, surprising. "I've simply missed seeing ye, I mean, since our business concluded. And ye mentioned wanting to see a film some time, and I had nae visits to make, and I thought perhaps it would be good for both of us to be able to enjoy each other's company without the stress of this or that... ye, know, to try to relax after all we've..."

So he was fudging on the truth just a little. The last thing he wanted was to blurt out the whole tale of how poorly he'd been treated by his overseer, or how saddened he was by people's inability to forgive and forget, or how frustrated he was with everyone and everything as of late.

He sighed. His omissions were hardly a crime, but they certainly were sin.

"Rose?"

"Yes?"

"Do ye think all sins are the same?"

She looked a little stunned at his question, but eventually, she did reply. "Ye mean like, is gossiping or being rude to someone just as bad as cheating on yer husband or committing murder?"

"Aye," Ian said.

"Sounds like a question I should be asking and ye should be answering instead of the other way around."

"I'm just curious to know what ye think aboot it."

"In the interest of being truthful, I have nae idea what the Bible says aboot all of this. Strictly my opinion. Okay?"

"Surely." Ian felt all the guiltier after Rose took such care to be truthful, but he wasnae ready to tell her what was upsetting him.

"Well, there are sins that only hurt the perpetrator, and sins committed against other people. I've always thought it's worse when what ye do hurts another person, even worse if that person is a child."

"Okay," Ian said. "So ye do think there are gradations of sin."

"I guess I must. So – now that I've told ye what I think – what's the right answer?"

Ian flushed. "Jesus said, speaking of those who taught children the wrong thing, that it would be better for them to have a great millstone tied around their necks and thrown into a lake. So I guess there's something to be said aboot hurting children, as ye mentioned."

Her face beamed. "Maybe I read those verses back in Sunday School and never quite forgot what they said."

"Much of our social, moral and legal beliefs come from the Bible, although fewer now than twenty years ago."

"I guess Biblical ways are engrained in our society then."

"Rose, would ye like to know more aboot the Bible? Is it something we could study together? We may nae be equals as far as our Biblical knowledge, but ye've a sharp mind, and a quick wit, and ye're very candid – all attributes I value in a study partner."

"I'd be honored. So tell me the rest. Is a teensy little lie of omission as bad as committing murder? In God's eyes, I mean?"

"Ye've heard it said, *'Thou shalt not kill, but I say anyone who hates his brother has already committed murder in his heart.'* And *'a man who looks at a woman with lust in his heart has already committed adultery.'* From the Sermon on the Mount."

Rose pursed her lips. "That's a bit frightening. But good to know, I guess."

They sat in silence for a few minutes. Rose was the first to speak. "So is this what pastors do? Contemplate theology, and banter on aboot how the Scriptures should be interpreted?"

"Sometimes. Rose?"

"Yes?"

"I've nae been honest with ye tonight, Rose. Something *is* bothering me."

"Is it something I've done?"

Rose spoke so sweetly, and with such concern, that he wanted to cry.

"Is it something aboot Digby?"

He could strangle those who doubted her sincerity and spoke ill of her. He truly could.

"No, and no. Nothing to do with ye at all."

Another lie.

He cleared his throat and forged on. "Several months ago, I was invited to be the keynote speaker at a regional conference for pastors." He went on to tell her aboot Benjamin's call.

Before he had even come close to telling the whole story, her face revealed that she had reached the same conclusions that he had.

"This is exactly what I was afraid of! And I will nae have it, Ian. I will nae be the one to ruin yer career, to cost ye yer call, to drive ye to financial and emotional ruin. I care aboot ye far too much."

She cried and he held her. He shed a few tears himself.

He stroked her back as tenderly as he knew how. And then he forgot aboot tenderness and pressed harder, because he wanted her to know how adamantly he felt aboot what he was aboot to say. "I cannae let them win. I will nae let them win. *'And if our God is for us, who can be against us?'"*

"Is that from the Bible, too?"

"Yes. It most certainly is."

"Well, there, then. The old biddies."

"This may be the first time my overseer has been likened to an old biddy, but I have to agree that it's an apt description."

She started to giggle then, and he joined in. Life would never be dull with Rose at his side. More importantly, she made him think aboot what he believed, really think.

Nae longer did he spout empty words by rote when he stood at the pulpit. His sermons were relevant, because he was. He was living life, struggling to do and give his best under adverse circumstances. He was focusing on what really mattered, because he had Rose. Dear, sweet Rose, who had opened his eyes to a whole new world. Dear Rose, so eager to please and open to learning. She had made him appreciate his Lord and life in a way he had never even envisioned. She had given him a whole new perspective on life.

They were sitting on a leather sofa in front of a small stone fireplace, basking in each other's warmth, Ginger sandwiched between them as far as she could wiggle in, when his mobile rang. He could see on his caller ID that it was none other than the old biddy himself.

He thought momentarily aboot ignoring the ring. That was why he had caller ID, wasnae it? He'd even assigned a separate ring tone to the senior manager to let him know when he was calling. He glanced at Rose and took a deep breath. Then, having given himself permission nae to answer, he decided to get it over with, here and now.

"Hello. Pastor Ian speaking."

His overseer didnae mince words. Some of the phrases that jumped out at him were "Putting up with this sort of nonsense, ye've left me with nae other choice, and what did ye expect when ye decided to force my hand?"

The one thing he could say aboot his senior manager's tirade was that they were all things he'd never expected to hear from his overseer's mouth – nae said to him anyway. Ian had gone from being the model child to the ideal seminarian to the perfect as perfect could be pastor without a catch. Why, he'd rarely even incurred the ire of his parents – certainly nae that of his teachers, mentors, or supervisors.

As a result, he had little practice defending himself against the slings and arrows of outrageous fortune, because until this time, he'd never been the target of such an attack.

"I've done nothing wrong," Ian said, his voice steady and calm even to his own ears.

But despite Ian's best effort to deflect the man's words and bring some semblance of order back to their conversation, his senior manager was still agitated.

"I've done nothing wrong." It's the overseer, he told himself. Ye may nae agree with his actions at this particular moment in time, but he has earned yer respect on plenty of other occasions. And even if he didnae agree with the man, he had to regard the office.

"What is it?" Rose whispered. "Who is it and why are they talking so loudly?" She looked miserable, like she already knew.

"It's nae yer fault," he whispered back.

"But it is."

"...the appearance of evil." The overseer's voice came back into focus and Rose's faded into the background as he contemplated what this could mean to his career, his calling, his chance of ever finding another church. He hadnae been paid more than a pittance in over three months, and although certain among the congregation had been taking care of his basic needs by bringing in baskets of eggs they'd picked, meat they'd butchered, and vegetables they'd grown in their garden, he would be hard pressed to pay a security deposit and first and last month's rent if he had to move out of the parsonage.

"I've already asked Rathborn to take yer place." The overseer sounded as stern and foreboding as Ian had ever heard him. "I will nae allow..."

And just as rightly, he was nae aboot to lose his honorarium or the chance to set wagging tongues at rest. "I will nae allow ye to banish me nor deny me an opportunity I have worked hard for and earned by meritorious service when I have done nothing wrong."

The overseer seemed stunned into silence, at least momentarily.

"If something I've said or done has appeared evil, I assure ye it is in the eye of the beholder." Ian looked at Rose, hoping to calm the wild look in her eyes. His efforts, nae matter how impassioned, were nae enough. He took her hand and pulled her close.

A second later, the overseer stated that he had a call waiting and would need to ring him back. The situation wasnae resolved, but he had earned a temporary respite, and a chance to speak with Rose before she totally freaked out.

Nae to be so.

"How could he? Yer behavior has been exemplary. 100 percent the gentleman." Rose railed on, defending him, extolling his virtues, and chastising the senior manager until he pulled her closer and shushed her with a kiss.

Their first. He supposed it wasnae the most romantic of precipitating circumstances, but he felt so full of love for her that he couldnae nae kiss her. It was as simple and as glorious as that.

"Oh, Ian." Rose moaned, and he kissed her again, as tenderly as he could.

Her lips were so soft. And she smelled of roses. Was he imagining it, or was such a thing possible?

Of course it was, ye dolt, he told himself, and kissed her again. And then he became very aware of the fact that if he didnae stop, and stop soon, he would soon be guilty of exactly what the overseer had accused him of.

"Rose?" He stepped back and used his thumb to trace the shape of her face, then to caress her neck.

"Yes?" She was breathless and obviously deeply affected by his kisses.

Nae surprise there. Ye saw how responsive she is. Saw her with... He hated himself the second the thought started to form. Would he ever get the pictures of her and Digby out of his brain?

"Rose. We cannae."

She stepped back into his arms and moved against him in response.

He moaned his anguish aloud. She was nae helping. And part of him didnae want to be helped. Part of him wanted her to tempt him beyond all chance of salvation.

"I know we shouldnae," she whispered. "My mind knows full well."

"I know." He grappled with her blouse until he found her nipple and teased it between his finger and his thumb. They were making decisions with their bodies. And they had to stop. But how, with their libidos waging war on the rational parts of their bodies?

If there were any rational parts. Sensations raced from one nerve ending to the next, down one side and up the other, every neuron tingling, every pulse spot surging.

"We shouldnae..." Rose kissed him this time, his neck, his ear lobes, his jaw. Who would have guessed feelings so exquisite could come from spots previously so dense and innocuous?

"We shouldnae..." she chanted, as though trying to convince herself.

"We cannae." He guided her to a chair, gently but firmly, in what he recognized as what might be his only chance at reasonable thought.

Her smile faded, and a forlorn grimace took its place on her face. "It's nae that I dinnae want ye."

"I suppose one has to practice what one preaches."

"Yes. Ye are beautiful, Rose. I've wanted to make love to ye since I first met ye, even more so since we've gotten to know each other and I've been able to see that ye're beautiful inside and out."

"I guess a planned seduction is out of the question, since ye've already seen everything I have to offer."

There was a lilt in her voice, but he sensed an underlying regret. Happy as he'd been to have a preview of what was to come at the time, he felt cheated by it as well.

He sighed. They'd needed to have this conversation. It was likely to be a passion killer, so he guessed the time was appropriate.

"Part of the reason I cannae, I mean, I will nae..."

"Yes?" She looked doubtful.

"It has nothing to do with ye."

"Nothing to do with me?" Now she looked offended.

"No." He gulped down a fresh lungful of air.

"I mean, I have to follow the rules if I want to keep my position, but it's more than that. I'm concerned aboot doing the right thing because I love the Lord, and I want to do what His Word says. I want to please him in everything I do and say."

Rose looked doubtful.

"I dinnae mean to sound overly pious. And I'm nae condemning ye if ye dinnae have the same convictions," he was quick to add.

"I assumed there would be nae pre–marital sex if I decided to see a minister." Had she emphasized the word decided, or was it his imagination? Like she might just decide nae to if he said a wrong word.

"Rose, we've never really talked aboot how ye feel aboot the possibility of ye and I having a relationship, or aboot the possibility of ye sharing yer life with a minister." He chose his words carefully. He wasnae ready to propose, still, serving God was his calling, and if she couldnae support him in his mission, there was little point in continuing their relationship. Please, Lord, let her answer be the one I want to hear.

"It is a bit daunting," she confessed. "I'm afraid my faith is nae as deep as yers. I mean, I know it is nae. And even if I try to, I mean, do some spiritual exercises, or take a class in Biblical wisdom, or start praying even when nothing is wrong, or try to love God more, or whatever people do when they're trying to enrich themselves, I'd never catch up to ye. Ye'd always be closer."

"But ye dinnae have to be–"

"Yes, I do. It's what people would expect."

"Is a surgeon's wife expected to know gross anatomy? Is an investor's wife expected to be a Wall Street wiz? Is a golf pro's wife expected to make a hole in one?"

"No, but–"

"But ye are nae me. Ye have nae been to seminary. Yer faith is what it is. It will grow at its own pace, maybe faster than it would under normal circumstances–"

"Because of the scintillating conversations we'd have aboot theology?"

He laughed. "We could pray together."

She looked uncertain.

"We could start right now." He reached out and took her hand. "I'll start."

"Ye're serious, are ye nae?"

He motioned for her to close her eyes, then sat down by her side.

"Dear Heavenly Father, Thank ye for bringing Rose into my life. Help us to honor ye in every facet of our relationship, and guide us in the way ye would have us to go." Ian squeezed her hand. "Amen."

"Amen." Rose blinked her eyes open and returned Ian's squeeze. Okay. So it was one of the weirdest things she'd ever done with a man. Any other man would be grappling on the sofa or rolling around on the floor with half their clothes off. And although it was hard to maintain a state of arousal during a prayer, part of her still wished Ian was kissing her instead of praying with her.

"Are ye okay?" Ian asked.

"Yes." And she was. "It was sweet of ye to mention me by name, I mean, when ye were talking to God."

"I've been praying for ye since the day we met."

"Ye have?" She assumed it was a compliment, that he'd prayed for her because he cared aboot her and wished her the best and nae because he thought she was such a basketcase that there was nae hope for her without divine intervention.

"Ye're in my thoughts constantly, Rose."

And she believed him.

The evening came to an end then. Nae sex. Nae staying the night. She kissed Ian good night. Ginger rubbed against his legs until he'd patted her head and scratched her ears. And then, Ian left to drive back to St. Conan's.

But she felt as though she'd been intimate with him. And a good feeling it was.

Chapter Twelve

Rose lifted her eyes to the very peak of St. Conan's auspicious rafters and prayed for patience. Then, for the hundredth time, she attempted to wrestle the thick yardage of tapestry wedged between the foot and the gripper thingamajig of her sewing machine into place. This was nae going well.

She'd thought driving up for quilting day at St. Conan's would serve as the impetus she needed to finish Lyndsie's pillows – and give her an excuse to see Ian again. But nothing aboot the day had turned out the way she'd hoped.

She looked down at the fabric and tried to remain positive. Besides being a pleasing mixture of pinks, greens and periwinkle blue – all Lyndsie's favorite colors – she'd thought the thick tapestry was a perfect choice for her niece's new pillows. *Just try chewing this*, she thought, looking down at Ginger fondly.

The only problem – well, it wasnae the only problem, but it was one of them – was that doubled up, good sides together to make a proper seam, the fabric was so cumbersome that it barely fit through her machine.

Just then, the needle arced in protest and broke in two. She couldnae say what she thought – although it was just she and Ian still at the kirk. The rest of the quilters had finished their projects, packed up their machines and gone home hours ago. But she was still in church.

She grabbed the thread and yanked, pricking her finger in the bloody process. And it was just that, as her finger began to ooze bright red blood.

She sighed mightily. Look on the bright side, she told herself, glancing over to see if Ian had noticed. (He hadnae seemed to, thank God.) At least the needle had just skimmed her finger and nae gone through it, like it had last week. Her new wound hurt far less than it had at the time of that incident, and far, far less than it had when the needle had accidentally punctured her fingernail. And when the red dried, it would be the same deep burgundy color as one of the background colors in the tapestry. So really, nae harm was done.

It still hurt like hell.

She used her thumb to apply pressure to her finger and started packing up the extra parts for her machine. She imagined they did wonderful things when one knew what to do with them. Maybe she should take a class. Someday. She'd had enough sewing for now.

She looked over at Ian again. Probably still hard at work on his sermon. Nae a good time to interrupt him. Her conscience started to throb right along with her damaged finger.

Wednesday was his pesky secretary's day off, and it was doubtful that any of the church ladies would pick this afternoon to drop by when they'd all just been there. It was so rare that they were alone, and she had to tell him sometime.

It was time to be honest with him. Number one, it was eating away at her. Her emotional fortitude was already severely diminished. She had so little meat left on the bones of her self–confidence as it was that she doubted she could survive another attack – even if it was by her own conscience.

Number two, keeping quiet aboot something this huge wasnae fair to Ian. She was falling in love with him, and if her instincts could be relied upon by any measure, so was he, with her. If he couldnae forgive her, couldnae bear the sight of her any longer, the sooner it was over, the better. Her secret had festered far too long already, and the more infected she let things get, the worse things would probably end.

"Ian?" her voice came out a squeak.

"Yes?" he called from the far side of the room.

"There's something I need to tell ye."

"I'm listening." He lifted his head, folded away whatever he was working on, and walked in her direction.

She was packing in earnest now – fabric, pins, patterns, odd sewing parts and utensils, broken things... "I'd put it out of my mind entirely until the day ye asked me how Digby and I happened to meet at St. Conan's."

Ian looked at her oddly. She supposed she might have led into the topic a little less abruptly, but in her defense, it was all she could do to muster the guts to tell him in the first place. The hows and whats of telling him were nae what was important here.

Ian looked thoughtful. "I'm sure Digby had set his sights on the place for some time. An undisturbed country location with a poorly kept yard, overgrown rhododendrons to hide his nefarious acts, the lack of a security system... Meeting ye here was a convenient cover so he could plot his next theft."

She said nothing for a few minutes. "Nae."

"Nae what?"

"Nae, that's nae the way it happened."

The silence was so changed it felt like the air could explode.

"It was me. I suggested we meet at St. Conan's," she said, gulping guiltily.

"Ye'd heard of the place and wanted to visit? Ye looked for halfway points and Google pinpointed our location?"

"No. I know – knew – someone who used to attend church here."

Relief flooded Ian's face. "That's good, then, is it nae? An auld uncle, a grandmother who's long deceased? The ladies at Missionary Society are always more forgiving when one of their own has gone astray than when an outsider steps in and starts causing trouble."

He must have seen her face then, and guessed that it was worse than that. "A tie to the congregation is a good thing. It will soften attitudes. They'll rally around ye when they find out. Ye'll see."

"No. They will nae." This was harder than she'd even thought. "Ian, I know I told ye that I wasnae in the habit of, well, having intimate relationships with men I'm not married to. And I'm not, not ever – well, except for Digby, as ye know."

"Yes?"

"Well, there was one other time."

Ian's face said it all. The trust he'd so tenuously clung to was nae doubt bouncing to and fro like an unbalanced teeter totter.

She'd lied. She'd hurt him. She'd implicated him in her mad scheme to get the tape back. She'd tried so hard to be good enough, to be deserving of his love, to be someone he could be proud of, to be someone he could trust, at least from now on. And now, she was going to shatter it all, ruin her chances for all time. There was nae way he would ever be able to forgive her for this. She could see it in his eyes and she hadnae even said a word. Or in this case, a name.

"Tell me," he said. Not cruelly, or cynically, but in a voice that was resigned and beaten.

She plunged ahead. It had to be done. "Ye remember when I first met the church ladies, and how high–strung I was feeling, and how nervous I was that they might recognize me? I mean, beside from being on the tape with Digby?"

"No. I wasnae aware that–"

"Well, I was. And at the time, I was so distraught aboot what had happened with Digby, and so worried aboot what ye must think of me that... And I didnae think it mattered anyway, because I never really believed that ye and I had any chance of..." She stopped and gulped air, afraid to continue.

She loved him! Who was she kidding? She was the worst possible candidate for a pastor's girlfriend – she was so unworthy that she couldnae even think the word wife – ever. Ever. She'd tried to talk herself into it, tried to visualize herself being good, and holy, and spiritual, the kind of woman that the church ladies could look up to, admire, and confide in, but she just... could nae... She just could nae do it.

Ian was sitting. Waiting, as patiently as ever.

"Ye know what?" She stood, her purse in her hand, her wrap half sliding down her shoulders. "This is nae going to work. I knew it from the start, but I cared for ye so much that I had to give it a stab." Tears started to stream down her face.

Ian rose to hug her, which made it worse.

"It's who ye are," she said. "It's the reason I care aboot ye as deeply as I do, and the reason I cannae let ye go on caring aboot me. I mean, assuming ye do. Because ye certainly act like ye do."

"Of course I care aboot ye," he said gently, urging her back into her chair. "Why dinnae ye tell me and let me decide for myself?"

"Because I already know what ye'll say."

"And what is that?"

"That it doesnae matter. That ye'll forgive me. That I'm perfect for ye just the way I am, and that if people dinnae like me, that's just their loss because I'm so wonderful and loving and... "

She could see the smile toying on his lips and it made her mad. "Just stop it!"

"But everything ye said is true!"

"Aye. That's the tragedy of it. I'm serious, Ian." Her voice grew so solemn and firm that it was scary. "No, Ian. Ye will nae forgive me. Ye will nae let me drag ye down. Ye will nae turn yer back on yer calling because ye had the misfortune to meet me. I will nae let ye."

"Okay," Ian said. "Let me see if I understand ye correctly. Ye've done something with someone, probably involving sex. Sorry to speculate, but I have nae choice since ye will nae tell me."

She tried to interrupt, but for what? He was right. He was always right.

"And that's nae all I dinnae have a choice aboot," Ian said bitterly. "I'm nae allowed to choose the woman I want to spend time with, nor the career I want, or where I want to live, or what I can say to people, or even what I think aboot things." He gave her a hard, no–nonsense–tolerated look. "Do I have that correct, Rose?"

She gulped. "Well, when ye put it that way..." She managed a half–hearted smile for all of a second. "But dinnae ye see? We could never have a life together. Nae really. There might be all kinds of good things happening between the two of us, but..."

He did his best to dissuade her, but she wouldnae listen, so he kept talking and she finally had to butt in.

"Let me say this," she insisted, when he tried to interrupt again. "Ye having to apologize for me, defend me, explain my motives... it's nae way to live my life, constantly being embarrassed and worrying aboot the negative way I'll impact yer career, I mean yer calling. I just cannae do it anymore."

"So this is because I'm a pastor?"

"No. It's because I'm a wild rose."

He came round and held her then, and she cherished every last moment in his arms, because ultimately, it changed nothing.

"So this is it? Ye're sure?"

"It's the way it has to be," she said in the same, hollow voice. "And really, the timing is good. I mean, nae that any time is good when it comes to something like this. But St. Conan's did get their grant."

"By a very narrow margin."

"Also my fault," she quipped. "But get it, they did. And the constable is happy with me."

"Well, happy might be a stretch. Appeased might be a better word." Ian gave her a concerned look.

"At least he's nae longer threatening to divulge my indiscretions to the world."

"Yes. There is that." Ian sighed.

"Nor are the church ladies quite so bent on revenge –

comparatively speaking."

"I do see them getting over the loss of the things Digby took and starting to move on."

"So my work here is done," Rose said.

"I guess if ye look at it that way. But that doesnae mean—"

"But I do," Rose said. "And really, it does."

And so she left to drive back to her B&B. When she arrived, her hostess was in the living room, so she was able to inform her that she would be checking out early. There was nae point in staying if she wasnae going to be seeing Ian.

Before she knew it, she had poured out her heart to the woman, mostly aboot her frustration with trying to sew Lyndsie's pillows and failing, even though she had tried her best, which she knew, even if the innkeeper didnae, was more aboot her disappointment over how things had ended with Ian than aboot some silly pillows. But they werenae silly to Kelly, and when the day was done, poor, little Lyndsie still had nae pillows, and nae hope of having any, ever, if it was left to Rose.

Before she knew it, she had her solution – at least for the pillow dilemma. A pity her problems with Ian couldnae be fixed so easily.

So, nae worries, except that now, she was nae only keeping an important fact from Ian, but a secret from her sister and Lyndsie.

When she'd spoken to the innkeeper aboot the designs she'd drawn up for Lyndsie's pillows and struck a bargain on the price, she went to her room and gathered up her things. She left enough money on the nightstand to cover the bill and the pillows and then some, got Ginger settled in her car, and drove back to Glasgow.

Chapter Thirteen

Later the next week, she was missing Ian with a passion, and doubly thankful that at least she still had Kelly and Lyndsie and the boys in her life. And now, at long last, she also had Lyndsie's pillows. It was like magic, really – her creative vision, the colors and fabrics and lace she'd chosen herself – sewn exactly as she'd envisioned them – and without any more broken machines or bleeding fingers or mental and emotional trauma.

Of course, there was still Kevin, who was currently standing with his square, blue–collar shoulders and mammoth upper body planted between her and the front door of his and Kelly's duplex.

"Is Lyndsie ready?" Rose said, trying to sound sweet even though the mere sight of Kevin made her bristle.

"She'll be down in a minute."

"Good!" She tried to peer around Kevin's hefty frame to see if the boys were around. She wouldnae have minded saying hello to them, even though it was just Lyndsie that she'd invited to lunch. She'd known Kelly was going to be gone – she'd said she'd taken an extra shift at the local hotel where she worked as a chambermaid. Kelly did everything she could to earn extra money for what she liked to call The Children's College Fund, although Rose suspected that the money went to buy groceries or things like Nikes more often than nae. The way Kelly told it, hand–me–downs didnae even work with their boys – Jaime had extra wide feet, Josh, narrow, Jace, long and wide, and Jack, short with stubby toes. The other boys called Jack their resident hobbit.

"The boys home?" She looked around and felt the usual mixture of wonder and revulsion she felt whenever she entered Kelly's world. Kevin was still half blocking the door, glaring at her like she was the devil incarnate. She didnae know how Kelly did it. And that included the unshaven hulk in front of her, who, by the way, still hadnae asked her to come in and have a seat – and obviously, wasnae going to.

He spoke. "Kelly got off work early and took the boys to get haircuts."

She tried nae to look at Kevin, which was her usual tactic. But something was different today. Something – other than the ordinary – was wrong.

"Nice weather out there, is it nae?" she said amicably.

"I asked Lyndsie to stay in her room for a few minutes so ye and I could get some things straight."

She sighed. *Oh, joy.* Been there, done that, never went well.

"Yes?" She tried nae to sound antagonistic. She really did.

"What yer dog did to her pillows hurt Lyndsie very deeply."

"I'm sure it did. That's why I'm here. To make amends. Her new, hand–crafted pillows are in my auto. I wanted to do more than drop them off – ye know, give us a chance to bond. As women."

"She's nae a woman. She's a girl. And so is yer dog, in case ye'd forgotten."

"I've nae forgotten." Nae doubt Kevin was alluding to a previous occasion, some years ago, when she'd also left Ginger with Kelly for a few days. Unbeknownst to any of them, Ginger had come into season for the very first time, and left tiny spots of red blood everywhere she went – until someone had discovered what was happening – including a trail of unsightly blemishes on the new Berber carpeting Kevin had installed just days earlier. "I paid for a complete shampoo of yer carpet."

"Which stripped it of its natural oils and left it prone to excessive soiling to this day."

Why they'd ever installed a creamy white rug when they had four rambunctious boys was beyond Rose. If they'd selected something practical, like rust, or even brown, nae one would ever have even known that Ginger was in heat.

"Is that what ye wanted to talk to me aboot?" she asked.

"She's very impressionable."

"Lyndsie, or yer carpet?" Okay. That was rude, but she couldnae help it. She could only take so much of Kevin's sarcasm before she started to hand it back, and she was nearing her limit.

"I dinnae want ye saying anything to her that will upset her."

"I always do my best."

"That's debatable," Kevin said.

Everything was with Kevin.

"And dinnae be filling her head with any of yer nonsense."

She felt her nostrils flare, her hackles rise. "I beg yer pardon?"

"Ye're a bad influence on the girl. She hangs on every word ye say."

"She adores me!"

"Which wouldnae be a problem if ye were a suitable role model for the girl."

"I – I..."

"Just keep yer trap shut aboot whatever mess ye're in the middle of at present."

Thank God he only knew the half of it. And the small half at that.

"And dinnae be filling her head with all sorts of mollycock aboot whatever man ye're dating. I dinnae know who ye've taken up with now that the bum who kept ye waiting in Loch Awe while yer dog was back here munching on Lyndsie's pillows has dumped ye, but whoever it is, keep it to yerself. Kelly and I want to raise the girl to have our values, that's all."

For a second, Kevin looked almost conciliatory, but since his words were delivered with yet another slam, she rejected his feeble, measly attempt.

"So what do ye think I'm going to say? 'Lyndsie, do ye know how much fun it is being regarded as the family floozy just because ye had enough guts to walk away from a man ye were with for all the wrong reasons and marry a man who ye loved with all yer heart? Except that nae one believed ye because he happened to be rich?' Or should I go into the fact that the very first time I went on a date in nearly two decades, the man just happened to be scum? Or do ye want me to give her a lesson in church politics and the fact that Christians seem to know less aboot forgiveness than anyone in the world even though their precious Savior died for my sins just as well as theirs?"

Kevin's eyes finally softened – ever so slightly – at the last bit. She hadnae been going for affect, but really, what could one say to that? It was true.

Really, she should file the thought away for future use and let the church ladies have it one day. Jesus had forgiven her. Why couldnae His people get the concept through their thick skulls?

"Lyndsie! Yer Aunt Rose is here!" Kevin's voice thundered through the halls. And then, in a stage whisper, "She'll tell us everything ye two talk aboot. Just remember that."

* * *

Rose gave Lyndsie the new pillows she'd made as soon as they were settled in the car.

"They're so pretty! Even prettier than the old ones!" Lyndsie exclaimed, fingering the pink ribbon and tiny, pastel rosebuds and buttons the woman from Corrie Bank B&B had sewn on to embellish the design.

"I wouldnae tell yer Mum that," Rose said. "I mean, it's okay to go on aboot the fact that ye like them, and that I did a wonderful job of erasing the trauma of Ginger eating yer pillows with my clever designs and deft workmanship, but I wouldnae be mentioning that ye like them better than the ones yer Mum made."

"Of course nae," Lyndsie said with a conspiratorial smile. "I wouldnae want to hurt her feelings."

She revved up the engine a bit and veered carefully onto the motorway. "Good. Good. Just so we're on the same page then."

The Willow Tea Room was just 6 or 7 blocks from Rose's flat, but it was on the opposite side of Glasgow from Kevin and Kelly's. Why Rose didnae dine at the quaint eatery three or four times a fortnight was beyond her, when it was so close. Their food was unrivaled. The décor was as fascinating as it had been in Charles Rennie Mackintosh's day.

A half hour later, they'd parked, walked down the pedestrian walkway to the tea house, and taken their seats. Lyndsie had filled her in on school, her summer activities, and her brothers' latest antics.

Rose listened intently, peering at the menu from behind her spectacles. How she wished she were young again. Just looking at Lyndsie filled her with longing. 20/20 eyesight, nary a worry when it came to anything, a trim, pert figure with nae sags or bags in sight, a totally clean slate upon which to write the story of her life... Lyndsie had it all.

Like so many women, Rose realized in retrospect how sad it was that she hadnae appreciated the first bloom of her youth when she'd had it. But now was nae the time to think aboot youthful figures. Nae when there were delicious goodies all around.

"I highly recommend the Scottish breakfast. And their scones are to die for. And we must have a spot o' tea. They make their own special blends to go with the seasons."

Lyndsie looked unimpressed but happy to be with her aunt nonetheless. Rose probably could have taken her to the new McDonald's Hamburgers down the street and gotten McCoffee and McPancakes with McBiscuits and McGravy and Lyndsie would probably have been more excited aboot the fare. That's what having four brothers had done to the poor girl.

"I'll feel so bad if I order something and then dinnae like it," Lyndsie fretted. "Because the prices are so high."

"Nae to worry dear. I'm picking up the tab."

"I'll bet my da could pay at least half the electric bill for our flat with what it will cost for the two of us to eat."

"Well, we're nae going to be feeling guilty aboot that now, will we? We're here to have fun. Just us girls."

"Mum would love this place."

"Well, ye said yer Mum wanted to get the boys haircuts this morning. It was her choice. Really, I think she thought it would be more special this way, if just the two of us got to spend some time together."

"I'm glad," Lyndsie said. "I mean, I love my brothers and everything, and my da, but I am a little outnumbered most of the time."

"Well, we're here to treat ye to whatever ye'd like."

"Mum was more upset aboot the pillows than I was," Lyndsie said. "And my da. I mean, I liked them and everything, because my Mom made them. But really, they were just pillows."

"I hope the new ones..."

"They're beautiful. When it happened... I mean, Ginger must have been so scared to have just lost it like that. Poor little baby. She was shaking so hard. I didnae even care aboot the pillows. Just her, ye know?"

"I know," Rose said, feeling the essence of a true kindred spirit, a very rare thing in her family – or in the world, really.

A waiter came by and took their order – two traditional Scottish breakfast plates. "I hear this is what they serve the tourists every single morning at every last B&B in the entire country." Rose said.

"I can see why. It sounds just luscious."

"The B&B that I stay at near Loch Awe prepares my breakfast just the way I like it – a cup of fresh fruit with a little yogurt on top, sometimes a scone, if I know I'm going to be able to take a long walk, a single egg, poached until it's firm all the way through."

"Ye dinnae like jiggly eggs?" Lyndsie's eyes opened wide.

"No! Ye?"

"The runnier, the better."

So much for the kindred spirit theory. "Really. Must be a trait ye inherited from yer father. Kelly never..."

"My mum is so grossed out by the way the rest of the family likes our eggs that she can barely stand to cook them for us. But that's okay. My da is the breakfast maker at our house."

"Really?" *Kevin?* She took a sip of tea. So the man had one redeeming quality – well, two actually. She looked across the table at her beautiful niece. The man made good babies.

Lyndsie looked up at her and smiled but said nothing. Rose twirled her spoon in her cup. Lyndsie looked at her expectantly. Rose did some more twirling and fiddled with the string on the tea bag. So there was a little lull in the conversation – that didnae mean that Lyndsie wasnae having a good time. She was nearly a teenager, that was all. Teenagers were known to be sullen and withdrawn, were they nae?

She searched for something to say. "Is nae it nice, that we live in a world where we can each enjoy our eggs exactly the way we like them?"

Lyndsie looked at her like she'd gone daft. Thankfully, their waitress chose that moment to deliver a china plate covered with hand–painted, pink cabbage roses to each of them. Each of the tiny plates cradled a smidgen of clotted cream and a freshly baked scone.

"Um..." Lyndsie inhaled deeply. "Still warm from the oven."

"That's the best way." Rose spread a bit of raspberry jam from a caddy she found on the table and some clotted cream on her scone and took a small bite. *See?* This was going just fine. Lyndsie didnae seem at all upset by the fact that her pillows had been destroyed. She'd confided in her aboot how she liked her eggs. *That was personal, yet safe subject matter, wasnae it?* Contrary to what Kelly claimed, the girl obviously still trusted her. Jiggly eggs. Rose could have laughed at her, or berated her for her questionable tastes, but she'd been gentle and responded in love and it had all worked out fine, hadnae it?

Lyndsie cleared her throat. "So, Aunt Rose, when ye want to

date someone, do ye think it's better to go out with a boy – um, man – ye're friends with, so that ye can talk aboot things, and study together, and stuff like that? Or, to go for someone who is so totally hot that yer knickers get in a wad every time ye look at him? I mean, even if ye dinnae have that much in common?"

Rose froze. Her spoon clattered against the side of her cup so loudly everyone in the room nae doubt heard it. "What?"

Lyndsie broke off a large piece of her scone, propped her elbow on the table, and started nibbling on it straight from her hand.

"Honey. Yer fork," Rose whispered.

"So what do ye think?" Lyndsie put her scone back on her plate and used her fork to lift a dainty bite to her mouth.

The pressure. Nae only was she asking her advice, she was almost certainly going to do whatever Rose said. Kevin would kill her. "Ah, dinnae ye think ye should be asking yer Mum aboot, ye know, things like this?"

"I tried. But Mum only ever dated Da since they were high school sweethearts, and ye've had so much experience with so many different men that I thought..."

Great. She was going to think positively and assume Lyndsie meant her words as a compliment, but really, wasnae that just the way it always was? Kelly and Kevin had only ever slept with each other, while she'd gone wandering from one man – one bed – to another. It wasnae just Kevin, or the people of St. Conan's judging her, or even Ian. Now, even her very own niece was doing it.

"And how do ye know ye will nae do the same thing as yer Mum and Da?" She tried to keep her voice light. "If ye choose well the first time, it could stick just like it did with the two of them."

Lyndsie wrinkled her nose and took another bite of her scone. "I dinnae want to spend the rest of my life with any of these guys. I just want to date someone, ye know, get a little experience with men."

Rose sucked in her breath in what she hoped was a non-conspicuous, ladylike way and tried nae to gag on her clotted cream. *What was that supposed to mean?* Experience as in holding hands at a rugby game, experience as in having a boy carry yer books home from school, or experience as in... *Oh Lord,* she prayed what was probably the most sincere prayer of her entire life. *Please help me to say the right thing!*

Thank goodness, a waiter chose that moment to bring the rest of their traditional Scottish breakfast. Black pudding, sautéed mushrooms and tomatoes, two sorts of bangers, a rash of bacon, eggs – Lyndsie's jiggly and hers, nae.

Lyndsie started in on her eggs and for a second, Rose thought maybe she would drop the subject. Today's children were known to have short attention spans, werenae they? It was what all the experts claimed. Nae doubt the fault of computer games over stimulating their wee, little brains.

"So what do ye think is the best way to get experience with men?" Lyndsie said, taking such a huge bite of toast that it would undoubtedly last the entire duration of Rose's answer.

Rose could feel her blood pressure rising, literally climbing off the charts. "Well," she said, looking round the room for someone to save her. "There are some sorts of experiences that make ye a better person, and enrich yer life, like visiting museums and going on a boat ride, or spending the summer working on a farm." (Or at a convent, she was tempted to say.) "But there are other sorts of experiences that only serve to sour ye, sometimes for the rest of yer life. It's what they call baggage, and the more men ye date, the more of it ye end up lugging around and taking into each new relationship ye enter in to, and eventually, into yer marriage."

"Seriously?"

"Yes! So I would definitely say to go for the guys ye're friends with. But dinnae go for them. Just be friends with them. All of them. I mean, nae one in particular, as in a close friend. Just casual friends with them all. Nae that there's anything casual aboot it. What I'm trying to say is that it's fine if ye want to be friends with the boys ye know – with whomever ye wish, really. Well, nae whomever. Better only a few, or maybe even just one. But even with that one, nothing serious. The important thing to remember is, nothing serious."

Lyndsie looked crestfallen. A bit confused as well, for some reason. Probably, her mother had told her the same thing. Probably, she'd thought Rose would spin some romantic tale and tell her what she wanted to hear.

"Ye can learn so much aboot a man when ye're friends, and then, even one kiss – believe me, that's all it takes, and yer head gets so clouded that ye cannae be rational, sometimes never again, and before ye know it, things get complicated – very complicated. And then, the whole relationship goes down the crapper. And if ye're in classes with the boy, or if ye work with him, or go to the same church he goes to, ye have to keep seeing him, or ye find yerself living in constant fear that ye'll run into him, and yer whole life is suddenly very, very messy."

Lyndsie was starting to look downright depressed.

"So that's why I dinnae recommend it. Dating, that is. But have fun! Enjoy yer school years. The experience part will come naturally, without yer having to do any plotting or planning at all. It will just happen."

Lyndsie's face softened and she took a bite of eggs.

Ugh, Rose thought. And smiled brightly.

"So Aunt Rose?" Lyndsie ate another bite of her disgustingly runny eggs. "Is there one man, I mean, besides Uncle Robert, who ye truly loved with all yer heart that ye would have liked to have spent the rest of yer life with?"

Rose chose to ignore the fact that the question was asked in past tense, like she was far too old to experience love at this advanced stage of her life. "Aye. As a matter of fact, there is someone." She tried to salvage her pride. "But we cannae be together because of what the man does for a living."

"Ye mean because he's a jerk who doesnae even have a job?"

So much for her pride. Rose ground her fork through the skin of a red tomato with her fork because she was too irate to risk picking up her knife. "Ye know aboot that?"

"I heard Mum and Da talking aboot this guy who was supposed to meet ye and didnae even bother to ring ye when he decided nae to come to the place where ye were meeting him. They thought I was asleep. It must have been kind of embarrassing. And it's sad that ye love him that much."

"It's nae him," Rose said. "That was Digby. I never loved him. The man I love is kind and sweet. He defends people even when they dinnae deserve it, and forgives them, even though they probably shouldnae be, and he's the most patient man ye'll ever meet."

"He sounds like a knight in shining armor, Aunt Rose."

"He is."

"So why cannae ye be with him?"

"Because... because he deserves someone who's as kind and sweet as he is... and well... someone who has nae been... ye know... someone who is... who has nae..."

"Ye mean, like a virgin?"

She choked. "Um, why, yes."

"I do know aboot sex, ye know."

"Of course ye do," Rose said, trying to recover. Oh, my. She hoped Lyndsie didnae know everything aboot sex. Of course she didnae. Her mind flitted from one thought to another, one position to another, involuntarily, hoping against hope that Lyndsie didnae yet know aboot this or that.

And Kevin. Oh my Lord. Kevin was going to kill her.

"It's too late for me, sweetheart," she told Lyndsie. "Ye can never go back. I mean to say, once yer innocence is lost, ye can never undo what's been done. And Ian, is so, well, special. He's a very dear man, and quite special, and he should have someone who is just as dear as he is, dinnae ye think?" She tried to speak brightly, as she always did with Lyndsie, to be positive and upbeat even though her heart was breaking.

"But ye are one of the dearest people I know, Aunt Rose."

"I'm glad ye think so."

"I cannae imagine that Ian would hold yer past against ye." Lyndsie sounded far older than her years. "Nae if he's as kind as ye say he is."

"He probably wouldnae. The thing is, I hold my past against myself. That's what I was trying to tell ye earlier, sweetheart. Once ye've written on a blackboard, ye can take an eraser and try to get it clean again, but ye cannae. Nae really. It will always be smudged and chalky. It will never be brand new again." Wait. Did the child even know what a blackboard was? They did still have them at school, did they nae? Or had they been replaced by some huge, big–screen version of an iPad or iPod or whatever they called them these days?

Lyndsie was giving her a bit of a blank look.

"Ye shouldnae be so hard on yerself, Aunt Rose."

"I'll try." That was all she could promise.

They finished off their traditional Scottish breakfast and splurged on a piece of Victoria Sponge covered with fresh strawberries, raspberries and powdered sugar galore. She might nae be able to forgive herself for sleeping with one too many men, but she had nae problem forgiving herself the a few extra thousand calories she'd consumed with Lyndsie on their girl's day out. *So there.*

Chapter Fourteen

It was Erika's day to come to her flat and work out of Robert's old office, but even so, Rose was still in bed, trying nae to think aboot Ian. She'd had big plans for the day in her mind, but the depression that had settled over her had such a paralyzing grip on the rest of her body, that it mattered little what her brain wanted.

Nae matter, she thought sleepily from just under the covers. Erika had a key, and the night before, when she couldnae sleep, she'd made a list of things to start on and left it on top of Robert's old desk where she knew Erika would find it.

"Bless that woman," she mumbled, just as she'd heard Robert say so many times when he was still alive and Erika was still his trusted personal secretary.

Erika would know what to do. She always did. The woman was a saint. She burrowed back under the covers, determined to have an extra hour or two...

"Mrs. Wilson?" A soft voice wafted through her dreams. Erika was the only one who called her Mrs. Wilson. She was just plain Rose to her mum, Kelly and the kids, and nobody to Kevin, who ignored her – unless she'd done something wrong, which as fate would have it, was often enough that she did get a fair amount of attention from him. The last thing Robert's boys, as he'd liked to call them, had ever wanted was to call her was Mrs. Wilson, an acknowledgment that cemented the fact that their father had married her. If they stuck to calling her Rose, they could pretend that she was some sort of detestable, distant cousin, twice removed – anything but the beloved bride of their father, step–mother to them.

She snuggled in a bit deeper.

"Mrs. Wilson? Are ye there? I need to speak to ye if I might."

She awoke with a jolt. "Erika?"

"Yes, ma'am. There's an urgent matter, I'm afraid."

She scooted up in her bed, reached back to plump up the two big pillows behind her, and tucked her coverlet neatly around her waist.

"Come in." Nae need to apologize to Erika, who knew full well what stress she'd been under as of late – even if she didnae know why.

"Ma'am. I hate to be the bearer of bad news when ye've already been feeling under the weather, but I thought ye'd want to see this morning's paper."

"Of course." She tried nae to yawn and vaguely wondered what could be so important that it merited awaking her.

And then, she saw the picture.

Pain shot through her body, physical pain. The picture didnae show anything, nae really. The important spots were covered. But it was obvious she was naked.

This couldnae be happening. *And why now? She'd gotten them the money, had she nae?*

"I'm so sorry, ma'am. The article calls it a major scandal. Sources say the photos of yer romp with a known criminal went viral in the wee hours of the night. Americans is my guess – like they dinnae have enough scandals of their own without butting their noses into ours."

She didnae try to explain. "Has there been any word from–"

"Robert called an hour ago."

"Nae surprise there. The man would have to gloat."

This brought a weak smile to Erika's face. "He did sound rather like ye'd made his day."

"Ecstatic, I'm sure. And Winston?"

"A few minutes ago."

"What aboot Kelly?" She moaned. "I should call her, before she hears aboot it from someone else."

"I'm afraid it's too late. She called aboot fifteen minutes ago, in tears."

"Oh, Erika." Tears were streaming down her face, too. "I'm so sorry to put ye in the middle of this. They've good reason to mock me, but ye shouldnae have to bear their ire. Ye should – ye should take the rest of the day off."

"I'll field the calls. Yer husband trained me well on many occasions when he, too, had a scandal to tamp down–"

"Like when he married me." She said it rather than asked. Oh Lord. The pain.

"That's what I'm here for." And then Erika left her alone, the newspaper still splattered across her bed.

* * *

"Yes, I've seen the papers," Ian said for at least the twentieth or thirtieth time that morning. "Yes, I'm well aware that this is exactly the kind of publicity that St. Conan's does nae need. Yes, I know the timing is unfortunate." He listened to the tirade on the other end of the phone with half an ear. "Yes, I know it's humiliating. I'll probably never view the flying buttresses in the same way again either."

At least they didnae have to begin every day looking out their living room window on the precise spot of grass on where...

He pulled his drapes shut and walked to the opposite end of the house, his mobile still tight to his ear. "And what precisely would ye like me to say to her?"

He listened well this time.

"No, I will nae tell her that she's nae welcome at our services. All are welcome. I for one, am always happy to see her in the congregation."

He watched as a blue jay flew from the kirk, across the motorway, to the forest beyond – and wished he could follow.

Instead, he paced. "But that's exactly where ye're wrong, Katherine. Ye maintain that this changes everything when quite the opposite is true. This changes nothing. We all already knew what happened under the flying buttresses. Although none of us were authorized to view the tape, several of us have already seen it. The rest have nae doubt heard graphic descriptions from those who have. Rose has already been humiliated. She has already apologized. She has already made every effort to compensate for the damages that were done to our building and our congregation even though she bears absolutely nae fault for what happened. She has gone above and beyond in her efforts to make peace including securing a sizable grant for repairs to the building."

His words were evidently nae persuasive enough, because the caller started another go round.

"Yes. Yes. Yes. I understand what ye're saying. But ultimately, the fact that yer daughter down in Edinburgh and a million other people scattered around the world are now aware of this disgrace thanks to the Internet doesnae change anything."

He listened to another string of arguments, each starting with the standard, "But pastor..." He bit his tongue so hard and so often that it hurt.

"Yes, it's embarrassing. But what's done is done. And more important, what's forgiven is forgiven – buried at the bottom of the deepest sea and forgotten according to God's holy word."

He was losing patience and fast. How could this have happened? He'd already rung up the constable's office to give the man a piece of his mind, but it had done nae good. The man maintained that there was nae leak in his office. Right. Ian was the only one outside the constable's office who could have had a copy of the tape, and he certainly hadnae released anything to anyone.

The phone started jangling again. This time, he ignored it and glanced down at his wristwatch. It was Thursday, a day that he often went visiting. And although none of his flock was in the hospital or at death's door, he did know of one parishioner who was having a very rough time of it and would probably benefit greatly from a pastoral visit.

* * *

A little while later, Rose was still snuggled up in her bed, on her mobile, talking to Kelly. First, they cried together, then they talked aboot what had happened – in detail. It was the conversation she'd longed to have with Kelly all along. She just hadnae known how to go aboot it.

In a way, she was almost relieved that everything was finally out in the open.

"Why didnae ye tell me?" Kelly kept saying.

Because some things were just too horrible to bring up, some subjects too mortifying to be broached. But now that the ice was broken, why nae blab all? She had nothing to be embarrassed aboot. At least, that's what she kept trying to tell herself.

Ian had said many a time that she ought to be commended for her bravery, that she deserved a medal for putting herself out there, for taking a risk again, for re–entering the dating world. Sure, things hadnae turned out the way she'd wished they had, but that was the way God worked sometimes.

"I'd never have met Ian if it were nae for Digby."

They discussed that thought for nearly an hour. God's ways were nothing if nae mysterious.

"Ye should use that angle when ye tell Mum," Kelly said. "Ye can say the whole thing between ye and Digby was destined to be – all part of God's perfect plan for yer life."

It was genius, really, except that... "I have to tell Mum?"

"Well, it shouldnae be up to me."

"Yer life goal for at least a decade was to find out what I was up to and tattle to Mum and Da."

"I've reformed."

"Right," Rose said facetiously. "And yer timing is so excellent."

They argued aboot how and when Rose should tell their Mum for another half hour after that.

"Ye know," Kelly said at some point. "The picture that was on the front page of the Star was quite flattering."

"Ye think so?"

"Definitely. I mean, nae that I'd ever want to be photographed doing what ye were doing, but if I were, I would chose exactly the same angle. Ye look so toned. Ye're really quite beautiful, especially in that one. And very sexy looking."

"Ye really think so?"

"I've always said ye have the skin of a woman half yer age. One of yer best features, really."

"Thank ye, Kelly."

"If the church ladies are saying bad things aboot ye, it's just because they're jealous."

"Ye really think so?"

She heard a string of harsh words in the background.

"Kevin's home. Got to go."

"Okay."

And then, she was alone again. The seductive, wine–colored walls, fluid silk window dressings, and romantic, goose–down coverlet of her bedroom mocked her. She thought aboot the supposed fairy tale life she led and the dull, mostly drab life most of the church ladies from St. Conan's lived, and thought that she would happily part with the cold, lonely finery of her life for a cozy evening cuddled up under an old quilt in front of the hearth with a man who loved her.

She thought aboot Kelly's life and wondered if she could find it in her to tolerate a man like Kevin if it meant having four strapping sons and a daughter like Lyndsie. Probably nae.

She'd been blessed to enjoy true love with Robert. The means he'd had – the means she still enjoyed, were a nice side benefit. That was all. She'd really been blessed. Maybe she was being greedy, wanting a man in her life again. If she'd been content to be Robert's widow, to enjoy the security and freedom from want he'd endowed her with, she wouldnae be in the predicament she was in, now would she?

Erika was still in the office working, nae doubt trying to do damage control, bless her.

She looked at the paper with Robert Junior's message and phone number written on it and crumbled it into a wad.

He would find her eventually, but she was nae going to make it easy for him. She looked at the next slip. Winston was another story. He was the chairman of the board, and had always been a very dear, very trusted friend of Robert's as well as their banker and financial advisor.

Erika buzzed to tell her that Kelly was calling on her land line. She hadnae looked at the charge on her mobile, but it was probably nearly dead after her and Kelly's previous conversation.

She heard Kelly's sobs before the phone was even half way to her ear. "Kelly. What's wrong?"

"Kevin doesnae want ye seeing the children anymore."

Her heart almost stopped beating.

Her sister sniffled. "Ye know I would never say what I'm aboot to—"

"Just say it," said a voice in the background.

"Fine!" Kelly spit out the words. "Kevin says to tell ye that he wants nothing to do with ye anymore, doesnae want ye to be seen with his sons or daughter. He believes ye are a bad example. Kevin says that he and the children are ashamed to be seen with ye."

"But—"

"Tell her the rest of it!" Kevin ordered.

More tears from Kelly. Then, in a muffled voice, amid more threats from Kevin, she said, "Kevin says that yer judgment is so poor that the children could be endangered while in yer company. Because who knows who else ye've met up with from the Internet. And that even if ye have nae made a practice of it before, now that every con man in the country knows ye're so gullible and lonely that ye're willing to... um... Kevin. Please dinnae make me..."

"Spread yer legs for any man who comes sniffing," Kevin yelled.

Kelly sobbed and hiccupped almost simultaneously. "Kevin says ye'll be a target for every loser within 200 miles of Glasgow – on top of all the perverts who live right there in the city. I am so sorry!"

Those were Kelly's final words before the phone clicked down and went dead.

She sobbed for almost an hour then. She hated knowing that she had caused Kelly any pain, and hoped Kevin had calmed down now that she'd been told off properly.

She tried nae to let Kevin's words scare her. Kelly would eventually find a way for her to spend time with the kids. Time was a great healer even for jerks like Kevin. This, too, would blow over. But knowing that and trying to look at things from a long term perspective didnae negate the fact that she hated Kevin for the way he bullied Kelly around, and almost hated Kelly for the way she let him. And it also hurt. Even though she had to consider the source, it still hurt.

That left Winston. It was late afternoon by the time she rang him up, hoping that the emotions he was feeling would have magically abated – even disappeared – by the time they spoke.

Winston had never been an emotional man. It was in his usual precise manner, clipped tones, and fair way that he said what he had to say.

"Rose, the Foundation is suggesting that you recuse yourself from the board for an indefinite period."

"Ye've had a meeting?" This shocked her, for some reason. It bothered her to know they'd been discussing her behind her back. But then, what had she expected? She'd known half the country was doing exactly that. Why shouldnae the board?

Because they were supposed to be her friends. Because they should have given her the benefit of the doubt. Because, supposedly, she was one of them. Because they should have stood behind her, nae matter what.

"Rose, I'm speaking for the entire board when I say that this would have saddened Robert Senior greatly."

"Of course it would have." Her response came so quickly and so forcefully that for a second, she wasnae sure whether she had said the words out loud or just thought them. "It would sadden him that he died and wasnae there to hold me when I needed a little affection. He would also have understood. He would have encouraged me to move on with my life and start dating again."

Winston plowed on in his typical businesslike way. "While we completely understand and fully support you, we don't believe that the majority of our stockholders and beneficiaries will, and thus, we would like to encourage you to withdraw from our governing board before any more damage is done."

Another knife wiggled into a spot just left of the one Kelly and Kevin had inserted.

She took a second to absorb the pain. "I understand that a scandal like this is unpleasant for everyone involved. But I dinnae understand why me being involved in an embarrassing but otherwise innocuous incident like this has anything to do with my being able to do my job as a board member. It is nae like someone is going to turn down a grant because they dinnae approve of my morals."

"It taints the organization and sullies our reputations – all of ours, nonetheless."

"But the organization was never perfect and still is nae. My husband wasnae perfect. None of ye are perfect."

There was a long silence. "Rose, I don't know how to say this gently, so I'm just going to say it. This really doesn't have anything to do with the photos, although they certainly aren't the kind of thing one wants floating around."

"Of course nae. I'm as mortified aboot it as ye are." *Times a million*, she thought.

"Rose dear, I know you already know this, but compensating for your transgressions is not a viable criterion for distributing a grant."

So it was aboot St. Conan's then – or rather, her efforts to make amends with the foundation's money. Of course, she'd acted with bias. She'd used the foundations money for her own gain – nae financial, but certainly emotional. She thought aboot it for a second, considered trying to explain aboot the constable's threats, and her hope that he would give the tape back if she cooperated. But it was all a moot point now.

Winston read a short statement from the board in which they let her know that she had cheapened the reputation of the foundation, and dishonored her husband's memory.

She swallowed her pride – what little remnant she had left. "Please let me sleep on it, Winston, and if ye would, please do the same. It's been a very hard day."

Resigning from the board went against every instinct she had. It would dishonor Robert's wishes and his memory. Sitting on the board allowed her to help people in a way she would never be able to otherwise. None of the other board members had her tender heart, which Robert Senior had known full well. The thought of any of them trying to do what she did was both laughable and heartbreaking.

Although she did have to admit that the thought of never having to walk into Wilson Enterprises again was certainly tempting, especially now that the board members all knew what she looked like naked.

Which is quite toned and very sexy, she reminded herself, trying to bolster her spirits.

Her mobile continued to beep. The subsequent messages she received from Robert's sons were nae nearly so kind as Winston's chat. Robert's hatred was palpable. Rodney joked and made his signature wise cracks. She certainly provided him with a bevy of new material. Robert threatened to take her to court and remove her from the board forcibly if she didnae voluntarily resign by the next morning.

Chapter Fifteen

"Mum? It's Rose." It had to be done sometime. Nae that it wasnae going to be painful. But the sooner the slice was cut, the sooner it would stop bleeding and the sooner it could start to heal. Besides, she was so numb already that it probably wouldnae even hurt.

"Oh, Mary Ann. It's so good to hear from ye. Ever since Robert died, ye hardly ever call. Ye'd think now that ye have nae one ye'd know how I feel."

"Sorry, Mum. I really do... It's been hard."

"Well, there's nae time like the present. Tell me what's going on. Have ye met someone special?"

Some things never changed. And some things changed all the time. And some things – things ye'd thought would last forever, or at least until ye were old and gray – didnae. Like Robert. Losing Robert had thrown this whole chain of events into motion. And she had nae clue how to bring her mother up to speed without totally freaking her out.

"Someone very special, Mum. But ye know what they say aboot the night always being darkest right before the dawn?"

"There cannae be a rainbow without a rainstorm."

"Yes, well. I have some bad news aboot that."

"Ye're in trouble? Oh, Rose, ye know I've always prayed ye'd give me a grandchild, but nae this way."

She almost laughed. How like her Mum, whose whole little world revolved around cute, little babies. "I'm nae pregnant, Mum."

"Oh."

A whole different kind of pain pricked at her when she heard her Mum's disappointment. And when she thought aboot where an unplanned pregnancy would fall on a scale of troubles, a surprise baby didnae sound half bad. Sure, there would be the usual troubles women went through when they got the order reversed and put the cart before the horse, and the pain of actual childbirth, but at least there'd be a bonus waiting at the end of the agony.

And what grandmother didnae get so excited aboot a new baby grandson or granddaughter arriving that they soon forgot at what time or exactly how the baby was conceived?

She could only wish her news was so good.

Maybe if she let her mother think she was having a baby, she would be so happy that she wouldnae care aboot all the other mucklehash going on.

Aye, right. "Mum, do ye remember when things would go wrong, and Grandma Mildred always used to say 'Tatties over the side?' Well, there's something in the paper today that ye should know aboot."

"I dinnae read the papers. Trash. That's all they print these days. That kind of filth, I dinnae need to know aboot."

Their mother had raised her and Kelly under that same premise. They'd been effectively shielded and sheltered from any knowledge that might harm them, any tales that might fill their heads with unwanted notions. They hadnae been taken shopping around the holidays or allowed to look at Christmas catalogs because they were only full of things they really didnae need anyway. They hadnae been allowed to go to movies or go to their friends' houses to play Barbie dolls or shop in stores with pretty dresses – nae sense dangling a carrot in front of their eyes when there was nae way they were ever going to have any of those kinds of things.

Those kinds of things was always said with a disgusted harrumph just like her mum was making right now. "I made a conscious decision years ago nae to include those kinds of things in my life, and my feelings have nae changed one bit."

Which effectively meant that her Mom didnae want her in her life. Rose was "one of those things" that her Mum had avowed to avoid at any cost.

"But Mom," she said quietly. "What's in the paper... It's aboot me."

Silence.

"God knows..." She was nae taking his name in vain, she really believed God was the only one who really knew how horribly she felt aboot all of this. "I'd rather ye nae find out aboot this. But people are going to be talking aboot it, and I think it's better that ye hear aboot it from me than them."

More silence. Finally, a stifled, "It's that bad?"

"Truly rag worthy."

"Well, whatever ye do, ye do in a grandiose way, Mary Ann Rosalie McCullen."

"That I do, Mum." She didnae go into any details that the paper already hadnae made public, which didnae leave much untold.

Her mother took a few minutes to digest the news. "I never thought I'd say this, but I'm glad yer father is nae alive to see this day."

"I know." It was horrible, but she felt the same way. Her da had thought the sun rose and set on her. Even when she'd left her Dad standing alone at the back of the church the day she'd abandoned Torey McDougall at the altar, he'd defended her decision. Nae one else had understood – he had.

"I've always tried to make Da proud, Mum. I still try, even though he's gone."

"Well, next time, try a little harder."

"I will, Mum." And then she took to her bed and after an hour or so, she was still wondering if she would ever again venture forth into the world.

She was still crumpled up in a heap on her bed with Ginger when the doorbell rang. Erika had gone home. She was so fearful of having to face paparazzi that she actually decided to use the peephole in the door for what was probably the first time in its hundred years of existence.

Ginger was barking her friendly welcome bark and nae her stranger danger bark, which should have told her that her visitor was a friend and nae a foe. But who could blame her for feeling a bit wary? And besides, she thought Ginger must be mistaken since she had practically nae friends, which, after all, was the reason she'd taken up with Digby in the first place.

She glanced through the peephole, saw Ian and was so happy that she almost lost her head, opened the door and catapulted herself into his arms right there in the entryway. But taking a second to look at where that kind of rash behavior had gotten her before, she thought better of her original plan and pulled him inside her apartment.

By the time the door was closed and re–bolted, she'd lost the nerve to hug him. He was wearing his clergy collar, which was just brill of him, really, in case her place was staked out, but also, a bit off–putting.

"Ian," she said casually, as though running into him outside her

114

door was the most normal thing in the world, as though she hadnae said good–bye to him for good, as though she hadnae been naked on the front page of the Sun, the Daily Mirror and the Morning Star.

Ginger, meantime, had nae such qualms aboot expressing her real emotions, and ran joyful circles around the two of them.

"I call it a rabies attack when she does that."

Ian smiled and reached down and tried to pet her, but she was off in a blur before his hand made contact. "How thrilling to get such an exuberant welcome."

Maybe if she were a dog. Dogs were seen naked all the time and nae one thought a thing aboot it.

"So ye were in the neighborhood..."

"And thought I'd pay ye a call."

"How sweet of ye." She truly meant it, too. It had been a hard day filled with great losses. Talking to Kelly had been such a balm to her spirit, and then... if she'd ever needed a friend, it was now.

She motioned to his collar. "Is this an official visit then?" It had been a month since she'd been up to Loch Awe. Maybe it was church policy – miss a month of Sundays, and ye got a visit, or something like that. Or maybe Ian was here because... And if he was, well, it was very kind of him, but her photos in the paper were the last thing she wanted to talk aboot right now.

"I'll bet the church ladies are craving to have me back to church now, then, are they nae?" She managed a wry smile.

"I'm sure they'd be happy to have ye."

"Happy as in Christian, dinnae–have–a–choice–because–we'll–go–to–hell–if–we–dinnae–do–the–right–thing–and–take–her–back happy, or happy because they like me and miss me?"

"Dinnae be so hard on yerself, Rose. I thought ye were getting on with the ladies at quilting quite well there at the end. I know ye've had a little setback, but–"

"I tried," Rose said, steering the conversation even further away from her naked pictures on the front page of the paper. "There was one, Amy, who was nice for a few minutes, but eventually she forsook me, too."

"And why do ye think that was?" Ian said in his gentle minister's voice.

"I have nae idea. I tried to be helpful, but they would have none of it."

"Helpful as in what way?" Ian looked suspicious.

"As in suggesting color combinations and so forth. Helpful things like that."

"Ah." He looked around her flat then, and nodded appreciatively. "Ye have a gift for arranging things. I can see that. And exceptional taste. But the ladies at church have gifts of their own. And they're very proud of the quilts they make."

"But they're ugly. Just between ye and me, of course." Ah... She breathed deeply. How good it felt to ignore her own faults and talk aboot someone else's for a change.

"I would never utter a word of it."

"My talents were being wasted, trying to work with those ladies. They're just so... I know what happened under the flying buttresses is part of it, but I dinnae think they'd listen to me if I were Saint Agnes herself. It was so frustrating! I have a real knack for fundraising ye know. It's what I do. If they'd have let me help, I could have raised three times the amount in half the time."

"I'm sure ye're very good at what ye do, Rose, but the truth is, so are they, in their own way."

Well, at least this was going well. Ian seemed so absorbed in the latest church lady drama that he'd totally forgotten the reason he'd visited, assuming it was her being seen naked in front of all Scotland.

"I see. Well, then, I'll just leave it to them like I have been."

"I'm sure in time..." Ian said. There was silence between them for a few minutes.

"How do ye do it?" She felt contrite, even though she hadnae been in the wrong with the church ladies and even though she'd been trying to deter him from talking aboot what really needed to be talked aboot. She'd just been trying to help the church ladies and who could blame her for nae wanting to think aboot the other?

"Each parish is different, Rose. For a pastor, and for anyone new trying to assimilate into the church, the skill lies in gauging the strengths and weaknesses of the congregation, learning to appreciate them for who and what they are, and helping them draw closer to God in whatever way befits their unique needs."

"Oh. I see." Rose sniffled and felt aboot ten inches tall. "So I guess that's why ye're a pastor and I'm nae."

"I've been doing my job for nigh on a decade. I know the church ladies can be a bit nebby at times."

"There are one or two who are downright nippy sweetie."

"But I would hope I've learned a wee bit aboot ministering to people's needs in that amount of time."

"I didnae mean to offend ye." She couldnae do anything right could she? Once again, she'd stepped into a hornet's nest, and instead of stepping away so she could heal, she just kept riling things up. Again and again and again.

"May I?" Ian stepped towards her with his arms outstretched. "Because based on my experience as a pastor, I'm sensing that yer unique need at this moment is to have a hug."

"Thank ye." She pinched away her tears. She'd wanted so badly to get the tape back, to protect herself from the very kind of embarrassment she'd been suffering since everyone had seen the newspaper this morning. And of course, she'd wanted to save herself from sure financial ruin. Who wouldnae? But it was more than that.

She wanted Ian to be proud of her. She wanted to fit in and be accepted. She wanted Ian to be able to hold his head high and say of her, "See? Ye must admit I was right aboot her all along. She's good people." She could envision it all in her mind, Ian bragging on her keen wit, and her canny ability to pick herself up, dust herself off, and put the pieces of her life back together after untold hardships. There would be a round of applause, and she would be given the award for "Best Thing That Ever Happened to the Congregation", and they would all gather around, thanking her for all she'd done to—

"Rose? Ye looked like ye were flying round the first star to the left of the morning there for a minute."

"Sorry. I can be a bit of an eedle–doddle."

Ian just smiled.

"Do ye think..." She paused. "...that if I started coming up again on the weekends and attending services that they would eventually grow to trust me?"

"Yes. But if it means torturing yerself, there's nae need."

"Yes, there is."

Ian waited before speaking, probably to see if she was going to tell him why. She didnae. Part of it was pure selfishness. Part of it was because... because... well, for reasons she wasnae even able to put into words. It was a good thing Ian was a patient man, she thought for the hundredth time.

"Perhaps we'll see ye next Sunday then." He looked very

pleased. And that pleased her.

He took off his clergy collar and opened the top few buttons of his shirt and hugged her again. Long and hard. Later, they sat on the sofa and talked and held hands and then she fixed a spot of tea, quite forgetting that she didnae want to talk aboot the photos.

"Oh, Ian." She moaned. "Do ye think it will ever go away, this colossal mess that I've made?"

"I think by this time next week, nae one will even remember what happened. It's nae like yer Princess Kate. There's nae ongoing drama here to keep the public's attention."

"I hope ye're right."

"Nae offense meant, Rose, but the looky lous who read the muckity muck in the paper dinnae really care aboot ye. People just love seeing other people's misery."

"Kind of like when there's an accident on the M8 motorway, I suppose."

"Exactly. They'll drive slowly and gawk out the window, and they may turn on the telly that night to see if there's mention of who was hurt, but they're nae going to continue to follow the person's progress or go visit them in the hospital or be there in court to see if anyone was issued a citation."

"So ye dinnae think people will cut my picture out of the paper, pin it on their corkboards and talk aboot me for weeks to come?"

Ian smiled. "No. I think that by tomorrow night ye'll be lining hamster cages or at rest at the bottom of the recycling bin."

She smiled and tucked her hand back in his. "That's the best news I've had all day."

Chapter Sixteen

Rose actually slept through the night once Ian had said good–bye and gone home. But that was as long as her peaceful state of mind lasted. Her escapades may have been a brief blip in the radar as far as the people of the UK and the world wide web were concerned, but to the board members at Wilson Enterprises, yesterday's news was still of utmost concern. Neither Robert Junior nor Rodney appeared to have forgotten all aboot it or to have lined their hamster cages with the newspapers she'd appeared in. Quite the contrary, what had happened seemed just the excuse they'd been looking for.

Rose looked at herself in the mirrored walls of the elevator on her way to the fourteenth floor of Wilson Enterprises and congratulated herself on having chosen the perfect attire. Her dull grey, wool suit was as drab and conservative as clothing could be. Her hair was combed and sculpted to perfection, her make–up, immaculately applied, her jewelry, staid and color–coordinated.

That was where the well–planned and perfectly executed part of her day came to a screeching halt.

She approached the front desk hesitantly. Good. Erika was working. If anyone would rise to the occasion and cover her back, or in this case, her front, it was Erika.

But today, even Erika looked embarrassed. Nae a good sign.

"Are they all, I mean, has everyone else arrived?"

"Yes. Waiting in the board room, I'm afraid."

Rose squared her shoulders and started down the hall with all the enthusiasm of a pirate walking the gangplank.

"Dinnae let them succeed, Mrs. Wilson," Erika said. Of course, Erika would be faithful to the last, nae matter what her personal feelings. She had loved Robert Senior, and had always been a mother hen of sorts to her.

She turned back at the familiar voice. "I'm so sorry, Erika. Nae for myself – I mean, it's been extremely embarrassing, and I'm mortified to the core, but I will survive. What I'm really, truly sorry aboot is that I will nae be able to continue my work with the charities." She lowered her voice a tone and moved a bit closer to Erika to prevent other ears from hearing what she had to say. "Nae to speak poorly of Robert's sons or the other board members, but they just dinnae seem to care in the same way that I do."

"Ye cannae resign!" Erika whispered back in a hushed voice. "Those children need ye. All of the less fortunate do. Ye've accomplished so much good. Without ye – it simply will nae happen."

"I appreciate yer vote of confidence, but I'm afraid they've already made up their minds."

"Then ye have to fight. Robert Senior's attorneys–"

"Are now Robert Junior's. It's hopeless. I am so sorry, but it's simply hopeless."

"Then we'll fight," Erika said staunchly. "I'm nae afraid to give them a piece of my mind."

"Is that allowed?"

"That bridge has been crossed, has it nae, dear? Ye may nae have intended to, but ye've opened Pandora's box. It cannae be closed now."

"I'm sure ye're right aboot Pandora, but I'm nae–"

"Dear, we're going to walk on in there and tell them... well, I'm nae quite sure."

Something clicked in her brain. Maybe Erika had a point. "Ye'll go into the meeting with me, then?"

"I'll be right by yer side. It's where yer husband would be if he were here." Erika came around from behind the gleaming curve of the secretary's desk and squeezed her hand.

"If my husband were here, I can guarantee ye I wouldnae be in this position."

With that, she opened the door to the board room. The voices inside stilled the second she started to enter, and the awkward silence continued until she and Erika had taken a seat. If anyone wondered why Erika was with her, they kept their curiosity to themselves.

Winston finally spoke, asking for a motion to call the meeting to order. Robert made the motion and Rodney seconded it. Nae greetings, nae small talk, nae even a smart remark.

Winston informed them that since this was a specially called meeting, for the express purpose of dealing with the "situation with

Rose", that no other subjects would open for discussion. All present nodded their assent. There was another awkward silence.

"We rather assumed ye would send a messenger over with your resignation," Rodney said. "So, I guess, kudos for having the guts to come in person, or, depending on your perspective, are you off your head?"

"Your being here does seem somewhat akin to jumping into the lion's den," one of the cousins commented.

"There's too much at stake. I had to be here."

"Rose, just so we're being clear..." Robert Junior said. "The board has discussed our options and everyone has agreed that no attempts will be made to revoke your monthly stipend once you've resigned."

"I will nae be resigning."

"I'm sorry," Robert said. "You must have misunderstood my intentions. As I was saying, the money you receive from my father's estate will not be revoked."

"Why would it be? Your father's love was never conditional on how I behaved, or what I said and did. It just was."

"You're clearly not understanding what I'm saying," Robert tried again, his voice growing more hostile with each clipped word. "And the behavior in question is not your lewd romp with Digby whatever his name is – although the pictorials have been most entertaining – but with your questionable judgment in the matter of the St. Conan's grant."

"I understand perfectly well, Robert. Winston was quite clear when he phoned me yesterday. Let me ask, how many of ye can say that ye have never used yer influence or clout to push through a pet project?" Nae one raised a hand. "I thought so," Rose said. "Rodney, I hope the MacIntires at Stanley Industries are enjoying their new wireless computer network?"

Rodney and Robert both started to squirm.

"And Winston." She looked to the head of the table and smiled innocently. "How are Silas and June Madsen doing after all these years? Still utilizing their two thousand square foot library, I hope."

"Theatrics always were one of your best assets, Rose," Robert Junior said, recovering his moxie. "But you still seem not to understand. The decision to demand your resignation has already been made and voted upon."

"As I said, I understand completely."

"Then how nice of you to come down here in person instead of sending a messenger. I mean, so we could *see* you one last time," Robert said. "How like you to favor us with a live resignation. Don't you agree, gentlemen? These little dramas that Rose seems continually to be a part of do keep things fresh – in this case, downright juicy."

"That's one of the things yer father loved aboot me," Rose said, turning his insult into a compliment. That got a smile out of Rodney, anyway. Robert Junior opened his mouth, like he was fumbling for a comeback. He said nothing, evidently stymied for once.

She took the reins again. "So for yer amusement, Robert, I will say once more, I have nae intention of resigning. As ye are so fond of reminding me, I have nae children of my own. And as long as we're being candid about things, I will tell ye that I am nae barren as ye've long speculated. Yer father was simply nae willing to risk losing me the same way he lost yer mother."

"That much is true," Winston said.

"That much?" Rose tried nae to flare. "Every word I'm telling ye is true. I may have tried to wrap a blanket around myself so ye all wouldnae see me naked on a few occasions, but I've never – nor would I ever – lie."

"I just meant, I mean," Winston stammered. "Robert Senior shared with me on occasion and he did mention that he couldn't bear the thought of your life being in any kind of danger, that after losing the boys' mother in childbirth, he just couldn't endure the thought of risking another such loss."

"It was a sacrifice for me to give up my dream of having children of my own, but I did it because I loved yer father. And I dealt with the grief I've carried around for years by throwing myself into my work with the Royal Aberdeen Children's Hospital, the orphanages I've volunteered at, the Ronald McDonald House in Glasgow, McKinley's Children's Camp for Underprivileged Children, and Campbell's School of Bagpipes for Tomorrow's Musical Prodigies.

"It's true," Erika said, jumping in on her behalf. "She's spent every Wednesday afternoon for nigh on fifteen years reading stories to the children at Aberfeldy Orphanage. She's been an advocate of literacy, and hosted fundraisers for Eye Glasses for Children and Immunizations in Third World Countries, after ye voted down her requests for funding."

"So I'm nae perfect." Rose looked Robert Junior squarely in the eye. "Although I dare to say yer father always thought so."

Another smile from Rodney.

"Who I choose to bare my body to, is really nae business of any of ye, I have much to contribute to this organization. My children need me. I'm nae going anywhere."

Nae one said a word. The seconds clicked by. Then Rodney started to clap. Sharp, punctuation marks, all in a row. At first, she thought he was mocking her. And maybe he was. But when Erika took up the chorus and joined him, many of the others did, too. And then, a few even stood. A standing ovation out of these gents? She was truly shocked. And truly humbled.

* * *

Almost everyone in the entire UK had seen Rose naked and yet, miracle of miracles, the world had continued to rotate on its axis. At least, the part of the globe that Glasgow was on.

St. Conan's was another matter entirely.

Rose had attended church a time or two and tried to be friendly, but people avoided her as though being glimpsed in the nude was the unforgivable sin.

Things were just as tense in the board room. She and Robert Junior were tolerating each other, but barely so.

In the meantime, life went on. She and Erika had continued to work on her charitable projects even though there would be no more board meetings until autumn. By that time, she hoped the issues surrounding their controversy would be as old, brittle and dead as the fall leaves that the west winds always blew in to congregate around her stoop.

Things were still tense with Kevin, and thus, Kelly. And because she felt so guilty about everything that had happened – because much as she hated to admit it, what she'd done with Digby had affected her relationship with Lyndsie and the boys, and she had been a bad influence – she was still trying to muddle through the task of sewing a pillow for Lyndsie.

The owner of the Corrie Bank B&B had sent her the scraps left over from the pillows that were already made so she could make one more – a crazy quilt – to give to Lyndsie. She hoped that making one last pillow all by herself would ease her conscience, and when she'd finally had it finished, help her to make amends... that is, until her next infraction.

She pulled her bathrobe snug around her waist and continued to think aboot the unfortunate events that had plagued her as she scrolled down through a list of Phaff sewing machine parts. The names were so foreign and the list so long that it made her head spin. She didnae need a double needle, she didnae need a convenient, soft–sided carrying case. She needed a stupid foot pedal. Plain and simple. One would think, being as it was essential to the operation of the machine, that it would be a popular item, but she hadnae found a single one on eBay. She'd even expanded her search to all countries. How could there nae be a single foot pedal on sale in all the world? Most likely hundreds of other women had also stomped on their pedals in frustration, just as she had, until their foot-feeds had also broken, creating a nationwide shortage.

Sewing machines were just that exasperating. Maybe instead of looking for a foot pedal, she should be looking for an online support group dedicated to people who had tried to learn to sew and failed. It was traumatic, feeling pressure from grandmothers, aunts, mothers, sisters, friends and dozens of church ladies who were somehow, incomprehensibly convinced that sewing was easy. To talk to them, one would think the art of sewing didnae even require a brain. That operating a machine as complex and complicated as her Phaff was so simple that any dolt could do it! How insulting!

She scrolled down to the next page – had she really looked at 20 pages of bobbins, no–slide feeders, and extra–large extender arms? This was insane. She should just buy a new sewing machine. She would have, before she met Ian.

She felt guilt aboot a lot of things since meeting Ian. How could she justify spending two hundred pounds on a new machine that she hardly ever used and didnae even like when Ian's church was so strapped for funds that they couldnae even afford to make the most minimal repairs? If Digby hadnae stolen the collection box, she would seriously be tempted to drive up there right now and stuff it with hundred dollar bills. Of course, even if it was still there, she could hardly be anonymous aboot giving when the place was wired with surveillance tapes running night and day. She should have stopped in and made a contribution the very first time she met Digby at the church. She flipped to the next page and scanned one more time.

And then the thought hit her... what if Digby had listed the artifacts he'd stolen from St. Conan's online? Enough time had gone by that he might have felt brave enough to test the waters. She thought for a second aboot what to search for. It would be awfully brassy of him to tag the item with the name St. Conan's. Subtlety was key. She tried artifacts and got over two million hits. On a whim, she typed in rabbit and copper. Bingo! She stared in disbelief. There it was! The famous rabbit rainspout, with his mouth gaping open as though he was as surprised as she was.

She stared at the page like she was at a store and the rabbit might get snatched up by another buyer if she didnae act fast. How did these things work anyway? Someone – probably Robert, years ago – had told her that if the seller listed a Buy It Now price, that someone could swoop in any time and close the auction just by meeting the requested price. Her heart rate sped as she searched the page, hoping she could buy the rabbit now, and nae have to worry aboot being outbid. Nae such luck. The bidding price had started at an outrageously high price, and there were already two bidders.

Ye've got to be kidding me, she thought. They must know it's stolen merchandise. If they had a conscience... and then she read the description. Hand–crafted copper rabbit downspout sculpted by Welch artist. Patterned after famous Scottish original.

Like hell... oops... like Hades? One more reason it was a good thing she'd given up on ever being suitable for Ian.

Nae matter, she was sure this was NAE an artist's reproduction. This rabbit was the real thing, and she was going to be the high bidder come hell or high water.

She looked around the site, patterned a profile that would hopefully give nae clue to her real identity, and placed a bid that was slightly higher than the existing one. Then, she called Ian to tell him the good news.

"Good work, Rose!" Ian's voice radiated enthusiasm, which in turn, warmed her heart.

"Yes. I'm sure it's our rabbit," he said after he'd connected to the internet. "Enlarge the photo and look at the tiny dent in his left ear. The week after the rabbit was discovered missing, Delbert

McCraddish confessed to making that very indentation when cleaning out the rain gutters in 1992. Poor chap had been carrying his guilt around for two entire decades, and thought the disappearance of the rabbit was God's retribution for his deeds."

"Ye're kidding, are ye nae?"

"No."

"Okay." If Ian saw nothing odd aboot someone feeling guilty over an unintentional dent in a rain gutter, how could Rose's sins ever be forgiven?

"But he didnae intentionally hurt the rabbit did he?"

"No," Ian said patiently.

He was too patient sometimes. It drove her crazy. And then there was God. Did God really keep a list detailing who had dinged this or dented that? If so, was it limited to people who damaged things on the church property, or in general?

Chapter Seventeen

Ian tugged at the hem of his jacket and touched his neck to make sure he had put on his collar. He had never before been nervous aboot attending a convocation of his peers. The gatherings were normally a time when he felt totally at ease, surrounded by friends and buoyed up by allies who understood the challenges of being a pastor as well as the joys.

But today felt very different. Neither Benjamin nor his overseer had ever called him back after they'd indicated, in their previous conversations, that he'd been uninvited to speak. He'd received one written communication from the general office, a flier publicizing the event, in which his name was listed alongside Rathborn's. Since nae agenda had been attached, he didnae know if his spot as keynote had been usurped, if he was to speak for 5 minutes or 2 hours.

He'd prepared his presentation as originally outlined. If he was nae allowed to deliver his lessons, he'd hold a seminar on evangelism at St. Conan's so his preparation time wouldnae have been for naught.

He looked down at his notes and silently rehearsed his opening line: Everything changed the day I met Rose Wilson. They all knew aboot her by now, didnae they? Nae sense trying to sweep things under the rug.

"Hello, David." He extended his hand to a pastor with whom he'd gone to seminary.

The man did nae take his hand, but acted though he was in a great hurry and rushed off without stopping to talk.

He looked back at his outline. He was so excited to share what he'd learned in the weeks since he'd met Rose. His whole perspective had changed and most certainly, for the good.

"Thomas! It's good to..." His voice trailed off as another old friend sped by. It was as though he were invisible.

He'd have to catch up to people after the morning session then, when they were nae so busy. He had his preparations anyway. The crux of his sermon was centered on the prophet, Daniel. He'd always had a great deal of respect for the man. He'd had a living faith, that one. Nae empty rhetoric when it came to Daniel's core values. He'd faced off with lions and seen his friends thrown into a fiery furnace and through it all, his faith had never faltered.

It was one thing to share yer faith with a stranger who would never be privy to the details of how ye lived out yer faith on a daily basis. It was another matter entirely to know that the person ye were hoping to bring to faith was watching ye like a hawk, circling overhead, spotting inconsistencies and hypocritical behaviors with their sharp eyes. Daniel had stood the test with his friends, his superiors, his employer – those who knew him best. Ian only hoped he would do as well.

Their senior manager entered the room and stopped less than six feet from where Ian was seated. Ian stood and headed in his direction. When he was two feet from the man, the overseer turned and began talking to someone else without even acknowledging his presence.

A shroud of cold enveloped him. So this was the way it was going to be.

He looked around the room at the faces of people he'd always felt close to and felt nae kinship with any of them. He felt a twinge of pain. He felt alone. And he felt more alive than he had in years.

Prior to meeting Rose, he'd surrounded himself with Christians who believed exactly as he did. While being of one mind with his companions led to a certain calm and predictability in his life, he had come to vastly prefer the exhilaration of being with Rose. She challenged his faith in many ways. Her candid observations of his lifestyle and what went on at church held him accountable. Her questions helped him hone his evangelistic skills and enabled him to better explain and defend his faith.

A few minutes later, the first session was called to order. He was introduced, and delivered his first address with as much passion as he could muster. His words fell on deaf ears, rocky soil. He could see it in their faces. Judging by the lack of any response to his message, or laughter at the jokes he'd so carefully inserted, he had to acknowledge the fact that he'd been blacklisted.

He'd gone from being the crown prince to being hung out to dry.

Benjamin was the only one who even spoke to him. His words

were hardly edifying.

"There are four or five women who attend my church in Inveraray who would be very suitable companions for ye, Ian. What ye're doing is cutting yer own throat, man. It's nae worth the price ye'll have to pay."

"Ye mean she's nae worth it, and I'm here to say she is the most beautiful flower, the most precious gem, and worth every iota." He thanked Benjamin for his advice and left the convocation feeling as alone as he'd ever felt. He would have liked to have spoken to Rose aboot it, but in the end, he decided nae to.

Rose's glasses were nae rose colored by any stretch. She was watching and assessing nae only the people of St. Conan's, but the church as a whole, trying to determine what she believed.

He would have to remind her, next time he saw her, that she needed to keep her eyes on Jesus. If she looked to man, even the best Christians among them, she would always leave wanting. She would always be disappointed. Turning her eyes on Jesus – and keeping them there – was the only way to find salvation.

He pulled his overcoat more tightly around his neck and ventured out into the chilly, late afternoon air. Behind him, the church shone with the impression of warmth like a mirage in the desert. From afar, it looked like a place that held great promise. Up close, the facade disappeared before yer eyes.

The most humbling fact of all was knowing that if he ruined things with Rose, he risked losing the one person in the world who was truly precious to him, and souring her towards Christianity for all eternity.

* * *

The next Sunday when Rose walked into church, she truly felt like she had reached a turning point. She'd been the high bidder on the rabbit and returned the beloved copper downspout to St. Conan's in a flurry of fanfare. Ian had put it out on the prayer chain as an answered prayer to make sure even those who hadnae been at Sunday services that week knew aboot it.

"Good day, Rose," Jaclyn, one of the younger quilters called out as she hurried by to get to her post at the organ.

"Hi ya, Rose," Angie, another young woman Ian had introduced her to, handed her a bulletin. "I need to speak to ye after church. I'm supposed to be organizing the harvest festival and fundraiser this fall and I'd love to brainstorm a bit. Ye have such fab ideas!"

"Why, thank ye." Rose nodded. "I'm honored that ye think so." She felt a moment of pure pleasure. At last, they were starting to trust her.

The mood changed completely when she entered the sanctuary. Who knew why? In her bliss, she actually gloated for a moment. At least they were nae talking aboot her anymore.

But they were definitely on to something. The longer she stood at the back of the pews, the more she felt like she was caught up in the midst of a scene from Bye Bye Birdie. Helen, who was sitting on the far right side of the pew, leaned over and whispered something to Janice, who in turn, leaned to her left said something into Phyllis' ear, who leaned over until her head was touching Christina's and so on until the whole row was abuzz with whatever it was they knew.

She hummed under her breath. "What's the story, Morning Glory? What's the word, Hummingbird?"

Then Katherine, who was at the left end of the row, made eye contact with Mildred, who was right across the isle, and nodded at the trio sitting in front of her. Mildred raised her eyebrows as if to say, "ah ha, so that's what everyone is buzzing aboot", then leaned to the left, and the whole thing started anew.

Rose stood at the rear of the church and watched until the news had assimilated its tentacles throughout the entire congregation. She rolled her eyes and headed for the row where she usually sat, aboot ten pews from the front. Her confidence started to falter. Maybe it was something aboot her and Ian. Wasnae it always?

She took a second look as she slipped into her pew. Surprisingly, it looked as though people were extremely interested in the tall gent with the straw blond hair between the two grey haired ladies at the front. One of them looked a lot like Margaret Ainsworth except that she had red hair.

Oh. My... She remembered nae to swear in the nick of time. She was in church after all. The scene before her was enough to make a sinner out of the most steadfast saint.

It was Patricia MacDougall and her son, Torey. She'd thought they'd moved! And Torey was – wasnae he supposed to be playing golf somewhere on the mainland?

Nae matter. He wasnae supposed to be at St. Conan's!

She faltered, tried to decide whether to sit or stand, and finally, sank into the pew. She had already been spotted by at least half of the congregation by the time she put two and two together. She could hardly get up and leave, now could she? She would simply scurry out and go the second Ian said his final amen so she didnae have to speak to anyone.

She had worked so hard to gain their trust! At the beginning, she'd feared someone would figure out that she was Mary Ann Rosalie McCullen. But the blond locks she'd had at twenty were back to their natural auburn now and she'd put on thirty pounds since then. Womanly curves had replaced the wispy, girlish figure she'd had twenty years ago, and nae one but Torey and his family had ever called her by her proper name.

If she could just get out before Torey got a look at her, all would be well. Torey MacDougall was a can of worms she dared nae open. Nae when things were going so well!

Who knew what hymns they sang, what Scripture readings were read, or what Ian said in his sermon. She was too busy fretting and stewing – and so busy plotting her getaway that she missed the benediction. She was sitting, deep in thought, hatching a hasty exit plan, when she noticed people milling around.

The service was over. Scrap that plan and move on to Plan B. She looked around, feeling more frantic with every second that passed. To her left, her pew and the aisle it led to were blocked by chatters. To her right stood Bertha Cleary, who was two or three of her wide. There would be nae getting around her. She could hardly leap a pew. She was trapped.

That was when she heard the dreaded words. "Mary Ann? What on earth are ye doing here?"

Perhaps if she acted the casual visitor, Torey wouldnae say anything more. She prayed that his mother wouldnae recognize her. *Please, Lord, if ye've ever listened to anything I've said, please let it be now. Those other requests? Move this one right to the forefront please. Number one priority, if ye know what I mean.*

But it was nae to be. Perhaps one day she would be able to acknowledge that it was all for the best – the whole truth coming out, total disclosure – but at that precise moment, when recognition dawned on the formidable Patricia MacDougall's face, all she felt was utter, abject humiliation.

"I think the question is what are ye doing here?" Rose smiled at Torey in what she hoped was an offhand way. "It was my understanding that yer mother nae longer lived in Loch Awe."

"We're visiting my aunt Margaret."

"Of course." Torey's aunt was one of the prime movers and shakers in the ladies group. She hadnae remembered that she was Torey's aunt. She sighed. It would have to be Margaret, wouldnae it, now?

She looked up at the cherubs in the stained glass round at the rear of the church. *I've only just redeemed myself in their eyes, Lord. I worked so hard to salvage my reputation. Was it really necessary to hurtle me back into a maelstrom of scandal?*

God evidently thought so. Recognition flooded one face after another as a chain reaction of memories rippled through the congregation.

"Rose is the same woman who left our Torey at the altar?"

"No, it cannae be."

"I knew she looked familiar."

The room was abuzz, their common shock echoing off the stone falls and bouncing back in her face.

"I felt so sorry for poor Torey, standing at the front of the church in his kilt, waiting, wondering, what had become of her."

"She's the same girl? Unbelievable."

"If Torey MacDougall wasnae good enough for her, well what does that say aboot her? If ever there was a perfect match..."

She'd nae been around to hear what they'd had to say aboot her on her aborted wedding day. She could only imagine what it had been like for Torey, if the venom and ire were still this strong, twenty years later.

"I am so sorry, Torey," she said for the first time. At the time, she'd written him a note, trying to explain aboot meeting Robert, and explaining that she had realized that she was making a terrible mistake. But she'd never said, "I'm sorry." She'd been too busy trying to justify what she'd done. She'd been too busy thinking aboot herself, and what it had felt like to dash her parent's hopes by leaving the perfect young man and taking up with someone twenty years her senior.

"He gave ye my grandmother's wedding ring," Patricia said stiffly.

"Which I returned."

"Our gift to ye was a surprise trip to the Cayman Islands," Patricia said in her formidable voice, with half the church listening in. "Everyone was so upset that the tickets went un–used."

"I'm so sorry. I didnae know."

"Would it have made a difference?" Torey asked, implying what they all thought, what everyone had always thought – that she'd married Robert for his money, for the things he'd bought her, for the life they'd led. The exact opposite was true, but they'd never believed her before. Why should they now?

And then she saw Ian walking towards them. Sweet, innocent, trusting Ian.

Her heart beat frantically. Would this be the straw that broke the camel's back? The final straw that made the whole heap tumble? He'd known she had some sort of history with the people of St. Conan's. She should have told him what.

The buzzing stopped. The room was as quiet as a morgue. Ian looked at her, then at Torey, clearly sensing something was amiss. He reached out a hand to Torey. "Pastor Ian. I dinnae believe we've met."

"Torey MacDougall. Margaret is my aunt." He took Ian's hand. "My mother, Patricia MacDougall."

Ian greeted Torey's mother. There was a pause. A very long, pregnant, pause.

Torey nodded at Rose. "Mary Ann and I were engaged to be married once upon a very long time ago."

"Mary Ann?" Ian turned and looked directly at her.

"Rosalie is my middle name. My da started calling me Rose when I was a wee lass. Everyone has always called me Rose. Everyone except–"

"I preferred Mary Ann," Torey said.

"She took his virginity and then emasculated him," Patricia said, taking it upon herself to make her confession for her. "Poor lad, left standing in his kilt at the front of the altar."

Well. Patricia wasnae mincing any words. Rose felt her cheeks flame red with shame. Embarrassment. Chagrin. Okay. So she had it coming. "Twenty years ago. We were so young." She smiled nervously. "And look what Torey's made of himself since then – a pro golfer playing at Carnoustie, St. Andrews, Turnberry. In the papers almost every week. Ye must be so proud, Patricia. We've both done well for ourselves, then, have we nae?"

To his credit, Ian tried to help diffuse the situation. "People who suffer a loss at an early age often turn out to be great achievers."

"I'd rather have been a mediocre golfer than to have my heart broken," Torey said, setting his jaw and refusing to cut her some slack.

What to do now? Rose had been afraid to look anyone in the eye, up until now. It was time. Unavoidable. Torey looked disgusted, which was fine. He never had been one to say much, and had consistently let her do most of the talking. She didnae expect or need his approval, although it might have made her feel less of a louse if he'd said something conciliatory.

Even after all this time, Patricia was obviously still infuriated and bent on knowing the answers to the most pertinent question – the one Rose had avoided thus far, the reason she was there. Patricia would have nae trouble finding out why Rose was back at St. Conan's once she was alone with her sister, or any other member of the congregation. They'd be happy to fill her in aboot her romp with Digby, her budding relationship with Ian, and anything else she wanted to know.

A quick scan of the church ladies' faces said the rest. They couldnae wait to tell all.

That left Ian. She lifted her eyes to meet his and for the first time, saw a flicker of disappointment. She could only hope it wasnae directed at her personally. Ian had been thrilled at the progress she'd made with the women of the congregation, and delighted that they'd begun to accept and appreciate her. Ian's untimely appearance would set her back, and then some. It was a disappointing development for both of them.

She looked at Ian again, and what she saw in his eyes chilled her to the core of her being. Futility. Despair. Fear.

She looked around the room one more time, at the handful of women she'd started to consider friends, at the ones with whom she'd felt a break–through was just a matter of time, and realized she'd come to the end of the road. It was never going to happen. Ian knew it. She knew it. The things she'd done – the cumulative sum of her transgressions was just too much to be surmounted. It wasnae that Ian didnae care aboot her. She knew he did. But the ill will she'd unwittingly bred would destroy St. Conan's if it was left unchecked, and the look in Ian's eyes said he couldnae let that happen. Nae matter how much he might wish things were different, the situation was what it was. And that was that.

She waited in Ian's office until the others had gone. When he finally appeared and found her waiting, she squirmed under his intent stare.

Ian tried to skirt her glance. "Ye should have told me."

"Yes. I should have." Any idiot would have said the same.

"So why didnae ye? Why did I have to hear it from them?"

"I dinnae know," she said. But she did, at least, to some extent. Who knew what the intricate workings of one's own mind were? The mind was a master at deception, wasnae it? A steel trap? How could she be expected to decipher her every motivation and deduce precisely why she did the things she did?

Ian was looking at her in his typically patient way, with an unaccustomed dash of irritation thrown in.

"Okay. So ye know." Rose said, "I've been afraid, ever since I started to care aboot ye, that there would be a straw that broke the camel's back. And the more I cared, and the more I opened my heart up to ye, the bigger risk I was taking–"

"This is nae aboot ye, Rose. I know ye'd like it to be, just like ye like everything else to be aboot ye, but it is nae. This is aboot me. This is aboot me looking the fool because ye did nae trust me enough to share an extremely pertinent piece of information aboot yer connection to St. Conan's."

"So then it is aboot me," she said, and wished she hadnae when she saw Ian's face start to turn purple. Well, deep red, really. "All I mean to say is that it's very difficult to tell someone horrible things aboot yerself when ye so very badly want to impress that person. And ye're trying so desperately to put forth yer best face because they already know so many awful things aboot ye that ye cannae bear the thought of them knowing one more horrid thing for fear they will finally turn their back on ye and walk away."

"Stop talking aboot me like I'm nae here," Ian said in a loud voice, nae quite angry, but very close. She suspected this was as bad as it got with Ian. "This is nae a hypothetical situation, and I am nae some third person extrapolation. I have been humiliated by ye over and over again. In each of those circumstances, I have shown ye

Sherrie Hansen

grace and acceptance. I have defended ye despite yer propensity to trouble, and despite all of that, ye still do nae trust me with the truth. An omission of the truth is just as much a lie as a blatant misrepresentation of the truth. Ye lied to me, Rose. Ye lied to me!"

There were tears streaming down Ian's face, and her heart broke into a million little shards knowing that she was the cause of his pain. And then she was crying, and trying to hug him. But he pushed her away. Well refused her advances, really. Because men like Ian were too nice to push a woman, nae matter how horridly that woman had behaved.

"I would have understood," he was saying over and over again. "I would have understood. If ye had only told me."

His eyelashes were still wet and spiky when she decided it was time for her to go. Because there was nothing left to be said.

She felt like a hurricane had just blown over. But it didnae matter how she felt. She knew that. She was the cause of Ian's grief, and it was up to her to make it up to him.

She did what she had to do. She said good–bye and left. Ian walked her to the door, but said little except that he was glad she had come, that he would always happy to see her, that she would always be welcome at worship – things he might say to any visitor. She understood. This was neither the time nor the place. Nae matter. There were nae words that would change any of it.

That night, she sat in front of the fireplace, with only Ginger to keep her company, watching the glow from the embers in the hearth. She was wrapped in an afghan she'd bought at the church bazaar that she called her Joseph's Coat afghan because it was made of so many different colors. At first, she'd thought it just as garish as the dreadful All–Inclusive Holiday Quilts. The woman who made it had admitted to using up all of her scraps of yarn on the project, a design method that went against Rose's very core.

But the longer she'd looked at the hodge–podge, mish mash of colors, the more she'd come to recognize a subtle beauty in the crazy kaleidoscope. She imagined it to be like the rings of a tree when it was cut down... a tribute to years of drought and excess, heat and cold, this baby blanket and that wedding gift, this Christmas present and that favorite design. While she might have chosen a single kind of yarn – one of the beautiful, multi–colored weaves she'd seen at the better shops – if she had been the one to knit the afghan, she had grown rather fond of this mixed breed mutt.

She thought at length aboot how she could make amends as she snuggled alone under her afghan. The only thing she could conclude, after thinking long and hard, was that Ian was better off without her. He deserved better. She'd known it from the start. Now, the proof was there. Having witnessed Ian's anguish, she couldnae delude herself into thinking differently any longer.

Chapter Eighteen

Rose stretched out her legs under the cherry wood desk in Robert's old office and slipped off her heels. She pushed the intercom on her desk and rang up Erika. "I forgot to mention that I'll need ye to have the paperwork ready by eight tomorrow morning. The courier will pick them up, deliver them to corporate headquarters for Robert Junior and Rodney to sign, pick them up again at noon when the board is through with them, then transport them to St. Conan's. Ye need to make sure they've arrived by half past six when the church council convenes."

Thank goodness for small favors. Erika continued to be a Godsend. Rose had always been welcome to utilize Robert's old secretary at corporate, but her requests had been secondary to a long list of executives and board members. Now that Erika was helping her out on a regular basis, she regretted nae hiring, well, borrowing one, years ago.

"I picked up yer dry cleaning on my way to work this morning and hung yer suits in the closet inside the front hall."

"Thank ye, Erika. I dinnae know what I'd do without ye."

"It's my pleasure."

She got back to business then, and dialed the number of the barrister she'd used to draw up the papers in the first place. Once she'd confirmed that everything was in order, she called Ian's office to confirm the delivery of the papers. She knew he had a standing game of golf set for each week at this time, so it was a given he wouldnae answer his phone. She left a message, concise, crisp and to the point. It occurred to her that she could ask how he was doing or inquire aboot some of their mutual acquaintances at St. Conan's, but the whole point of calling when she knew he wouldnae be home was to avoid dredging up the past, was it nae?

Erika buzzed her when she was done with her call. "Yer masseuse is here, and has his table set up."

"Thank ye. Tell him I need ten minutes to shower and I'll be in."

It wasnae her short–lived fling with Digby that had reawaked her senses, it was her feelings for Ian. In many ways, the grief of losing Ian hurt more acutely than even Robert's death. The heartbreak of it was numbing. But she still had needs – skin hunger, her sister called it – and she'd found some practical ways to meet those needs. Much safer than trolling the internet or going on blind dates. She really had nae desire to be in a relationship with anyone. Been there, done that – twice. She wasnae willing to subject herself to that kind of risk financially, physically, or emotionally ever again.

She slipped out of her clothes and walked into the double, Italian quarry tiled shower Robert had installed just before he died. Ten minutes later, she was lying face down on the massage table, having her needs met by a professional whose every touch was carefully measured and without fault. Nothing was left to chance. There were nae risks involved. Nothing messy, nae possibility of getting hurt – every touch totally predictable. Her masseuse would spend the first ten minutes getting the kinks out of her shoulders, the next ten, getting rid of the knots in her back. Her calf and thigh muscles were next, then her feet. He was very thorough with her feet. She was on them a lot these days. Pounding the pavement, Robert would have said. And he was right. She was working harder than she ever had. She'd gained a new confidence in her abilities, even if her step–sons and the board members didnae agree with her assessment.

And that's why she felt nae guilt aboot splurging on her weekly massages.

When he was done with her feet, her masseuse said the exact words he always did. "I'll wait outside while ye roll over and make yerself comfortable." When he returned, he did her hands, her arms, and her neck. Her favorite part was when he massaged her head, her temples, and her forehead. Her head throbbed constantly these days. Nae surprise there. She was nae sleeping well.

By the time her masseuse was done with her legs, she was almost asleep, a warm towel over her eyes. He said nothing when he was done and locked the door on his way out. Erika had been instructed nae to awaken her, assuming she was still there. Those times of utter relaxation were rare, and she coveted the moments.

She was still on the table, soft, warm, flannel sheets beneath and above her, when she heard her mobile ringing. She thought at first that she was dreaming. She always put her mobile on silent before she went to bed. Now that Robert was dead, nae emergency was that great that she needed to be awakened once she'd finally gotten to sleep.

Where was she? Ian's song was playing, she thought drowsily. He'd helped her program it one sunny afternoon after they'd been trekking in the highlands. He'd chosen a rousing Celtic melody. So like him. Always upbeat and cheery.

She awoke from her slumber, leaped up from the massage table, dragging sheets and towels with her in her disorientation.

"Ian?" Why be coy? She knew it was him.

"Rose. I was hoping ye'd answer."

"It's good to hear yer voice." It was. He'd caught her at a vulnerable moment. Her defenses were down, and so was the ire that had kept her going the last few weeks.

"Rose–"

"Yes?"

She heard the doorbell ring once, then twice, then a third time. Was she still dreaming? Was this all part of a dream?

"I need to... I want to..."

The doorbell rang, again, and a few impatient seconds later, again and again.

"Someone's at the door. I need to go. I'm nae dressed." The doorbell rang again. Whoever was there was nae going to go away. "May I call ye back?"

She raced around the room as soon as they'd disconnected, throwing her clothes on as quickly as she could. Ginger had started to bark midway through the clatter, and kept it up until her head felt like it was aboot to explode.

When she got to the door, and nae one was there, she wanted to scream. She even opened the door to see if whoever had been knocking was still in sight.

That was when she found the rose, a single red rose, with a white ribbon tied around it. Her heart leaped with joy at the familiar sight until she remembered that Robert couldnae possibly have sent his trademark gift to her. When she finally regained her wits and read the card, it was Rodney's name, nae Robert's, that greeted her.

What on earth? It was a kind gesture, she supposed, but it seemed a little too familiar, a little too intimate, considering the antagonistic relationship she'd had with Rodney – more specifically,

Robert Junior, but still...

She thought aboot calling Ian once the ruckus had settled down.

But–

But what? She didnae quite know. All she knew for sure was that her brain was on overload and her head was throbbing and she didnae want to hurt any more. What she wanted was another massage. The soothing benefits she'd reaped from her earlier session had already been eradicated.

* * *

Ian disconnected his mobile and cursed the fates for their bad timing. For a moment, he allowed himself to question whether the rude interruption of Rose's doorbell had been God's way of saying that he shouldnae be speaking to her. He'd resisted ringing her up for two entire weeks. Why backslide now, when he was past the worst of it and finally starting to move on?

Because he loved her.

At first, he'd been relieved to put the whole messy affair with Rose behind him. He'd wanted her to stop involving him in her muddled life, had he nae? It was he who'd wanted things to go back to being normal, had he nae? To be able to enjoy quiet, peaceful evenings by the fire with his books and the occasional visitor. It was what he'd wanted. Now he had it.

Except that he couldnae stop thing aboot Rose.

His phone rang and he jumped to answer. It was only an acolyte, calling to tell him she wouldnae be able to be there on Sunday.

He tried relaxing in his recliner. He flipped on the golf channel. He scanned the channels for a good film and found nothing worth watching. When all else failed, he tried to pray.

But tonight, nae even God could set his mind at ease. What he needed was to speak with someone on earth. Nae offense to God, but he needed someone who might understand what he was going through, someone who might have some specific insights into the psyche of a woman.

It took him a moment – he'd been so preoccupied with thoughts of Rose of late that he'd barely spoken to anyone except to carry out his pastoral duties – but he eventually remembered his friend and fellow pastor, Vivian. She was serving a church in Oban – if she was free, she would probably meet him halfway.

An hour later, he was sitting in a roadside pub across the table from his friend, Vivian. As always, she was one to get to the point quickly.

"Can I ask ye a question?" Vivian twirled her tea bag around the curve of her spoon.

"Sure." Ian was eager to hear her thoughts. If he hadnae wanted to know what she made of his dilemma, he wouldnae have called her in the first place.

"Why Rose?"

"Why nae?" Ian tried nae to bristle, but he was tired of people who didnae even know Rose casting dispersions on her.

"Okay. That sounded negative. Let me rephrase the question. Ye've told me that Rose didnae attend church regularly before she came to St. Conan's and probably is nae going anywhere now. She memorized a few Bible verses when she was a wee one, because of her Grandmother's influence, but has nae read or studied the Bible since then. She doesnae understand the whole concept of being actively involved in the life of the church. To her, church is a place where ye're wet, wed, and dead." Vivian paused and squeezed her tea bag against the side of her cup. "Is that a fair assessment or am I being too harsh?"

"No. That's pretty accurate. But she has been trying, was trying..."

"So what is it aboot Rose that attracts ye to her, Ian? Why nae one of the women ye met at seminary or someone from the area who's a devout Christian?"

Ian was silent while he searched his heart and thought of how he would answer.

"Rose is..." He paused. Rose defied description. Or at least, what he felt for her did. "I find her... I find her refreshing."

"Sexually?" Vivian never had been one to mince words.

"No. I mean, yes. Although we have nae..." He re–gathered himself, and tried to stop sputtering. "Personally. I find Rose refreshing personally."

"In what way?"

"In every way!" His mind flashed back to the last visit he'd made to a family from his parish – a young family that was struggling financially. When they'd asked for assistance with their utility bill, he'd gone to visit. He flashed back to the conversation he'd heard when he'd reached their home.

"Mind yer manners, Laurence. The pastor's here. Be on yer best behavior, Charlie. Cannae ye see the pastor's visiting?"

They were taught young and taught well. Even children felt constrained when Pastor Ian was present. When aunts and uncles came over, the children nae doubt ran free and wild, screaming with delight, but Pastor Ian walked in the door and everyone was required to stuff their emotions in a box, reign in their instincts, and behave appropriately.

"What I usually see of the people I interact with is some sort of superficial shell of who they really are. I'm the one they're trying to impress, the one they would never dream of offending with coarse words. I'm the one with whom they'd go to any length to avoid being honest aboot who they really are and what they really think."

The irony of it hit him like a kick in the gut. It was exactly the opposite of how it should be. Nae one would dream of openly lying to the pastor, yet that was what they did every day, cheating him with half–truths and teasing him with their Sunday best behavior. At times, he wondered what on earth he was doing, why he continued to devote his life to the pretense that was the Christian life.

"She... she was naked. Her vulnerability... it was a beautiful thing to behold."

"So go to the pound and adopt a puppy," Vivian suggested, always the pragmatist. "If ye want to take care of someone, or feel needed, or rescue someone who's hurting, there are many ways to do it without being saddled with a loose cannon like Rose for the rest of yer life."

For the eighth or ninth time in as many days, his anger flared. "I'll nae let ye speak of her that way. She's nae rope around my neck if that's what ye're trying to imply. I love being with her. Her candid speech is a pleasant change from the molly cock mush I'm used to hearing from people."

"So she engages ye on a personal level. That doesnae mean she's a positive influence on ye."

"She makes me feel alive. Real."

"The people we choose to permanently associate with should enhance our strengths, Ian. Ye've counseled more couples than I. Ye know it as well as—"

"Since when is being honest a detriment?"

"Honest, yes, but with a healthy dose of decorum and propriety. Ye know the drill, Ian."

"I have nae broken any rules. I've never broken any rules. I've always been the good boy. I've never ever done anything really wrong." He put his head in his hands. His admission pained him more than if he'd been confessing a cardinal sin. "I have nae been inappropriate. Nae with Rose, nae with the members of my church, nae with..." He struggled with his conscience. Was what he had done so wrong? Lord, the years and years he'd gone without sex, resisted normal human urges, and turned down countless opportunities to stay true to his calling. Even now, he hadnae done any bodily wrong. All he'd done was think aboot it. But thought aboot it, he had. And now, he, who had the power to forgive and absolve by virtue of his ordination, was due to confess.

The number of times he'd watched the actual tape was irrelevant. It was etched in his mind forever, to be replayed again and again, at will.

"I cannae stop thinking aboot her."

"Naked?"

"Yes."

"And ye're absolutely sure that yer feelings for her are genuine, that ye're nae just trying to convince yerself that she's the right woman for ye so ye can have sex with her?"

"Absolutely certain. I feel equally enamored of her heart and mind and soul as I am of her body. I've met my soul mate, Vivian. I truly have."

"Does she know?"

"No." His greatest fear was that she would laugh, or run when he said the words. Intellectually, he was confident she would nae. Regardless of what people thought, Rose was a lady, polite to a fault. If she were put in a position of having to let him down, she would do it gently, with the same thoughtful tenderness she brought to every conversation. "I'll tell her when I'm sure she feels the same way."

"Is she even open to the idea of being a pastor's wife?"

"I dinnae know," he admitted glumly. He couldnae honestly imagine why she would be after the way the church ladies had treated her.

"Do ye love her enough to resign yer call if she doesnae want to be a pastor's wife?"

"I hope and pray that's a choice I do nae have to make."

"Ye'll be in my prayers, friend."

As he drove home to St. Conan's, he thought long and hard on Vivian's words and wondered why he couldnae have fallen in love with someone like her.

He tried to talk to God aboot Rose, and found that the conversation didnae come any easier than his relationship with Rose had.

He well understood that matters pertaining to his calling and pastoral roles needed to be discussed with God, and did so on a regular basis. But, Rose... could he tell God how much he wanted to kiss her breasts? That more than anything in the world, he wanted to touch her until she moaned with pleasure and called out his name and pressed herself against him and begged him to take her? Could he really talk to God aboot all of that?

Chapter Nineteen

By the time Ian answered the phone and found Rose on the other end of the line – exactly one week to the day after she'd promised to call him back – his mood had changed. It changed three or four times a day, these days. From black to blue to hazy and opaque to sizzling, red hot or icy cold – if there was one thing he could count on, it was that his moods were volatile and unpredictable.

Today's mood was intolerant of the molly cock notion that there was any chance he and Rose might still end up together, an idea that might have seemed perfectly plausible at another time.

Of course, he'd had so little sleep he didnae know whether he was coming or going. So when Rose identified herself, she didnae exactly get the warm welcome she'd probably hoped for.

"Sorry to be so slow in calling ye back." She didnae say what had taken her so long.

The reason he'd called her a week ago nae longer applied. What he wanted to know today was, what had happened between her and Torey. Or perhaps he should say Mary Ann and Torey. Whatever. "Just tell me what happened between ye and Torey MacDougall," he said. "I'm sick of feeling the fool, tired of every woman in the church and half the men being privy to information I dinnae have. Like it or nae, this whole mess involves me. I should know what transpired."

Rose was hesitant, probably rightfully so. His demeanor was so antagonistic, even he could feel it. She must be petrified.

"All right then," she said slowly. "Where would ye like me to start?"

"How did ye meet?"

"It was my freshman year in college. I volunteered to work at a golf tournament – a fundraiser to raise funds for the Scottish Children's Hospital. I was the scoreboard carrier for Torey's twosome. By the time we got to the eighteenth hole, we were so enamored of each other that it took him five putts to hole out."

"Ouch."

"I know. He should have walked away from me – nae run, as fast as he could – right then and there."

"How long did ye date before ye made love?" Why he wanted to torture himself with the knowledge was beyond him. But he wanted to know.

There was a long silence. "Nae quite a week. And it didnae have anything to do with love. It was sex. Wild, uncontrollable sex. Rash, regrettable, never–should–have–happened sex."

"So it was a bad experience."

"No. It was an amazing experience. Probably the best sex I've ever had in my life. Mind–blowing."

"Then why did ye regret doing it?"

"Because that's all it was. And from that moment on, that's all it ever was. Every time we saw each other, we hopped into bed and made love. Actually, that's nae true. We very rarely made it to bed. We did it in his car. We did it in parks under the fir trees – or nae. We did it in the yards of complete strangers in the neighborhood around the college, presumably while they were at work. We didnae talk. We didnae date. We didnae go out to eat. We didnae do things with friends. We didnae get to know one another. We just made love, each time better than the last."

"Were ye a virgin before ye met him?"

"Yes. So was he, according to his mother."

"So I heard." Silence. "What made ye realize that ye wanted, needed more than wonderful sex?"

"That's the trouble with great sex, now is it nae? It warps yer perspective. It turns yer brain to mush. Every ounce of the blood supply that should be fueling yer cognitive senses is spent thinking aboot sex – what wonderful thing happened when ye last had it, wondering when ye'll have it again – until ye can barely remember yer name, say nothing aboot reasoning out complex emotional issues."

"So ye got engaged."

"It's addictive, I tell ye. I could nae bear the thought of nae having constant sex with Torey MacDougall. Nor could he dream of being without me."

"A short engagement then, I presume?"

"Miniscule. My poor mum, trying to pull together a wedding in less than a fortnight. She still has nae forgiven me. And then when I left him at the altar..."

"Why rush the wedding then? It wasnae as though ye'd pledged to abstain until ye were wed."

"I was afraid of getting pregnant outside of marriage, a sin for which my mum and granny would never have forgiven me. Torey, who was brought up to be good and honorable and dutiful, was filled with guilt for taking my virginity to gratify his needs and thus felt compelled to marry me, especially after his mother got involved."

"Patricia, is it?"

"Yes. Ye wouldnae have believed the steamroller of wedding plans, engraved announcements, bridesmaid dresses, kilts and cummerbunds, china, crystal and sterling patterns, flowers, music that I was faced with. My mum and dad didnae have the funds for a large wedding, Torey didnae care aboot any of it, and I had so little time, with my studies, that it all fell to Patricia, which was exactly the way she wanted it. Torey is her only child, and her husband was gone, and I was the daughter she'd always dreamed of..."

Ian could imagine, knowing Mrs. MacDougall's sister, and having dealt with a fair number of mothers of the brides over the years.

"Then came the talk of children. I was to have four or five, most of them girls so Patricia could dress them in ribbons and lace and bows and butterfly wings. The one and only thing of a personal nature that Torey ever did confide in me was that he did nae want children."

"Why was that?"

"Who knows? I'm supposing it came down to the fact that he didnae love me, nor I him. I think we both knew it by that time. Oh, and the fact that being pregnant would mean I couldnae or wouldnae want to have sex three times a day, 365 days of the year."

"So the day of yer wedding came. Did ye come to the church and then bolt or were ye a nae show? Was Robert involved? Where was he when all of this was going on? I'm assuming ye knew each other by then. Were ye having sex with him, too?"

She winced at that. He couldnae see her of course, but he heard the sharp intake of air over his mobile.

"No. It was only Torey who made me crazy with lust. And yes, Robert was at the church that day. Robert was my best friend. We could – and did – talk aboot everything. I would have liked him to have been my male *maid of honor*, but it just wasnae done back then."

"How did ye meet?" He was starting to soften, to feel sympathy for her, which wasnae what he'd intended. What did he want then? To hate her? To find just cause to walk away from the woman? His life would be a lot less complicated.

"I was taking a class on Shakespeare. He was a visiting guest lecturer, an amateur literary buff who had earned a great deal of acclaim for his interpretations of Shakespeare's plays. I asked a few questions during class, and a few more afterwards. He suggested we continue the discussion over a spot of tea at the local tea house."

"What play were ye studying?" Nae that it mattered. He was getting into the story. He was curious, that was all.

"King Lear. He likened his sons, then in their mid–twenties, to Regan and Goneril, which I thought an overblown assessment – until I got to know them. His wife had died in childbirth only 6 months earlier – an unexpected, late–in–life pregnancy gone wrong – the baby died as well. Robert lamented the fact that their stillborn daughter could have been his Cordelia."

She paused, perhaps to see if he knew the play well enough to get what she was saying? Yes, of course he did.

"So ye were Cordelia, and he, yer King of France."

Oh, he got it all right. He quoted from King Lear, "Fairest Cordelia, that art most rich, being poor; Most choice, forsaken; and most lov'd, despis'd! Thee and thy virtues here I seize upon."

"I was standing at the back of the kirk at St. Conan's in my gown – a monstrosity of virginal–looking white froth, hand selected by Patricia, looking down the aisle at Torey, who looked absolutely miserable – like a trussed turkey just aboot to be baked. And Robert turned around and caught my eye, and smiled, ye know, in an encouraging, ye–can–do–it sort of way. He knew how nervous I was."

"But ye couldnae."

"No. It was Robert I loved. My dear friend, Robert. Our relationship was the complete antithesis of what I shared – or more accurately, didnae share – with Torey. I had nae idea if Robert and I were even compatible sexually. And it didnae matter. All I knew was that I wanted to spend the rest of my life with him, my best friend."

He had tears in his eyes.

"So I ran. Robert followed. Drove the getaway car, we always said when we looked back on that day."

"When did the two of ye marry?"

"We didnae until years later when we were on a trip to Tobermory, on the Isle of Mull. They're famous for their weddings and we just decided it was time."

"I've heard it's a wonderful place."

"The last thing I wanted back then, after my tête-à-tête with Patricia and my near escape with wedded bliss, was another wedding. And suffice it to say, we encountered considerable resistance from Regan and Goneril, as well as from the Dukes of Albany, Cornwall and Burgundy, er, um the board of directors."

There was a bit of mirth in her voice now, and he loved hearing it.

"My mother was heartbroken. Kelly thought I was insane. I mean, Torey was even better looking back then than he is now, and certainly at the height of his masculinity. Every woman who came within sight of him swooned. He had a promising career in golf, and was undoubtedly everyone's idea of the perfect suitor."

"Except yers."

"Yes. Kelly and Kevin still have nae read King Lear, to the best of my knowledge. I tried to explain my actions, but it fell on deaf ears. I still dinnae think they understand what possessed me. Nae really."

"Rose?"

"Yes?"

"It took courage to do what ye did that day."

"Thank ye." Her voice was weepy with emotion now, and despite everything, including the debacle at church, he wished he could hold her in his arms once again.

"Thank ye – for sharing yer heart, for being honest with me." And then he forgave her, extended her the grace he should have a fortnight ago.

How and when they would see each other again was left open for discussion, but see her again, he would. Perhaps it would be best were it nae at church. Then again, it might be better if they all got right back up on the horse again. He would have to ponder it.

* * *

Rose hadnae been back to St. Conan's since the day Torey and Patricia had outed her as Mary Ann Rosalie McCullen, dasher of boyhood dreams – except the once when she'd gone to pick up her sewing machine. But that didnae count, because Ian had made sure nae one was there when she stopped by.

If it had been up to her, she wouldnae have been there today. But it wasnae up to her. The bottom line was that Ian knew aboot Torey, and he still cared for her. His forgiveness – along with God's – was a gift she didnae take lightly. She would have done nearly anything to try to repay the debt she owed him – both of them, really.

So here she was, at St. Conan's again, trying to do what God, and Ian, wanted her to do. It was too bad following the Lord's divine leading didnae guarantee ye an automatic sense of the warm fuzzies. She felt quite the opposite. It was summer's end, the rhododendrons had faded, and even the greenery around the auld kirk looked tired and dusty. She walked up the stone steps and stepped inside the sanctuary, feeling a sense of latent hostility rather than warmth. Sadly, as she looked around, it seemed like the stone interior was as cold as an early ice storm, the soaring ceilings aloof and distant, the floors unyielding and hard.

She could feel the collective stares of the congregation boring into her back as she made her way to the front of the church. She could have sat in the back, but she wanted to be as near to Ian as possible. In fact, if there was nae one between them, if she could keep her eyes on him – and of course, the cross – and pretend nae one else was there, all the better.

She held her head high and tried to stop the shaking in her hands. Her legs felt like jelly, and the air felt stuffy, and she started to sweat. The horrid things the church ladies had said to her reverberated in her ears so loudly that she could almost hear them over the prelude. Ho–ho–ho–hosanna. Ha–ha–halleluiah. He–he–he–he came to save. And it wasnae aboot the joy of the Lord. They were mocking her, laughing at her, tittering aboot her behind her back and silently heckling her. She couldnae endure it. She really couldnae.

"Welcome to St. Conan's. A warm greeting to any guests who are with us today." Ian's voice was like a fire in the hearth, the sun breaking through the clouds on a rainy day.

It was too late to leave. She tried to shut everyone but Ian out of her head, but it wasnae enough, so she concentrated on the music, and the organist, who had never said an unkind word aboot her to the best of her knowledge.

She closed her eyes when the acolytes came to the front of the church to light the candles. It was just her, God, and Ian. And the nice organist. She repeated it so many times that she almost believed it.

She settled deeper into the wooden pew and prepared to listen to Ian's oratory. If it had been her, and she'd known that a known sinner was coming back to church for the first time, she might have chosen the text aboot Jesus forgiving the prostitute, or maybe the tax collector. Or maybe the bit aboot David sending Bathsheba's husband off to war to get killed so he could have her to himself. What she'd done in the name of sex wasnae half as bad as what David had, and God had still used him to accomplish great things. Right?

But Ian didnae preach on anything that had to do with her – nae forgiveness, or acceptance, or redemption or anything of the sort. The message was aboot the little children coming to Jesus. Innocents. Nothing to do with her at all.

All was well until it was time for the communion to be served. Ian nodded to her, seeing as she was sitting up front and would be the first to go. So she stood. That's when the buzzing began.

"We have to share the Lord's table with her, then?" an old lady said, in what she probably thought was a whisper.

"Shhhhh." She could hear the woman's daughter chastising her as she glided across the length of the pew to the center aisle. She froze two feet from the end.

"All are welcome at the Lord's table," Ian said in a kindly, but assured, nae nonsense voice.

When she still hesitated, he came down the steps from the front of the church where he stood, and took her hand. "Rose, do ye want to partake of the body and blood of Christ?"

"Yes," she whispered.

"Come."

He led her front and center and placed a crumb of bread in her hands. "Body of Christ, broken for ye." She took and ate.

"Blood of Christ, shed for ye." A woman she recognized from

Circle handed her the cup, her hands shaking, her eyes looking past Rose, wildly scanning the crowd as if to say, "Pastor made me do it! There was nothing I could do aboot it!"

Good grief! Were the theatrics really necessary? Rose was tempted to storm off in a huff, but Ian had said that forgiveness begat forgiveness and that she shouldnae stoop to their level, and that someone had to be the bigger person – all of which she was fully prepared to do until the woman holding the chalice made a big production of wiping Rose's germs off the rim of the cup. Nae just a cursory wiping either – the woman was scrubbing the thing with so much gusto that she nae doubt wore the silver plating right off. It was downright embarrassing – like they might all perish from some dreaded infectious disease if so much as one stray cootie was left behind to contaminate them.

To make matters worse, nae one else had come forward to receive communion. Ian smiled and motioned to the usher, who stood rooted to his spot like a tree.

Rose rushed back to her seat, her cheeks ten shades of red.

"Fine," Ian said at last, his voice stern. "It is our custom to bring communion to those who cannae come to the altar by their own power, and I will be happy to do so once ye who can walk have come forward."

Nae one moved, and the church was quiet except for the buzzing of a honey bee who'd evidently decided to attend worship that day.

"Mrs. McDaniel. I know ye can walk."

A middle–aged woman stood reluctantly, and slowly made her way to the front of the church.

The silence thundered in Rose's ears – complete silence, punctuated only with the clicking sound of each excruciatingly slow step against the cold stone floor.

Where the hell (*excuse me, Lord*) was the nice organist? Wasnae she supposed to be playing a hymn to muffle the sound, to soothe and to calm?

"I will fear nae evil." The words were out of her mouth before she consciously decided to say them. "Thy rod and thy staff will comfort me. Ye preparest a table before me in the presence of mine enemies. Ye anoint me with oil. My cup runneth over. And I shall dwell in the house of the Lord forever. Surely goodness and mercy shall follow me all the days of my life."

She probably hadnae gotten it word for word, but it didnae matter. She fell to her knees right there in the pew and started to weep, quietly of course, because it was church. But really, it wasnae her decision to speak or to cry, she just did. It must have been the Spirit.

"Amen," Ian said quietly.

"Amen," another voice chimed in. "Amen, amen, amen." A chorus of voices repeated the refrain. An elderly man squeezed past the others in his row and started toward the front of the church. A few others followed, their footsteps creating a din that filled the quiet church with life and momentum.

She stayed on her knees until communion was finished. The closing hymn was sung. Her brain was in such a flurry that she couldnae have said what day it was. Ian had gone to the back of the church, and was nae doubt greeting people – if she knew him, making an appropriate comment or two to some.

She finally rose and turned, lifting her eyes and focusing on the circle of angels in the stained glass window to the rear of the kirk. Oh, to be able to start over again, to be like a babe, with her whole life before her – to make choices afresh, to have one more chance to do the right thing.

But ye can, a still small voice said to her.

She looked around, but nae one was near.

Ye can start over – be born again. It's just like I told Nicodemus a few centuries ago. "But ye cannot go back and reenter the womb," Nicodemus said. *And I said, "Of course not, but ye can start out fresh, sins thrown into the deepest sea, forgiven, forgotten, brand new, clean slate, the whole kit and caboodle."*

"Really," she said, her eyes narrowing, wishing she had paid more attention in Sunday School all those years ago. "Because when David killed that Hittite guy so he could be with his wife, Bathsheba—"

"Forgiven," God said. (Yes, she knew it sounded weird, but somehow, she knew it was Him.) *"Forgotten."*

She thought for a moment and tried nae to be intimidated by the fact that she was having a conversation with the Creator of the Universe.

"So David was forgiven, and what he did was forgotten." She gave God a look that said "ah ha". "Except that it's in the Bible, so every person who's read the thing in the past three millenniums knows aboot it."

"This is true," God said, smiling.

And the weird thing was – even more weird than the fact that she was talking to God, was that she felt Him smile. Like a sunbeam hitting a prism and bursting into a million, rainbow–colored fragments. She felt God smile.

She felt so flustered that she nearly forgot what she was trying to say, what with trying to wrap her head around the fact that God had a sense of humor, and that something she'd said had actually made Him smile.

"Ye know what I'm trying to say," she finally said.

"That I do," God said. *"But if it will make ye feel better to get it off yer chest, I'm happy to listen."*

"What I'm trying to express is that forgiven as David might have been, there were still ramifications for his actions and a price to be paid for the evil acts he committed."

"That's very astute," God said.

"Like his baby died, and own son tried to kill him."

"True."

"Ian preached aboot it a couple of weeks ago. He practices his sermons on me," she confessed.

"I know," God said. *"He does to me, too."*

She felt a real kinship with God then, because they both loved Ian. "So, tell me. I can take it. Are they ever going to forget what I've done, or will I always be the woman who left their favorite son at the altar and then reappeared out of nowhere two decades later and spread her legs for a thief under the flying buttresses?"

"Sadly, they will never forget. What do ye expect? They're only human. And yes, there are always ramifications. What do I look like anyway? A magician?" God laughed. *"I gave ye free will, memories, intellects. With the privilege comes responsibility and those pesky things ye called repercussions. Once things start playing out – the things ye set in motion by yer choices, I cannae just yank the needle off the record and stop the music."*

"Well, ye could if ye wanted to."

"But I choose not to," God said. *"It's the way of the world. I made it. I should know."*

That took her aback. First off, didnae God know aboot CDs? Of course, the illustration wouldnae have worked as well with CDs as it had with records. And second, she thought it was pretty cool that God knew she was old enough to remember her Da's record player. But she digressed.

"So what do I do now?"

Apparently, God didnae have to think aboot his answers, even when it seemed a loaded question to her.

"Next time, come to me for advice before ye act. Ye'll save yerself a lot of trouble if ye remember to pray before ye get yerself in a fix instead of after."

"Sure," she said. She might be a tad bit stubborn at times, but she recognized good advice when she heard it.

"And don't worry aboot what other people think. Concentrate on me and ye'll be just fine," God said, as if to have the last word.

And then Ian was at her side, and God fell silent, although now that the lines of communication had been reopened, she felt sure she hadnae heard the last from Him.

Ian put his arms around her and gave her a hug – long, tight, and personal. The church was empty now. The others might have drunk from the same cup as she, once cleansed from germs, but nae one had offered an apology or even spoken to her.

"I rarely find myself without adequate words," Ian finally said, "but I'm afraid I dinnae know what to say."

She looked around his shoulders and kept her eyes focused on the cherubs again. Would she ever feel free of guilt, free of censure? Would she ever feel free just to be herself?

"Dinnae let them bother ye, Rose. Be proud of who ye are. I am."

"I'll try." How could she nae when God had just told her the same thing? But she was still human. "Even when I appear to be exuding confidence on the outside, on the inside, I'm desperately craving approval. I may act like I dinnae care what anyone thinks of me, but really, truly, all I've ever wanted is for everyone to like me."

She thought aboot what God had said. She would try to do what He'd asked of her. She really would.

And then Ian invited her to join him for lunch. And since he didnae seem to care what anyone thought, neither did she.

Chapter Twenty

Two days later, Rose still felt like she was off to a fresh start. The weather was fair and filled with sunshine, there were birds chirping outside her window, and she'd awakened to a call from Ian. He'd called to say that he had nae meetings to go to, nae one in need of a visit and nae weddings or funerals to attend to. And then, he'd declared it a "play day" and invited her to drive up to Loch Awe to share a picnic with him.

She wore her favorite sundress – the one with the thin straps and comfy green bodice and the full, flowered skirt rimmed in bluebells and wild roses and yellow buttercups – because it felt and looked festive and she was in such a happy mood. She took a pretty pink sweater that matched her earrings just in case a chill should develop later in the day.

When she arrived at the parsonage, it was nearly midday and getting quite hot, so Ginger settled down in front of the fireplace to enjoy the cool, stone hearth, and Ian put some beef on the grill. In the back of Ian's refrigerator, she found some sharp Cheddar from one of the English islands and cut the round into tiny, bite–sized squares. She stirred the cheese into a pasta salad that she made with little corkscrew macaroni, fresh peas from the garden, and mayonnaise.

When she was done, they sat on the patio table under the wisteria that hung in purple wisps from the arbor and waited for their steaks to reach medium well. There was the perfect amount of sunshine and shade and their lunch smelled heavenly and it seemed like a dream because they were so happy, and it was only the two of them – nae church ladies, nae overseers, nae criminals, nae law enforcement officials, and nae wicked step–sons.

The same sense of intimacy that she'd felt the night they'd prayed together instead of making love had returned. The sense of well–being had them wrapped so snuggly in its arms that everything finally felt right with the world – except for one last little thought that kept niggling in the back of her brain.

"Ian?"

"Yes, dear?"

"Um, being as ye're a pastor..." Rose inched her seat over a little to the side of the grill opposite the way the wind was blowing. "I'm wondering what ye would do if I wanted to go to a sex store and buy a teddy."

She fiddled with the salad, tossing it a bit more, and tried to act as nonchalant as possible.

"Like Victoria's Secret?" Ian's face alternately blanched and blushed until he looked quite splotchy.

She steeled her heart and resisted the urge to shush up and comfort him. "No. Nothing classy and pretty and pink. Something smutty and hardcore sexy to appeal to my baser instinct."

Had she really just said the word smutty? To Ian?

Where had that come from?

"Ye have them then?" Ian stammered.

"Baser instincts? Yes," she confessed. "Sometimes, I do." Truth was, she'd never once set foot in a sex shop. But that was beside the point. She wanted someone who would – could – live it up with her, didnae she? "So would ye? Go in with me?"

"Perhaps if we drove down to England." Ian's face was pinched and drawn. "I couldnae around here. If there are even such places nearby."

"Glasgow is nae far enough away then? The parish has spies there as well?"

"They're hardly spies. Nosy, old busybodies, perhaps, but nae–"

"Got it."

Ian said nothing for a moment. "It's nae aboot who might see me – although we've certainly proven that there are moments in our lives that we would rather nae one knew aboot."

He was certainly right aboot that.

"It's aboot my conscience. How can I in good conscience preach the word of God if I'm willingly transgressing?"

"So if we were legally, ye know, and I wanted to wear sexy nightclothes for ye, that would be a sin?"

"Of course nae." He looked a bit flummoxed. "Is there an online shop or mail order catalog where ye could discreetly purchase yer...?"

"But then, there would be a record of it on file. If I skulked into a store in a costume of some sort and paid cash, there would be nae way to substantiate–"

"Couldnae ye just sleep in the buff?" Ian asked hopefully. "I would find that very sexy."

"But..." That wasnae the point. "So we have to be perfect, then?" Her mind reeled with the injustice of it. "And I can never indulge in..."

"Nae one expects us to be perfect, least of all God, who knows how impossible that would be. But we have to try – nae to be perfect – but to do as God's Word instructs us." Ian stood and started to pace. "It's nae that we have to be good, it's that we want to be good and do right, because we love God, and want to try to emulate his goodness."

"But how do we know God doesnae have a bit of a kinky side? We are created in his image, are we nae?"

Ian looked at her like he couldnae believe she'd just said the words God and kinky in the same sentence.

"Yes, we're made in God's image. But we also have sinful natures. That taints everything we do, and means that we have desires that go against God's laws."

At that point, she started to wonder what she was doing. First, Ian had a ready answer for everything – she was obviously in over her head. Second, she was picking a fight over something inconsequential. She had scores of sexy nightgowns that she'd never even worn. Truth be told, she preferred sweet to smutty.

That was her intellect thinking. It was her emotions – wild and fluctuating – that she couldnae bear to abandon without at least giving them a chance.

"So what if I wanted to have a ménage a' trois?"

Ian choked. "I couldnae." Now he looked splotchy and shocked. "This is what ye want?"

"I dinnae know. Probably nae. But if I did?"

"Rose, my sweet, beautiful Rose. I would do nearly anything for ye. Ye know that, dinnae ye?" His words tried to make light of her request, but his eyes – such sadness, such heartbreak.

And in that instant she understood that asking him to do something – anything – that was against his convictions, would destroy him, absolutely destroy him. "Forget I even asked then. It's nae really what I want. I just..."

"I love ye sweetheart. If ye have a wild side when it comes to sex, that's fine. All I ask is that ye give me a chance to satisfy ye before ye look elsewhere for pleasure. Agreed?"

She nodded. "All I really want is ye. I'm just trying to adjust to the notion that..."

"I suppose it's an intimidating thing, the thought of going round with a pastor."

"It seems to come naturally enough to some."

"Ye care aboot people so deeply, Rose. Ye have the heart for it."

"But nae the body."

"Yer body is perfect."

"Then maybe it's my stomach. Maybe I have the heart but just nae the stomach."

The wrinkles on either side of his eyes seemed to deepen right then and there.

"I cannae make the decision for ye, Rose. I want ye to be happy. If being with me would cause ye that much anguish..."

"It's nae that at all. But in yer position... It's like I'd be committing nae only to ye, but the entire church. It would be like carrying on with a man who has a dozen children, except that in this case, they're old and obstinate instead of cute and cuddly."

He laughed and took her in his arms.

"Ian?"

"Yes?"

"What if I wanted to vacation on the French Riviera? Ye know, nude sunbathing. Just ye, me, the sun, the wind and the water."

"I could do that," Ian said. And this time, his face was only a little pinched.

* * *

Another few days had flown by, and the rhododendrons were completely done blooming for the season, but the wild roses along the narrow lanes and byways in the country were still in full flower. There had been nae more fiascos of any sort and nae more flack from anyone they knew, although most of the people at Ian's church probably assumed that their involvement had come to a natural end.

On one of her mornings to help, Erika had even remarked on how fortunate Ian was to have found an honest, loving, caring woman like Rose. And she meant it. And she hadnae retracted her statement even when Rose had pointed out the various troubles she'd brought into Ian's life.

Granted, Erika was a bit biased, but still, since approval from at least one person whose opinion they respected, and nae protests from everyone else in their lives was likely as good as it was going to get, Rose took it as a sign that they finally had the green light to proceed with their relationship, at least at cautious speeds.

So they were still running into the occasional roadblock and hitting a few speed bumps – those things happened in any budding relationship, didnae they? Ian had made it perfectly clear that he accepted her just the way she was. Perhaps that was why Rose felt comfortable starting to assert herself in the relationship. Wasnae it best that Ian knew exactly what he was in for if he continued to spend time with her?

Besides, if things between them kept progressing, didnae they need to venture out into the real world and test the waters there, too? It wasnae as though they were going to spend the entirety of their lives making small talk after church or hobnobbing in the board room. At least, she hoped nae.

Ian had been the one to suggest that he drive down to Glasgow and take her to a discothèque, nae doubt because she'd mentioned that dancing was a little indulged passion of hers that she missed. Nae that she and Robert had ever gone to dance clubs. And nae that she'd dared to go by herself in the years since he'd died. And nae that she wanted to lead Ian astray or fill his Godly head with temptations that couldnae be acted upon or anything of the sort. But she was so excited!

The strobe lights danced to the beat of "Hey now, you're a rock star, get your game on" until the entire room seemed to pulse around them. Her skin tingled with the thrill of it.

A rainbow of colored lights kissed her cheeks and then went on to swirl around the dance floor. She really should have done this months ago. If there was ever a time to do it, it should have been then, nae now, when she'd taken up with a prim, proper pastor. Of course, Ian's conservative lifestyle was entirely his choice. That didnae mean she had to choose exactly the same, did it?

She looked up at Ian. It was really too noisy to talk, so their occasional glances took on a whole new meaning. She smiled at him and thought anew that he was one of the most gorgeous men she'd ever seen or known.

And then he tried to move his shoulders to the beat and her illusion of perfection was shattered entirely. Ah, well. If the man had been blessed with rhythm, he would have been too near faultless for anyone's good.

And then she lost herself in her thoughts.

In her daydream, she'd met a gent who liked to dance as much as she did. They danced together every Tuesday night and again on Saturdays. He wasnae a minister, so they could stay up as late as they liked on Saturday nights. They'd even taken a class to learn all the latest moves.

She pinched herself, reeled back from her imaginary trek to *Dancing with the Stars*, and again, wondered why she hadnae taken up dancing years ago. It was much more fun than trekking, wasnae it?

It hadnae been aboot being proper. That much she knew for sure. She supposed part of it had been Robert's age, and eventually, hers. She glanced around the room and took in the spiked, purple hair–dos, the depressing Goth get–ups and the insanely short skirts of their fellow revelers. She and Ian looked more to be parents than comrades of most of the people there. Robert would have appeared ancient.

But the music was so – she loved the music, the beat, and the simple act of wading in the waters of the wild side.

"I dinnae believe I've ever heard this song." Ian practically screamed, which was the only way to be heard over the band.

Of course, she thought. It's hardly what they play on the Christian radio station. Nae matter. Even if she didnae get to dance, it was such a thrill, such a boost to the old juices, just to be here. She tore her eyes away from the sparkling lights, glanced at Ian again and gave his hand a squeeze. The man was a doll even though he did look absolutely stilted and as though he was in great pain.

It was enough to drive her to drink. "Is a glass of wine okay then? I mean, since we're in Glasgow?"

"Wine is always okay. I have a little every Sunday, now, dinnae I?"

She smiled. "One of those pastors, are ye?"

"Rose, I do like wine, and a glass or two is fine even at the pub at Loch Awe, if I wish. But I've nae urge to get inebriated, nae matter where I may be at the moment."

"Yes. Moderation in all things," Rose said, her heart sinking, because a few glasses of some extremely potent wine might have loosened Ian up a bit. Nae that she had ever had more than a couple of drinks herself – three was her absolute limit. And she couldnae recall a time that she'd ever been inebriated – a little tipsy, perhaps, but never drunk. And really, it should please her that Ian wasnae a drunkard, shouldnae it?

A gent in a stiff white shirt and a plaid cummerbund with a matching bow tie appeared with a tray in his hand and a white towel draped over his arm and asked them what they would like to drink.

"A glass of Madeira for me," Ian said, after a slight pause.

"Um, that sounds fine for me, too," Rose said. "No. Wait. I think I'd like a Tequila Sunrise."

Ian raised his eyebrows, then smiled, although it seemed a bit forced.

"Just feeling a little exotic, I guess." What was wrong with her? She never drank hard liquor. What was she trying to prove?

The music had quieted for a moment, but when the band swerved into their next selection, it was *Mony Mony* and she couldnae help moving her shoulders and grooving to the tune.

Ian still looked a tad uncomfortable. Well, vastly uncomfortable, if ye wanted the truth.

"Ye look like ye'd like to dance."

"I love this song. Dinnae ye?"

"Oh, I dinnae know. I think I'd prefer to wait for another. Something slow and sensual might be more my speed," he teased.

"Why, sure. Silly song. *Mony Mony*, I mean. It's a favorite of mine but I've danced to it a million times. Certainly dinnae need to dance to it again." She swallowed her disappointment.

"We can if ye want to," he said again, his reluctance obvious.

"No. Really. It's fine." Much as she loved the song, she couldnae imagine a worse torture than to be on the dance floor with someone who didnae want to be dancing. The thing aboot *Mony Mony* was that it demanded that ye lose yer inhibitions, throw yer cares to the wind and give yerself over to the beat. Someone who really didnae care to be on the dance floor would only spoil it for the rest of the dancers, now would they nae?

Ian gave her a grateful look, as though he appreciated her

understanding. Which was fine. She'd always prided herself on her empathy and really, Ian nae wanting to do the pony was hardly a deal breaker, was it? I mean, what was she going to do? Dump him because he didnae have the same exact songs on his iPod that she did? If he even had one. He probably only listened to praise and worship tunes, old hymns, Gregorian chants and whatnot. Nae that there was anything wrong with that. She smiled reassuringly at Ian and looked back at the dance floor, watching the moves, the people, the band.

"Excuse me, miss." A tall man, blond, blue–eyed, younger than she and Ian, was standing beside their table. "I was wondering if you'd like to dance."

He had the cutest accent. The lad smiled and nodded at Ian. "If your brother doesn't care."

"I'd love to!" She jumped out of her chair and reached out to place her hand in the one that the stranger was extending.

Oh. Ian.

She turned. Ian's face was a bit crestfallen. Well, more shocked, really. "Is it okay with ye, Ian?"

Did they really look like siblings? She guessed maybe they did. They were both tall. Their noses were a little alike across the bridge.

"It's one of my faves," the blond gent said.

They were wasting precious time. Ian managed a half–smile, which she took as a yes.

Two seconds later, her skirt was swirling around her as she spun round and round in the blond gent's arms, shaking her booty and having a hi–o time.

"Ye're an excellent dancer," she told him. And he was. It was pure fun with him – the rhythm, the silliness, the be–bopping. It was just what she needed. Nae for the rest of her life, mind ye, but right at that moment. Another of her favorites started, the band skillfully blending one song into the other so the dancers didnae miss a beat. She turned and waved at Ian, who was nae looking happy. But if he didnae like dancing to *Mony Mony*, he certainly wouldnae be comfortable discoing to *Stayin' Alive,* now would he?

"What's your name?" The blond gent asked, the first words he's spoken since he'd asked her to dance.

"Rose."

"Mads."

She must have looked dazed, because he said, "I'm Danish."

She said nothing more as Mads twirled, dipped, and swirled her around the dance floor like they really were celebrity contestants on *Strictly Come Dancing*. She hadnae had so much fun in ages. By the time the music switched to another golden oldie, *How Deep is Your Love*, it felt perfectly natural to slip into Mads' embrace. He pulled her to him until their cheeks were touching, and she followed suit, melting into the music.

She didnae even see Ian approaching them. "The first slow song," he said, his deep voice just loud enough to be heard over the music. "I believe I promised ye the first slow song."

"Of course!" She jerked away from Mads and smiled warmly at Ian before turning back to Mads. "Thank ye. It was a pleasure. Ye're an excellent dancer."

"The same is true of you," Mads said, with a bit of a bow.

He had to be fifteen years younger than she. Nae that she gave a hoot. Dancing with him had been pure ecstasy, but it had also been just that. Dancing. She wasnae looking to connect with him for life, just to share a dance or two.

Ian took her firmly and drew her to himself, his wounded ego on his sleeve. Her body surrendered to the familiar rush of warmth, comfort and security she always felt when he hugged her.

Mads looked on and smiled knowingly.

She caught his eyes. "He's my... my..." Boyfriend? Pastor? Friend? "He's nae my brother."

Mads smiled and turned away.

"Is he gone?" Ian said softly.

"Yes."

"Good. I want ye all to myself."

"Isnae being selfish a sin?"

He didnae answer, but staked his claim on her lips.

Definitely nae her brother.

Chapter Twenty–One

Rose sighed and settled more deeply into Ian's arms. Would she ever get this right? Sometimes she felt like she might as well paste a sign on her forehead saying "BEWARE – UNSUITABLE TO BE WITH A PASTOR. PROCEED WITH CAUTION!!!"

"Feeling better now that ye got to dance to some of yer favorites?" Ian rubbed the small of her back, always considerate, while she secretly wished he were fuming with jealousy. Why did he always have to be the good, patient, longsuffering one, and her, the bad, impatient, selfish party?

She was tired of being a wild rose, that was all. Even as a youngster, she'd been the sister who was always getting in trouble. Kelly had never done anything wrong. Kelly had married her high school sweetheart and given their Mum five lovely grandchildren. Rose had left perfect Torey MacDougall at the altar. Enough said.

She'd definitely been the wild one of the pair where she and Robert were concerned. Now, here she was again, the one who was getting Ian into trouble with his parishioners, tempting him to do things he shouldnae be doing and luring him into situations he would never encounter if it werenae for her.

Well, she was tired of always having to apologize for her actions, tired of being criticized and looked down upon and made to feel as if she were the rotten apple in the barrel, the too ripe banana that spoiled the rest of the bunch.

She was sick of feeling inferior, nae good enough. She would nae drag Ian down to her level, and she would nae be made to feel as though she wasnae a proper match for him. If she couldnae find her equal, then she should have someone wilder and more wanton than she was. It only seemed fair – mostly to her, but to Ian, too.

She looked up at Ian. He responded by swirling her around and catching her again – almost quickly enough to keep up with the beat of the music. Maybe Ian did have potential. They'd never be asked to be contestants on *Dancing with the Stars* like she and Mads might have been, but with a little practice, Ian might turn out to be a fair dancer. And she would always want more. Because she still had a hankering to be wild. Because despite her reputation, she'd never really given it a try. Nae really. She'd been daring a time or two, but that was it, especially once she'd married Robert. She'd done everything she could to make him proud – acted the perfect lady, entertained his family and friends, and pandered to his business associates and board of directors.

In fact, she'd taken double care nae to give anyone cause to criticize her because Robert's sons had hated her so. She'd practiced frugality. She'd conducted herself in such a way that she would always be found to be above reproach. If awards had been given for the perfect society wife, she'd have been given the gold medal. She'd lived and loved Robert impeccably.

The music changed to a version of Rod Stewart's *Have I Told You Lately That I Love You.* Ian gave her a little off–tempo squeeze and she drifted back to the history channel for another episode of her life.

Unwittingly, the next role she'd assumed was that of a grieving widow.

Neither of them had guessed Robert would die by sixty. Friends had warned her that when Robert was a tottering old fool with spittle dripping down his chin, she'd still be in her prime, a vibrant young woman, raring to do and go. They'd said she'd be forced to spend her days attending to an invalid. They need nae have worried. Robert had matched her step for step until the day he keeled over of a heart attack. A widow maker they'd called it. Quick. Severe. Nothing anyone could do to save him. Almost always fatal.

Acting the wild widow would nae only have been inappropriate, it was the furthest thing from her mind. She'd grieved for Robert with every ounce of her being. Acting out some latent desires left over from the youth that had been cut just as short as her marriage was nothing she'd even considered. Nonsense! Rudely as Robert, Jr. and Rodney had treated her, they'd had nae basis. She'd married Robert for love, been true to him for love, and grieved him just as acutely as she would have had she been his precise age.

After nearly three years of weeping for the man, she'd done one wild thing, and it had been caught on camera for all the world to see. Even then, she'd had a plausible reason to act as she had, and it had

had nothing to do with being wild. She was nae a trollop and resented being pegged as one.

The band slid into their next selection, *Should Auld Acquaintance Be Forgot...*

There were so many things she'd longed to have a taste of. She and Robert had traveled to some very exotic locales and taken a few cruises. But they'd never hiked a ben or taken a bike ride round Scotland or camped under the stars. Their trips had been planned by travel agents, with activities and adventures arranged round the clock, their time scheduled and micro–managed just like the rest of their lives.

She had nae desire to go dancing every night or sleep with a different man every time she went to bed, but she also didnae want to live her life wondering if her actions would be a detriment to her mate's career. Was it so wrong of her to want a little spontaneity, to be able to have a little spur of the moment fun or act on her whims once in a while? How could she explain all of that to Ian?

"Earth calling Rose... earth calling Rose..." Ian's voice pervaded her thoughts slowly, surely, and gradually, just like everything he did. Nae abrupt, sudden actions from this one – that was fact. Everything Ian said and did was carefully considered and thought out in advance.

She rubbed his arm. "I have a question for ye. Totally off topic. Is that okay?"

The band was taking a break, so Ian guided her off the dance floor and back to their table. "Of course."

"Just wondering, when ye preach a sermon, are ye speaking off the cuff? Or do ye have an outline? Or do ye write every word down in advance?"

"What brought this on?"

"Just curious," she said, hoping he was going to say his method was extemporaneous. If it could be called a method. Quite an oxymoron, really, was it nae?

"I start by reading the Scriptures several times and writing down my thoughts, usually quite early in the week."

"And is the first draft just brill, or do ye make revisions?"

"I send it off to my critique partner."

"Ye have a critique partner?" She felt a surge of irrational jealousy.

"A friend of mine who's a pastor in Edinburgh. I reciprocate."

"And then?"

"Once I've made revisions, or scrapped the whole thing and started over, whatever the case might be, I commit it to memory, or at least the bulk of it. I make an outline, so I dinnae forget any key points or references, and then..."

"So ye're nae reading from a text?"

"No. Does it sound like I am?"

"Of course nae," she said. "I never thought it did."

"What comes out at the end is a combination of what I've committed to memory, with some last minute inspirations thrown in compliments of the Holy Spirit."

Hmmm. She hadnae expected that. She grappled with the image of the Holy Spirit hovering over Ian's head and every so often, dipping down to whisper in his ear. "So, He, I mean, the Holy Spirit, speaks to ye in the middle of yer talk?"

"I can only hope," Ian said. "My sermons should never be aboot me, or what I think. I'm just a vessel."

Okay. Being led by the Holy Spirit wasnae exactly like doing yer own thing, or saying, in this case, but she supposed it did allow for a little spontaneity of thought.

She leaned into Ian and snuggled against him. She wondered what the Holy Spirit was saying aboot her. It wouldnae surprise her if He were telling Ian to watch out, that she was trouble. She could just imagine what they thought of her in heaven. *WILD ROSE. Thorny. Do nae touch.*

She didnae want to hurt Ian. She didnae want him to hurt her either. She'd had enough hurt to last a lifetime.

Ian stroked her hand. She didnae know what to say. When she looked at Ian, it was obvious that he was passionate aboot his mission, that he truly loved God. She enjoyed the church services he led, especially the music. She was open to what the Bible had to say aboot things – whether or nae she believed it was the absolutely authority on things the way Ian did was still open for discussion. Her fear was that if she didnae believe exactly as Ian did, that he would nae longer be interested in continuing their relationship. And despite her doubts, she wanted to be in relationship with him.

"Is something wrong, Rose?"

She still couldnae find the words to answer.

It could be worse, she told herself. He could have a rebellious 13 year old son or daughter. It could be, *love me, love my child.* Instead, it was *love me, love my God.* God was love, was He nae? It had to be easier to love God the Father, and his Son, Jesus Christ, than to love an angst–filled teenager whose mother had been intimate with yer man, didn't it?

The thing was, ye might be able to fake it with a teenager. Well, probably nae, but ye could try. With God... Ian was devoted to God. If she wasn't, it would show. And God, being God, would know.

If she ended up being a lukewarm, half–hearted kind of Christian, or worse yet, an imposter married to a pastor, everyone would have it figured out in nae time. She would be the worst kind of hypocrite, guilty of pretending to be something she wasn't for romantic gain. And Ian – Ian would end up hating her if she tried to play the role of a devout Christian to earn his love. He was a man of integrity. He would respect her more if she didn't believe and chose to be honest aboot it than he would if she opted to lie aboot it for his behalf.

She could try to be a prim, properly pruned, domesticated rose, but if she were a wild rose at heart, there would be nae camouflaging it when all was said and done.

"Ian? Can we pray again?"

He looked at her, surprise obvious on his face.

"Is there something ye'd like to pray aboot?"

"Yes."

"Would ye like to talk aboot it first?"

"Nae really," Rose said.

"Okay. Let's talk to the Lord."

She bowed her head right there in the discothèque. "Lord." She swallowed and tried to think of the words to express her feelings. "Please help me to get to know ye better." There it was. The love would have to come in its own time, and naturally, if it came at all. She had the desire. She wasnae sure how these things worked, but she had the feeling the rest might have to come from God himself.

After they prayed, Ian made a couple more stabs at conversation and finally gave up. She was off in her own world tonight – and would freely admit it to anyone who hadnae already figured it out, including God himself.

Thankfully, Ian was ever the gentleman and didnae seem to mind too awfully much.

Chapter Twenty–Two

It had been a week since Rose had seen Ian. They'd kept in close touch, speaking on their mobiles at least twice a day and sending cards back and forth through the post.

She felt highly motivated to put the past behind her and move on, and if possible, to improve her self–confidence when it came to her relationship with Ian. Although she knew he liked her just the way she was, she truly wanted to learn more aboot the God he worshipped. Towards that end, she'd joined a woman's Bible study at a church in Glasgow. She planned on driving up to Loch Awe over the weekend to attend church at St. Conan's and spend some time with Ian Sunday afternoon and Monday, his day off.

Slowly but surely, she was healing from the negative effects of the traumatic turns her life had taken when she met Digby.

She'd just had a long chat with Kelly and a brief exchange with her Mum, so when her mobile chirped its friends and family song, she assumed it was Ian.

"Rose?"

Digby's voice cut through her newly–acquired sense of well–being like a knife with a dull, serrated edge.

"DIGBY?"

"Hey, babe," the slime said, like months hadnae passed without word from him, and crimes hadnae been committed, and her life hadnae been an exercise in humiliation a dozen times on his behalf.

"I'm surprised to hear from ye, that's all," she said, coming to her senses before she accidentally hung up on him or told him what she really thought of him.

Play it cool. This could be yer chance to put him behind bars.

"I've been missing ye bad, baby," Digby said, and she wondered for the millionth time what she'd ever seen in him.

"Me, too." *Play innocent.* "I didnae know if ye still wanted to see me after ye..."

"Are ye kidding? Ye're all I can think aboot," he said. "Ye're so beautiful, Rose. I'm sorry aboot the way we left things. Something came up and I couldnae contact ye."

"Ye couldnae have called just once and let me know what was going on? Ye couldnae have emailed?" It wouldnae seem natural if she wasnae a little bit angry, would it?

"I said I was sorry. And I'll make it up to ye if ye'll let me."

"Are ye sure everything is okay now?"

"My schedule is still a little unpredictable, but I could squeeze in a quick visit if ye're willing."

"I'm nae sure," Rose said. She didnae want to sound too eager. He'd spurned her, and it might seem suspicious if she acquiesced too easily.

"What I'd really like to do is to pick up where we left off." Digby's voice was low, suggestive, riddled with innuendo. "If ye know what I mean."

"How could I forget?" She had to fight nae to gag.

"If I remember right, ye were just aboot to..." He purred. "... when we left off." He let his voice trail off, waiting for her to fill in the blanks.

"Ye'll have to wait and find out where things might have led when we see each other next. A lady has to have a few secrets." *This was what she'd wanted wasnae it? An opportunity to lure Digby back to the scene of the crime so the police could nab him?*

"That sounds perfect, Rose. I cannae wait to make love to ye."

She stifled her gag reflex once again. "Do ye want to meet at St. Conan's again?" She couldnae let on that she knew.

"Let's try somewhere different this time."

The jerk probably wanted to scope out a new place to rob. "Sure. Where?"

"How aboot the Ardanaiseig Hotel? I'm told the gardens are beautiful this time of year."

Her mind whirled with the pros and cons. The hotel was at least seven or eight miles off the main road on a single–track lane, the last few miles of which were extremely bumpy. That alone should make it an ideal spot for the police to apprehend him, should it nae? The Ardanaiseig was known for its seclusion, but at least it was inhabited. That would certainly aid the police when it came to being in a position to help her. They probably even had a security camera. Digby could have chosen an abandoned castle, ruins or someplace in the wild where she'd be completely alone and vulnerable.

"Certainly. I've heard their gardens are a masterpiece – 19th century if I'm nae mistaken."

"Meet me at the boatshed, then. They say it's a romantic bolthole for couples. If we're discovered, we'll just say we're guests." He named the time, the day after next.

Good. What if she hadnae had time to contact the authorities? She was starting to shake just thinking aboot it. "I'll be there."

"I promise ye, nothing will keep me away this time."

"I believe ye." But only because he wanted sex. Nae because he cared aboot her, really cared, like Ian did. She tried to envision her and Digby praying together. Digby had never been rude to her, or rough, either physically or verbally. She never would have agreed to meet him in the first place if she'd sensed any sort of danger. But that didnae change the fact that he was a thief. A thief with honor? All she knew for sure was that he had hurt Ian, hurt St. Conan's, hurt people she cared aboot, and that she would love nothing better than to help bring him to justice.

When she hung up the phone, her heart was pounding. This was the day they'd been waiting for, was it nae? This was what they'd hoped, even prayed for. She tried to decide whether to call Ian or the constable. He'd been her go–between since day one.

She dialed Ian's mobile and told him aboot the meeting she'd set up with Digby.

Ian felt the same dread she did. "Why now, after all this time? Did he say what he wanted?"

"I think he wants to finish what we started."

"What? Under the flying buttresses?"

She let her silence answer his question. A fresh wave of shame washed over her. She hated dredging up reminders of her with Digby... especially now, when her indiscretions were finally forgotten, or as close as they ever would be.

"Well, the man has good taste. I'll give him that," Ian said begrudgingly.

"Will ye call the constable, Ian?"

"Of course." Ian was rather quiet, probably trying to process the fact that Digby had reappeared when they'd finally given up on ever hearing from him again.

She tried to swallow around the lump in her throat. "Whilst ye're at it, ye might alert the owners of the Ardanaiseig aboot what's going on – maybe send them my photo so they'll know I'm on a mission. If possible, I'd like to avoid any further bouts of false imprisonment, or even general humiliation for that matter."

"Of course. Ye dinnae want to be detained for loitering should Digby be late. They should also be on the look–out for yer safety, along with the police."

"If they have a security camera, and if they have it focused on the boatshed, they'll likely capture something helpful."

She wanted to be vindicated, did she nae? To be documented at her best and most courageous just as she had been at her worst and most vulnerable?

"Yer safety has to be the utmost concern."

"Thank ye. The owner of the hotel should also be notified that Digby might attempt to steal property – either before or after we meet."

"That is his pattern."

She was suddenly exhausted. She needed to prepare herself, to compose herself, to diffuse the emotions that were threatening to undo her.

She could sense Ian's anger simmering even before he spoke. "I know ye have to do this, Rose. But if I could, I'd stop this whole charade before it ever gets started and forbid ye to go anywhere near the man."

"Ye're right, of course. It's a horrible mess nae matter how ye look at it. But Ian?"

"Yes?" He sounded uncharacteristically sullen.

"Promise me ye will nae do anything to disrupt our rendezvous, please?"

"I suppose I have nae choice."

"Neither of us does. That's why I need ye to let me do this. And if I'm worried aboot ye or know that ye're looking on, I'm afraid I will nae be able to play my part. Do ye understand?"

"Again, do I have an option?"

"I dinnae want ye watching me with Digby. I dinnae want ye ever to see me or view me in that light again." She felt like she had finally won Ian's respect. She feared that seeing her in a compromising situation with Digby at this point could ruin their relationship.

She said her goodbyes reluctantly. Ian was nae happy and

probably wouldnae be until the whole scheme was over and done. There was nothing she could do aboot that either. If it had been up to her, she would have slammed down the phone when Digby called. She didnae care to see the man ever again, say nothing aboot pretending that she was willing to provide a release for his sexual frustrations. But she had to have a go at bringing Digby to justice. It was the only way to redeem herself.

* * *

Ian opened the door to the constable's office and waited for the room to fall silent. It was like magic. He was greeted by loud, raucous voices, off–color jokes and liberally sprinkled curses every time he entered the building, but as soon as they saw who was calling, the conversation was shut off as curtly as a click of the light switch.

Today was nae exception.

"Um, Reverend MacCraig." The constable hadnae been expecting him.

Ian assumed the man with the deep red face was the one who had delivered the particularly bawdy punch line right before he'd rounded the corner.

"Rose has heard from Digby."

"So it's Rose now, is it?" The muffled whisper from the far desk wasnae muffled enough.

"Aboot time," the constable said. "So is she cooperating?"

"Of course she is. She's as eager to see the scoundrel behind bars as we are. More so, if possible."

"I wasnae sure what she would do if she heard from him." The constable's eyes were hard and skeptical. He wasnae kidding. "Just because she didnae aid and abet him with the actual crime doesnae mean she wouldnae be sympathetic enough to shelter him from the law."

"Ye neednae worry. She has nae feelings for the man."

"Be careful, Pastor. I'm betting she had a few as recently as – oh, let's just say the day she spread her legs for the man." Contempt oozed from his words.

Ian clenched his fists and reined in the impulse to strike the man. "It wasnae like that." But even as the words left his lips, he knew that nothing he said would change the man's opinion of Rose. Only Rose could do that. Even that wasnae a given. Their prejudice against her might be impossible to reverse. The thought saddened him greatly.

"Doesnae matter." The constable took a pad of paper and a blunt pencil from his desk. "The important thing is that she's finally doing the right thing."

"Finally?" He flared. "What else – how else – could she have done anything sooner? This is the first she's heard from him."

"So she says."

Ian wanted to punch the man. "I trust her. She's telling the truth."

"Fine. As I was saying, the important thing is that she's doing something to redeem herself."

"She's already redeemed."

They glared at one another with such hostility that the room felt in danger of combustion. Ian imparted the date and time of the rendezvous Rose had arranged with Digby and turned to leave.

"One more thing." Ian turned back and looked the constable in the eyes. "I'm holding ye personally responsible for her safety. Rose should be shown the same consideration ye would a policeman or woman going undercover. If yer men will be carrying guns, I'd like her to have a bulletproof vest."

The constable's face softened perceptibly. "So that's the way it is. I understand. But do nae say I did nae warn ye."

Ian knew he should choose his words carefully. Up until now, only a few people from church were aware of his feelings for Rose. And those were just speculation. He hadnae publicly declared his intentions. Those from his congregation who did know – or thought they did – hadnae bragged aboot the fact that he was associating with Rose. Quite the contrary.

"The woman has come to mean a great deal to me. Think of her as ye will, but what ye think and say aboot her, ye think and say aboot me." He was tired of pussyfooting around his feelings for Rose. "Am I understood?"

"Perfectly. But let me also be clear. This is nae Glasgow. We do nae have a bulletproof vest."

"Then there will nae be guns?"

"That's a promise I cannae make."

He left the office filled with dread. To the constable and his men, Rose was expendable. They didnae value or respect her. If it were any of these people's mothers, aunts or wives that were to be involved in a sting, he had nae doubt that they would lay down their lives to protect their loved one. They had nae such affinity, nae such loyalty to Rose. To them, she was a worthless piece of trash, deserving only of their scorn. If anything went awry, the price for their indifference could be Rose's life.

* * *

Rose awoke early after hardly sleeping a wink. She'd already programmed the address of the Ardanaiseig Hotel into her GPS even though she knew exactly where it was and how to get there. She'd known she would be nervous and nervous she was.

She chose a slightly seductive looking blouse to wear – low necked, cherry red roses burned on a slinky, lightweight, black velvet – and purposely didnae wear a bra. She wanted Digby to be so mesmerized by her... assets that he would be distracted and off his game. She needed to be at her most alluring to accomplish her goal.

She also intended to be careful. That's why the top she'd chosen had nae buttons and therefore, nae easy access. It was possible that she'd need to stall for time – if so, every deterrent would help. If she had the opportunity, and she hoped she did, there was nothing that would make her happier than to eke a confession out of Digby.

Ian had insisted it was too dangerous, but she felt she had to try.

An hour later, she was on the road to the Ardanaiseig. She checked in with Ian, and then the constable, on her mobile as she was leaving Glasgow. It had been agreed that she would have nae contact with anyone once arriving at the Ardanaiseig.

The local police didnae have the equipment to fit her with a wire. In their view, a confession wasnae necessary anyway. They already had Ian's surveillance tape showing Digby stealing artifacts. They had Rose to place Digby at St. Conan's. It was all they needed.

Her agenda was a little different. She'd purchased a small recording device and tucked it in her pocket. If she could get Digby to confess, Ian's surveillance video wouldnae have to be admitted to evidence. She was happy to testify against Digby, but she did nae want Ian's video introduced. They would only use it to discredit her as a witness, and she'd been discredited enough already because of what they'd caught on tape.

The constable had said his men would be in position before dawn in case Digby had staked out their rendezvous. The one thing none of them could be certain aboot was whether or nae Digby knew that she had been arrested, or that she knew he was a criminal.

Dinnae think aboot it, she told herself. Nothing she would be doing in the next few hours would change. She was determined to help the police bring Digby to justice.

She parked her car behind some bushes in the parking lot. The hotel grounds were set up to accommodate nae only their overnight guests, but tourists who visited their dining room, a drawing room, and a bar that was renowned for its open fires and the popular snooker room in the basement. At this time of day, however, the place was practically deserted.

She resisted the urge to peer in this direction or that, trying to spot the constable's men. Digby could be watching. If so, it wouldnae do for her to act as though she expected company.

She walked to their agreed upon meeting place. The boatshed was right at water's edge – a stand of pine trees created a cozy canopy of green over and around it.

A bird broke the unearthly silence and whistled.

Thank goodness for that. It was too quiet, too unearthly tense. Her nerves were jittery and almost painfully alert. Would Digby see that, too? She'd never been a good actress. If she had been able to act like everything was okay and pretend to be a perfect little angel, like Kelly, she wouldnae have gotten into half the trouble she had as a child.

Her face had always been readable – from miles away according to her mother, who used to say she could take one look at her and know when she'd been bad. Maybe that was why she'd been avoiding her mum. She smiled, comforted by the memory.

She tried to keep smiling, to look happy and relaxed instead of tense and terrified. Yeah, right. *Just let him come soon,* she prayed quietly. Waiting was the worst part. At least she hoped it would be the worst part.

She was just aboot ready to hyperventilate from the tension when Digby stopped out from behind a bush. Right. That relaxed her.

"Digby!" She stood and gave him a hug, being careful nae to

press her hips against him; one, because the thought repulsed her, and two, because she was afraid he'd feel the recorder.

And then, he kissed her. She'd miscalculated when she'd assumed he would be satisfied with a hug. She couldnae make another mistake. So she kissed him back. She tried her best to be convincing but what she was thinking was that now would be a good time for the constable's men to nab Digby, cuff him, and drag him away to prison.

She felt Digby stiffen, and nae in a romantic way. This couldnae be good. That's when she felt something very hard against her thigh. It was too unyielding to be... She glanced down. *A gun?* Nae one had said anything aboot a gun!

"Dinnae say a word," Digby snarled in her ear, ex–lover nae more.

"Is that a gun?"

He reached into her pocket and grabbed hold of her recorder. "Is this a sting?"

"Lord, save me." She wanted to see Digby held accountable for his crimes as much as the next person, but this, she had nae signed up for.

"I dinnae know anything." Was it a sin to tell a lie under such duress? She would have to ask Ian. If she ever saw him again. Digby was yanking her along a muddy pathway, into the forest, away from the loch, waving his gun menacingly, yelling obscenities.

"Try anything, and she dies."

Dies? Seriously? It had come to that? "Why are ye doing this?"

"I will nae go back to prison," Digby said.

Back? She'd thought him a petty thief. Was he, had she... oh, Lord. She'd given herself to a hardened criminal?

The underbrush tore at her legs, each thorn hurting more than the last, but she kept quiet and sucked it up. She deserved as much and more, did she nae?

And then, Digby was spreading her legs again, this time, to shove her on the back of a motorcycle. He took off so quickly that her only thought was to instinctively clutch at his waist to keep from falling. He was driving at such high speeds that all she could do was to hang on for dear life.

And pray. She felt a little awkward at first – I mean, who was she to invoke the Lord God Almighty's assistance? But pray, she did.

179

She prayed as bushes whizzed by and mud pelted her shins and loose rocks went clattering aboot. She prayed for Ian, that he wouldnae do anything foolish and get himself killed in the process of trying to save her. She prayed for Kelly and Lyndsie, because she knew how distraught they would be when they heard the news, and she prayed for the constable, that he and his men would catch up to them quickly and rescue her. She even prayed for Digby, that he would drop this insane idea and figure out another way to solve his problems – one that didnae involve her.

She couldnae speak to the state of mind of the others she'd prayed for, but Digby appeared unfazed. She didnae get mad at God for nae answering right away – she just prayed harder. So while the world went by in a dizzy blur, while Digby dodged potholes and careened around curves and even went airborne a couple of times, she prayed, nae for her safe escape, although that's what she wanted most, but that she would live to tell Ian that she loved him. She should have said it when she'd had the chance. Should have said and done a lot of things. And now, she might never have the opportunity.

The praying helped to calm her jangled nerves. But even with the Lord God Almighty's comforting arms of protection aboot her, she still had to fight back tears – which would make a real mess of her face, what with all the dust Digby was stirring up from the edges of the motorway.

So she prayed some more, and tried nae to blubber. If she'd ever needed her wits aboot her, it was now. But she couldnae seem to help herself. Yes, she'd gotten herself into this mess. But still, it didnae seem fair. She'd just wanted a little love. Was that so terrible?

* * *

The constable and his men looked at Ian like he was the biggest fool on earth.

"Ye saw the way he kissed her."

"There is nae way she would have gone with Digby willingly. She did nae plan this!" Ian tried to keep the desperation out of his voice. Impossible. "I know the woman. She would never–"

"Well the way she was clinging to him on the back of his motorbike would suggest otherwise." The constable's jaw was set.

"Why would she have told us when and where she was meeting

him if she intended on running away with him?"

"Because she planned on leaving with Digby voluntarily all along. She's trying to get her hands on more of her late husband's money."

"That's ridiculous." Although, in retrospect, it should have occurred to someone that Digby might have found out that Rose was a wealthy widow. "She detests the man."

"The two of them are in cahoots, I tell ye. And according to Ms. Wilson's stepsons, there's every reason to believe Rose's motivation is a bigger piece of the pie. She's been kept on a very short financial leash since her sugar–daddy died."

"Rose is in mortal danger, and ye're thinking ill of her instead of attempting a rescue? If anything happens to her, I swear I will–"

"Ye may be a good pastor, but a detective ye're nae." The constable stared him down. "Ye've been hoodwinked, man. Admit it."

"Ye're the one who botched Digby's capture and let him get away with kidnapping Rose." The constable's men had been prepared to apprehend Digby on foot. By the time they'd scrambled back to the parking lot to retrieve their vehicles, Digby had been several miles out.

"We could have had a road block set up and he still would have dodged us on that motorbike."

The constable was probably right aboot that much, but there was nae way in hell Ian was going to give the man the satisfaction of admitting it. He resisted the urge to cuss at the man. He'd been watching from the gate and had seen them leaving together. Digby had been driving so fast that there was probably nae way anyone could have caught up to them.

"If one of my men had caught up to them and tried to drive them off the road or cut them off, she'd have been killed. With nae helmet, and speeds that high..."

Right again. Ian's heart sank lower and lower. He'd tried to follow in his car, but the lane had been so small and tight, with such dense hedges on either side, that he'd nae been able to dodge the potholes and ruts the way Digby had.

"If ye hadnae lost the chase, we wouldnae be having this conversation," the constable yelled.

Ian had never even made it to the main road thanks to a large rock lurking in the middle of the lane. His little car was low to the ground, and he'd nae seen it in time to swerve around it. He'd never even had a chance.

He'd watched, helplessly as Digby's motorbike had disappeared into the distance, his car hung up in the middle, rocking back and forth like a pathetic teeter totter, his motor spurting liquid. And to add indignity to indignity, his mobile service had been dead. He'd nae even been able to call for help.

His soul felt anguish anew as he relived the horror of watching Rose disappear with Digby. But it was anger that spurted past the rest of the emotions he was fighting and won the race. "I wasnae even supposed to be involved. And now ye're blaming me? It's yer own ineptitude that's put Rose at risk, nae mine!" Nae that yelling would bring Rose back, but–. No. He couldnae even say that he felt better. He could nae lose her. He would nae lose her.

Lord, please bring her back.

Oh, Lord. All this time, and he'd never even thought to pray. He should have been invoking the Lord's help from the first second he saw Rose fly by on the back of that motorbike. She'd looked so terrified, so small, and vulnerable. The thought of her nearly ripped his heart in two.

He couldnae lose her. He never should have let her meet Digby in the first place. Worthless artifacts. A few dollars in a donation box. A baptismal font that could be replaced with one call to the religious supply. None of it was worth her life.

The only reason she'd done it was to win approval from the church ladies. She'd been trying to prove to the church ladies that she was worthy of their acceptance – to justify herself in their eyes, to redeem herself from their judgment when she was already justified, already redeemed by the Lord God and Creator of the entire universe.

He stormed out the door and, when he got to his car, wept.

Chapter Twenty–Three

Digby looked at Rose expectantly from across the tiny room, his face in bas relief against the tattered remnants of peeling, sky blue paint. "Scream all ye want, Babe. We're miles from the nearest house. Kind of like that old Fleetwood Mac song, '*We're All Alone. Turn the lights out, close your eyes...*'"

There was nothing romantic aboot the situation, but Rose wasnae aboot to give Digby the satisfaction of hearing her state the obvious. Better to ignore him. The slime ball wasnae worthy of two seconds of her time or energy.

"How aboot we act out one of those kinky fantasies we talked aboot online?" Digby stooped down in front of the chair he'd tied her to, his face just a few inches from hers.

"Are ye insane? I'm tied up here."

"Exactly. There are people who would find that extremely sexy." He brushed his hand against her cheek.

"Nae when they've been kidnapped at gunpoint."

"Some women get turned on by danger, too."

"Well, I am nae one of them." She snapped her head away from him. "Ye should just let me go, Digby. Ye've made yer escape. Taking me was a good way to avoid being shot at while ye got away. But ye've got nothing to gain by holding me hostage. If the police knew where ye were, they'd be here already. Just drive me into the some random town and give me my mobile back. Ye can be long gone by the time they come to retrieve me. All's well that ends well."

"Ye've got it all figured out, dinnae ye?" Digby laughed. "Except for the part aboot me nae having anything to gain by holding ye hostage."

Her heart lurched in her chest. Digby couldnae possibly know, couldnae possibly have found out that she, that Robert was, had been...

"So what are kidnapped heiresses worth these days, do ye

think?" Digby smirked at her from the far corner of the room, which wasnae nearly far enough. "One mil? Two?"

She struggled to keep her cool. *And if she couldnae?* Nae much she could do with her hands tied behind her back. Seethe, boil, devise ways to hurt him in her mind... and who would that benefit?

"I dinnae know who ye think has that kind of money. My step–sons, perhaps, but they hate me... always have, even more so now that my name has been linked to yers. They'd sooner pay ye to do away with me than give ye money to bring me home. I mean, if Robert was still alive... but he's nae."

"Then I'll go to the board of directors. They will nae stand by and watch one of their own raped, tortured, or murdered."

She cringed in spite of herself. Nae that she really thought that Digby would hurt her – at least she hoped he wouldn't. But she could only imagine the grief and anxiety Ian and Kelly and the kids would feel if such a threat were made public.

"Forget them. I'm afraid they have much the same opinion of me as my stepsons."

"Ye've got a family, dinnae ye? How aboot them?"

"Poor as church mice. My mum lives on social security and a tiny pension and my sister has 5 kids and a husband who works for the trash company."

"Nice try."

"It's the truth! That's why Robert's sons think I married their father for his money. I come from nothing." Except love, she thought. Her family had always been good at love. Of course, if Kelly ever found out that she hadnae really sewn Lyndsie's pillows, even that would be in question. And if her Mum ever found out exactly what she'd done under the flying buttresses – well, she didnae even want to think aboot that.

Digby slapped her out of nowhere, probably to get her attention, which he certainly did. "So ye're telling me that the only people in the world who care aboot ye are destitute?"

She gritted her teeth and refused to give him the satisfaction of seeing her whimper. "Yes. And the money from my late husband's estate is in a trust that's controlled by my stepsons and a board of directors who would just as soon see me dead."

Digby swore and paced the tiny patch of floor. "Ye can say that, but there's nae way they would actually let anything happen to ye.

The public outcry would ruin their reputations. Rich people are very big on protecting their public images. I'm sure they'd pay at least 50 grand just to prove that they're nae heartless ogres."

"Are ye kidding? These men dinnae care what people think of them. They're cruel bastards and everyone already knows it. Adding one more dastardly deed to their already long list of sins will nae faze them one bit. Ye should just let me go. I mean, the kidnapping was a very good idea, or would have been if I were from a rich family or something like that. I mean, ye had nae way of knowing I'm more despised than naught."

"I have to try." Digby's eyes were a maze of tortured rage. "Ye dinnae understand. There are other people involved, and they're planning on this ransom money. If I were just to let ye go, they'd kill me."

"Oh, Digby." This did nae bode well. Digby might be a jerk, but he wasnae a killer. And while she might nae like the man any longer, she certainly had nae desire to see him dead. Unless it came down to her or him, and then, she had to admit she preferred nae to be the one to die.

"If ye tell me what's going on, maybe we can put our heads together and think of some way out of this mess."

"I have to think," Digby said. "If I tell ye they might kill ye whether they get any money or nae."

"Why did ye ever get involved with these people? Ye're nae an evil person, Digby. I learned that much when we were getting to know each other online."

"I owe them money." Digby ripped a shard of loose paint from the door frame, then smacked the palm of his hand against the rock wall. "That's why I started stealing things. I was trying to raise money to pay them off."

"So I was just part of yer plan to get money?" Her voice sounded small and tiny and vulnerable, even to her own ears. She'd been such a dunce!

"No. I didnae know ye were rich until after ye were arrested."

She gulped.

"Ye know aboot that?"

"I was just running a little late. When I got to the church, I saw all the cops and turned on a police scanner to try to find out what was going on. I mean, I didnae know why they'd be arresting ye." For a second, his apparent frustration faded to a look that was almost apologetic. "It took them aboot two minutes to run a make on ye and find out that ye were the rich widow of Robert Wilson, head of Wilson Enterprises."

"Okay. So I have a lot more money than my sister Kelly and her family do. But, Digby, my funds are strictly regulated, doled out monthly. It's enough to maintain my present lifestyle, which I'll admit, is generous by most people's standards. But I only get a stipend to cover my expenses each month. If my refrigerator stops working or if I need new tires, I have to submit a request for extra funds, which has to be approved by the board of directors. I certainly dinnae have an extra million pounds lying around in case of kidnapping."

"How aboot 50 grand?"

"I've got a thousand pounds in my checking account."

He was pacing again, except the room was so small that circling was more like it. He looked like a big, black vulture, swooping in for a bite. "What aboot yer credit cards?" His face lit up and for a second he looked downright cheery. "Ye must be able to get cash advances."

"I could when Robert was alive, but I have this tendency to shop when I'm feeling down. After Robert's death, I got a little carried away. When the bills started to come in, my stepsons had all of my credit cards cut off and closed the accounts. All I have now is my debit card, and it has a two hundred a day withdrawal limit."

"Great," Digby snapped. But he looked more forlorn than angry.

"Please just untie me, Digby. Let me go. Ye're only making things worse by holding me. And if things keep escalating, ye're risking both of our lives."

"Let me think. I have to think." Digby snarled and disappeared into what she assumed was the living room.

The light was starting to soften, so she assumed daytime was fading to afternoon. Was she supposed to sleep sitting up? She had to go to the bathroom in the worst way. Would Digby untie her long enough to use the loo? She was hungry, too. *Oh Lord,* she prayed. *Please help me. And please help Ian nae to be worried, or Kelly, or Lyndsie. Lord, please give Digby the courage to do the right thing. And please give me the words to help instead of hinder. Oh, Lord, save me.*

She thought for a moment. She'd never been one to pray except before meals when she was wee. Had she left anything out? Was there something else she should be saying? She felt nae need to make rash promises of things she would do if God answered her prayers. It went without saying that she was going to make God proud if she got out of the mess she found herself in.

She only hoped she would do the same if she didnae. She'd been hanging around Ian long enough to know that God cared aboot her and was watching over her. She felt certain that Ian was praying for her even now, and that despite the trouble she'd made for God and Ian on previous occasions, that God was listening. Listening and loving her.

She sat praying, her hands tied, but her mind as free as it had ever been, until minutes had turned to hours. Had Digby gone? She thought aboot yelling for help to see if he would come, but figured that her silent prayers to God would ultimately be of more help than screams to Digby. When nae one came to feed her or to let her relieve herself, she finally dozed off, her empty stomach making loud protests and her bladder suffering silently. Her head sagged uncomfortably, her neck was stiff and sore from the strain, and her arms were still tied behind her back.

* * *

"It's very nice to meet ye, Kelly." Ian nodded at Kevin. "Although I deeply regret the circumstances that have brought us together." It was the same thing he said when he met the family of the deceased before performing a funeral for their loved one. The thought chilled him to the core.

Kelly's eyes glinted with tears. "Pastor Ian, this is our daughter, Lyndsie, and our boys, Jaime, Josh, Jace and Jack."

Each of the children nodded, their faces scared and ill at ease.

"They suggested we bring all of the children along," Kelly explained. "Since Rose doesnae have any of her own. I mean, unless ye count her two step–sons, which Rose never did. They're nearly the same age she is and have never regarded her as a mother."

"Yes, she mentioned that her relationship with them has been more antagonistic than nae."

Kelly looked uncannily like Rose, except that she looked tired, even a bit haggard, if he was honest aboot it. To be expected, he guessed, when yer sister had gone missing and was being held captive by a madman. Although, looking at the boys, he found himself wondering if Kelly always looked a bit exhausted, short on patience, and pushed to her limits.

"They thought having the children here might soften the man's heart," Kelly's husband, Kevin said.

Kelly looked up at him with concern. "And impress upon them that we're nae rich, and do nae have a lot of extra money lying around."

"I was told specifically nae to wear a suit," Kevin said, looking like a cement block in a work shirt emblazoned with his name and the City of Glasgow Public Works logo.

"A good thing," Kelly said. "Ye've gained thirty pounds since yer da's funeral. Ye'll need a new one when the children start to marry, but until then..."

Kevin looked directly at him for the first time. "Guess it's jeans and a sweater for Sunday services then."

The look in the man's eyes said he hadnae darkened the door of a kirk in a long while and probably wouldnae do so again until forced to. Ian could only hope that the first occasion would indeed be the marriage of one of his sons or daughter, and nae Rose's funeral.

"The children have all been confirmed," Kelly said, as if to defend Kevin's lack of involvement with a parish and inadvertently confirming Ian's suspicions. "At St. Vincent's, just up the street from our duplex. Except Lyndsie, that is. She's still in the middle of her instruction."

"Good. It's an important step in a child's spiritual growth."

There was an awkward silence, in which he deduced none of the boys had been back to church since the day they were confirmed either. Thankfully, the station manager chose that moment to invite them to enter the ready room. Ian had delivered a weekly radio address at the local station while at a former parish, so he knew a little of the way things worked. This would be his first television appearance, and his first experience speaking to a market the size of Glasgow.

"Our sister station in Edinburgh has agreed to do a live simulcast. Thought we might as well cover all the bases while we're at it."

"He could 'ave her anywhere by now. If she's even still..."

"Kevin." Kelly cut him off, looked over her shoulder at Lyndsie, and reached back to take the girl's hand.

Ian looked on and said nothing. There was something aboot

Kevin's attitude that had been bothering him since the second he met the man. It was almost as though the gent thought Rose had finally gotten what she deserved. He bristled, and thought aboot taking Kevin aside to set him straight, but the station manager was shushing them with his pointer finger and motioning at the spot where they were to stand.

So Ian put Kevin out of his mind. He had bigger worries, far more worthy of his attention. He had to convince Digby to release Rose. The producer arranged him in the front, with Kelly, Kevin, and the children standing behind him. Their positions would reverse when he had said his part. The copywriter at the station had written scripts for each of them, but he had opted to speak in his own words. He recalled his discussion with Rose aboot extemporaneous or spontaneous sermons and how the Holy Spirit could and often did work though the words of a willing servant. And that, he was.

A large light flashed from red to yellow to green. The program director took the microphone, introduced himself and explained the details surrounding Rose's kidnapping for those who were new to the story. He then reiterated the part of the story that had already broken. Rose's stepsons had received a ransom note and had chosen to reply with the following message: "To whom it may concern. Although we sympathize with the family and friends of our late father's wife, Rose Wilson, and wish to express great concern for her safety, we cannot in good conscience give in to the terms of a kidnapper. Our father abhorred violence of every kind and would not wish for us to give into the demands of such a person or to propagate extortion as a means of terrorism. We therefore refuse to cooperate in this scheme and respectfully request that Rose Wilson be returned to her family, unharmed, without further delay."

The announcer then introduced Ian as a close friend of Rose's and handed him the microphone.

He closed his eyes for the briefest of seconds to pray, then put the mike to his lips. "Digby, and any others who may have assisted in the kidnapping of Rose – I'm speaking to ye." *Be firm. Let yer compassion, even yer desperation, shine though.* That's what the station manager had recommended. Nae acting required there. He would do anything to hold Rose in his arms again. "I live on a limited income. I have nae money for ransom. But I love Rose more than anything in the world. I'm begging ye to please send her back!

Ye've heard the spiel from her stepsons. Ye've nothing to gain by holding her and much to lose by continuing this ill–fated attempt at coercion. Rose's family needs her. Her friends and co–workers need her. I need her."

His eyes felt wet. The people and room décor blurred around him. He handed the microphone to Kelly and took a step back to make room for her and Kevin.

The girl – Rose's niece – slipped her hand in his. "Aunt Rose loves ye, too. She told me the day we had breakfast together."

"Thank ye." He squeezed Lyndsie's hand. Why hadnae he told Rose that he loved her? He'd had millions of chances. Now... The tears he'd been holding back slipped down his cheeks for all the world to see. And he didnae care.

Kelly spoke next. "Rose is my only sister. If I had the means, I'd pay twice what ye're asking to get her back. But I dinnae, and the foundation will nae. I've pled with them myself and they will nae budge."

Ian wiped his eyes and looked at the monitor to see Kelly rolling her eyes in a very sincere gesture of her frustration, disgust even. "So ye're nae getting any money. We just dinnae have it, and we've nae way to get it either. That's the facts. So I beg of ye, please return my sister to me and my daughter and my sons. Our da is gone and our mum is very elderly – Rose is the only family we have. So we would very much appreciate her safe return, and we promise ye that if ye do the right thing, the police will forget the whole thing ever happened." Kelly looked up at Kevin and nodded. "And just so ye know, the police told me I could say that last bit. All that matters to any of us is that ye return Rose."

Kevin leaned over to speak into her microphone. "That's right. And if ye dinnae do the right thing, ye'll have both the police and me to answer to. God, too." He put his arm around Kelly and led her back to the children.

The station manager called a wrap and looked positively gleeful as soon as the lights faded. "Good job, everyone. That couldnae have gone better. Ratings will be through the roof! Which will only help yer cause, of course. We'll replay yer appeals throughout the day to maximize our chances of the kidnappers seeing the spot." He shook each of their hands. When he got to Ian, he added a few words especially tailored for him, "Keep the faith."

Chapter Twenty–Four

"So who's this guy Ian who claims to love you so much he's willing to do anything to get you back?"

"What?" The sound of Digby's voice cackling loudly from the other room awakened her. She was cold, stiff, and disoriented.

"It was on the telly just now. First your sister, crying like a baby, and your niece, looking all red–eyed like she'd been at it, too. And your brother–in–law. What a piece of work he is."

"What are you talking aboot? Are they okay?"

"It's on the national news. Pleading to get you back alive. See? You have more people who care aboot you than you thought."

"Of course they care aboot me, you numpty. That doesnae change the fact that they have nae money."

"So tell me aboot this Ian."

She clamped her jaw shut and said nothing.

"He certainly looks like a gent who's well–off. Nice wool jacket, sporty hat, leather shoes."

She had nae intention of discussing Ian with Digby.

"Definitely wore a look of desperation. He's a man in love, if I'm nae mistaken. And I dinnae believe I am."

She held her tongue until it hurt, determined nae to give Digby the satisfaction of...

"I must say, it didnae take ye long to spread yer legs for another man. And here I was feeling a bit o' guilt aboot what happened between us. But now that I know ye forgot me with a snap o' your fingers and moved on to another man within the space of little more than two months, well..." Digby raised his eyebrows suggestively.

Okay. Now she was mad. "I did nae such thing!"

"A man with that look in his eyes... and the pretty speech he gave... he's had a taste, all right."

"Maybe he loves me just for who I am. Did ye ever think of that?"

Digby just smiled. Which was fine with her. Let him think what he wished. The kind of relationship she and Ian shared was far more than an oaf like Digby could ever understand.

Digby kept smiling at her, like he was envisioning her and Ian in bed. Honestly, it gave her such heebie jeebies that for a moment, she was tempted to tell Digby aboot how she and Ian had prayed together. She opened her mouth to try, but found the memory too precious to talk aboot with the likes of Digby.

"I'll wager he's a doctor," Digby said, straddling the back of a straight–backed chair across the room from her. "Maybe even a surgeon. A plastic surgeon. Big money there from what I hear."

"He's nae a doctor."

"Maybe a barrister then. Nice herringbone coat like that must cost a pretty penny. He probably has a nice little estate somewhere outside Glasgow. And a summer house on Loch Lomond."

"Dinnae be ridiculous. And will ye please untie me so I can go to the loo? I will tell ye one thing aboot the man, and that is that he's fastidiously clean and well–groomed. If ye care anything aboot the possibility of him wanting me back, ye'd better take excellent care of me."

"All righty, then." Digby untied the knots at her wrists and jerked her to the back of the house. He shoved her into the bathroom, closed the door halfway, and told her she had two minutes.

* * *

Ian was just aboot ready to leave the radio station and set out for Loch Awe when the station manager stepped out of his office and asked him, Kelly, and Kevin and their family to step into his office. "The constable from Loch Awe would like to have a word with ye while ye're all together."

Kelly gave a little gasp. "Is it Rose? Have they found her? Is she okay?"

"Nae to worry, ma'am. They assure me that there's been nae change in the situation. At least nae to the best of their knowledge."

He spoke into the mouthpiece of the telephone then. "Do I have everyone's permission to put the conversation on speaker phone?" Kelly and Kevin nodded. So did the station master, so it was evident that the constable had agreed.

"Better let the constable know there's a young girl in the room."

192

He assumed the boys had heard worse at school. He certainly hoped Lyndsie hadnae heard the likes of the man's tongue.

"Done." The station master passed along his message and flipped a switch on the phone.

"I dinnae even want to know which of ye idiots is responsible for yer little parade on the telly, but it's going to stop right now." While the constable refrained from using out and out swear words, his intent was clear. "I am running this investigation, nae the media, nae the good pastor, and nae the family. If I am made aware of one more instance of any of ye compromising this investigation, I'll press charges and send the whole lot of ye to jail."

He, Kelly, and the station master all looked at one another in disbelief. Although for a second, Ian thought the station master looked a little guilty.

"What did we do?" Kelly spoke. "We thought we were helping."

"Helping the television station get better ratings, most definitely. I just hope ye have nae done irreparable damage to our case in the process."

"Why would what we did hurt Rose?" Kelly started to cry once again.

"With all due respect," the constable said, without the slightest trace of it in his voice, "our goal is to keep the kidnappers believing that there is money, and that they are going to be paid the ransom money."

"But that's nae possible," Kelly said. "None of us has any extra money, or a posh house to mortgage, or anything of the like. And the foundation—"

"We all know that, but we dinnae want them to know it." Irritation dripped from his voice. "Let's use our heads here, people. They've kidnapped yer sister. They've promised to give her back if ye give them the money they've demanded. We want them to give her back. So we pretend we have the money. Maybe it's counterfeit bills, maybe it's a few bills treated with a chemical that permanently stains their hands when they touch it so we can catch them later. We get yer sister back. We catch the crooks. It's called a sting. But now, we have kidnappers who know we have nae real money. That changes everything. Do ye understand?"

"Cannae we say we found some money somewhere that we didnae know we had, or that the foundation changed their minds and decided to pay the ransom?" Kelly's voice was verging on hysterical. Ian mentally kicked himself.

"And ye think they'd believe us now? Let me explain it another way. These men or women took a calculated risk when they kidnapped yer sister. There was a possibility they would get caught and go to prison, but it was worth it because they thought they were going to get the money. Now that they've been told there's nae money, they've got nae motivation to continue to take the risk."

"And that means getting rid of Rose." Ian's words left a trail of regret, of sour, acrid bile in his throat.

Kelly sobbed.

"We've been running a blankity blank investigation while ye people have had yer heads up yer butts. This Digby may have acted on his own when he kidnapped Rose, but there are other people involved. Dangerous people who would think nothing of killing both Rose and Digby if it serves the bigger picture."

Kelly's face blanched white. His probably did, too.

"What is the bigger picture?" Ian asked. Nae that it would help to know. But he had to ask.

"Oh, Lord," Kelly sobbed. "Please save my sister. Keep her safe. Bring her home."

"Digby owes them money. They're out of Germany. Gambling debt." The constable wasnae yelling any more. He sounded as weary as Ian felt.

"We're devoting every possible man to solving the case," the constable said curtly. "We've called in Scotland Yard. We're getting help. But we need time. If ye do anything else as stupid as what ye just did, I will press charges."

"We will nae," Kelly cried. Kevin stood beside her like a dolt, and Ian wanted to scream at him to hold her, to take her hand – anything.

"And if I find out that Rose has anything to do with this – that she's trying to help Digby get his hands on her money, so she can share it, get him off the hook financially, whatever – she will pay. If I have to hand her over to the cartel myself, I will, but she will pay."

"What is he talking aboot?" Kelly dug a tissue out of her purse.

For one second, Ian entertained the fact that Rose may have helped Digby. She had such a compassionate heart. Was it possible she'd learned of Digby's financial plight and resolved to help him?

She had talked aboot wanting to live on the wild side for a change. Maybe she'd given up on church – with the way they'd treated her at St. Conan's, he could hardly blame her.

"They think she's in cahoots with Digby." Ian shook his head.

"But she doesnae love him," a quiet voice said.

"What?" He turned toward Lyndsie.

"What did ye just say, sweetheart?" Kelly stopped crying and focused on her daughter.

"She told me. The day she gave me the pillows she made for me, the day we went to the tea house."

Ian had to smile in spite of the gravity of the situation. He was undoubtedly the only one present besides God who knew that Rose had hired the innkeeper at Corrie Bank B&B to make Lyndsie's pillows, after multiple attempts to do the work herself, all resulting in failure and considerable damage to her sewing machine.

"What did Rose say, sweetie?" Kelly knelt down in front of her daughter.

"That she loved him." She pointed at Ian. "She was feeling sad because she was in love with a man that she couldnae be with. I remember that. There were a lot of reasons she couldnae be with him but the only one I remember is the one aboot nae being a virgin."

She had everyone's attention, including Kevin's, who did nae look happy.

"She talked to my daughter aboot sex? I warned her. I told her she was treading on thin ice. I told her–"

"What exactly did she say, honey?" Kelly glared at Kevin, then encouraged Lyndsie in a reassuring voice. "It might help the men to find her if ye try to remember everything that ye can."

"I heard ye and Da talking aboot Rose being with a bad man, so I thought the reason she couldnae be with the man she loved was that he was in jail or something, but she said no, she never loved the bad man."

Kevin paced the floor, looking fit to be tied.

"She said she loved Pastor Ian, but she couldnae be with him because he needed a virgin."

"Well, that ship sailed a long time ago," Kevin said.

"Kevin, shush yer mouth for heaven's sake." Kelly gave her husband a dirty look and then glanced questioningly at Ian.

"I assure ye, I was well aware of the fact that Rose was nae longer a virgin, and thought nae less of her for it. Nor did it deter my efforts to court her."

Kevin snorted. "I'll bet it dinna."

"Kevin!"

"Oh, all right." Kevin slouched into the nearest chair and bit his lip.

"Then what did she say, sweetheart?"

"She said Pastor Ian was so good and nice that he deserved someone very dear, and I said she was the dearest person I know, and that Pastor Ian probably wouldnae hold her past against her if she asked him real nice."

His heart smashed into a million smithereens. *Oh, Rose. Dear, sweet, Rose.*

"Which I'm sure she would have if she hadnae gotten kidnapped," Kelly said. "Ye gave her very good advice, sweetheart. I'm very proud of ye."

"Ye have to find her." Lyndsie turned to him. "Because, because she's my aunt, and Mum and I need all the girls we can get in our family. But also, because she loves ye and really, really wants to be with ye."

"I will do my best, Lyndsie. Thank ye for telling us what Rose said. Ye've been a big help."

Ian took the phone from the station manager and spoke directly into the mouthpiece. "Did ye hear that? Tell me what to do and I'll do it. Now."

Chapter Twenty–Five

"So tell me aboot this Ian person on the telly." When Digby returned from wherever he'd gone, he sounded even more menacing than before. He looked angrier, too. Something had changed. She didnae know what.

"I asked ye once. Nice like. Now I'm telling ye that ye need to tell me who he is."

"Why dinnae ye tell me? Ye obviously know far more aboot me than I thought. And I know next to nothing aboot ye. Is that fair?"

"I'm the one whose hands are untied so I get to decide who talks and who doesnae. And I say this: we're nae on a date trying to get to know each other better. This is nae a give and take situation. Ye spill the beans. I keep quiet. That's the way it's going to be because what I say goes."

His voice grew louder and louder with each sentence until he was nearly screaming. Fine. So at least she knew what she was dealing with. Digby was starting to show signs of stress. That much was obvious. He was truly frightened of the men to whom he owed money. And that frightened her.

* * *

"What now?" Ian put down the receiver and turned to face Kelly, Kevin, and Rose's niece and nephews. "They want me back in Loch Awe. But first, I'm to visit Robert, Jr. and Rodney at Wilson Enterprises. Something aboot it being harder for them to say nae to a man of the cloth than the constable."

"Or the kidnappers," Kelly said. "It makes sense. Would it help if I came along?"

"Absolutely nae," Kevin said, stepping between them. "Things like this are best left to the men folk, dinnae ye think, darling?"

"Contraire." Ian smiled. "I think it might be just the thing to soften their hearts."

"But I just heard ye say that ye would nae do anything without consulting the constable." Kevin scratched his head. "Hardly seems worth ringing him up again when ye just got off the phone. Especially when he's likely to say nae."

"I would like to check with the constable first. I promised nae to do anything else involving the investigation without running it by him." He tried nae to let the desperation he felt creep into his voice, if for nae other reason than to protect Lyndsie from the terror he felt.

"I'm so sorry," Kelly said. "It was Kevin's idea that we go on the telly and make a plea for Rose's release, but I'm the one that drew ye into it."

"Ye would blame me," Kevin said. "How was I to know? It's what they do in all the movies."

"Nae to worry," Ian said, even though he was. "It was as much my fault as yers. I saw nothing wrong with the idea until the constable called."

He pulled his mobile out of his pocket and rang up the constable. "Permission granted," he said a moment later. "He also suggested that Lyndsie accompany us, if that's okay with ye and Kevin."

"Lyndsie? Would ye like to come with us to speak to Aunt Rose's stepsons at their office building?"

"Yes. If it will help Aunt Rose."

"Now here is where I 'ave to put my foot down." Kevin seemed to be growing more agitated by the minute. "It is bad enough what the girl has already had to endure thanks to her Auntie Rose."

Kelly glared at Kevin, then smiled and patted her daughter on the shoulder. "Kevin, will ye please take the boys home? I'll ride with Pastor Ian if that's all right with him."

"Of course it is."

Kevin scowled but reluctantly complied.

Kelly smiled and retrieved her purse. "I feel so bad to think we may have hurt Rose's chances. This... Well, hopefully we can persuade the Wilsons to work with the constable and undo some of the damage we did."

"Have ye ever met the terrible two?" Ian grimaced. "I've spoken to them on one previous occasion and it didnae go well."

"They were there at Robert's funeral," Kelly said, "acting like it was Rose's fault that the man had died of a heart attack. Other than that, I've had nae previous encounters with them."

"I'm still nae convinced that this is a good idea," Kevin said, his voice tinged with an uncustomary, high pitched jitter.

"I'm nae afraid to talk to them," Lyndsie said. "Neither was Aunt Rose. She said once that the younger one, Rodney, kind of liked her, at least some of the time."

"That's good to know." Ian smiled for what seemed like the first time in weeks. Time was like a bat in that respect. It had a way of both creeping and flying in the midst of a crisis. He'd thought the same thing many a time when sitting at the hospital with a parishioner, waiting for news, hoping and praying...

He guessed now it was his turn. And in theory, the overseer was his pastor. Somehow, he doubted the "old biddy" – to quote Rose – would be making a house call, or even a phone call for that matter.

He nodded at Kevin and the boys as they prepared to depart, then extended an arm to Kelly. "Let's go, ladies."

"It will be fine, Mum," Lyndsie said. "Rose always said their bark is much worse than their bite."

"Ginger!" Kelly screamed. "Ginger! Where is Ginger?"

"I – I – I should have thought..." Ian couldnae have felt more disgusted with himself. What else had he neglected to do? Or done wrong? Losing Rose had him so discombobulated that he had nearly lost his wits.

"Poor baby," Lyndsie said. "How could we?"

The clamor of each of them realizing that Ginger was probably locked up, alone, in Rose's flat, rose to a roar.

"Does she nae have a housekeeper?"

"Yes, but she only comes once a week. I have nae idea which day it is."

"Did anyone let her know that Rose had been kidnapped?"

"For goodness sake, I've been so distraught that I didnae even remember that she had a dog. How would I have thought to have contacted her housekeeper?" Kelly looked more frantic with each second that passed. "I have a key. We'll go there now, on the way to speak with the men at the Foundation."

"Didnae she say something aboot hiring a personal assistant nae too long ago?"

"She didnae exactly hire her. She borrowed her from the corporate office for one or two days a week so she could work from her office at home."

"So she would be aware that Rose had been kidnapped."

"Yes. But if she had thought to go and take care of Ginger, wouldnae she have called?"

"She probably assumed we would take care of it."

Lyndsie said, "I hope she's okay."

Kelly grabbed Lyndsie's hand and headed for the door. "It's only been two days. Rose always left her plenty of food and water."

Lyndsie's face scrunched up with worry. "But what if she had to piddle in the house? Or..."

"Then we can only hope it wasnae on one of the Persian rugs," Kelly said.

"Ye." Kelly stopped in her tracks and pointed at Kevin. "Ye follow us in the car with the boys and take Ginger to our house while we go to the Foundation."

"I said that dog is nae longer allowed in our house—"

"That dog is coming home with us and that dog will stay with us until Rose is returned." Kelly railed at Kevin, then turned to her sons, who each had a quip of their own. "There are four of ye. One of ye will walk her every four hours. One of ye will stay with her at all times. And keep her out of Lyndsie's room. Rose sewed those precious pillows with her very own hands. They may be the last thing we have to remember her by. Ye will make certain that dog doesnae put so much as a tooth mark in a single one of them. Do ye understand?"

The one he thought was called Jace looked skeptical. "But Mum, the car is crowded as it is. Where are we going to put Ginger?"

"Hold her on yer laps in the back seat. If all else fails, it's a hatchback. If she doesnae fit in the boot, one of ye will."

Kevin, who looked like he knew it would do nae good to argue when Kelly was in her present state of mind, simply said, "We'll make it work. Anything for our dear sister, Rose." And left the room.

* * *

"Are ye absolutely sure ye dinnae want to have sex one last time?" Digby stood in the doorway of the room where she was being held captive looking at her lustfully. Which was saying a lot since she hadnae showered, combed her hair or brushed her teeth in however long she'd been tied to her chair.

She thought at first that he was kidding, but nae, there was definitely a hopeful glint in his eyes.

"Digby, we've been over this. I am nae aroused by being tied up."

"My Mum used to read romance novels. Had them lying around the house – t'was a good way to educate myself in the finer points of how to make a woman happy."

The look on his face would have made her nauseous if she'd had anything in her stomach to regurgitate.

"Ye're a masterful lover, Digby. It all makes sense now. I mean, ye really know how to treat a lady." So she was feeling a bit facetious. Good grief. What did he expect from her?

But at least he was asking, and nae demanding. Another blessing in disguise.

"So, in one of these novels, a woman was kidnapped by a renegade American Indian. He held her captive, but for a very noble reason – to arrange for the children of his village to have food."

"They were probably starving."

"Yes. It was a hard winter, and the Indian reservation they'd been assigned to was in a place where there was nae game to be found and nae way to grow crops. The American government had reneged on its promise to send supplies.

"So in desperation, he kidnapped a woman and demanded food for the children in his village."

"And this relates to us how? Do ye have a passel of hungry children that I dinnae know aboot?"

"Nae, but–"

"Because last time I knew, ye kidnapped me because ye gambled all yer money away on the mainland and were stupid enough to borrow money from the mafia so ye could gamble some more to try to recoup yer losses, and then, as gamblers are inclined to do, lost all of that."

"The lady in the book fell in love with him."

"Ah. Let me guess. Every time he untied her so she could go the ladies room to freshen up, she made wild, passionate love to him."

"Exactly," he said, for some reason, looking very pleased with himself.

"Well, dream on, Digby. I am nae falling in love with ye and I am nae going to make love to ye. I do nae relish being yer captive and there is nae one thought of either passion or compassion towards ye in my pretty, little, romantic, womanly head. Which, speaking of, I do need to go to the ladies room in the worst way, so if ye would please..."

"But what if we die?"

Digby didnae give up easily. She could say that much for him.

"These men will stop for nothing. If yer people dinnae come up with the money soon, they'll kill us both. Think of it this way – wouldnae ye like a wee bit of satisfaction before ye breathe yer last?"

It was too ludicrous to dignify with an answer. But she screamed "NO" nonetheless. "A wee bit of food, and a wee bit of water, YES! But a wee bit of sex with my kidnapper, nae thank ye!"

For that, she was granted two minutes in the privy with the door cracked open a smidgen in case she tried something.

"Hardly worth untying ye for," he groused.

Lord, please rescue me, she prayed. It was the only thing she could think to do.

* * *

Kelly rang the doorbell in the hallway of Rose's flat twice before turning the key in the lock and pushing the door open. They knew she wasnae home, but it was still her house, and they all felt she deserved the same privacy they would have shown her had she been home.

Ginger was barking frantically from the other side of the door. Once she saw who had come to rescue her, she raced from room to room at incredibly high speeds, her ears flying behind her, her neatly trimmed claws and furry paws alternately clicking and sliding on the wood and tile floors.

"Aunt Rose used to call it a rabies attack when Ginger ran around like this. She always used to have one when Aunt Rose came back from a trip or something, or even a long day at the office."

He almost chastised Lyndsie for talking aboot Rose in the past tense but didnae have the heart.

"Ginger was so happy to see her that she just went a little crazy. Didnae ye?" Lyndsie tickled the dog's head and scratched her ears when she finally stopped running.

But today, Ginger's joyous yelps and whimpers were mixed with fear. He could see it in the dog's eyes. They told a story more compelling than happy. A tale of confusion and wary enthusiasm. *Where was her mother?* Exactly the question they all wanted answered.

When Kelly had calmed Ginger down, had a few more terse words with Kevin, and sent her off with the boys to be walked, they set aboot the unpleasant task of cleaning up the inevitable messes.

"Poor puppy. She never would have done this under normal circumstances."

"Rose said she never had accidents, even when left all day long."

"She has a bladder of steel that one. Rose has commented on it many a time. But nae one could have expected her to hold it for two days, poor thing."

"What choice did she have, when nae one came for her? I feel so awful."

"We were so concerned for Rose that we could nae think of anything else."

"I'm just relieved that ye thought of her when ye did."

"Are ye sure she'll be okay at yer house?" Ian blotted, then scrubbed a spot on the small rug just inside the front door. "She knew she was supposed to go outside. She just couldnae open the door."

It was eerie being inside Rose's flat when they all knew – or more precisely, didnae know, where she was. Reminders of her loving spirit, and evidence of her creativity and passion everywhere he looked – on the wall, a painting of Tobermory's colorful harbor on the Isle of Mull that Ian recognized from a pilgrimage he'd taken to the age old religious community at nearby Ionia. A plaid, wool shawl draped over a chair, a cluster of nubby, wool flowers, a painting of a man in kilts playing a bagpipe with a picture perfect rendition of Eileen Donan castle etched in stone behind him... The scene looked precisely as he remembered it from a sight–seeing tour years earlier. Some things never changed. How he hoped nothing aboot his life with Rose would. Her flat was so desolate without her.

He wandered to check the rest of the rooms. Rose's office reflected another side of her altogether. Neat as a pin, organized, tidy, businesslike – all adjectives that described the wonderful woman whose life he was honored to be a part of.

"Oops. I found a little pile of ye know what," Lyndsie said.

"I'll get it." Kelly took a paper towel and knelt to clean the spot. "Ye know what's truly amazing? Ginger didnae eat a single pillow or bedspread or anything made of cloth."

"I hear tell that Rose had quite a talk with her after the incident at yer house." Ian chuckled.

"Whatever she said must have sunk in. I imagine she had a good talking to her when she was making Lyndsie's new pillows. Rose knows full well how to sew, but she does nae enjoy it like I do."

It was at that exact moment that Ian spied the receipt on the kitchen table. The name at the top caught his eye first. It was the woman from Corrie Bank B&B. He scanned the cursive script. Four pillows in shades of pink @10 pounds each. And in parenthesis: (Must be hand–sewn, but nae too perfectly so as nae to make the sister suspicious.) The too was underlined. He smiled and closed his hand over the incriminating evidence just as Kelly walked towards him.

"Found something helpful?" Kelly started to rummage through the remaining papers and a few unopened envelopes that must have come in the mail before she left sitting on the table. "I keep thinking that there could be a phone number or something written down that would help the constable's men find her."

"No. Nothing of the sort unfortunately." He didnae want Kelly to see him slipping the paper inside his coat pocket, neither did he dare risk putting it back on the table.

"Almost forgot what I came for," Kelly said, giving up her search. "I need another cleaning cloth."

Ian cleared his throat – a sure sign of guilt – which thankfully went unnoticed. Kelly didnae suspect him of anything, and probably wouldnae ever – he was a pastor, of course. Pastors were always given the benefit of the doubt.

"Can I help with anything more?"

"Just make sure there are nae any more messes around the flat. I think we have them all, but if ye dinnae mind double checking..."

He glanced around while Kelly washed her hands and wiped down the sink. They had nae reason to stay any longer. Ginger had been taken for her walk, and was safely on her way back to Kelly and Kevin's house with the boys. Kelly had checked the apartment to make sure there were nae other problems set in motion by Rose's unexpected absence. The iron was off. Stove burners nae leaking gas, toilet nae running, answering machine set with a new message asking callers to dial Kelly's number or the Wilson Foundation if they needed immediate attention until Rose returned from her *travels*.

They'd collected Rose's mail and left a note for the mailman to temporarily hold any other deliveries. Although what good that would do when they'd announced on national television that Rose had been kidnapped and was being held for ransom, he didnae know. With the luck they'd been having, it wouldnae surprise him if someone robbed Rose's apartment while she was away.

Maybe that was why he was so hesitant to leave. If he couldnae protect her, the least he could do was to guard her things. But that too was ridiculous. Her things didnae matter. Her life did. He had to figure out a way to save her.

She's already saved. The quiet voice whispered to him as he turned to go. *Trust me.*

I'm trying. He really was.

And then, he ignored God's voice and listened to his heart for a moment. Her bedroom. He went under the guise of making sure there were nae puddles or messes on the floor.

He sucked in his breath and let his emotions wash over him. Rose's bed was unmade, so casual and just–slept–in looking that he almost expected to hear her voice calling out from the bathroom. A Ginger–sized wallow punctuated the quilt. Smart dog. He'd have done the same if given the chance – anything to feel close to her again.

"All set, Ian?"

"Coming." He brought his fingers to his lips and blew Rose a kiss as he backed out the door.

Chapter Twenty–Six

Rose awoke – if ye could call her fitful rest, punctuated by hunger, thirst, and the constant urge to go to the bathroom, sleep – to the sounds of voices. She could hear Digby's and at least two others, all speaking in another language. She narrowed it down to German as the guttural sounds slowly made their impressions upon her sleepy mind.

She felt so weak, both in mind and body. If she had had any chance of plotting an escape or overpowering Digby and making a run for it, she should have done it at the start, before Digby wore her down with nae food, very little water, and nae sleep. Her only beverages had consisted of drinking what rusty tap water she could cup in her hands when she was untied and allowed her brief visits to the bathroom. How many days had it been?

What little energy she did have was devoted to trying nae to throw up or wet herself – if there was even enough moisture in her dehydrated body to do such a thing. Her brain and her body were turning to mush. Recognizing it didnae help, but depressed her even more.

She tried to focus on the conversation she could hear through the thin walls, to recognize a familiar word or two. She knew a few words of German from trips she'd taken with Robert over the years – mostly terms of endearment or polite reassurances – please, thank ye, I beg yer pardon, excuse me and other common civilities she had taken care to learn so as to be a gracious guest when in a foreign country.

These voices did nae sound polite, or even civil. What she did hear was a battery of vulgar, American expletives. Although she couldnae understand what they were saying, they were clearly unhappy with Digby, threatening him, even roughing him up, if the thunks and moans she heard were any indication. Would she be next? She thought aboot what she would do – or try to do – should they try to rape her. Try? She managed a weak smile. If they made

206

the attempt, they would succeed. She had nae strength left to fight. Perhaps her dulled senses would negate part of the horror. Ah. Another blessing in disguise.

She heard the sound of a boot hitting the door to the small bedroom where her chair sat. The door jerked open. A heavy–set man with short–cropped, dark hair, multiple scars on his arms and a ski mask over his face held up a camera and started to snap pictures. She could only imagine how lovely she must look. But then, her deteriorating condition was nae doubt what they wanted to impress upon the people who had the means to save her.

The man barked a command in German. Digby appeared in the door briefly, his face bloodied and bruised. He held a newspaper in his hands. She flinched in anticipation of being hit with it. But nothing happened except that the man issued another directive, and Digby moved behind her, out of her line of sight.

"They're going to make a video of the two of us. They want ye to say that ye're okay, but that ye will soon look like me unless Wilson Enterprises pays the money they have requested. Please do as they ask or they will kill me."

"All right. Sure." She wrenched her neck and tried to see Digby over her shoulder but could nae. Maybe she didnae want a closer look. These men were definitely serious – that much she'd seen from the quick glimpse she'd gotten when Digby first entered the room.

The man motioned for her to begin.

"Hello. My name is Rose Wilson." Her mind groped for some way that that she could send a secretly encrypted message with her words. Something that Ian or Kelly would pick up on and understand that her captors wouldnae. She couldnae think of a thing. What could she tell them even if her brain could manage such a feat? She had nae clue where she was or even what day it was. What could she possibly say that would help?

Digby poked her in the shoulder from behind.

"Please give them the money."

Digby poked her again.

"Or they'll do to me what they just did to Digby. Please give them the money. I want to come home." She could feel her tears wetting her face, hot, smooth, and desperate. She had nae way to wipe them away. "I love ye, Ian. I should have told ye when I had the chance. I just wanted ye to know in case, in case I never... Kelly,

I love ye, too – so very much. I know ye know–"

The man with the camera turned and left the room. She had nae way of knowing at what point he'd stopped recording.

* * *

The gold letters of the sign at the corner of the building that housed Wilson Enterprises, Ltd. gleamed in the sunlight. Ian relished the cheery welcome while he held the door open for Kelly and Lyndsie, realizing full well that the reception he got on the inside of the building would nae doubt be considerably more icy.

"Was Uncle Robert the owner of this whole building?" Lyndsie asked.

"Yes, dear, he was."

"And now it all belongs to Aunt Rose?"

"No, dear. Uncle Robert left Aunt Rose enough money to care for her very nicely, but Wilson Enterprises now belongs to Robert's two sons. It was a stipulation of their mother's will, since the money came from her family originally."

"But they dinnae like Aunt Rose very well."

"No. Sadly, they dinnae. But she works with them on a lot of projects that help a lot of people, and they all get along just fine, so nae worries."

"But they dinnae like her well enough to give the kidnappers the money so they'll bring her back?"

"That remains to be seen." Ian pushed the button for the elevator and gave Kelly and Lyndsie each a squeeze on the shoulders. "That's why we each have to do our best to persuade them to do the right thing."

The elevator door opened soundlessly and they climbed aboard. A few seconds later, the door opened again and they were standing in an opulent reception area on the 14th floor.

"Reverend Ian MacCraig to see Robert and or Rodney Wilson, please."

The receptionist smiled at Lyndsie. "And who might this bonnie wee lassie be?"

"I'm Kelly Morris. This is my daughter, Lyndsie."

"Ye're Rose's sister then? And her niece?" The woman's face beamed with delight. "She always spoke so highly of ye." She stood and extended her hand. "I'm Erika, Robert's old secretary – the one who's been working a day or two every week at Rose's flat. My, the two of us can get a lot accomplished without the phone ringing every two minutes and the men going in and out." Her face fell. "Could." She looked for a moment like she could cry. "Nae to be negative. I so hope and pray that Rose is found and returned to us safely, and soon."

"Thank ye." Kelly smiled and wiped a tear from her eye. "Now, if we could..."

"Oh, my." Erika paused, as though considering what to do. She obviously cared deeply for Rose – and had probably been given orders nae to interrupt the crown princes. "Come right this way." Erika stepped out from behind the desk with a determined look and waved her arm to the right.

Ian exchanged a glance with Kelly and followed Erika's quick clip down the hall. Their first big break.

Erika gave a quick rap to the double doors at the end of the hallway and opened the door. "Sirs, ye have guests. Ye know Pastor Ian, of course, and this is Rose's sister, Kelly and her dear niece, Lyndsie."

Rodney, who was facing Robert's desk, turned. A flustered, apprehensive look flashed across his face when he recognized Ian.

Robert Junior never flinched, his features hard and cold as he gazed at Kelly. "I've made it clear on more than one occasion that Rose's relatives are not eligible to receive any of my father's money. It's strictly forbidden by the terms of my mother's trust."

"Of all the..." Kelly sputtered, a shocked look on her face.

"The Morris's have nae and are nae asking for any money," Ian started, in her defense.

"Perhaps not today," Robert interrupted. "But I have had several conversations in the past with a Kevin Morris, whom I assume is a relative of yours."

Kelly's face turned a deep shade of red, and she lowered her eyes.

So this was how it was going to be.

"Kelly's husband is nae the issue here today, and ye know it full well." Ian took a step forward and let the full wrath of his best hell and brimstone voice be heard.

Robert flinched and jerked back as though he'd been slapped.

Which, in Ian's opinion, was exactly what the man deserved.

"We've made our position quite clear on the matter of Rose's kidnapping, if that's what you're alluding to," Robert said defiantly.

Ian stepped another foot closer. Robert's chair tilted back as far as it would go. "Ye know that's what I'm talking aboot, Wilson, and I'm telling ye that yer position is aboot to change."

"Oh, yes?"

Ian noticed Rodney's amused look for the first time.

"Yes." Ian scowled. "Ye're going to cooperate with the constable to the fullest. Ye'll do whatever the authorities ask, including coughing up the full amount the kidnappers have requested. Whatever it takes to get Rose back."

"Perhaps if we took the monthly stipends Rose receives for her living expenses and paid them out in one lump sum?" Robert toyed with his pen. "The money is hers to use as she wishes. If she desires to be freed, she would then have the means to secure her own release. Her choice. And from what you say, I'm sure she would choose to—"

Ian extended his arms, leaned on Robert's desk and looked him square in the eye. "That's nae what I had in mind."

"Perhaps the money that was earmarked for St. Conan's grant could be diverted to fund Rose's release." Rodney chimed in, looking more like a cat playing with a mouse than a serious contender in the battle they were waging. The only thing Ian couldnae decide was whether or nae Rodney's suggestion was for the enjoyment of seeing Ian squirm, or his brother.

The door to the office opened and Erika rushed in.

"Sir," she said to Robert, Junior. "There's a phone call from a Herr Heinz on line 3. He says he's got Rose, and that he wishes to speak to ye immediately."

"I'm sure every crackpot between here and north Africa has heard aboot the kidnapping by now thanks to Pastor Ian's little stunt on national television. Am I supposed to give them all money?" He stood, turned on Ian, and unleashed his furry. "How many millions do you want me to cough up, Pastor? They'll all be claiming responsibility before we know it, all wanting money, all promising to return her if we pay them." He threw up his hands. "What exactly do you want me to do?"

"But sir," Erika said meekly. "Ye have to speak to him. Herr

210

Heinz said that Digby is deposed at the moment and is finding it hard to converse without his teeth."

"The whole world knows Digby's name. That proves nothing."

"But sir, he put Rose on the phone. I heard her voice. It was her, sir. I know it was." Erika's face was pale and drawn.

"What did she say?" Ian asked gently.

"She said to tell Robert Junior that she would sooner die than have ye give this oaf a single pound of Robert's money. She said to give the ransom money to St. Conan's in her memory. She said..." She turned towards Ian and took his hand. "She said to tell ye she loves ye, more than anything in the world, and that's assuming that God is in his own category entirely, because she knows it's a sin to love anyone more than God."

A smile flashed over Ian's face in spite of his efforts to remain stern. "That's Rose all right."

"Fine then." Robert stood tall and straightened his vest. "We'll do exactly as she asked. Even she knows what a travesty it would be to hand over a million pounds to a kidnapper when there are so many deserving people in the world in need of money."

Ian reached out and grabbed the man's arm before he knew what had come over him. "Are ye saying Rose is nae worthy to be saved?"

Robert smirked. "Well, she did bring her troubles upon herself."

First, Ian punched him in the gut. Then, while Robert was falling back into his easy chair, rolling across the floor, and clutching his left side, he told him why. "Rose was lonely, nae doubt in part because ye two have treated her so abominably since yer father's death. Nothing she did in her attempt to find a little affection rendered her unworthy. She had nothing – absolutely nothing – to do with the artifacts being stolen from St. Conan's. And she was trying to help the authorities and the people of St. Conan's when she was kidnapped. What in any of that makes her unworthy?" he was yelling, and he didnae care, except for Lyndsie. How he rued his decision to bring her into this den of iniquity.

"As one who knew and loved yer da a lot more than the two of ye ever did, well said!" Erika said to Robert and Rodney. She nodded at Ian, then handed Robert the phone.

Robert mumbled a few distinguishable words but for the most part, just listened to whatever Herr Heinz was telling him. The rest of them were quiet.

"What's the number for your mobile?" Robert barked at Ian.

Ian gave him the number.

Robert repeated it to the man on the phone. A few minutes later, he clicked the cordless off and handed it back to Erika. "They have a video of Rose holding today's paper. The video will be played on the six o'clock newscast on the same station you dealt with earlier. Proof that she's still alive, or was, earlier this morning. Oh, and more news. They've kidnapped the kidnapper. Digby is there, but nae longer calling the shots. These men are German mafia. Digby owed them money. They probably stepped in to keep him from botching the heist."

Kelly looked as impatient as he felt. "So what aboot Rose? What do we have to do to get her back?"

"They want a million in cash. I'm to deliver a bag filled with unmarked bills in hundred pound increments to Ian, who's to head northeast on the 809 from Glasgow, at 5 pm tomorrow. They'll call his cell phone with further directions once he's en route. We call the police, and Rose is dead."

"They didnae say nae to call the constable." Lyndsie's small voice eked out from the corner to break the silence.

"Why Ian?" Rodney asked. "He's got nothing to do with it, does he?"

"Better Ian than we." Robert answered, nursing his left shoulder. "All we need is to give them the opportunity to make off with one of us."

"She loves him," Kelly said. "If she knows he's the one bringing the money, she wonae try anything funny for fear he'll be hurt."

"You're saying she'd not give a rip if anything happened to the two of us, eh?" Rodney seemed to find Kelly's implication extremely amusing.

"Can ye blame her?" Kelly glared at him.

Ian was tempted to say a few words on the subject of being a better step–son, but Robert Junior was on the phone with his banker, and there was nae need to beat a dead horse. He only hoped that the lessons they'd all learned today would help them mend some relational fences in the days to come.

"Ian?" Lyndsie brushed his sleeve. "Ye have to call the constable. Ye promised ye wouldnae do anything else unless ye asked him if it was okay."

"I know I did. But the Germans said..."

"But ye promised."

"But Robert promised nae to call the police."

"Nae he didnae. They told him nae to call, but he didnae promise them. And they didnae say he couldnae call the constable, just the police."

"The constable is the same thing as a German polizei."

"I know that. We're studying German in school." For a moment, she looked like a sassy teenager instead of a sweet ten year old.

Okay, so he was missing the point. He had promised, and Lyndsie was watching to see if he followed through on his commitments. He opened his mobile, slowly, thoughtfully. He'd tried the route of taking things into his own hands and it hadnae gone well. The constable and Scotland Yard were trained to spot pitfalls in a plan and make sure things turned out the way you wanted them to. They didnae need any more disasters.

Lyndsie peered up at him, her eyes wide. He stepped into the next room. His hand was trembling as he punched the constable's auto dial on his mobile.

He would never forgive himself if the decision he was making hurt Rose in any way. But he had promised. And how could he live with himself if he played the fearless cowboy and things went wrong?

When the constable picked up, he repeated the terms that the kidnappers had made for Rose's release and confirmed that Wilson Enterprises would supply the money. He gave the constable Winston Glenn's name. He'd met the man on his previous visit and remembered well that he was nae only the Chairman of the Board but the president of Robert's bank.

So what was done was done. Now, he could only trust the Lord to bring Rose safely back to him.

Kelly stepped into the room and walked slowly toward him.

"Are ye all right?" He put his arm around her shoulder when she was near enough and squeezed her arm.

"I was just thinking aboot those stupid pillows." Kelly sighed. "I made such a big deal aboot Ginger eating them and Rose having to replace them when I know sewing is pure torture for her. And really, what did it matter? Ginger was just being a dog, and Lyndsie survived just fine, and I could have made three times the pillows we lost in under an hour if I'd set my mind to it."

"None of it much matters now, does it?" Ian took her hand and held it tightly. "I was thinking aboot the church ladies. And my overseer. I mean to say, in the big scheme of things, who cares what they think of my choice of a wife?"

"Ye're going to ask Rose to marry ye?"

"I should have done it a month ago."

"It's so romantic," Lyndsie said, walking toward them. "Rose will be so happy."

"All that matters now is that we're together again – and soon."

Chapter Twenty–Seven

Rose hadnae seen or heard anything from Digby or the Germans since the night before. What had precipitated the change, she did nae know. Her need to use the loo had diminished right along with her intake of food and water, which had been next to nil for however many days she'd been tied up, but her muscles were cramped and stiff and cold and she longed to be free to walk the few feet to the rest room, even if it was only for two minutes.

She'd gone from being hungry to lethargic. She was doing her best, but her instincts told her she couldnae go on this way much longer.

What had they done to Digby? She'd hardly expected him to be her savior, but she trusted him infinitely more than the Germans.

She started to rock back and forth on the legs of the wooden chair she was tied to. Something, anything to flex her muscles. If she got their attention, all the better.

When she stopped, the room was still filled with the deathly quiet of nothingness. A cow mooed in a nearby pasture. Sheep bleated from afar. The house creaked. Nae signs of human life except for her ragged breaths. *Oh, Lord*, she prayed. *Please let them come for me. Preferably Ian. But really, anyone will do.*

Even the Germans? Her eyes flew open and her senses sprung to life when she heard the first boot hit the floor. Angry voices filtered through the door like sharp–tipped knives. They were fighting aboot something. She could hear it in their intonations even though she didnae understand 90 percent of their words. Frau, Digby, dummkopf, Wilson Enterprises, polizei, autobahn, geld, euros. They were talking aboot her.

Was this a good thing or a bad thing? She prayed some more. The door burst open. Men in masks grabbed the ropes binding her, untied them, and unceremoniously yanked them away. A pillow case over her head prevented her from seeing anything. She was wrapped from head to toe in what felt like a blanket. A soft, warm blanket.

She was already half gone when her head hit the floor. She felt a prick of pain, a gush of sticky warmth – oh, the relief – and finally, blessed blackness.

* * *

A guard stood by as Winston Glenn put a cloth bag on the seat beside Ian. Just like in the movies – the kind he couldnae bear to watch because they were so bloody tense. He glanced at the bag – the thing looked like the one he'd used to cart his dirty laundry home to his mother when he was in seminary.

His mind jerked obediently back to the task at hand. Robert and Rodney stood nearby, watching, Robert's face swathed in disgust, Rodney's in his typical laissez faire attitude.

"God be with you," Winston said. Both men nodded.

And he was. Ian felt that much, deep in his heart anyway. The rest of him, including his brain, was half numb. Kelly had insisted he stay in Roses' guest room the night before to avoid having to pay for a hotel. In the end, she and Lyndsie had returned with Ginger to spend the night in Roses' big, king sized bed. Ian suspected that what Kelly had learned aboot her husband's shenanigans had something to do with that, but he hadnae queried as to the reason behind her decision. He was sure Ginger had been happier in her own bed in her own home, amongst people who loved and welcomed her, than she had with the men of the Morris household.

But that was neither here nor there – now, he simply needed to concentrate on diffusing the supreme stress he was under while maintaining an alert state of mind. His gas tank was full. His mobile was at the ready, on the seat, next to the money. He'd worn comfortable trekking shoes in case he should need to make a run for it. He had nae idea what to expect, which all told, was probably for the best.

He drove north on the A809 for forty–five minutes, give or take a few seconds, the exact amount of time Map Quest had said it would take for him to reach the B8050 Roundaboot, where he was to head northeast on the A 81 towards Mugdock.

He made the turns as directed and continued going toward the Trossachs until his mobile rang again.

"Veer left and go towards Dumgoyne." Click.

He did as they said. His mobile rang again. Nae chit–chat, just,

"Follow the sign to Brig o' Turk."

The pattern repeated itself six or seven more times. Turn right. Then left, then right again, twice, then left once and right once more before veering to the left. He tried to remember the sequence. It seemed important, in case the constable should ask him for the information. But try as he might, his mind couldnae seem to muddle through the maze of keeping the old data straight while simultaneously following each new directive.

His mobile rang once again, when he was a few more miles down the motorway. There was nothing for miles around. Somewhere in the Trossachs, he guessed, north and east of Loch Lomand, but he had nae clue where.

"You'll come to an overpass in 28.2 miles. Stop in the middle of the bridge, get out of the car, and drop the bag off the left side of the bridge." Click. So that was why they'd wanted a bag and nae a suitcase.

The final click echoed in his head as he realized he'd been given nae instructions on where to find Rose, nae opportunity to demand her release.

He drove through a desolate series of outby fields for what seemed like an eternity until he saw a rise in the distance. Yes. There were guard rails, and quite a drop off underneath if the sharp descent of the hill was any indication. He put the car in park, left it running, grabbed his mobile and the money, and got out of the car.

The wind whipped at his jacket as he leaned over the side of the bridge. He bent as far as he could without toppling and saw nothing. With nae other alternative, he extended his arm, prayed that this was the right spot, and let go of the bag.

Splat. The bag stretched, scrunched, expanded, contracted, but didnae break.

A man dressed in black wearing a ski mask scrambled out from under the bridge like a rodent waiting to raid a dumpster. When he'd retrieved the bag, he scurried back under the bridge and disappeared.

Ian listened for some sign of Rose, and heard nothing but the squeal of tires as her kidnappers exited the opposite side of the overpass. He skirted the car and ran to the other side of the road but they had disappeared into a cloud of dust by the time he got there.

The authorities had told him to ID the car, to get the license plate, to tell them everything he could, to call the constable's men as soon as the drop had been made.

But all he could think aboot was Rose. "Rose! Rose!" He yelled into the wind, glancing frantically from left to right. Wasnae the girl supposed to come walking down the center of the bridge right aboot now? There should be a mist. She should be appearing any second.

But she did nae.

There was nae access from one road to the other, except to climb down the rocky incline on either side of the overpass. He did, grasping at bushes and even a thistle to keep his balance. "Rose! Rose!"

Nothing.

He reached the bottom of the hill. Nae Rose. Some scrubby underbrush, some wildflowers, another patch of thistles. "Rose!"

And then he saw it. A blanket, raveling around the edges. Rolled up like a Cuban cigar. Oh, no.

He tried nae to fear the worst as he pawed at the blanket. A stain. He rolled her over and over, trying to avoid the rocks, trying to be gentle and quick aboot his task. *Lord, please...* he begged.

And then he saw her face, smudged in blood. So quiet, so still. So ghostly white. And then, her eyelids fluttered. Blessed life. Like a butterfly kiss against her own cheek. He grabbed his mobile and called for help. He could nae carry her up the hill, he could nae drive the car down to get her without traveling around the lochs and bens for Lord knew how many miles, maybe never to find her again. The emergency crews would locate him with his signal, could they nae? He scanned for a road marker and saw a small number etched on the base of the bridge.

Rose moaned and tried to open her eyes, saw the light and must have thought better.

She was alive. All that mattered was that she was alive. Now he just had to keep her that way.

* * *

Rose opened her eyes to the gleam of white, bright, celestial light. Well, at least if she was dead, she'd ended up in the right place. That would make Ian happy. Robert, too. Hopefully it meant that she would never have to see Robert Junior again. *Wait a minute...* if she really was in God's presence, would thoughts like that be allowed?

Probably nae.

She was wondering who she would end up spending eternity with if she and Ian and Robert Senior all ended up in heaven. *How would that work?* And then, she saw a face. She squinted and tried to remember if she'd ever seen the person before. It wasnae Digby, wasnae the Germans, wasnae anyone she remembered seeing recently. Her granddad come to welcome her? Saint Peter?

Peter was a man she'd always felt a certain kinship with. It would be fitting if he were the one to welcome her to heaven. He'd blown it – in a very big way – and God had let him back into the fold. If it had worked for Peter, certainly God would give her a second chance, too, would He nae?

Second chances... actually, she might need a third, fourth or fifth. Okay, so maybe a tenth, a fortieth, or a fiftieth. The first thing she was going to do when she got home to her own cozy flat was to get out her Bible and count out how many times Peter had done stupid things. If Peter hadnae flubbed up enough, she would read the story of David. If she remembered right, David's life had been so colorful that it made her transgressions seem downright tame.

"Ian?" Her eyes focused for a moment then faded and blurred like an app on the moviemaker on her computer. For a second, she thought she'd seen Ian's face. *Oh, God,* she prayed. *Please let it mean that I'm alive, and that Ian's nae dead, too.*

She could just see it – him rushing in to rescue her, the Germans capturing him, tying him up and making him watch while they tortured her, then shooting them both. Thank goodness she'd been unconscious through the worst of it.

"Rose?"

"Ian?" She tried to form the words, but her tongue was too thick.

"I'm here, Rose."

"What happened?" Had she really said the words, or just thought them?

"The Germans dumped ye along the side of the road somewhere in the Trossachs and made off with the ransom."

"They paid?" Now, this was news. She was incredulous. Even more so because Ian seemed to be able to hear her – which meant she was talking. She was alive!

That was the good news. The bad news was that she hurt like, well, hell.

Sherrie Hansen

"Did they catch them?"

"No. Nae yet. I wish I had thought to bring my camera. If I'd gotten a photo of the back of the car as they drove down the road, I could have zoomed in on the license plate and–"

"Ye and yer cameras." An image floated in front of the haze that used to be her field of sight... a room full of constable–types zooming in on her erogenous zones, looking for clues, taking notes. "Enough already."

And then she heard the most magical sound – Ian's laughter, floating through the room, merging with the light, wafting into every pore of her being.

"Oh, Ian. I'm so happy to be alive."

"Me, too. I am so glad ye're okay. Ye are okay, are ye nae? The doctors say yer head will be fine, but yer top was torn, and the bruises on yer wrists... I am so sorry ye had to go through this ordeal."

"I'm fine. My blouse tore the very first day when Digby was struggling with me, trying to get me on the back of his motorbike. I tried to fight, but he had a gun." Tears threatened to overwhelm her as the horror of what had happened to her – and the relief that she was safe again – started to sink in. "They didnae hurt me, nae really."

"Ye must be very sore. The bruises on yer wrists look so raw."

Her mind clicked and a wave of hysteria assaulted her. "Is Ginger... Did someone think to get Ginger? I told her I would be gone for only a few hours."

"Safe and sound with Kelly's boys and Lyndsie."

She expelled a long sigh. "Thank God."

"More than ye'll ever know." Ian stood back and looked her over thoroughly. "Ye're certain ye're feeling well enough then? The doctors say ye're very dehydrated."

"Hungry, too. May I have something to eat?"

He leaned over her and kissed her cheek. "I'll check with the nurse."

"Ian?"

"Yes?"

"Is Kelly...? Is she mad at me?"

"No, no, sweetheart. We're nae in Glasgow, that's all. They took ye to Inverness, which was the closest town with a hospital. She's on her way right now."

"Ian? Could I please have bangers – the Cumberland type – and mash – and a couple of rashers?"

"I'll check with the cafeteria." He turned to go, his reluctance plain on his face. "I'll go see then."

"Ian?"

"Yes?"

"If they have it, a little smoked haddock pie would be nice as well."

Ian started towards the door. "We'll soon find out."

"Oh, and do ye think they stock sweets? Because if so, I've got the worst craving for Mr. Kipling's Exceedingly Good Battenburg Cakes. I thought of them the whole time I was tied up. One of those things that really kept me going. Ye know – I must live, or I'll never taste another mini–battenberg."

"Perish the thought! How would one survive?"

"T'would be a tragedy. Like the poor Americans nae being able to get their Twinkie fixes, I suppose. I pray every night that Mr. Kipling never goes out of business like Hostess did."

"I'm nae sure how the Americans will get on without Wonder Bread."

"I'm sure it's a trial." She brushed her brow and winced when her fingers ran into what felt like a very nasty bruise. Probably better there were nae mirrors in the near vicinity.

She looked up at Ian, who was still at her bedside – stalwart, steadfast, strong, and so very, very dear.

"Rose? Why are we talking aboot food?"

Her eyes met his and she felt her face crumpling. "I was so scared. I thought I'd never see ye again."

And then he was hugging her and kissing away all the hurt – well, almost all of it – and she didnae care how hungry or sore she was as long as he was there.

"Do ye want to talk aboot it?" Ian asked, ever so gently.

She ignored him. "All this talk of food has made me even hungrier."

Ian straightened up. "Fine, then. Somehow, I dinnae see battenbergs sounding like pro quid hospital fare, but I will specifically ask if they're on the menu."

"They have them at Marks & Spencer, if there's one nearby."

"Right–O."

"It's the sheets of sugared almond marzipan on the outside that make them so delicious. Quite addicting, really. But – if there are none to be found – I could settle for a smidgen of sticky toffee pudding, or even some caramel shortbread."

"It's always good to have a solid Plan B in place in case the worst should happen."

"Ye're so right. Thankfully, I've always been known for my flexibility. I know it's nae in the same class of virtues as say, meekness, or gentleness, or goodness–"

"Or humility," Ian said.

"Yes. But it's an asset nonetheless."

"One ye're to be commended for."

"Thank ye." She snuggled back into the tall stack of pillows at the head of her hospital bed. She thought aboot closing her eyes, but it was so comforting just to look at Ian that she resisted the urge.

"I'll check with the cafeteria straight away and be back in a few minutes then," Ian said. "I promise."

"Me, too." The light was starting to fade. "And I promise to be good until ye get back. But dinnae be too long. The odds of my acting up increase exponentially with every second I'm left to my own devices." She smiled. "At least that's what my da always used to say."

"Rose?"

"Yes, dear?"

"I love ye."

"I love ye, too, Ian."

Chapter Twenty–Eight

It was the time of day when the sun would already have set in most parts of the world. A family of rabbits was playing hide and seek in the fading light and the clouds hovering over the loch were overlapping one another in shades of purple, pink and blue.

Rose could see the concern on Ian's face as they walked along the side of Loch Awe. She tried to smile. It wasnae that she wasnae happy. She was fine. Just a bit subdued at the moment. She had a lot to mull on, now that her adrenalin rush had gone down a notch. All she really wanted was to get back to normal and resume her schedule. Sadly, she knew she wasnae there quite yet. She'd been scared silly, and she wasnae ready to be alone just yet. Maybe when the Germans were apprehended... Maybe then she'd start to feel a bit safer.

Ian started to say something, then stopped. Then started again. "So what are ye thinking aboot, sweetheart? Yer eyes radiate emotion like the clouds reflected on the waters of Loch Awe."

She wasnae sure what to say, so she said nothing. It was like that lately – so many words wanting to be said aloud and heard, yet when given the chance, none came out.

"It's quite an ordeal ye've been through."

She looked at Ian and loved him even though he sounded more like a pastor than a lover at that precise moment. But that was okay. He was a gem with many facets, just as she was.

Ian prodded gently. "Would it help to put it into words? Maybe to share something ye've learned from all the things ye've been through in the last few days?"

There it was. The magic key. All week, people had been asking her how she was or how she felt, general questions to which she had nae clue how to respond. This one specific question she knew how to answer.

She thrust her chin up and out. "I've learned to quit apologizing for myself. Roses come in all sorts of pleasant varieties, and I'm proud to be one of the more exotic bushes in the garden."

Ian smiled, delighted, if she was any judge. "Maybe I'll do that some year for yer birthday. Contact a horticulturist and have them develop an exotic hybrid. Name it after ye."

That brought a smile to her face. "Wild Rose, then? Or Rambling Rose in honor of my da?"

"Ye're both, and more. I'll have to wait and see how the mood strikes me at the time."

"Brave words for a staid, play–it–on–the–safe–side pastor."

"If ye can be diverse, so can I."

"Wasnae there an American pop singer years ago who had a hit that said "I'm a little bit country, I'm a little bit rock and roll?"

"Marie Osmond. She has nae been heard from in years, at least nae in the UK. Probably should have picked one or the other and gone with it instead of trying to dip a toe in each pond."

She made a face at him and he smiled. Comfortable, content, relaxed. How she loved him! And then, she said, "But I like variety. This morning I was on Facebook, and one of my online friends had posted a banner that said, 'Pray like Jesus. Pray all the time.' So I liked it – because I do, and I need to, and I did. But another friend posted a photo of a very cute, very studly guy in his underwear, sprawled out on his bed giving the camera an absolutely wicked "come hither" look – pure eye candy – and I liked that, too."

"Should I be jealous?"

"No, because jealousy is a sin and I'm trying very hard nae to be the cause of any more transgressions on yer part. It's a full time job just keeping track of my own comings and goings. I dinnae need yer failings on my conscience."

"So ye like candy."

Rose reached down to scratch Ginger's ears, and straightened up slowly, so as nae to make her head throb any more than it already did. "Well, actually I didnae like it on Facebook, because I'm friends with some of the ladies from church and I didnae want to give them one more thing to talk aboot. But I liked it on the inside."

"So, if ye're praying all the time, what were ye praying aboot when ye were looking at the handsome gent on Facebook?"

"Grace." She grinned. But nae guiltily.

He roared at that, and his laughter echoed across the loch, up the ben and back. "Good answer. Ye'll make a great pastor's wife yet."

"Right." She laughed nervously. It was hysterical, really, the thought that she would ever... but Ian's eyes had gone from laughing to serious and he was looking at her with eyes so full of heat that they could melt a Cadbury chocolate egg.

She smiled up at him. "What? Was that a proposal?"

And then he bent to pick a stem or two of wildflowers, and got down on one knee, right there along the edge of the road.

"I wasnae hinting, really, I wasnae."

He pulled out a box.

"Oh, Ian, please tell me it wasnae yer mother's, passed down from generation to generation since the time when metal was first forged."

He grinned and started to open the box.

"Nae that I wouldnae be thrilled. I mean, I'm sure yer family is just peachy, but–"

"Chosen and designed especially for yer finger."

"Oh. Oh Ian." The front of the ring was shaped like a rose, its soft petals shaped in gold, and a diamond nestled at its side with a pair of leaves wrapped cozily around the base.

"I had my grandmother's wedding band melted down and reshaped into a setting that would be uniquely yers."

"Perfect." Just like Ian. The man was perfect. He thought of everything.

"Because traditions and continuity are wonderful things, but we're treading new ground here and it seemed that like ye, and our love, everything aboot this ring should be bright and shiny new."

She took a deep breath and tried nae to hyperventilate. "What a delightful surprise, Ian. I love ye so much."

"So ye'll do it? Marry me?" So hopeful, so excited, so perfect. The exact opposite of her.

"Of course I will," she said, while her brain screamed, *are ye crazy? Ye, a pastor's wife?* And, he's already married to God. How is that going to work? And, what if someone from church drives by and sees us?

A million other questions – some quite valid – assaulted her consciousness. She pushed them aside. Her brain was too muddled to process them anyway.

And then Ginger went to Ian, put her paws on his knee and licked his cheek. For the millionth time, she envied Ginger her ability to express how she was feeling. Everything would be so much simpler if she were a dog.

And then she followed her very wise dog's lead. She motioned Ginger to her side so she could sit on Ian's knee, and kiss him.

* * *

Rose had been back in her flat in Glasgow for nearly two weeks and everything was almost back to normal. Kelly called to say that Lyndsie had a school holiday, and asked if Rose would like to drive up to show Lyndsie St. Conan's.

Ian had tea set for them in the courtyard outside the parsonage when they arrived, a cozy bit of lawn surrounded on three sides by ten–foot trellises covered in wild roses. The stems were thorny – some capped in persimmon–colored rose hips and others bursting with new blossoms, singing joyously in the breeze, celebrating their second chance at life before the cold days of winter came.

Rose wrapped her sweater a little more tightly around her shoulders and snuggled back into Ian's cushy patio chairs. Ian had gone inside to brew a fresh pot and dish up some of the dainties the quilters from church had sent home with him the day before.

Kelly looked at her quizzically. "Can we go back to what we were talking aboot in the car for a minute? It's still chipping away at my brain."

"Of course." Rose winked at Lyndsie. "Ye cannae afford to lose any more of yer mind."

"Ha. I'm serious." Kelly looked intense. "I just keep wondering – do ye think God orchestrated the entire thing with Digby to get ye and Ian together?"

"That's a zinger all right." Rose shivered even though there was barely a chill in the air. "I must admit I've been trying to make sense of that, too. And no, I dinnae think God wanted me to do what I did under the flying buttresses." She wondered for a second if she should have said what she did in front of Lyndsie. Kelly had made sure she didnae see the photos that were in the paper, and the sites on the Internet that published the photos were barred from the Morris computer. But Lyndsie knew most of the story anyway. She'd obviously picked up bits of it, overheard here and there – hopefully nothing in graphic detail, but enough to know what they were talking aboot. And really, Rose thought it better that she heard it discussed from an honest perspective than to overhear whatever it was that her enemies or people who didnae know her were saying.

"God didnae want Digby to steal from the church, or to get hurt, or to hurt ye" Lyndsie said.

"No, of course nae. I dinnae think God wishes any of us ill. Digby clearly chose his own path, and paid the price when things didnae go as he planned. And I'm the one who chose to do what I did with Digby. My choice. And I bore the consequences for that, too." She sighed. "Free will and all that it entails."

They were all silent while they pondered the fact that every action has a reaction, and more importantly, a consequence.

"So how do ye think God intended it to happen?" Kelly asked.

"Probably something innocuous like Ian and I bumping into each other as one of us entered and the other exited the church."

"But ye do believe that God wanted ye together, dinnae ye, Aunt Rose?" Lyndsie piped up.

"Oh, yes. When Digby first asked me where we should meet, the thought of St. Conan's sprung into my mind after nae thinking of the place for almost 20 years – I truly believe that was God."

"That is so exciting," Lyndsie said. "I hope God talks to me like that someday."

"I'm sure He will, sweetheart." Her Mum patted her on the arm and gave her a quick squeeze.

"Especially if ye're listening for Him," Rose added. "Some of us are so stubborn and independent and quick to follow our own hearts that we hardly give God a chance. More often than nae, I'm going at it so fast that I forget to stop, stand still and listen. But ye're so smart and clever and eager to know God better that ye'll probably hear him right off."

"Before ye get into any trouble at all," her mum added.

Lyndsie just smiled.

The sun came out from behind a cloud and they basked in the warm light.

Rose put her hand on Lyndsie's arm. "So, Lyndsie, ye are going to tell yer da that I've been a good influence on ye today, are ye nae?"

"Of course, I am."

"And ye'll tell him we talked aboot God at least half the time we were together, and that I had many inspirational things to say?"

Kelly started to giggle. Lyndsie followed suit. Rose was the last to succumb, but when she did, she almost split her side laughing.

"What's all the commotion out there?" Ian leaned his head out the window and started to laugh with them.

It was infectious. In a good way. A very good way.

"Oh, nothing," Rose said. "Just trying to score some points here. As we all know, I'm a wee bit behind."

Lyndsie rolled her eyes and Rose could almost see the pre–teen oozing from her soon–to–be oily pores.

"So are ye going to get married at St. Conan's, Aunt Rose?"

"No." She didnae even hesitate.

Kelly made a face. "Too many bad memories."

"That's part of it. The main thing is that here, in this building, Ian is Pastor Ian. And that's nae who I'm marrying. Right Ian?" she said loudly.

"Right," Ian said from the kitchen.

"Agreeing with everything ye say. See? He is so ready to be a husband." Kelly had a tinge of envy in her voice.

"Do I need to come out there and pray with ye ladies?" Ian called.

"Do ye nae have a sermon to work on?" Rose asked.

Ian's chuckle faded into the walls of the parsonage as he went back to work.

"So the wedding is going to be in Glasgow?"

"No. Tobermory, on the Isle of Mull."

"Oh, how exciting! Will we take the ferry, Mum?"

"I'm sure we will." Kelly sounded hesitant. "If we're invited. Ye're nae going to elope again, are ye?"

"Next thing to." Rose already felt slightly guilty. "It's the only way I can keep the church ladies away. Nae that I havenae forgiven them – I have. But that doesnae mean I want them marring my wedding day. And, I'm afraid one of them will give me one of those crazy "All Inclusive Holiday Quilts" they're famous for, and then, I'll have to hide it away in a dark trash bag, because they absolutely make me nauseous. But I would still have to drag it out whenever we have company from church coming, which could be any time, really, since the parsonage is right next to the church. And before ye know it, it would be on our bed all the time in case one of them should drop by unannounced, and suddenly, we'll find ourselves unable to have – um – marital relations because sleeping under it is so traumatizing, and then one day I'll throw it away, accidentally, of course, because we were storing it in a dark trash bag."

"And then what?" Lyndsie looked mesmerized.

"And then I'll feel guilty for the rest of my life. So ye see, we really cannae have a proper wedding with guests, because nae matter how we handled it, church ladies would be offended." She took another sip of tea. "Or, I would be offended. Either scenario could happen at any time. That's why Ian thinks the more distance he keeps between us, the better."

"So that's why ye're nae going to quilting." Kelly said, looking mollified for the moment, anyway.

"Yes, but they'll think it's because I have guests up from Glasgow, or a dentist's appointment – nae a doctor, lest they think I'm having a late life pregnancy, or wasting away from cancer, or unstable emotionally."

"Dentists are fairly safe when it comes to quelling rumors."

"Although, someone could spread the word around that ye're in need of dental implants, which would make everyone very nervous since they'll eventually be paying for my health and dental insurance."

Kelly started giggling again.

"How I wish I had a sister," Lyndsie said, bringing more peels of laughter from her and Kelly.

"So where are ye getting married in Tobermory? They're quite famous for their weddings, are they nae?"

"We're debating. The options are a quaint Victorian Gothic Church, Parish Church – Ian knows the pastor from seminary – or the lawn at Glengorm Castle. The grass slopes down to the bluest span of sea ye've ever seen, and the rhododendrons are beautiful in the early spring just like they are at St. Conan's."

"Ye're waiting that long then, are ye?"

"Time will tell."

"Do nae tell me there's another debate going on aboot the date?" Kelly smiled sweetly.

"Wouldnae have it any other way," Ian said from the house, where he was evidently listening.

"Ian would prefer sooner. The sooner, the better."

"How aboot tomorrow?" Ian called out from the kitchen.

229

"But I really want a nice wedding, even though it's going to be small. Ye know, a piper, some Tobermory Chocolates with our initials and some sweet little hearts on them, a hand–engraved silver chalice for communion, a wedding cake made to taste and look like a giant Mr. Kipling's Exceedingly Good Battenberg, and flowers. Lots of flowers."

"Wild roses," Ian said. "I can pick ye a bouquet, de–thorn the stems, and have ye at the ferry stop by three if ye'll let me. Kelly and Lyndsie can be our witnesses."

"What aboot my cake?"

"If we swung by Marks & Sparks and bought all the mini–battenbergs they have in stock, we could layer them four wide and eight long and make our own."

"The top would be beautiful decorated with sugared roses. I could dip them in the back seat on a smooth stretch of road," Kelly said.

"Hmmm..." Rose mentally weighed the pros and cons. "The cake would have much more marzipan in it if we went at it that way."

"I'm certain if we called the people at Tobermory Chocolates, they'd have yer sweets all ready for ye by the time ye arrived."

"I'm nae sure we can get a license or a minister by this afternoon," Ian said. "How aboot if I book two rooms at a B&B for tonight so we can be married tomorrow?"

It was all planned then. There was nae reason nae to. It would make Ian happy. Lyndsie would think it was the dreamiest thing ever. The boys wouldnae be there, but they'd be bored stiff sitting through a wedding anyway. Kelly would be at her side. Kevin nae. She and Ian would finally be able to make love, and in little more than 24 hours. What could be more perfect? It was everything she'd ever wanted, was it nae?

She felt, rather than saw, Kelly's eyes on her.

"Lyndsie? Let's take a little stroll so Ian and Rose can talk a wee bit by themselves, shall we? It looks like a lovely walk into the village."

"Sure, Mum." Lyndsie gave a cute little wave and sashayed off with her mum.

Chapter Twenty–Nine

And then, it was just the two of them.

Ian took her hand and looked into her eyes. "Something wrong, Rose? Those pink cheeks of yers that I love so much are suddenly looking a little green."

"I'm fine. Really. It sounds like a delightful plan."

"But..."

"Nae buts. Truly. I couldnae be more thrilled with the way things are coming together. I guess that's one more advantage of marrying a minister that I hadnae thought of."

"I've been helping plan weddings since the time I was ordained."

"Which was when, exactly?"

Ian looked at her quizzically. "Seven years ago."

"Oh, so ye must have waited awhile before going to seminary."

"No. I went as soon as I'd graduated from college."

"Oh, so ye're one of those who took a few years after yer undergraduate schooling to decide what ye wanted to do with yer life."

"No. I knew from the start that I wanted to go into the ministry. Rose – what is this aboot?"

"I dinnae even know how old ye are! And in light of what ye've just revealed, I'm nae sure I want to know any longer."

"I'm 34. My birthday is February 24th."

"Ye're six years younger than me? See, I knew it. There are all kinds of things I dinnae know aboot ye. All kinds of reasons we shouldnae get married."

"Ye married someone twenty years older than yerself. Ye, of all people, should know that true love is blind to age differences."

"Within reason. Older men marry younger woman all the time. It's far more acceptable than a woman marrying a man half her age."

"Ye're making me out to be a teenager!"

"Well, ye practically are in man years! Everyone knows that it takes men decades longer to grow up than their female counterparts."

"I've always been told that I'm quite mature for my age."

"Fine then. But when I'm 60 and ye're 54, I'll look old and haggard and ye'll still look distinguished and dashing. It's a fact that women age much faster than men. And, and, what if ye want a family? I'll be forty in a few months. What if I cannae have a bairn? I'm nae sure if I even want to anymore."

"Rose, are ye really so upset that I'm a bit younger than ye are, or is there something more that's bothering ye?"

She looked away from him then, because she couldnae bear the thought that he might use his magical powers of intuition and understanding to see inside her heart.

"Rose, if ye have objections to getting married, we need to talk aboot them."

"And then what? We cannae live together first to see how we'd get on together, now can we?"

"No. We cannae. But we can continue to date for however long it takes for me to prove to ye how much I love ye."

"I've nae doubt of yer love.

"Tell me what's bothering ye then."

"I've never even met yer mother. After what she's heard aboot me from her cousin, Sally, down at the constable's office, I can almost guarantee ye that she's nae going to think much of the idea of having me for a daughter–in–law. And young as ye are, she's probably right at aboot my age."

"If she was 6 years old when she gave birth," Ian said. "And she'll love ye once she gets to know ye."

"Then what if I dinnae like her?"

Ian sighed. "There's only one way to find out. I'll arrange a meeting with her and my sister as the earliest possible moment."

"Ye have a sister? See?!!!"

"I never told ye aboot Melinda?"

"What else dinnae I know aboot ye?"

"It's going to take us each a lifetime to learn everything there is to know aboot each other. Do ye really want to wait that long before deciding if I'm the right one for ye?"

"Aboot that..."

"Yes?"

For the first time, Ian almost sounded angry. Which, strangely enough, pleased her greatly. The man was so near perfect that she was scared to death of being married to him.

"So what if I'm walking down the isle and I see another Robert? I mean, I think ye'll be just a wonderful husband, but I do have a history of leaving men at the altar–"

"One man. But he was in his kilt–"

"Yes. And a fine sight he was, too. Yet I walked away because someone better came along."

Ian's face was stormy, but he said nothing.

She envied his blind faith, but she hadnae quite arrived at the same place. "So how do ye know, if we each commit ourselves to spending the rest of our lives with each other, that someone even better willnae come along? Like someone who has all of my finer points, but who never seems to get into trouble, and who is loved by the church ladies? Or someone who has all of yer attributes but can also do the pony to Mony Mony?"

"Ye would walk away from me because I'm unable to pony?"

"Of course nae."

"Then why are we talking aboot it?"

"Because we're two very different people, and we have to be sure that we're doing the right thing."

"Well, there's something we can agree on."

"Yes. I definitely agree with ye."

"No, I agree with ye."

They both laughed. And then Ian's face turned seriously cloudy and he said, "It's my turn now."

And her turn to feel a little worried.

"This conversation we're having – the conversations we're always having–"

"Yes?"

"I'm trying to think how to put it." His face was serene, but etched with the effort he was making to formulate his thoughts. "Ye walked away from a man who was perfect for ye on paper to be with yer best friend, the one ye could talk to aboot anything. Robert wasnae right for ye in many ways, including the difference in yer ages and the antagonism of his family, but ye knew that ye were meant for each other because ye could talk aboot anything and everything with each other. Ye could share yer souls."

"Yes."

"And that's why I know we'll be happy together."

"Because we come from different generations and yer family is set to dislike me?"

"No, silly. Because we can talk aboot anything."

They really could, could they nae? She smiled. Warmth flooded over her.

"The very fact that ye feel free to share yer concerns – some bizarre, some zany, some very astute – with me, says that we're where we need to be."

It made sense. Adrenalin raced through her veins. Ian was her new best friend. He wasnae any more perfect for her than Robert had been, but he was, because their souls had connected, because they truly loved each other.

"So there's one other thing, if ye're still listening."

Now he looked worried, and she couldnae blame him one bit.

"This whole thing aboot being a pastor's wife–"

"But we've already talked aboot–"

"I wanted to have one more go at making amends with the church ladies. If I marry ye tomorrow, they'll all be nice to me, but I'll never know if it's because they really like me, or if they're just playing nice because I'm the pastor's wife."

"I suppose that's one possibility."

"Right. And the other one is that they will nae be nice to me even though I'm the pastor's wife. Which would really be frightening."

"So ye'll go to church somewhere else. It would make me sad, of course, but I would understand. I will nae walk away from my calling, but I promise ye that if things cannae be worked out at St. Conan's, that I'll start looking for another congregation straightaway."

"Ye'd do that for me?"

"From now on, it's whatever we decide is best for the both of us."

"I do love ye, Ian. I really do."

"I'll even take dance lessons if that's what ye want. I'd do anything for ye, Rose. Ye have to know that."

"As long as it's nae illegal."

He laughed. "Yes. Been there. Done that. Nae a good idea."

"The wedding's still on then?"

"If ye'll have me."

She smiled. "I will."

Ian kissed her then. And it wasnae the kiss of a best friend. Although it had elements of trust, and overtones of that comfortable feeling ye get when ye put on yer favorite sweatshirt. It was pure passion – a hot, sizzling, let's get naked right now, kind of kiss. The only reason they stopped was because Kelly and Lyndsie were suddenly back from their walk and they had three church ladies in tow.

* * *

This was really the way to get off on a fresh footing with them, was it nae, with her lipstick smudged and her hair all askew and her dress twisted from all the groping they'd been doing. "Um, hello."

Kelly took in her appearance and Ian's rumpled look and said, "Is this a bad time? Because we can go on another walk."

But the church lady who headed up the procession evidently felt it was now or never, because she plowed on ahead. "I'm sorry we misjudged ye, Rose," she said, all the while looking like she was thinking, *It appears we were right all along.*

Rose patted a stray hair out of her eyes. "Nae need to apologize. Ye really didnae misjudge me. Ye just saw the true me, instead of the trumped up, perfect image I – all of us, really – usually like to project."

"Right. Which of us have nae done something we regret?" the second of the church ladies said, looking like she was thinking, *ah yes, but none of us has gone as far as Rose did. I mean, ye simply cannae put my little lies of omission on the same level as her romp under the flying buttresses.*

"I'd be ashamed to tell ye some of the things I've done in my years," the third admitted.

And Rose wanted to scream, because her sin was probably another doozy like the man who'd confessed to scratching the copper rabbit downspout when he was cleaning out the gutters at St. Conan's.

The first of the delegation nodded and said, "I've heard say that when we dare to show people our true selves, including our vulnerable spots, that it only makes us more dear and loveable to those who know us."

The second took the ball and ran with it, patting her friend on the arm. "I'm sure that's why everyone loves ye so much, dear. Ye're a bit like Princess Diana, are ye nae? Flawed as she was, people adored her."

"So ye're saying that it's a good thing Rose was– um– in the papers, because now she's going to be more dear to people...?" Kelly said.

"Dinnae make me out to be so noble," Rose said, finally finding her voice. "It's nae like I was so brave and daring that I didnae mind being exposed – notoriety was forced on me against my will."

"Yes," Kelly said, slowly and succinctly, like she was imagining the finish line in her head and trying to figure out how to get there. "But I'm sure ye feel more cherished than ye did before all this happened. Right, Rose?"

"Certainly."

"Well, there's that then," the last of the women said.

The garden fell quiet, and a calm, almost boring sense of stability filled the walls, in a good sort of way of course.

"So it's all settled then?" Ian asked.

"Yes. Oh, yes. Definitely," they murmured collectively.

And for once, even Ian looked bewildered.

Chapter Thirty

An hour later, they'd arranged for a piper to play the postlude at Parish Church the next day at half past two in the afternoon. The pastor who was going to marry them was a friend of Ian's from seminary, and had kindly offered the praise team to provide music for the vows and processional, seeing as they always practiced at that time anyway. Ian choose "How Deep the Father's Love for Us", "10,000 Reasons", and "Lord, Reign in Me" from their repertoire, which was fine with her.

And when she said, "If God is going to be an integral part of our relationship and yer life's calling, then He might as well be included from the start."

Ian beamed.

Tobermory Chocolates had been called upon to make hand dipped delicacies for a small reception dinner, which was to be held at a newly refurbished pub called the Bluebell. A photographer had been engaged to insure they'd have remembrances of the day, and all was in place. A local florist agreed to make her a nosegay of pink roses.

Ian was on his mobile with the ticket order for the ferry company in Oban. A few seconds later, he nodded to confirm that their spots were reserved for the last crossing that night. He'd already reserved two rooms for two nights at a pet–friendly B&B and confirmed that the registrar's office would be open long enough for them to get their marriage license when they arrived in Oban.

"I've nothing to wear!" They were almost ready to go when the realization hit her.

Kelly's face fell.

Lyndsie's eyebrows scrunched up. "None of us do."

"How could we have forgotten something so important?"

They'd driven up expecting to spend the day. They hadnae packed so much as a fresh pair of skivvies.

"My kilt is at the ready," Ian said.

"Well, is that nae nice," Kelly said, making a face at him. "And I'm sure a dashing groom ye'll be. But we cannae have the groom looking more bonny than the bride, now can we?"

"T'would never be. Rose is the fairest flower in the garden nae matter what she has on."

"Or doesnae," Rose said. Someone had to.

They all had a laugh, but really, what was she going to do? "Do we have time to run back to Glasgow before we go to Oban?"

Ian looked at his wristwatch. "There's nae way we'd make it to the ferry on time."

"Is there a dress agency in Tobermory?" Kelly asked.

Ian did a quick search on his mobile. "None in Tobermory. But here's a dresswear hire in Oban. Geoffrey Highland Crafts on MacGregor Court." He punched a few more buttons. "Sorry. They'll be closed by the time we can get there. Here's another though, Ruche – A Vintage Inspired Bridal Collection. Will nae work either. Every dress a custom made creation just for ye."

"Wait," Kelly said, peeking around Ian's shoulders to see the screen. "Look at that one. If I just had a little lace, or some organdy, I could make an overlay just like in the picture."

"That one", Lyndsie said, looking on from the other side. "It would be perfect over the dress Rose is wearing."

"She's right," Kelly said. "I'd have to undo the bodice to tuck in the overskirt, but it would be beautiful on ye, Rose."

"But where would we find lace at the last minute?"

Ian looked sheepish, but finally spoke up. "If it's nae too cheeky a suggestion – think Scarlett using the drapes at Tara like in *Gone with the Wind* – I have a couple of my grandmother's old lace table clothes in a chest in the dining room. My mother said there'd be occasions when a pastor – even a single one – would be expected to entertain guests."

Kelly squealed. "Sounds perfect. Let's have a look." And she and Ian went rushing into the house.

Rose just smiled and looked at Lyndsie.

"Dinnae ye want to see, Aunt Rose?"

"Nae really. I'm fine with whatever yer mother comes up with just as long as I dinnae have to sew it."

"But ye're a wonderful seamstress. Ye made my pretty pillows all by yerself, didnae ye?"

"Yes. Of course I did. I mean, I picked out the fabric and the ribbons, and envisioned them in my mind, and worked up the design. But..."

Lyndsie smiled, unsuspecting.

"As long as I'm turning over a new leaf here." Rose paused and weighed her options. "Okay. Out with it. I started to do the actual sewing and damaged my machine so severely that it couldnae be repaired. So I hired the lady from Corrie Bank B&B to finish the job."

"It's fine with me," Lyndsie said, "but Aunt Rose, ye really must nae tell Mum."

"Wise words, young lady. It can be our secret, then."

Lyndsie lifted her hand and linked her pinkie finger with Rose's.

A few minutes later, her niece went to see what her Mum and Ian were up to, and Rose was left to her own devises.

Which was fine with her. The world was spinning a little too quickly at the moment, and she needed time to think.

All she really wanted to do was to put the past behind her and get on with it. A fresh start. A clean slate. Why she hadnae thought of it that way before was a mystery, because it was clearly what she needed.

"Aunt Rose, Ian said we should pack some of his shirts to sleep in while we're in Tobermory," Lyndsie called out from the house.

"Good idea. I'll be in in a minute. Did he say which drawer he keeps them in?"

So the thing was, marrying Ian was just brill. First and foremost, she loved him with all her heart. And, although secondary, a nice side benefit would be that once she was married to Ian, her name would be different, her address would be different, her daily (and nightly) routines would be different – everything aboot her would be different.

"Aunt Rose, Mum says ye need to put on one of Ian shirts right now so she can work on yer dress in the car. And Ian said ye can borrow a pair of his running shorts. He says the elastic is tight enough on them that they shouldnae fall down."

There was silence for a few minutes and then she heard the door clanking shut. Or open.

The most wonderful thing was that once she was married to Ian, she'd be a whole new person. She'd be a floundering widow nae more, but a wife – a purposeful pastor's wife. As such, she'd have a proper mission, and people would look up to her. She'd be respectable, respected. And nae one would think she'd married Ian for his money, now would they, since he didnae have any to speak of. She'd be poor. Her connections to the Wilson's would be severed once and for all – nae reason she couldnae continue to help others through the foundations – but her personal ties would cease to exist. She'd be penniless, but happy. It all sounded so wonderful.

She was rooting through Ian's drawers for something suitable when she heard the door again.

"Rose?" Kelly's voice echoed from the front of the house.

"I'm back here changing."

"Ian said I could wear some of his things, too. I've been doing some cutting and measuring over at the church and there's enough lace for me to fancy up my dress a little, too."

"Great. I'm glad we at least wore dresses."

"Yes. Good thing Ian suggested treating Lyndsie to a fancy tea party or I'm sure we would have worn jeans."

She showed Kelly where Ian's shirts and running shorts were. She picked out a matching pair and started to strip down.

"Is Ian still over at the church?"

"He and Lyndsie are looking through the quilting cupboards for some needles and thread for yer dress. I even found some pretty ribbon and an old hat that I can adapt for a headpiece for yer hair."

It was all so perfect, the way things were working out. Despite all her troubles, she'd never been happier.

Kelly had just slipped out of her dress when they heard a mobile ringing in the next room.

"Yers or mine?"

"Mine," said Kelly. "I left my purse on the kitchen table. I should get it, too. I called Kevin a few minutes ago and told him to call as soon as possible. I need to tell him what's going on and that Lyndsie and I will nae be home for a couple of days."

"Better run, then. Who knows what the reception will be like between here and Oban."

"But I'm in my skivvies."

"Just go. Nae one's here but us."

Kelly dashed off to answer the call. Hopefully Ian would stay at the church at least for a few more minutes.

And then, her mobile rang. Thankfully, she had hers in her pocket.

"Ms. Wilson?"

"Yes?"

"Please hold for Scotland Yard."

"What on earth?"

She was put on hold and forced to listen to Handel's Water Music for a few seconds. She had just decided to hang up and finish getting dressed when someone picked up, and asked to speak to Rose Wilson.

They both identified themselves. There was an awkward silence.

"Ms. Wilson, I hate to be the bearer of bad news, but yesterday some trekkers discovered a body in an old farmhouse up in the high country, and preliminary findings indicate that the deceased was a friend of yers."

Her heart thudded in her chest.

"Ma'am, we have it on good authority that ye were the last person seen with Digby Bentworth, and that, in fact, ye may have been the last person to see him alive. We'd like to ask ye a few questions."

A million emotions ran though her head like a video on slow rewind. Thankfulness that she was still alive. Regret. Could she have done anything different, something to prevent Digby's death? Fear that whoever these horrid men were, they might still come after her. She felt pity. She'd wanted Digby captured. She took nae joy in his death. For a second, she thought she might be ill.

"I cannae," she stammered. "I'd like to help, but I'm getting married tomorrow, and there are a million things to do before we catch the ferry. I'd be happy to contact ye when we return."

"I'm nae sure ye understand, Ms. Wilson. This is a murder investigation. My supervisor has requested that ye be in Edinburgh tomorrow morning at ten sharp. If ye'd like to bring yer barrister–"

She thought she heard a noise and instinctively clutched her free hand to her breasts. "My barrister?" she whispered. She didnae want Kelly to hear. And a barrister? Whatever did they need to speak to him aboot? She'd told them what happened while she had been held captive several dozen times. While she felt horrible to think that Digby had been murdered, his turning up dead didnae change anything that had happened. "I'm so sorry. Please tell yer boss that

I'll be in touch as soon as I return from my honeymoon."

She clicked her mobile shut and dressed as quickly and as quietly as she could.

* * *

Ian needed to pack a few things but Rose and Kelly were in the house and Kelly didnae have much on in the way of clothing if he was to understand correctly. He was told that Rose had on Kelly's dress so Kelly could pin things which she planned on sewing in the car on the way to Oban, and on the ferry if the seas were calm.

He could hear Lyndsie oohing and aahing and making suggestions on where to pin the lace. Although he was tempted to tell them they needed to hurry so they didnae miss the ferry, he'd also wanted a moment to ring up his Mum and this seemed like it was the right time. The garden was quiet and the scent of the pink roses climbing up his fence by the gate cloyed with his senses.

His mum answered her mobile. "Oh, sweetheart, I'm so glad to hear from ye. Ye've been so scarce lately."

"Sorry, Mum. I've been–"

"I know. Ye've been busy. Always so busy."

"And how do ye think I got to be the way I am? Ye certainly never let any grass grow under yer feet."

"That was then. Truth is, I've gotten lazy in my old age."

Ian laughed. His mother might be slowing down a little, but she could still run circles around most people half her age.

"Mum. I'm calling for a reason, and I dinnae have much time." He often called for nae reason, but today...

"I'm sorry, sweetie. Go ahead."

"Mum, I'm getting married."

"Ye are?"

"I know it's a bit of a shock."

"Ye've never mentioned..."

"Her name is Rose." He purposely didnae mention her last name. His mother never watched the telly, and wasnae tremendously computer savvy, but she was on Facebook and she knew how to Google things when she had reason to. The last thing he needed was for his mother's first impressions of Rose to be what had been documented in the national rags.

242

"Have ye known her long?"

"No. A few months. But I know – I mean, I'm absolutely sure. She's wonderful, Mum. Ye're going to love her."

"I hope to get to meet her soon. Have ye set a date?"

This was going to be hard. "It's a long story, Mum. And I will tell ye all aboot it one day. But I dinnae have time to talk now."

"And why is that?" His mother was a smart woman, and she knew him well.

"We're leaving for Tobermory in a few minutes. I'm sorry I dinnae have time to explain. And I promise I'll make it up to ye later. But for now–"

"Ye're eloping?"

"I'll tell ye all aboot it as soon as we're back. Until then – just dinnae say anything to Melinda. Awrite?"

"But, Ian, ye know she's going to–"

"That's why ye're nae to say a word."

Chapter Thirty–One

Rose awoke to the smell of rashers and bangers and Kelly's perfume. Lyndsie had slept on the floor, and she and Kelly had each had a twin. Tonight, she would be sharing the double bed in Ian's room with him. She couldnae wait.

Lyndsie was stirring but nae quite awake. Kelly was still sound asleep – she'd probably been up half the night finishing their wedding dresses. They'd all slept in old shirts of Ian's so that the underwear they'd worn the day before could be rinsed out and hung to dry overnight.

She looked up at the dress Kelly had altered for her to wear as a wedding gown, hanging on the closet door. It truly was a thing of beauty, and just one more bit of proof that everything was going to be fine.

She pushed the call from Scotland Yard out of her brain for the hundredth time since she'd received it. She hadnae mentioned it to anyone. Why mar an otherwise perfect occasion? There would be plenty of time to deal with Scotland Yard when she returned.

She heard a rustling noise and turned to see a news paper being eased in under the door. Nae that she cared aboot the news. Who worried aboot what was going on in the world on yer wedding day?

She decided to jump into the shower before Lyndsie and Kelly woke up. If she waited, they'd probably be all queued up wanting to use the loo at the same time.

Warm water was streaming down her shoulders when she heard Lyndsie scream.

* * *

"It's horrible!" Lyndsie sobbed.

Rose looked at Ian helplessly and glanced from him to the newspaper on the edge of the bed. So much for nae seeing the bride before the wedding. Her hair was wet from her attempted shower, and she was wrapped in a bath towel. Kelly was still in one of Ian's shirts, her bare legs tucked under her, and her arms around Lyndsie. The headline read 'Merry Widow At It Again. St. Conan's Romp, Act II.' A picture of a woman whom everyone would assume was her, in her skivvies, this time, in the kitchen of Ian's house, topped the article.

Except that it wasnae her.

Ian scratched his head. "I dinnae understand how they could have... I mean, I know a skilled person can do wonders with Photoshop, but how on earth..."

"Nobody photo–shopped anything. Kelly and I were in yer bedroom, slipping out of our dresses so Kelly could do her magic with the lace tablecloths when her phone rang. They must have been waiting outside the kitchen window."

"Okay, then. That much, we know. But all this hoopla aboot Digby has to be–"

"How could they?" Kelly moaned. "Kevin is going to kill me."

"It's nae like ye were doing anything wrong," Rose said. "Ye were talking to him."

"Now I know how ye must have felt."

Lyndsie sniffled. "But Mum, nobody will even know it's ye if ye dinnae tell them."

"Yer father had better recognize me."

"But I thought ye didnae want him to know."

"I dinnae know what I want." Kelly burst into tears.

"At least ye had on a matching set of lingerie. And pink lace at that. It's a beautiful set."

Which the church ladies were going to think were hers. Which was nothing compared to the probability that they were going to assume that she'd been seducing their precious pastor and leading him astray just like she had young Torey MacDougall.

"It will be fine, Kelly. Are ye nae glad ye lost that last ten pounds ye've been trying to get off?" *At least they didnae see yer bare bahookie*, Rose thought, but didnae say. "It's really a very flattering photo."

"But I'm a mother! What if the boys see it? And that pink lace is so pale it almost looks as though I'm naked." She grabbed the newspaper and rattled it in Rose's direction. "It's one thing for ye to be photographed in the nude. It's quite another–"

"Ladies, please," Ian said. "Let's try to calm down and get our bearings. We will get through this. As we've so graphically learned in the past few months, there are plenty of worse things that could happen."

And sadly, it appeared that one of them already had. Because Rose's / Kelly's revealing photo wasnae the only thing in the paper. Under the first headline, in slightly smaller letters, was more breaking news. 'Wilson Widow's Lover Couldn't Take the Heat. Body Found Stashed in Secret Hideaway.'

"What are we going to do?" Her voice eked out, half wail, half nails. She was mad all right. "They make it sound like the man keeled over because he couldnae handle the heat of having – um – been with me." The article was very lurid. "And the implication that the ropes at the cottage where I was held captive were used to tie me up while I participated in, um, certain games. It's ludicrous is what it is."

"So," Ian said. "We've established how the mishap with Kelly occurred. But all this mess with Digby is quite another thing entirely. How on earth–"

Three sets of eyes turned on her.

"Aboot the same time Kevin called Kelly, Scotland Yard rang me up to inform me that Digby's body had been found. I assume from their description, at the same house where I was held captive."

"But ye didnae say a word aboot any of this." Ian's voice sounded strained.

Which was exactly what she had tried so hard to avoid. "I just wanted our wedding day to be perfect."

"So, what else did the man from Scotland Yard say?" Ian said, with a what–other–tidbits–have–ye–nae–told–me look in his eyes.

"Nothing that cannae wait until we get back from our honeymoon."

"Rose."

"Just that they wanted to talk to me, and that I could bring my barrister with me if I wanted to."

"That doesnae sound good," Kelly said.

"Are ye a suspect?" Ian looked worried, which really wasnae good.

"It's ridiculous is what it is," Rose said. "First they think I'm in cahoots with the man. Now they think I killed him? Make up their minds is what I wish they'd do."

"What is wrong with these people?" Kelly looked almost as irate as she felt. "Ye're one of the most truthful people I know. And when ye make a mistake, ye take responsibility for yer actions and do the honorable thing."

"I certainly try." *Dinnae go there,* Rose pleaded silently. *Please – just – do – nae – go – there.* Because it was one thing, hiding the truth from an unsuspecting person, when ye knew that telling them what really happened would only hurt them, and ye. But it was quite another thing to come right out and lie aboot it. Especially when yer impressionable niece was looking on.

"Like when Ginger ate Lyndsie's pillows. Ye were going to buy her some new ones, but when I insisted ye replace them with handmade pillows, because of all the work I'd put it to them, ye got out yer sewing machine and made them yerself." Kelly beamed at her proudly. "And I know sewing is nae yer favorite thing to do."

"Well, yes." Now what was she going to do? "Aye. I did get out my sewing machine. And aye, I did replace the lovely handmade pillows that Ginger ate with pillows that were also handmade."

"With yer own two hands," Kelly said. "And didnae it make ye feel good to sit down and sew them, knowing how much Lyndsie would cherish them because she knew they were made by her own dear auntie?"

Lyndsie was giving her a look – a very fearful look. *Dinnae do it, Aunt Rose... Trust me on this. Ye really must nae...*

Ian was staring holes through her, too. *What was that aboot?* She'd specifically asked the woman who had sewn the pillows nae to mention it to Ian. *Their little secret.* The woman had promised.

"Okay! Okay! I didnae make the pillows. I bought the fabric, and the ribbons and the trim, and designed each one, and tried to sew them. I really did. But my machine broke. And I couldnae fix it. And if I had bought another machine just to make three or four pillows, it would have been so wasteful. And as ye know, Grandmum taught us always to be frugal."

Kelly was moving toward her now, her face a mask of fury.

Rose backed away, trying to explain. "And if I had borrowed someone else's machine, I probably would have broken it, too, and then what would I have done? Grandmum always said that's why ye should never borrow things in the first place, because they always get broken!"

"Dinnae ye go bringing Grandmum into this, Mary Ann Rosalie McCullen Wilson. Why if she were here, she'd wash yer mouth out with soap right this minute. And she'd tell ye the story of Pinocchio again and again until ye could repeat it by memory. And, she'd send ye to bed without supper." And then, Kelly burst into tears once again. "Rose, I swear I will never ever be able to believe a single thing that comes out of yer mouth, ever again. Maybe ye did murder that man. How would we know? We cannae believe anything ye say." And she dissolved into more sobs.

For once, even Ian seemed nae to know what to do.

"Dinnae look at me," Rose told him. "Ye're the one who's trained in counseling."

"Maybe Kevin is right." Kelly's whole body was racked with tears.

"So just volunteer to throw the switch on the electric chair, why dinnae ye?"

"I told ye." Lyndsie said. "Dinnae tell my Mum. Those were my exact words."

Rose sucked in a breath and held it. She could hear the hiss of air as Ian briefly did the same.

"Ye've had a very hard start to the day, Kelly," Ian said in his most soothing, pastoral voice. "The photos, the paper. It's all getting to ye."

And then the damn broke. Kelly's face turned an uncomplimentary shade of purple. "Lyndsie knew? Now ye're using my innocent daughter to cover up yer lies? And asking her to lie to her own mother so yer sins will nae be found out? For shame, Rose. For shame. What would mum say if she knew?"

"Oh, good grief." Rose had finally had enough. "This is supposed to be the happiest day of my life."

Ian just shook his head. "I didnae know Scottish people behaved this way."

"I know." Lyndsie's eyes were wide. "It's like that movie – *Big Fat Greek Wedding* – except that we're nae Greek."

"Maybe we should be," Rose said. "Because then I could throw something against the wall and break it."

"Our heirloom china from three generations back, I suppose?" Kelly huffed. "Grandmum would roll over in her grave if she could hear ye now."

"Oh, no, she wouldnae. Grandmum would say, 'Crying is for sissies, and ye need to get up and wash those silly tears off yer face right now and march right in there and stand up for yer sister and act like ye love her even if ye dinnae.'"

Kelly made a face at her. And it wasnae pretty.

"And Grandmum would say, 'Stop making that face unless ye want it to freeze that way,'" Rose added.

"Or 'Ye'll look that way for the rest of yer life,'" Lyndsie said. "Mum has only told me that aboot a million times."

"Ladies, we are going to be late getting to the church if we dinnae finish getting dressed and hurry on over to meet Pastor Fergus."

"Fergus, schmergus," Rose said. "I want an apology."

"Well, ye're nae getting it." Kelly glared at her.

"Well, I am going to go to my room to put on my kilt." Ian's face looked nae like that of an eager groom, but like a man who was suffering from a severe headache.

"Now see what ye've done?" Rose stormed back into the loo, slammed the door behind her, dropped her towel and resumed her shower before anyone could say another word.

* * *

If Ian had seen the thorny side of his beautiful Rose that morning, he was aboot to get a glimpse of the most beautiful flower in the garden.

"Dear Lord." He was bowed down on a kneeling stool at Parish Church, looking up at the intricate stained glass. The midday sun streamed through the window facing east and flooded his soul with every color of the rainbow. God's promise.

"Lord, I felt an incredible sense of peace as soon as I woke up, and again, when I walked into yer House. Even with everything Rose and I have already been through on this fine morning, I feel very strongly that I'm right where ye want me to be, and that marrying Rose is exactly what ye want me to do with the rest of this day.

"I'm nae so sure aboot Rose. Lord, please give her a sign, something tangible that will assure her of yer love for her, and mine, despite all the bad things that have happened to her in the last few months. Amen."

He stayed on his knees until he heard the clatter of the praise band starting to arrive. Pastor Fergus had called them the night before to let them know that they'd been asked to take part in an impromptu wedding. He could hear the excitement and jubilation in their voices as they entered the sanctuary.

All was well then, at least he hoped so. He'd eaten his breakfast in the dining room at Brockhurst, and taken the liberty to request the remaining breakfasts be sent to the ladies' room on trays to be enjoyed at their leisure, which was probably wishful thinking on his part, having been witness to at least part of what had transpired in their room earlier that morning.

Then, he'd hiked down the hill to walk along the harbor, where he'd seen his first rainbow of the day in the brightly colored array of shops and pubs lining water's edge in Tobermory, reflecting down in the calm water of the bay. He'd ducked under an awning while a quick shower passed overhead, and seen the second a few minutes later when the sun came out to chase the clouds away – hopefully for good. But most likely, nae.

He doubted Rose had seen the rainbow, although it might have been visible from the window of their rooms at the B&B. *Lord, give her a sign that ye love her, that ye're with her, and that a life with me is what ye intend,* he prayed again, this time silently. He didnae pray that God's Will would be done, because he already felt complete assurance that things were working out exactly the way God had intended them – despite the obstacles that seemed always to be in their path. That was life, was it nae? Rocky, winding pathways, just like the sometimes perilous roadways Scotland was famous for. Nae wonder his homeland had bred men and women of such strong faith.

He saw a man in black enter the rear of the sanctuary and assumed it was Pastor Fergus. He looked a bit taller than he remembered, but it had been years since he's seen him, and then, they'd been students together rather than close, personal friends.

He was halfway down the center aisle before he confirmed that the man was indeed nae Pastor Fergus. By the time he would have reacted and slowed his approach, the man was upon him and flashing a badge. Scotland Yard.

Lord, give me strength, he prayed again, and nae for the first time that week. "Can I help ye?"

250

"I'm looking for a Rose Wilson," the man said. "Her name was on the ferry manifest from late yesterday, and I'm told she's to be married sometime today."

"Yes," he stammered, a sense of foreboding trampling his high spirits like a Shetland pony forging a new path through a virgin field of grass.

"Ye the pastor?"

He wasnae wearing his collar, but he supposed he still had the look. "No. Today, I'm the groom."

"Oh, my apologies – I mean, congratulations, then." The man extended his hand to shake his. "She looks to be a beautiful woman."

"Yes," Ian said. The man would have seen the photos, he supposed, and probably the tape as well. "So what can I help ye with?"

"Ms. Wilson was asked to be in Edinburgh this morning."

"Today is her wedding day."

"The invitation wasnae so much a request for her presence as a summons." The man's eyes took on a menacing look. "Declining to appear was nae an option. As was made clear, she was expected to be there."

"So, she's what? A fugitive fleeing from justice because she wanted to honor her commitment to be married?"

"Basically, yes."

At least the man had enough sense to look chagrinned.

"And what is yer mission, then? To bring her back to Edinburgh?"

"Precisely. I have a warrant for her arrest."

Chapter Thirty–Two

A surge of heat coursed from Ian's heart to his head. "Ye plan to jail Rose on her wedding day?"

"That will be determined based on the results of the interview."

He struggled to maintain his composure. Being antagonistic would nae help Rose's case. "Is there nae way ye could conduct yer interview at the constable's office here in Tobermory? I mean, ye are already here, and it is our wedding day, and we do have other plans in mind for this evening."

The man looked at him, taking in his kilt and his cummerbund, his knee socks and his tassels as if judging his sincerity, his trustworthiness, his intentions. What he saw must have convinced him. "I supposed that could be arranged."

"Wait in the narthex then, if ye must. The wedding is at two. Hopefully she'll assume ye're one of the musicians or someone on staff at the church. I'd rather she didnae – I'd rather we were allowed to conduct our vows..."

"I understand."

"I appreciate yer consideration." Even his voice sounded stiff.

The next thing he saw was Pastor Fergus approaching them. The agent took his leave before the Pastor joined them. Hopefully, he would assume the man was part of the wedding party and wouldnae ask for an explanation.

"Bit of a rough morning, I presume," the pastor said, gripping his hand with one arm and his shoulder with the other.

So he'd seen the photos in the newspaper and put two and two together. "More than ye know," Ian admitted.

"I regret nae having time for premarital counseling," the pastor replied. "Under normal conditions, I insist upon it, but seeing as ye're a pastor, I assume..."

"Thank ye." He didnae know what else to say. "I'm sure we would have made an interesting case study."

"I'm sure." The man smiled. "Maybe another time."

"Yes," Ian said. "We love Tobermory. Perhaps on a future visit."

"I guess I didnae mention that this is my last week at Parish Church. I've accepted a call at St. Cuthbert's in Edinburgh. My wife and I have loved it here, but the Ministries Council thought I was ready for a larger congregation and recommended me for the position."

An honor Ian could safely assume would never be bestowed upon him given his recent go round with his overseer. "Congratulations."

"They're a wonderful group of folks." Pastor Fergus nodded at a cluster of musicians, who began playing quietly in the background. "I wish I could say I was leaving them in the capable hands of another minister, but ye know how that goes. It can be hard to find someone willing to accept a call on one of the outer islands. Everyone loves visiting for a fortnight, but living in such a remote place is nae for everyone, especially come winter."

The blazing heat that had burned through his consciousness a few minutes earlier was replaced by an electric zing akin to a shock. "We'll have to pray aboot it then, will we nae?" He choked back tears. "I mean, that God will send the right one to shepherd them."

"Thanks. Speaking of, has the bride arrived?"

"Um, no. Not yet." He'd left a generous tip and the keys to Rose's car with the host at their B&B and asked the gent to bring the ladies round at the proper time, which was – he glanced at his wristwatch – five minutes ago. Nae need to panic. He'd allowed plenty of time before the ceremony was scheduled to begin.

Ten minutes later, he was congratulating himself on remaining calm, because there was still nae sign of Rose.

Pastor Fergus crossed the length of the church to speak to him again. "I think I'll tell the praise team to start in on the songs ye requested. If they end up having to repeat them, they'll thank ye – all the more practice for them."

"Certainly. I dinnae wish to detain them or ye. I'm sure Rose will be here momentarily." He glanced to the rear of the sanctuary to make sure their friendly representative from Scotland Yard was still accounted for. He was.

"Wait," he said to Pastor Fergus. The two of them talked. He filled the good Pastor in on a few facts. A tentative plot was hatched. Of course, at this point, everything was contingent on Rose. His plan would be a moot point if she didnae show up soon. Where was she? He pulled out his mobile and checked to see if she'd left a message. None. Had being in Tobermory stirred up memories of her wedding to Robert? Had she changed her mind?

I do have a history of leaving men at the altar.

So this is how Torey must have felt standing in the front of St. Conan's, in his kilt, Ian thought, except that poor Torey had had the whole church looking on, and family and friends whose opinions mattered.

Rose's words rang in his ears like a train whistling as it approached a busy intersection.

Could someone have tipped her off, told her there was a man from Scotland Yard waiting to apprehend her as soon as the ceremony was done?

He waited a few more minutes and tried to ring her up on his mobile. Nae answer. He started to pace. Pace, nae panic. He'd never before realized that the words were so similar. He searched through his recently dialed numbers, found the number of the B&B, and tried to ring them up. Nae answer.

He paced some more. The man from Scotland Yard had watched him very closely while he'd had his mobile to his ear. If he left to try to find Rose, he'd nae doubt deduce that it was part of some hastily planned escape from justice. He would just have to be patient.

Another five minutes passed. Pastor Fergus was pacing now. Probably wondering why he'd ever agreed to get involved in such a mess. The praise team was carrying on with their music as though nothing was askew. If only they knew.

Why could he nae do the same?

Nae need for alarm. Keep calm. Carry on. It was what he, as a pastor, would tell a groom in a similar position. But how in God's name was he supposed to carry on when his bride had gone missing?

"Ian!" He turned and saw Rose running down the aisle, her nosegay clutched in her hand, the lace from his Grandmother's tablecloth clinging to her and trailing behind her, a vision of loveliness.

"God spoke to me again, Ian! I've had an epiphany."

"He did? Ye have?" His heart pounded in his chest.

"I've been out in the car. And I just couldnae think. Kelly has been at me nonstop aboot those pillows. Says if my machine really was broken – like I would make up such a thing – I should have sewed them by hand, like she did my dress – which may sound simple enough to her, but–"

"And yer epiphany?"

"Oh yes. Well, there I was, sitting in my car, listening to Kelly's caterwauling, unable to stand it for a second longer, but for some strange reason, unable to get out of the car. It was like I was paralyzed, ye know?"

"I'm sure ye were," Ian said.

"And then, I started to pray, *Lord, if ye're listening, give me one reason, just one, that I should nae kill my sister...*" She laughed.

Ian hoped the man from Scotland Yard hadnae heard.

"Dinnae go all queasy on me now. I'm just teasing. What I really prayed was, *Lord, give me one reason, just one single reason I should walk into that church and marry Ian MacCraig, when ye and I both know that I'm the most miserable wretch there is, and completely unworthy of yer love or his.* I was really at my wit's end. Ye know?"

"Yes, dear, I know."

She kissed him then, so hard that it almost didnae matter what kind of epiphany she'd had.

"And suddenly I found the strength to get out of the car, and walk in, and all the way, I'm still praying, *Just give me one good reason* and then, suddenly, I heard the song they were playing, and–"

"What song?"

"Ye didnae hear it? Ye, standing right here?" She started to sing, "You're rich in love and you're slow to anger. Your name is great and your heart is kind. For all your goodness, I will keep on singing. 10,000 reasons for my heart to find."

As if on cue, his ears were opened and he could hear the praise team joining in on the chorus of what he knew to be Matt Redman's 10,000 Reasons. He had nae doubt that it was probably the first time Rose had heard it. "Bless the Lord, oh my soul – Oh my soul. Worship his holy name. Sing like never before – Oh my soul. I worship your holy name."

Coincidence? He thought nae. And the timing? That could be nae other than God answering his prayers – and Rose's. Perfectly.

* * *

Kelly and Lyndsie finally appeared. Although Kelly was still noticeably peeved, her scowls became less frequent, probably because it was hard to be unhappy when the worship team was singing so beautifully. After a quick conference with the pastor, he and Rose walked down the aisle to *How Deep the Father's Love For Us.*

When it was time for them to say their vows, Pastor Fergus said, "Please repeat after me."

And Rose said, "If ye dinnae mind, I'd rather nae."

Ian's first thought was, always the picture of politeness. His second, *why am I nae surprised?* "Did ye have something different in mind, dear, or have ye changed yer mind aboot marrying me?"

"Of course nae, silly."

He smiled down at her and adjusted the pouch of his kilt. "Did ye write yer own vows?"

"No, but I've always been good at extemporaneous speech."

"Very well, then. Whenever ye're ready."

Rose gave her hair a little fluff – right in the front, in just the way he'd come to love, and smiled. "Ian, I'm sure ye'll say it much better than I when it's yer turn, but I am forever thankful that ye've come to love me and continued to love me even when I've been at my most unlovable. It's called grace, and ye've obviously learned it from the Master.

"But I'm nae here today because I feel gratitude towards ye. Yes, I love ye because ye're my hero, my defender and my knight in shining armor, but I really love ye because ye listen to every word I say – even when I'm rambling. I love ye because ye treat me with respect nae matter how wild I might act, and ye never back away from me, nae matter how prickly things get. Ye're my best friend. And, ye're the hottest thing in a kilt since Sean Connery, and ye make me feel like smiling all of the time. And the fact that I love ye enough to marry ye even though ye're a terrible dancer says something, too, dinnae ye think?

"Ian, the only thing I worry aboot – even though ye've tried to reassure me near ten thousand times – is that I'm going to be a smudge on yer good name." She looked around the room as though it encompassed the entire world. "Well, if we're honest aboot it, and I think we need to be, given our location and the company we're in, I already have been. So I guess that's where the better and worse part comes into play for ye. For me, well, I'm sure I'll eventually discover one or two things aboot ye that are nae perfect, and I promise ye, I will love ye through and in spite of all of them."

She winked at him and whispered. "Am I forgetting anything?"

Kelly leaned forward and whispered in her ear.

"Oh. Right – O."

Rose leaned forward and spoke directly to Ian. "And ye have my vow of faithfulness, even if someone more perfect than ye comes along. Which is hard to imagine. But if it should happen, rest assured that I will nae even look. Well, actually, I might. But I would never act on anything inappropriate. Although I might share a dance with the man if he's a good dancer, and only if we were in Glasgow or Edinburgh where nae one from St. Conan's would see us. But ye'll still be my husband and my only lover from here on out – forever – unless one of us dies first, which I certainly hope doesnae happen anytime soon."

Kelly nudged her from behind and whispered in her ear one more time.

"Oh, and I pledge ye my chastity."

Kelly shook her head, lifted her knee and booted Rose in the buttock.

"Oh wait, we dinnae have to do that anymore." Rose was still facing him, and the look that passed between them said the rest. "What I meant to say was that I pledge ye my charity, which is the kind of love that God has, right? The kind that's unconditional, and encompasses every part of ye.

"I think what ye're trying to get at is agape, but charity is good, too," Ian said.

"Good," Rose said. "It's all settled then. I do."

The minister waited a few minutes and then said, "Ian? Would ye like to repeat after me, or do ye also have other plans?"

Ian continued to hold Rose's hands in his. "Ye're a hard act to follow, Rosalie Wilson, but I'll try. Okay. I'm nae a pastor today. I'm a man. And since I'm marrying a woman who's honest to a fault–"

"Except when it comes to sewing pillows," Kelly said under her breath.

He smiled – couldnae help himself. "As I was saying, I may as well be honest since Rose has been. Rose and I havenae been together yet, in the Biblical sense, but due to some unusual extenuating circumstances, I have seen Rose naked."

"Ian!" Rose said.

"Well, it's true. And everyone knows it."

"See." Rose smiled, but he could see it was as fake as smiles come. "I knew there would be times when I would discover little imperfections in ye that would require me to overlook yer faults and–"

"What?" he said. "Ye can talk aboot dancing with other men but I cannae talk aboot being naked?"

"So this is still aboot the pony."

"And the pillows." Kelly harrumphed.

"Ladies and gentleman," their pastor said. "Rose, it's Ian's turn to speak his vows."

"Thank ye." Ian tried nae to sound sanctimonious. "I was going to confess that Rose's and my unique relationship began when I fell in love with her body. I know – exactly backwards. Then I got to know Rose at her most vulnerable, and I fell in love with her mind – the way it works, the way it processes information, the way its categorizes emotions. The whole kit and caboodle."

"Ye did?"

"Yes."

"That is so sweet."

"And then, it was her soul. We've spent hours together, talking and sharing and learning aboot each other, and I can honestly say that I love this woman with all my heart, soul, body and mind, like I've never loved anyone ever before. Rose, we are very different people, but I believe we are a perfect match for each other."

"Amen to that," Kelly said.

"I agree as well," Lyndsie said in her most lady–like voice, still determined to be proper.

"Well, then, while we're all in agreement–" the pastor started to say.

"Which really doesnae happen all that often," Rose interjected.

"It would seem like a good time to pronounce ye man and wife. Are there rings?"

"Yes, but she's already wearing it."

"No. I have nae had time to go shopping."

"Okay. We can work with that." The minister took both of their hands, and placed Rose's in Ian's. "Blessings, then on yer ring, on yer love, and on yer future together. Forever. Nae refunds. Nae returns. Understood?"

"We do." Rose and Ian said in unison.

"Then I now pronounce ye man and wife. What God has joined together, let nae man put asunder."

"Amen!"

"If ye'll just step into the sacristy to sign the marriage license, it will be official. Witnesses, too." Pastor Fergus motioned to Kelly and Lyndsie to follow him.

The musicians burst forth with a rousing rendition of *Lord, Reign in Me* and the piper stood at the ready for the recessional while they made their way into a tiny room. Pastor Fergus closed and locked the door.

"Rose, Kelly, please dinnae ask questions." Ian tried to look stern enough to command their immediate attention when what he wanted to do was to dance with joy. "I need ye both to remove yer clothes. Now!"

"Wha–?" Rose only got the word half out when he shut her down.

"Strip. Now."

Chapter Thirty–Three

Rose took one look at Ian's face and started to unbutton her dress.

"Kelly, ye put on Rose's clothes. Rose, ye wear Kelly's."

Kelly looked a bit shocked, but she turned so Lyndsie could unzip her.

Good. For once they were all listening, more importantly, doing what they were asked.

"Lyndsie, ye're to go home with Pastor Fergus and stay with him and his wife until yer Mum comes to get ye. The owner of the B&B we stayed at last night will be bringing Ginger over to join ye and I'd like ye to keep close watch over her for yer Aunt Rose. Is that okay with ye?"

"So she doesnae chew anymore pillows?"

"Exactly. Just until yer Mum comes to pick ye up. It may be later tonight or it may be tomorrow."

Rose was in her bra and panties, her wedding gown in her hands, motioning for Kelly to take it and give her her bridesmaid dress.

"Close yer eyes then, Ian MacCraig, or yer little plan will nae be happening." Kelly's eyes looked thunderous, but she hadnae refused to go along with the plot. Yet.

"Kelly, there's a man in a black suit at the back of the church. He's from Scotland Yard."

Both of the women registered shock.

"He'll be taking ye into custody in a few minutes. Ye'll be taken to the constable's office here in Tobermory for questioning. Let them think ye're Rose for as long as ye can continue the ruse. Ask for a solicitor. It will take them some time to bring one in, which will buy us time. If ye can answer their questions, based on what Rose has told ye, do so. If nae, say ye dinnae remember."

"Will they nae ask where ye are?"

"Tell them I've gone to make arrangements for Kelly and Lyndsie and see to things at the Bluebell, where we had reservations for a wedding dinner. Tell them that I'll be there shortly. Say ye dinnae know where I am – that I must have been detained."

"But what aboot the piper?" Rose asked. "He came very highly recommended, and he was very dear."

"Where will ye and Rose be?" Lyndsie asked innocently.

"On our honeymoon."

Rose had just stepped into Kelly's dress when he spun her around and pulled the zipper up. She didnae say another word – a miracle in and of itself – when he whisked her behind what looked like an angled bookcase.

He reached into his pocket and pulled out a key. The bookshelf slowly closed behind them.

"It's like magic."

"Come." He flipped on a flashlight and urged her down the steep incline of the secret passageway that led from the sacristy to the parsonage.

"We might only have a few minutes depending on how long it takes the agent from Scotland Yard to get suspicious."

She gripped his hand and trailed behind him while he shone the light down at their feet, then straight ahead. The air was filled with particles – must and mold and age old dust if his tickling nose was any indication.

Rose sneezed. "Here I am, dragging ye through the muck again."

He ignored her implication. It was her fault that they were being forced to flee like a couple of most–wanted fugitives. Which in the strictest sense, they were – or at least, she was. Although he would soon be added to the ranks once they discovered he'd aided and abetted. But none of that mattered now. "I'm supposing the caretaker at the church doesnae include this route in his regular cleaning regimen."

She laughed. "That seems to be a fair assessment."

"I love ye, Mrs. MacCraig."

"I'm hoping we dinnae have to spend the night down here."

"Nae to worry. But if we did, I can promise ye ye would nae be thinking aboot a wee bit of dust for very long."

"I like the sound of that, Mr. MacCraig."

The path sloped sharply upward. When they'd reached the top, he winched the rusty, antiquated locking devise up, opened the creaking door and peeked out into the sunshine.

Sherrie Hansen

Their getaway car was parked just where Pastor Fergus had promised it would be.

"Welcome to the adventure of our new life together." Ian took her hand and they ran.

* * *

A few hours later, Rose was nestled in Ian's arms on the sand at Calgary Beach. It was unseasonably warm, and the afternoon sun was perfectly hot. She was in her bridal panties and bra, which Ian didnae seem to mind one iota. They didnae look that unlike a swimsuit, and from a distance, she was sure nae one would ever guess. The beach was deserted except for a few sheep roaming aboot, but she was still thankful she'd worn her lovely but conservative burgundy lace set and nae the sexy, crotchless, see–though set she'd thought aboot wearing. It wouldnae have boded well to shock Ian too much on their first night together.

And nae matter, they'd only stay on for a minute anyway.

"Ye might have mentioned I should pack a swimsuit."

To which Ian said, "Ye might have mentioned we'd be evading Scotland Yard."

"Who knew?"

"Nae I."

Ian kissed her hand. "Besides, ye didnae pack. We eloped."

"Oh, that's right. It seems forever ago, doesnae it – all our plotting and planning back at St. Conan's?"

"I hope Pastor Fergus and his wife and Lyndsie enjoyed our wedding dinner and hand–dipped Tobermory chocolates at the Bluebell."

Rose tried to smooth the crinkled hairs on Ian's chest with her finger tips and finally gave up. "Speaking of, I'm a bit curious as to how Kelly is getting on with the man from Scotland Yard."

"Please love, let's nae go there."

"She's going to hate me forever, ye know."

"But it will all be worth it because ye got to go on yer honeymoon and make love to yer husband for the first time instead of being behind bars."

"And what a pleasure it's been," she said. "Well worth the wait."

She rolled over on top of him and relished the feel of his chest curls against her bare skin. Then, she thanked God she had a husband who wanted her so badly he would risk life and limb and his good reputation – and possibly jail – for aiding and abetting a known criminal, to be with her. And then she kissed him.

"A bit of heaven right here on earth."

Ian squeezed her hand and she leaned down to kiss him one more time. And then, she looked out over the expanse of white capped blue sea and pale sand, and puffy little sheep grazing contentedly. Life just didnae get any better than this, she mused – except for the Scotland Yard thing hanging over her head.

"It's all so beautiful." She sighed as one wave after another lapped at the sand, and she thought of Ian, and the way he'd made love to her. She'd never felt so cherished. "I feel like we're wasting a perfectly wonderful room, but being out here in the sunshine is so dear."

Two cars rounded the corner of the road that led to the beach and slowed as if trying to decide whether or nae to stop. It was almost as though they were looking for something – or someone.

She could see Ian's eyes following the cars, and heard his sharp intake of breath when the black one stopped on the far side of the parking area. Two men got out.

"Ye know – I think I would like another go at celebrating our marital bliss before I start to fade. Nae much sleep last night and I dinnae want to doze off while ye're..." Ian stood, grabbed her hand, and wrapped one of the towels they'd brought from their B&B around her. He pulled her towards the path that led to their hideaway like he was so ready to have at it again that he could hardly wait to get back to their room. Warm, romantic feelings flooded her psyche and then, she realized Ian was afraid of the same thing she was – that the men were from Scotland Yard, come to take her away.

"Ye are so handsome, Ian, and I want to make love to ye again so badly, but–"

"Yes?" He sounded slightly out of breath as they headed up sand and stone walkway to the cottage they'd rented for the night.

"But I think I should turn myself in."

He didnae miss a beat. "First thing in the morning, love. I promise. We'll have a proper breakfast and–"

They reached the gate, and made sure to close it behind them so that nae sheep escaped – nae more, judging from the ones that wandered the beach. A few yards later, they were climbing the stile over the last fence before they came to the door of their cottage. They both looked over their shoulders before they went inside. Nae one appeared to have followed them, which either meant the men werenae from Scotland Yard after all, or that they had watched where they went, and would be over to nab them as soon as they'd finished running the license plates of the other of the cars parked at the beach.

"I feel so badly. Ye worked so hard to make our honeymoon perfect."

"Perfection is unattainable. It doesnae exist. Think how boring it would be if it did. Foibles and flaws are what make life exciting."

"What? Waiting for the other shoe to fall?"

"No. Being at the ready. Because ye never know what grand adventure lies just around the bend."

Rose was quiet for a moment. So was Ian. She took the opportunity to kiss him. "So I have nae spoiled anything?"

"Of course nae! Ye've just made it what it is."

"And what is it now?" She moved toward him, her eyes focused on his.

He slowly unwrapped her towel and let it fall to the floor. "It's our first evening together as man and wife."

"And we're in a lovely room with a cushy bed piled high with pillows – pillows that look handmade, which makes them especially dear." Rose giggled as she took up the story.

He reached around her and unsnapped her bra.

"And for now, at least, we're alone."

He let his lips do his talking. And his tongue, and his hands. And when he lifted his head to take a break, he said. "We overcame so many obstacles to get here. We may as well enjoy it as long as we can."

He stroked her nipples into peaks. "And if those men should be from Scotland Yard, and if they do end up knocking at our door, we may as well give them something to talk aboot when they're back at the station bragging aboot how they've captured one more fugitive and brought her to justice."

"Two more," she murmured. "Ye helped me escape."

An hour later, she was counting her blessings because she'd had the best sex of her life for the second time that day, and nae one had knocked so she was still cuddled in Ian's arms under a pretty handmade quilt in cheery shades of blue and yellow. How could anyone be sad or worried or have a care?

"I told ye we were a good match," Ian said, still stroking her in places she hadnae known she had.

"Who says perfection is a myth?" Rose said.

His response only served to prove her right.

Another hour passed and they were still snuggled up tight, with several more things to be thankful for.

"Rose, I was just thinking..."

"Yes?"

"Ye know how it is when ye've seen a movie, and it just is nae that good, so ye have a hankering to read the book, and ye do, and it's so wonderful that ye forget that ye even saw the movie because it's nothing compared to how wonderful the book is?"

She smiled. "Yes, dear. I know exactly what ye mean. Do ye know what I was just laying here thinking?"

"I have nae idea. Oh, I could imagine a few things given what ye were just doing."

She reached down and found him thick and hard again. "I was just counting my blessings."

"As in?"

"All ten inches of them." She teased him with her hand and listened as his chuckle turned to moans. "What I mean to say is that a few short months ago I would have been crowing aboot lady luck and fate smiling down on me, and the stars finally being aligned, and now I know that it is nae anything to do with any of those things. It's God loving me so much that he wants the very best for me, is it nae?"

"By His mighty power at work within us, He is able to accomplish infinitely more than we would ever dare to ask or hope. Ephesians 3:20."

"See now, that's what I love aboot ye, Ian MacCraig. Quoting scriptures while ye're–"

And that was the last coherent thought she had until late that night.

Chapter Thirty–Four

Rose was more afraid of Kelly than she was of the constable or Scotland Yard.

Ian patted her hand and tried to reassure her as they walked the gangplank that led to the constable's office. "We're nae even sure Kelly will be here. They probably released her hours ago."

"I hope ye're right. Because if she had to spend the night in jail, we can skip Scotland Yard and take me right to the torture chamber. I've nae doubt Kelly will volunteer to do the honors herself."

"If she's so mad at ye, why do ye think she agreed to switch places with ye?"

"First, because ye didnae give her adequate time to think aboot it. Because if ye had, she definitely would have said no. And second, because ye asked her to. We McCullen women all have trouble saying nae to a handsome man."

Ian grinned. "That statement both pleases and worries me."

"Ha ha."

"At least ye've only Kelly to contend with, and nae Kevin."

"Oh, that cheers me nae end."

Ian laughed and grabbed her hand. "Let's get on with it then. At least now, if they arrest us, they'll have to charge both of us."

"Yer overseer would love that."

"I'm sure he would – t'would be a good excuse to get rid of me once and for all, since that seems to be what he's inclined to do anyway."

"And that doesnae worry ye?"

"Nae anymore. I'm at peace with whatever the Lord has for me."

Rose didnae even try to camouflage the shock from her eyes. Was he serious? There was a warrant out for her arrest – perhaps his, too. Nae only had they willfully evaded Scotland Yard, they had Kelly to contend with.

Ian was at peace? Well, wasnae that jolly wonderful! She smiled and pretended that his sense of calm had rubbed off on her even though she was a nervous wreck.

Ian waved at a man wearing a sweater vest and a plaid tie. "There's our solicitor. Just remember to let him do the talking and nae doubt he'll have us out of here in less than an hour."

She tried to smile, to emulate his confidence, but her insecurities chipped away at her again.

The water in the harbor was sparkling like a million diamonds as they approached the steps to the constable's office. Ian was bubbling with the same sort of effervescence, looking like he was some sort of Norse god that could skim over the surface of the water on a jet ski if he was so inclined. Except he would have to be Jesus walking on the water, now wouldnae he, because everybody knew Ian was perfect and that meant he would never glorify a pagan deity.

All she could think was that she felt like she was drowning. She hoped Ian's confidence in their solicitor was well founded and that everything would be all right, but she certainly didnae feel all cheery like Ian did.

Which may have been because a bigger problem was niggling at her conscience. Here they were doing the same old thing their relationship had been founded on – Ian defending her – again and again – at great cost to his good name and his reputation.

She wasnae proud of what she'd put him through. She might have joked aboot it back at their honeymoon hide–a–way, but it mortified her to think that if things didnae go the way they'd hoped, Ian could lose his vocation on account of her. She couldnae bear the thought.

The solicitor introduced himself and started to ask her questions. But when he tried to reassure her, all she could think aboot was, what did she have to offer Ian? Once again, she found herself indebted to him, and wondering what she could do for him. How could she help him? How could she ever pay him back? And could their relationship continue to bear the imbalance of her always needing and him always helping?

She was just wondering what on earth Ian saw in her when she heard Kelly's voice. "How a nice man like Ian ever got involved with the likes of ye, I'll never know."

Kelly charged out of the door sounding exactly like their mother. And it wounded her to the core. Because she would have expected it from her mother, had she been there, but right now, she needed a sister –

an understanding, compassionate sister with soft arms and a big heart.

She didnae see Lyndsie, thank goodness, because she wouldnae have wanted her to hear Kelly's rants – the child heard enough insults aboot her from Kevin. She also didnae see Pastor Fergus, which was wonderful, because if she could keep from further humiliating herself in front of another of Ian's peers, that was a good thing, right?

But there was someone following close on Kelly's heels, someone she didnae recognize, but who looked eerily familiar. And she was screaming at her, too. Something to the effect of "Are ye insane? Think of yer career." And then she realized that the woman was talking nae to her, but to Ian. "People will never accept a woman who's behaved like such a floozy."

There was more, but aboot that time, Kelly wonked the woman with her purse, which was really Rose's, because Kelly had needed to prove her false identity, and because it matched her dress, which was really Rose's, because of course, they'd switched at the church before she and Ian had escaped through the secret tunnel.

And then she vaguely heard Kelly saying something like, "I can say anything I want to aboot her – she's my sister. Ye cannae!" And Kelly wonked the woman again. And then, the solicitor was trying to stop them from scraping, and the strange, but vaguely familiar looking woman was calling out to Ian to "get this crazy woman away from me" and screeching something to the effect that "if this cretin is any indication of what sort of gene pool Rose Wilson comes from..."

Her mind was mush by that time. She probably should have come to Kelly's defense, since Kelly had come to hers, even if it was in a bit of a roundaboot way, but she didnae. Couldnae. What she did do, without even thinking aboot it, was to run. She wasnae dressed for it, and God knew she wasnae good at it, but all she could do was to try.

She ran past the Bluebell and along the slippery cobblestones, by the clock and the rainbow colored shops and the old church that was now an art gallery. The smells of a half dozen pubs and, Lord, help her, a bakery, wafted into her consciousness. But nothing slowed her down – nae even the thought that the bakery might have freshly made battenbergs, although it did occur to her as she ran by.

And then she came to the end of the harbor and the ferry terminal, and beyond that, forest, and there was nae where left to go but up.

She tried to scramble up the hill that led away from the harbor, but she was in heels, and a bridesmaid dress, and instead of making a dashing disappearance, her lungs were being torn in two and her hair was nae doubt a fright and...

And suddenly, Ian's arms were around her, and the shouts and noises she'd heard were nae armed guards jumping out of their armored vehicle, hell bent on capturing her, but her loving husband coming to retrieve her.

And Kelly. "It's okay. It's going to be okay," her sister repeated over and over again until her heart finally stopped pounding.

Ian kissed her head while Kelly soothed her and then everything was almost fine again. But nae quite, because she still had to turn herself in, and because there was evidently another woman in the world who hated her.

It wasnae hard to figure out why, but who she was remained a mystery until a few seconds later when Ian said to Kelly. "What is Melinda doing here? How on earth... When did she..."

Her brain was still mostly numb but a corner must have been thawing somewhere because it was all starting to make cruel, awful sense. "Ye know her?"

Of course he did. She'd spoken directly to him. She'd called out to him for help. And – the horror almost made her topple – she looked like Ian.

"Melinda is my older sister." Ian did nae look happy.

Kelly looked suddenly sympathetic. Rose was mortified.

"I'm so sorry, Rose. I know the timing is a bit unfortunate, but I'm sure that once the two of ye get to know one another, ye'll be best of friends."

"Are ye away with the fairies?" For a second, she thought a blood vessel had burst in her brain. *Okay.* She took a deep breath. *Ye can handle this. Think of all Ian has put up with to be with ye. What's one measly, mean sister–in–law compared to all of that?*

Ian reached out his hand, looking sheepish and just as dear as always and said, "I guess now we're even."

"Aye. Right." So much for marrying the perfect man. "As long as yer mother is nae..."

"I'm afraid Mother also has her moments–"

"Which moments? Good moments or bad moments?"

"Bad moments."

"So she's predominantly prone to good moments, with only occasional bad moments?"

"Yes. I think I can safely say that–"

"And what would ye safely say aboot yer sister? Melinda, is it?"

"Yes." Ian looked over his shoulder, presumably to make sure Melinda hadnae followed him up the hill. "I would say that Melinda may be prone to having more bad moments than good, and that's why one of my daily prayers of thanksgiving is that I have a sister who lives in Edinburgh."

"Well, at least there's that."

"The only time we'll even see her is the occasional holiday," Ian said.

"I'm very possessive of family holidays," Kelly said. "Ye'll be spending them with me and Mum."

Rose looked at Ian. "Family traditions must be maintained, now must they nae?"

"Melinda and my mother will just have to understand." Ian was sweating just as heavily as she was – perhaps for different reasons, but the outcome was the same.

She looked up the hill. Going down had to be easier than trying to make it the rest of the way to the top. And then, she looked down. Their solicitor was ambling up the hill.

As opposed to the rest of them, he'd nae even broken a sweat. But she forgave him when she heard what he had to say.

"Rose, they've dropped the original charges. The only evidence they had was yer hair on Digby's clothing and yer fingerprints on the murder weapon, which was the chair ye were bound to. There were witnesses to yer abduction, including the constable's men from Lochawe, so there's a perfectly adequate explanation of how yer hair got there. And the chair–"

"He was bludgeoned to death with a chair?" Ian's face was a mask. A sweaty mask.

"Scotland Yard is calling it the hot seat."

Rose's stomach turned sour and she buried her head in Ian's shoulder.

"Their whole theory that ye were in cahoots with Digby went down the crapper when yer sister got a hold of them."

"How long did it take them to figure out ye were nae Rose?" Ian asked.

"Long enough to get me good and hot around the collar." Kelly harrumphed. "The things they said to me aboot ye..."

Rose lifted her eyes tentatively. "Probably nae worse than what ye've thought on many an occasion."

"A sister's allowed. They are nae."

Their solicitor smiled. "Kelly here was like a mad mother bear. Yer sister made such a compelling case aboot the trauma ye endured whilst they were holding ye hostage, and so stirringly convinced them of yer love for Ian that they soon dropped any notion that ye were in cahoots with Digby."

Kelly smiled smugly. "Of course, there was Ian's sister, who was screaming that the marriage had to be annulled post haste and trying to undermine every good thing I said aboot ye."

Their solicitor smiled. "Kelly handled her like a pro."

Ian said, "So the purse bonking didnae start up until–"

"I didnae say that," the solicitor said. "But I eventually managed to get the charges against the both of them dropped as well."

"He hardly even earned his pay," Kelly said.

"I'll freely admit she did most of the work for me."

Kelly grinned. "Ye should put me on retainer."

"Believe me, I'm tempted." The solicitor turned to Rose. "Rarely have I seen such a compassionate orator."

Rose turned to Kelly and gave her a hug. "Thank ye."

And Ian hugged them both for a long minute and then asked, "Ye said they dropped the original charges. Have they charged Rose or me with anything else?"

"They're nae at all happy with the way ye handled things, although one or two of the local gents expressed a keen understanding of yer motivation for doing what ye did."

Ian looked at Rose and took her hand. "I'd do it again if it meant spending my honeymoon without Scotland Yard looking on."

"They do want an apology."

"That's it?"

Rose felt her first glimmer of hope that the past might finally be behind them. "Then what are we waiting for?"

Chapter Thirty–Five

When the constable and the man from Scotland Yard finally told them they could go, and Ian had convinced his sister that he had nae intention of annulling their marriage, they walked down from the far side of the bay, along the harbor, to the Bluebell.

Ian had asked that they might have a few minutes alone, so the others had gone on ahead.

"Take a good look around, Rose, and tell me what ye see."

"I see color and light." She turned in the direction of the harbor. "And history and tradition. And sanctuary. I see wonderful new beginnings..." She turned around and lifted her eyes to the top of the hill. "But nae without a steep price."

"Why do ye say that?"

"I dinnae know. It just came to me." A chill washed over her.

Ian cupped her chin and lifted her face to kiss her. "Could ye be happy here?"

"I think I could be. I'm sure I could be with ye here."

"Then we could be happy anywhere."

She looked out at the water – smooth, gentle water, cradled by the bay, protected from the winds. "If ye're thinking what I think ye are, I wish... What I mean to say is that I wish what happened in Loch Awe wouldnae have been in the papers here in Tobermory, and that the constable's office here need nae have gotten involved and – well that we could have had a really fresh start here. If that's what we decide to do."

Ian sighed. "It's a small country. But Rose?"

"Yes?"

"I believe that something good comes out of everything that happens."

"Even the bad things?"

"Especially the bad things."

She thought for a moment. "Like maybe Lyndsie will choose a better man for herself because of what she's seen me go through."

"Perhaps. She's seen what happened to Digby, and how trusting the wrong person hurt ye."

"She's watched how her da handled things, and how ye did."

Ian nodded. "Each of us – and the things we do and say – makes an impression on the people around us. Especially tender–hearted little ones like Lyndsie."

They fell into a comfortable silence, breathing in the smells of the harbor and listening to the sound of the sea lapping at the docks.

"Rose?"

"Yes?"

"It may be days from now, or weeks, or months, or even years, but someday, I believe that God will be able to use ye to help someone else because of what ye've learned and gone through these past few months. I dinnae know what her name is, or where she is, or how ye'll meet her, but I have a very strong sense that somewhere out there, she's there, and that she'll be needing ye."

"Oh, Ian. Ye give me shivers."

A moment later, they reached the door of the Bluebell and found Kelly, Lyndsie, and Pastor Fergus and his wife – and Melinda – waiting inside. She and Ian joined hands and walked in together.

"Hi. My name is Logan. I'll be yer waiter today."

"We're with the folks over in the corner," Ian said.

"Aye. The lucky bride and groom," their waiter said, his spirits so high it was hard nae to respond with a smile.

Which Ian did. "Luck had nothing to do with it, my good fellow."

Lyndsie came running up to them with Ginger in tow. "I had a wonderful time on yer honeymoon. Did ye? We got to watch the *Sound of Music* and when the Von Trapp family escaped from the Nazis, it reminded me of ye and Ian slipping out through the secret passageway in the sacristy. Were there rats in the tunnel? What aboot bats? I hope none of them bit ye! Because I read a book at school and it said that there have been several recently confirmed incidents of bubonic plague. Just like in the Middle Ages."

Rose smiled, knelt down to pat Ginger, and hugged Lyndsie to her side. "Ye know, someone once told me that 9 out of 10 children get their awesomeness from their aunts."

"Or," Kelly said, "Their stubbornness, their willfulness, their wild imaginations, their tendency to ramble on and on with barely a chance to come up for air..."

Ian turned and kissed Rose. "She's a wild rose. One of the most beautiful, tenacious species in the universe. And I love her – thorns and all."

"Aunt Rose, did ye know that Pastor Fergus is moving to Edinburgh? So the church needs a new pastor, and I thought, if ye moved here, I could come and stay with ye when I'm on holiday from school and we could explore the secret tunnel."

Rose looked at Ian and smiled. "It sounds perfect, Lyndsie." Really, the child could care less aboot pillows or even fancy tea rooms. All she wanted was to spend time with her dear Auntie Rose exploring musty old hideaways and other scary places. "I'd love it."

"Ye are the most awesome aunt," Lyndsie said.

"And wife," Ian said.

"And sister." Kelly winked.

Ian's sister said nothing, which given the options, was just fine with Rose.

Rose wished that she could think of something wise to say. Something quotable, something that would put the finishing touch on their entire experience. But she couldnae think of a thing. Surprisingly, all that came to her mind was the thought to pray. And so, right there in the front entry of the Bluebell, with this Logan gent and whoever else happened to be around looking on, she did. "Thank ye, Lord, for wallowing through the worst days of my life with me and bringing Ian MacCraig, the best friend and bonniest man alive, into my life."

Ian took her hand and raised their arms aloft like they'd just scored a winning goal. "Give thanks to the LORD, for He is good. His love endures forever. Give thanks to the God of heaven. His love endures forever."

And they all said, "Amen" except for Ian's sister, whose lips didnae move one iota.

Now Available

Blue Belle
by Sherrie Hansen

Included as a Bonus Section:

Chapter One

She was having a panic attack. He was sure of it. The classic signs—shortness of breath, chest pains, trembling, sweatiness, a sense of terror, numbness—were either written on her face or obvious in her gestures. What had set her off? The Blue Bell was as safe a place as he could imagine.

Michael St. Dawndalyn resisted the urge to jump up and go to her rescue. He wasn't a doctor in Scotland. He was a contractor. And not even that, if ye wanted the truth. The last thing he needed was to draw attention to himself, make people wonder how a common rock layer would know so much about anxiety disorders.

Logan approached the booth where the American woman was sitting with a pot of tea and what appeared to be sticky toffee pudding. It was the first time Michael had seen the lad in an apron and he did look a bit scary, his large girth criss–crossed with strings like a trussed side of Angus Aberdeenshire beef. But even that didn't account for...

He looked on helplessly as the woman cowered, recoiled, tried to compose herself and failed. He watched as she fought for breath after panicked breath. It was Logan—kind, gentle giant, harmless as a mountain hare, Logan Galbraith.

Doing nothing, when he knew he could help, was driving him crazy. Two Americans, both living in Tobermory, Isle of Mull, Scotland, and he'd been all but rude to the woman because he was afraid she'd Google him and find out he was wanted in Wisconsin. He wanted to help, but he had to keep his distance.

Screw propriety. He leaped to his feet and catapulted himself in her direction. At the very least, he had to get Logan away from her. Poor fool was hovering over her like Algernon with his mouse, trying to make her feel better, never in a million years guessing that he was the cause of her angst.

The crowd parted instinctively as he approached, not because they knew he was a doctor, but because he was their leader. They trusted him to help. He was their boss, their provider.

He nudged past Logan until it was he who filled her frame of reference.

"Isabelle, is it?" Everyone at the pub knew her name. Small town, just like Oconomowoc. He used his most reassuring, kindly voice, the one he'd been told could just as likely melt a woman's heart as soothe a patient.

He stroked the back of her hand. "Take deep breaths. Think about yer favorite spot in the world, the place where ye feel safest and happiest and free from any cares." He whispered so only she could hear.

He could feel her trembling, her shallow gasps changing to deeper, fuller breaths.

And then she lifted her head and locked her blue eyes directly on his. He felt it happen, the bonding, the imprinting, the life–altering zing of energy that passed between them.

A tall gent that he recognized as the new pastor at Parish Church came alongside him. "Pastor Ian MacCraig. Anything I can do to help?"

A woman with dark auburn curls whooshed up and wedged herself between them. "Sweetheart, it's going to be okay. I promise ye, it's going to be awrite."

Isabelle's eyes flickered away from his. She glanced at the other woman and then back at him, the blues of her eyes even bluer against her pale skin, pink cheeks, and soft red hair.

The auburn–headed woman smiled brightly. "Ye're too young and pretty to be having a cardiac episode, so I'm assuming what ye're experiencing is a good, old–fashioned panic attack."

Isabelle looked up at the woman, her face showing obvious relief. Michael continued to block Isabelle's view of Logan, and when she wasn't looking, motioned for his young charge to return to the bar and give the woman some space. What about Logan had set her off, he could only imagine.

"I'm Rose. Rose MacCraig, Pastor Ian's wife from Parish Church."

Michael backed away when he saw the look of relief on

Isabelle's face. The important thing was that she got help. It didn't have to be him that healed her. This woman, Rose, might not be professionally trained, although for all he knew, she had more degrees than he did. What did matter was that Rose was confident of her ability to help. Her positive approach was in turn instilling confidence in Isabelle. Isabelle appeared to trust her. It was Logan who had set her off. Maybe another woman's touch was what she needed.

He stood quietly by, watching, as Rose took charge. Isabelle's eyes searched for his one last time. He met and held her gaze while Rose talked her down from her hysteria. When her breathing had returned to normal, he left the pub, content not to tempt fate. He needed to be in Scotland, and he needed to keep his identity a secret. There was too much at stake.

#

"So what's the matter, sweetheart? I'm happy to listen if ye'd like to talk aboot it."

Isabelle MacAllister put her hand to her chest and felt her heart rate slowing to normal. She looked at the woman in front of her and sensed only the purest of intentions. She looked around the room, searching for the man who had been so kind to her a few minutes earlier.

What could she say? She wasn't keen on opening up to a complete stranger for obvious reasons. But then, she really didn't have anything to hide except... and if she thought about that right now she'd be in the throes of another panic attack. So she would just tell them enough to satisfy their curiosity and deal with the rest later. She didn't want to seem rude when everyone had been so kind to her.

"I was going to ask the tall waiter in the apron if I could take his photo for an article I'm working on."

"Ye're a reporter then?"

"Yes. For Insight magazine. My office is in Roanoke, Virginia. I'm writing an article about the recent problems that have beset the United Kingdom's farmers."

"Yes." The woman named Rose twirled a tendril of hair between her thumb and first finger. "First mad cow disease, and then hoof and

3

mouth. The prices for wool and beef keep dropping lower and lower."
Isabelle gulped another breath of air.

Rose nodded. "Logan was a farmer, was he nae?"

"That's what the woman said when I was at the bar looking at the specials and the day an' daily's on the board."

"So ye were going to take his photo."

"That was the plan. We hadn't gotten much further than 'Sae do ye fancy a wee drum?'" Her heart shivered in her chest. "That's when I turned my camera on and discovered that the memory card was missing."

"Had ye filled it and forgotten to buy a new one, or taken it out to download the photos on it?"

"No. I download the photos with a cable that hooks directly into my laptop. And I rarely even use this camera." Her mind flitted to Ben—the last place on earth she wanted her thoughts to travel—as the sickening truth hit her. That, and the realization that Logan's large size, broad shoulders and short, Marine–style buzz made him look the spit and image of Ben, at least at a distance. She grimaced and felt a fresh batch of shame wash over her.

She looked up at Rose. There was definite empathy in her eyes. She didn't know why, but she knew instinctively that she could trust her. "A man I know—knew—used my camera once or twice. He must have taken it."

"Why would he have wanted the memory card? Was there something valuable on it? Evidence that could have incriminated him?" Rose's eyes looked serious, but there was a spark of something else that she couldn't quite put her finger on. "Sorry. I have a bit of a wild imagination."

Isabelle's head started to spin again and this time, her stomach followed suit. Ben had pictures of her—pictures that would leave nothing to the most vivid imagination. How could she have known that Ben was... How could she have trusted him? She was smart, savvy, an investigative reporter. And she'd been hoodwinked by a two bit criminal, a conman who now, apparently had photos that he could use against her.

"Are ye okay?" Rose asked. "Not to alarm ye, but yer face turned the slightest bit green there for a second."

"I'm fine." But she wasn't. She'd traveled to what was practically the end of the earth to get away from the man, yet here he was, stalking her electronically and emotionally.

"I'll be fine." She hoped she would be. When she'd first met Ben, she'd been proud of the fact that he'd served with the Special Forces. Now that she knew he was a trained assassin and computer espionage wizard, she was scared of her own shadow. She knew she'd done the right thing by turning him in to the police, but she'd always been terrified that he would make her pay. Now it would seem he had just the ammunition he needed.

Rose continued to try to reassure her. She looked up at the bar, but the man who had helped her was gone. Not that it mattered. No one could help her now. But she was curious. Maybe it was just the fact that she'd been so out of it at the time, but she could have sworn he was an American.

#

The next day, Michael headed back to the Blue Bell as soon as they'd finished their day's work at the castle.

"Guid day, Michael," One of the farmers who worked for him called from across the room. "Bevvy up—the ale's oan me tonecht!"

Michael nodded and paused to survey the eclectic mix of people perched on stools, plopped on chairs, and straddling benches around the circumference of the Blue Bell. Both the people and the pub had a comfortable, well–worn feel about them – despite the fact that Damon Hermance, the new owner, had recently had every seat in the place reupholstered.

He took the frothy drink the barmaid handed him, settled into his seat, and swiveled into position so he could see who was there. The stools that lined the bar had been topped off with just enough padding to take the pressure off a man's weary haunches at the end of a long, hard day. The dappled tones were just right for camouflaging the ever–present muck and mud brought in by his stone layers.

No matter what the locals thought about Hermance—most of it not good—it was clear that careful thought had been given to every detail of the pub's refurbishing—far more thought than Michael had given to any of the specifics involved in his own remaking. He had to give Damon credit for that.

He ran his hand over a set of age–old initials carved in the soft, smooth pine of the bar. They could have belonged to a friend of his great–grandfather's. Thankfully, Hermance's controversial efforts to pretty up the place hadn't included redoing the surface of the well–dented bar, except to buff it up a bit.

"So ye're staying out at Bluevale Castle, are ye?"

Logan Galbraith's voice was so loud that for a second, Michael thought he was asking him about Cnoc Fuar, the cottage where he was staying down in Bluebell Valley, on the far side of the castle grounds—which made no sense. Logan knew exactly where he lived.

He turned and watched as Logan handed a cottage pie with a thatched roof to the same American woman he'd been bothering the night before. And why? Logan wasn't even a waiter. He couldn't enjoy being trussed up in a too small apron cutting swaths around his middle. What was he up to?

"I'm in one of the cottages." She glanced around uncomfortably, looking as though there were a stray upholstery tack sticking out from her seat. But at least tonight, she was keeping it together.

"Must be the whitewashed but and ben below the garden wall that looks down to the sea," Logan said.

Her eyes looked downright panicked at the speed with which Logan had put two and two together. She'd learn. People were no different in Scotland than they were in America. Everybody knew everything about everyone.

Why on earth had she come back if Logan bothered her so? She'd only begun to frequent the Bell and she wasn't meeting a friend. She always sat alone—by choice, if Michael knew anything about human behavior—and he did.

"So what brings ye to Tobermory and the fair Isle of Mull, if I may ask?" Logan's brogue was loud enough that Michael could hear him clearly. He had to strain to hear the woman's replies.

"The rainbow–colored buildings along the waterfront, I suppose. And the castle. The way it guards the inlet made the island seem—I don't know—safe."

Michael grunted. Probably the same URL he'd looked at back in his office in Wisconsin. Not that he was inclined to argue with her assessment of the place. He couldn't deny that the island was picturesque. And it had been the perfect haven for him.

"Sae ye're not after the gold then, eh?"

"No." She looked a little less ill at ease. "But it didn't hurt that you have a chocolate factory."

Michael swiveled around to the face the bar before Logan could spot him eavesdropping, but he could still hear Logan going on about the local legend that there was a sunken Spanish galleon from 1588, filled with gold coins, buried in the bottom of Tobermory Bay.

He should have realized it was the gold. Logan and his mother thought every stranger who came into the pub more than twice was involved in a plot to unearth the gold and abscond with the buried treasure.

He smiled in spite of himself. This Isabelle's rosy cheeks and girlish, reddish blond curls made her look the least likely pirate he could imagine. Although there was something lurking beneath the careful, Southern facade she wore that was a study in complexity. Maybe that was why he'd yet to tire of looking at her.

He tried to look stern and aloof as Logan passed the door to the kitchen and squeezed between the edge of the bar and the liquor–lined wall behind it.

"So you've stooped so low you were willing to don an apron just to get near the lady," Michael said. He felt only a tinge of guilt about teasing Logan, though truth be known, he was the last one who should be hassling someone for pretending to be an expert at something he knew precious little about.

Logan grinned. "My Mum's the cook. Ye canna sae I dinnae have a good excuse to be helping out."

Michael shook his head. "Your get–up has nothing to do with your Mum, and you know it." The younger man's bulky frame and elongated hands were far more suited for hefting rocks, mixing mortar and fitting stones than maneuvering around a slippery–floored kitchen or navigating the obstacle course of chairs and customers that packed the pub. If Logan had grown up in Wisconsin instead of Scotland, he'd probably be clutching a football and dodging a blitz of linebackers from whatever team the Green Bay Packers happened to be playing that week.

"The wee bit o' pride I had to set aside to accomplish my task has been weill worth it." Logan lowered his head and jabbed Michael's ribs with his elbow. "I'm the first person she's bared her soul to since she darkened the door."

Telling Logan she was staying at Dunara Cottage hardly qualified as an inside scoop—the whole town had known since five minutes after she'd arrived—but Michael didn't want to burst Logan's bubble, so he just smiled. "You're a pro at getting the ladies to open up to you, all right."

His young employee smiled broadly. "My mum thinks she works for the Spaniards who want to scour the bay for the sunken treasure."

"You thought the same thing about me when I came to the island. If I remember right, your Mum had me pegged for a sonar technology expert because of my refined mannerisms and scholarly good looks."

"G'wa," Logan said, with a laugh. "No one said a thing aboot good looks to the best o' my recollection."

Michael followed Logan's eyes back to the booth.

"She's eye–sweet, a right," Logan said.

The strappin' laddie was right about that. She was pure Southern belle, warm and dewy–looking as a sultry night laced with the scent of cherry blossoms – a true lady, if her shy but charming gestures said anything at all. Definitely not an agent of subterfuge. But he'd never convince Logan of it.

Michael let his eyes roam back to the booth. There was still something about the woman that was not quite right, assuming his instincts hadn't dulled too much in the last nine months. Maybe it was the way she kept clutching at her bag. He would have written it off as the jittery habit of someone who'd lived in a big city too long if she hadn't looked so stiff and... Downtrodden? Deflated? He didn't know quite how to describe it. For whatever reason, Isabelle looked as blue as the wildflowers blooming in the pasture behind his cottage.

He took a sip of ale and tried to analyze his fascination with the woman. He couldn't deny that she'd set his senses singing the moment she'd walked into the pub. But then, he'd been working for almost a year with piles of unyielding, gray stones, and a randy bunch of men with heads as hard as the rocks they wielded. It was probably a natural reaction.

By the time Michael thought to tear his eyes away from her, Logan was back at her side.

"Ye've caused quite a stir with the locals," Logan was saying, cozying up to her like they were buddies from way back despite the fact that she looked increasingly ill at ease. "I dinnae mind telling ye they've all been doing their best to find out who ye are and what ye're up to."

They've been? Michael rolled his eyes. Like you're not one of them?

She looked around the room as if gauging—no, doubting—the trustworthiness of each face. "I suppose their curiosity is understandable." Nor did she care to be forthcoming about why she'd come to the island. Logan might not see it, but it was crystal clear to Michael that she valued her privacy just as he did.

Logan inched closer and topped off her water glass. "My mum's got you pegged for a barrister come round to try to persuade the town board to reconsider their decision to forbid dredging for gold in the bay. What's got them in a flap is yer six–month lease. Folks are a–clattering aboot it aright. Most goer–byes stay no longer than a fortnight or two."

Her eyes opened wide, apparently shocked to find out that Logan knew the terms of her rental agreement. Might as well get used to it, Michael thought. Logan was obviously going to keep pecking away at her until she coughed up the rest of the story.

"You can tell your Mum I'm from Virginia. I'm a writer," she said in a resigned voice.

Logan's face lit up. "Aye," he said, drawing out the short word as if that explained everything. "A poet here to walk the same ground Robert Burns once trod? Or a novelist looking for your inspiration in the old haunts of Robert Louis Stevenson or Sir Walter Scott? Wait. Now that I think aboot it, you look a mite like a J. M. Barrie type."

Her? A Peter Pan fan? With that skittish look in her eyes? No way. Michael's favorite Barrie line played itself in his head like a well–worn record... Every time a child says, "I don't believe in fairies," there is a fairy somewhere that falls down dead. Sorry as he was to say it, her blue expression alone could slay dozens.

"I usually work as an investigative reporter, but I'm here on temporary assignment writing travel articles for Insight magazine. I'll be traveling all over Europe while I'm here."

See, he'd known there was something. The fact that she carried a laptop around had made him nervous from the start. Michael stifled a groan and tightened his fist around his ale. Damn. The last thing he needed was some journalist sticking her nose where it didn't belong. The slightest bit of curiosity on her part could ruin everything.

"A remote island that's only accessible by ferry seems like an odd place to settle if ye're planning on traveling aboot while ye're here." Logan said.

"I do a lot my research online," she said. "The internet is a gold mine. My goal is to lure American travelers back to Europe, particularly the British Isles, in light of all that's transpired in the last few years."

Logan nodded. "Ah suppose ye mean Mad Cow. Hoof and mouth."

"Not to mention airline safety concerns due to terrorists, SARS, Iceland's volcanoes, and the whole situation in the Middle East."

Logan sighed. "Aye. And rightly so. The whole hoof and mouth debacle hurt many fine folk. The restrictions they put on hiking and traveling to keep it from spreading aboot dinnae even apply to this area, but the trekkers stopped coming nonetheless."

The woman took a sip of water. She looked passionate in her desire to help—he'd give her that. "I'm sure it's been terribly hard on the farmers who had both infected animals on their land and bed and breakfasts in their homes. To lose their herds, then have tourism drop off to almost nothing..."

"Aye. Many are still in dire financial straits. That's why Michael St. Dawndalyn, the American sitting over at the bar, has been such a godsend."

Michael twisted around as fast as he could and grabbed a newspaper from the barstool next to him. He took a deep breath and tried to appear as though he were nonchalantly reading the news.

"The one right there—the tall gent with the fair hair who's wearing the wool sweater," Logan said. "I'd be happy to introduce ye."

"Maybe later," she said, in a half–strangled sounding voice, to which Logan appeared oblivious.

"When Michael set aboot recruiting stone layers to work on the keep, he went straight to the farmers—said they're the hardest–working, most dependable gents aboot no matter what part of the world ye find yerself in."

So Logan was making him out to be a hero. The muscles in Michael's jaw clenched and unclenched as he momentarily recalled the stack of subpoenas he'd left cluttering his desk when he'd walked away from Oconomowoc. There were some who would disagree.

"Mr. St. Dawndalyn's efforts sound very admirable," the woman was saying. "I'd like to think I can help by writing articles that will put a positive slant on the opportunity to see the British Isles now, while prices are reasonable and accommodations are readily available."

"The reporters who've come before ye seemed more intent on getting the public revved up than on helping." Logan's voice sounded as wary as she looked. "They knew good and weill how rumors would gae aboot once they get people clacking about herds being burned to stave off hoof and mouth. It was tragedy enough without the muckle hash journalism that came with it."

"I've got my work cut out for me then—proving I'm different from my unscrupulous associates," she said calmly. "I value the truth above everything else. If my stories don't sell because they're not scandalous enough, so be it."

"I hae ye." Logan sounded unconvinced.

Michael looked over his shoulder as discreetly as he could. The woman was taking a bite of the steaming hot mashed potato and cheddar cheese crust that topped her meat pie. He could smell the succulent filling as she poked down through the top—pungent leeks and green peas fresh from the garden. He loved the Bell's food.

"Weill, enjoy yer champers," Logan said, and "Go n–eiri an t– adh leat. Good luck in Gaelic." He extended his hand to her. "I'm Logan Galbraith, by the way. Ye might mention that the queues are blissfully short at the ferry terminals and Historic Trust sites."

"Good idea." The woman extended her hand and smiled, looking as though the effort of talking to Logan had drained her. "Isabelle MacAllister."

By the time Logan returned to the bar, he looked like a cat who'd been in the cream, lapped a little too much, and gotten indigestion.

"She canna have come here just to write about Mad Cow Disease, can she?" Logan asked, glancing back at Isabelle. "She would nae come all the way to Tobermory to do something she could have done from London."

Michael glanced at the blackboard on the wall behind the stools, with its neatly printed list of the pub grub that was available that week. He'd already ordered the same vegetable strudel he'd had twice earlier that week. It was hard to improve on perfection.

"She must be connected to the blokes who want to dredge the bay." Logan fumed. "There's nae other explanation for it."

"All the more reason not to be spilling your guts to the woman," Michael cautioned him. That was the problem with Southern belles—they lured you into complete and utter surrender with their sweet–as–honey voices. Then, when it was too late, you realized you'd been had by a mind as sharp and acute as a shard of fine Irish crystal.

His stomach rumbled more from nerves than hunger. Damn it anyway. He would not let some reporter ruin the idyllic life he'd forged for himself over the last nine months. He loved working with his hands again, breathing in the fresh, outdoor air, feeling the wind in his face and the cool Scottish sun warming his shoulders while he worked. Better yet, he liked seeing the immediate, tangible results of his labor, watching the walls of the keep grow higher and stronger with every week that passed.

There was no way in hell he'd risk all that. For years, he'd earned his living maintaining a psychological interest in people and still remaining professionally detached. How hard could it be to do the same where Isabelle McAllister was involved?

He let his eyes linger on her for a second longer, just to prove to himself that he could do it. Her high–necked, long sleeved sweater covered her from the soft curl of fabric under her chin to the rolled cuffs that hung down over the tops of her petite hands. He could almost feel his finger slipping under the soft bit of wool, tipping her chin up a notch and lifting her face to meet his.

Fine. So there was something about her that threatened his objectivity. That didn't negate the fact that she was a reporter, and as long as he was obliged to keep the confidences that had brought him to Scotland in the first place, there could never be anything between them.

"If I have to watch you mooning around in this apron much longer I'm likely to lose my appetite." Michael scowled at Logan. "Tally up your lady–friend's tab and be done with it, will you?"

Logan pushed away from the bar and strode over to her booth just as Mrs. Galbraith appeared with Michael's food. The enticing aroma of steamed carrots, loamy mushrooms, and zucchini wafted out from a slit in the pastry on top. The warm steam bathed his face as he used his fork to make the opening wider.

But even with the distraction of food, he could not keep his eyes off her. When he looked back, she had picked up her fork with her left hand and her knife with her right. Not a good idea. Just because the Brits could wrestle peas and champers and tiny bits of beef onto their forks with their knives, and feed themselves with what seemed like the wrong hand, didn't mean she could.

Michael grimaced as a pea slid down her chin and fell to her lap. He watched out of the corner of his eye as she daintily dabbed at her mouth with her napkin.

"Logan?" Michael heard her say, when she'd discreetly recovered the wayward legume.

If Logan had had a tail, it would have been wagging.

"Would you mind if I tried to snap a quick photo of you to send in with my next article?"

"Me?" Logan blushed as he reached behind his back and attempted to untangle the strings of his too–small apron.

"No, leave it on. That's the point I'm trying to make," she said. "Farmers are going to any means necessary to support their families."

"So I'm to be the sympathetic gent who's eking out a living on the wee tips I earn serving skoosh and fortifiers?"

"Something like that." She smiled.

Logan smoothed his apron and struck a pose.

She raised her camera to her eye and snapped.

Made in the USA
Columbia, SC
02 May 2021